GIFTS FROM THOL

BOOK 2 IN THE THOL SERIES

DAWN GREENFIELD IRELAND

CONTENTS

Please visit my website and leave a review: http://degreenfield.com/

Sign up for my newsletter and get the latest news before the public.

❀ Formatted with Vellum

ACKNOWLEDGMENTS

The cover was designed by yours truly, me, the author who struggled and stumbled all through the AI cover creation. The character is Stanley, he's the scientist who tagged along with the Jacksons to the land of Thol.

The paperback cover was put together by Brandon White www.victorylaurel.com

I wanted a map of Thol, but I'm not even capable of stick figures. Thank you Scott K. Leslie www.theadventurerspack.com the cartographer who tackled the Map of Thol.

Creatures, creatures, creatures... A hearty thanks to Alex Gravalis (Fiverr.com) for Ghury, the Egrom creature; AskOrbin (Fiverr.com) for my diwal dog; and my son George White for Jakla Bosakin. The borjo creature was created by me via an AI program. YAY me for figuring this out!

The glossary for the Thol book series was created by Ayshaarias from Canada. Man oh man, that gal had her work cut out for her, and she did a fabulous job. Many thanks that I found her!
https://www.fiverr.com/ayshaarias
Want to get to know me better? Read my newsletters, and check out my website www.degreenfield.com

Quotes

When you realize that other dimensions exist, You'll never think of life, death, yourself, or the universe in the same way again.

The Afterlife of Billy Fingers
… A true story by Annie Kagan

*We must be willing to
get rid of the life we've planned,
so as to have the life that is waiting for us.*

Joseph Campbell

ALSO BY
DAWN GREENFIELD IRELAND

PROLOGUE

*V*ictor Bennett and Dr. Ben Joplin stood on the blacktop parking lot at Katy Mills Mall in Katy, Texas on Interstate 10 just west of Houston.

Victor, the twenty-five-year-old sandy haired physicist that was on loan to Dr. Joplin, hung on to Buffy, the Jacksons' faithful two-year-old pit bull.

Ben and Victor stared as the flash of bright light forever changed all their lives—the five people who went through that portal to the Thol dimension, and the two left behind with an inconsolable dog.

"I don't know how we're going to explain this to Joe. What do I tell the team?" Dr. Joplin asked. He was more or less just thinking out loud. His mind raced with ideas about what was on the other side of that bright light. What was Thol really like? Did Stanley make the right decision?

As the head of the physics department at Rice University, Dr. Joplin felt the weight of the responsibility for this investigation. How could he possibly explain losing a member of this team? He wondered if he would be fired, or held accountable in other unforeseen ways, such as criminal charges. His mind raced with implications. At sixty-two, he was too old to even consider job hunting. Who would hire someone who lost a team member?

Victor knelt beside Buffy and patted her. "Looks like it's you and me, girl."

Buffy whined and struggled to leap forward to join her family.

"How do we explain this, Victor?" Dr. Joplin asked.

"Science. Plain and simple. A true scientist wants only the facts. He wants to prove theories. I'd say Stanley is the luckiest man alive," Victor said.

CHAPTER ONE

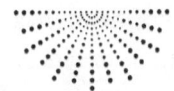

The bluish-silver, moss-covered ground was littered with the dead: Ciertrons, the dark-haired soldiers of the Tholian city of Ebscalon; Egroms, the white, furry, mystical creatures; Plotals, the reptilian creatures; Kudaja, the tiny forest people similar to Ciertrons, and other tribes of the northern hemisphere of Thol.

Borjos, the animals the Kudaja rode, and pakows, the large beasts the Plotals rode had also fallen in the battle.

Deactivated, smoldering black robots were scattered across the vast battleground.

D'laine pulled out of Trakon's embrace and led him over to her stunned family. Lee Jackson, D'laine's father who recently celebrated his forty-sixth birthday, and her younger brothers, Brian, who was ten years old and Jamie who was six, were slowly taking in the world of Thol.

Stanley Daigle, the scientist who chose to join them, digested everything his senses captured. While he was only twenty-five, the scientist held two PhDs. He was considered a genius and the scientific world embraced many of his papers and experiments as groundbreaking.

The Earthlings had arrived on the battlefield where the survivors of the robot invasion from the Zan dimension gathered their wounded and dead.

"What happened here?" Lee spread his arms wide, taking in the battlefield. "Was there a war?"

"It was a fight for our survival," D'laine said. "These robots are the same ones from my dream, daddy. They're from another dimension and they broke through a portal. They wanted to conquer us, like they did their creators."

Stanley appeared stricken. He grabbed his head while he took in the dead across the vast field. "This may be my fault. We were investigating your disappearance and discovered a portal. I was face to face with a robot before Victor and Dr. Joplin pulled me back. I had a feeling that perhaps I had disrupted the balance."

"I don't think you did anything to cause this, Stanley. I'm sure my father told you about the accident that killed my mother, and the coma I was in for months. When I woke from the coma the dreams started, and the big robot was one of the four beings that visited me nightly. Don't worry. I sealed the portal to their world, and we killed their leader," D'laine said.

She pointed to Zandal, deactivated on the moss. "He's the much larger robot. I hope the humans on that world will be able to take back their society. I don't know how many robots were there. We were overrun by them. But, as you can see from these decommissioned ones, we knocked out quite a few who came through the portal."

Lee's jaw dropped open. "You did what?"

D'laine fidgeted. The seventeen-year-old had been living without her father's supervision since her journey to Thol. "Healing's not the only gift I received from Thol, daddy. I'm sort of like a weapon of mass destruction."

"We'll talk about this later," Lee said.

Stanley relaxed a bit. "I saw some people on that world. They were hiding and scared. They were skinny and seemed to be dressed in rags."

Jor-Dan, Ghury and Jakla Bosakin gathered around D'laine's family.

"Welcome," Ghury said in guttural English.

Lee and Stanley studied the white creature. Their eyes travelled two feet over their heads. The Egrom was at least eight feet tall with two sets of arms. Ghury's red glowing eyes seemed at odds with catlike ears on the side of his head. A distinct nose and mouth similar to a feline from Earth softened his face.

Before either could say anything, Ghury spoke. "My language would be similar to what you call bird, cat and pig sounds."

"Did you just read my mind?" Stanley asked.

Ghury nodded.

"Oh, yeah, the Egroms rely heavily on telepathy," D'laine said.

Lee and Stanley shared an expression of awe.

Stanley rubbed his hands together. "I can't wait to learn that!"

D'laine placed her hand on one of Ghury's arms. "This is Ghury, one of the elders of the Cember Forest Egrom tribe. The Egroms took care of me and taught me how to survive here on Thol."

Lee nodded to Ghury, relief visible in his expression. "Thank you for taking care of my daughter."

Ghury turned to D'laine. "I think it would be best for your family to stay at my village while they get acclimated. Otherwise they will not be able to communicate with anyone."

D'laine nodded. "I agree. There's a lot to learn and I don't want them to be overwhelmed."

"Who are all these people and creatures?" Jamie asked.

"Wait a minute, Jamie. You just got here." D'laine turned to Trakon, grabbed his hand and tugged him forward. "Everyone, this is Trakon, son of Jor-Dan and Kitry, the rulers of Ebscalon, one of the largest kingdoms of Thol."

Trakon, the eighteen-year-old prince of Ebscalon, wore the traditional black hair down to his shoulders. His battle uniform didn't hide his physically fit, muscular body. His dark eyes smoldered when they rested on D'laine.

Jamie snickered behind his hand. "Is he your boyfriend?"

D'laine blushed. "We'll talk about that later. I'll have to interpret for all of you until Ghury provides everyone with translators." She pushed her hair aside and showed them her translator behind her ear. "Introductions are formal here, and they don't shake hands. It's similar, but you'll see."

She moved to Jor-Dan. "This is Jor-Dan, Trakon's father and the king of Ebscalon."

The king was ruggedly fit for sixty-six. His shoulder-length black hair didn't show any gray at all. His face held a few battle scars from long ago.

"Wow, a king!" Brian said as he fidgeted.

Jor-Dan appraised the newcomers. Lee and the boys were blond, but Stanley had dark brown hair. "The people from earth have different hair coloring?"

"Yes. There are many different colors, including shades of red," D'laine said.

Jor-Dan nodded as he took in her wavy white-blond hair that reached her waist.

D'laine rested her hand on Jakla's forearm. "This is Jakla Bosakin, the commander of the Plotal army."

Brian, Jamie, Lee and Stanley took in the large fearsome alligator-like creature that towered over them. Jamie clutched onto Brian as they studied the massive Plotal. His tall battle helmet added to his immense height alongside the Egrom. Jakla's massive form was all muscles under reptilian scales. His snout held long, sharp teeth and his long, thick tail ended in a pod.

Brian and Jamie watched as the pod opened and closed, exposing deadly barbs on the Plotal's tail.

D'laine then turned to the group of native Tholians and introduced them.

"This is my father, Lee Jackson, the celebrated engineer and inventor of my home world space agency called NASA. These are my brothers, Brian and Jamie. This is Stanley Daigle, a distinguished scientist, inventor and investigator from the state of California on Earth."

Trakon grasped Lee's arm.

Lee awkwardly returned the gesture. Stanley watched.

"Welcome, Lee Jackson! We have a lot to talk about," Trakon said.

D'laine translated for her father.

"Thank you. Yes, we have quite a bit to talk about." Lee looked from D'laine to Trakon.

D'laine turned pink. "Daddy!" She then translated what her father had said to Trakon.

Trakon realized what Lee meant regarding D'laine, which caused his face to flush. He nervously met D'laine's eyes.

Stanley grasped Trakon's arm. "I'm so happy to meet you, and to be here on your world! What do you have planned for these robots?"

D'laine translated.

Trakon shrugged. "We're going to study them."

"We need to keep a couple of the regular ones and this bigger one, so we can dismantle them. Let's find out what type of circuitry was used to create them." Stanley looked up at the hovering crestriders and motherships. "I was worried that I didn't bring any tools with me. I'm guessing you have everything I'll need to tear one of these robots apart."

Trakon nodded. He pressed his communicator. "I want to take this big robot and two others back to our workshop."

A midsized crestrider hovered close by. Zandal and two of his slave robots disappeared.

Stanley and Lee gasped.

"Did they just beam them up?" Stanley asked.

"Oh, yeah," D'laine said. "Like 'Beam me up, Scottie' on *Star Trek*."

"Wow!" Stanley said.

While the adults talked, Brian and Jamie watched the borjos carry the Kudaja through the air.

"Wow, they sort of look like little dragons, but more like dragonflies," Jamie said. "I wish they were bigger!"

"I wonder if those guys are fairies." Brian watched the Kudaja soar through the air on the borjos. "Look at that giant cow thing." Brian pointed to a pakow foraging for food.

Brian and Jamie wandered over to the beast. It had six legs, feet like an elephant, long shaggy hair, and a cow-like tail. The beasts looked like cousins to the wooly mammoth, except for the fly-type eyes.

"Look at how big this thing is," Brian said.

Jamie pointed to a Plotal on his pakow. "Wow! Look at that, Brian. I wonder if we'll be able to ride one of these animals." Jamie reached out and touched the front leg of the pakow. The pakow turned its head, stuck out its long, rough tongue and licked Jamie's face.

"Gross!" Jamie squealed and wiped the side of his face. "Brian, Jamie, stay away from the pakows—the animal you're near. If they get scared they stampede and you could get trampled," D'laine said. "Stay near daddy."

"How are you going to get rid of the rest of these things?" Lee asked. The sea of black shiny robots told a story in and of itself.

Ghury nodded, chirped and sent a silent message to the Egroms on the field. The surviving Egroms spread out. They held their four hands in front of themselves. Within moments, the robots disintegrated, and all that was left were the slight indentations in the moss. Slowly, the moss was restored to its former beauty.

Lee and Stanley could hardly believe their eyes. "Will we learn how to do that?" Stanley asked.

"No, that's one of the many Egrom talents," D'laine said.

"It is time to go." Ghury silently communicated to his tribe.

They held out their four hands. Suddenly, the Egroms and their dead were no longer on the field. The only Egroms that remained were Ghury and three others.

All the newcomer's eyes swung from the field devoid of white forms and robots to the Egrom elder. No one said a word. They digested what had just happened and the power used.

Plotal troops gathered their dead. The other groups did the same.

"We can help by transporting you, your pakows and your fallen on the motherships," Jor-Dan told Jakla.

Jakla nodded. "That would be most helpful."

Jor-Dan pressed his communicator and gave the order. Within moments, two motherships hung over the field. Then all the Plotals and their pakows, except Jakla, vanished.

"Daddy, that's like the mothership in *Close Encounters*," Brian said in a reverential voice.

Lee and Stanley gaped at the ship.

Stanley rubbed his hands together. "I can't wait to get my hands on some tools!"

"And to think we thought *Star Trek* make believe," Lee said.

While the men stared at the ship overhead they noticed the two suns, the flashing sky and clouds that held wisps of pink and blue streaks.

Jakla Bosakin grasped Jor-Dan's forearm. "I am grateful for your assistance. It would have taken hours to gather our dead and transport them to our home bases."

"We're in this together, Jakla," Jor-Dan said. "It's what neighbors do. They help each other in times of need."

Soon, all that was left on the field were the Tholian leaders, Ghury, his three kin and the group from Earth.

"Would you like me to fly D'laine's family and their companion to your village?" Trakon asked Ghury.

"The journey is important so we will walk through the field and forest," Ghury explained.

Lee suddenly spotted the bluish-silver groundcover. He knelt and ran his hand over it. "Is this moss?"

The colorful ground covering stretched as far as he could see. He stared off into the distance and saw the vast forest as if for the first time.

Brian, Jamie and Stanley became more aware of their surroundings as if they hadn't been standing there for ten minutes.

"Wow! Look at this stuff!" Brian ran his hand over the moss. "It's so soft and fluffy."

"It's pretty!" Jamie said.

"It changes colors in different areas," D'laine said. "The whole planet is extremely colorful. I can't wait until you see hosks!"

Ghury grumbled with a memory. "Let's hope your family doesn't share your first experience."

"That's not fair," D'laine said. "My circumstances were quite different from my family's and Stanley's trip through the portal. They came willingly; mine was more like a hijacking."

Ghury grumbled.

D'laine hugged and kissed her father and brothers and patted Stanley on the back. "You're going to love it here."

Trakon communicated with a ship and he, D'laine, his father and Jakla were beamed up.

THE EARTHLINGS STARED UP AT THE RETREATING SHIP WITH mouths hanging open.

The Egroms and newcomers walked across the field of moss. By the time they reached the small watering hole, Lee and Stanley were sweat-soaked, and Jamie was ready to fall asleep on his feet. Brian, surprisingly, held up through the heat.

The pond was surrounded by tall flowering plants with immense blossoms in vibrant shades of red, pink, orange and yellow. Spiny land coral and wide, flat, smooth, black rocks were scattered between the flowers.

They collapsed to their knees and slurped the brilliant turquoise water.

Lee splashed water on his face. "Better get wet and cool down."

Soon, they were all splashing the water on their faces, necks, arms and chests.

Lee studied Brian. "You must have gotten some kind of boost when your sister healed you. This heat doesn't appear to have any effect on you."

Brian shrugged. "I don't know. I don't feel all that hot like you do. It's a different hot from back home."

Ghury held out a hand and scanned Brian. "You are in the process of an internal healing. I see your sister repaired your heart and other problems. When you have rested overnight, you should be in good shape."

Lee's eyes misted. "D'laine showed up at the right time. We almost lost Brian."

Ghury nodded.

Stanley studied a handful of water. "This water is so pure." He stood and wiped his hands on his slacks.

They continued their journey. About a mile from the pond they came across a large colony of hosks. The boys dropped to the ground, giddy with excitement over the fluffy spider-like creatures. The hosks fled from Brian, but they swarmed Jamie, scampering all over him. He giggled and shrieked as tiny hosk babies tickled him with their little spider legs.

"How come they don't like me?" Brian asked, disappointed.

"Animals have always liked your brother. You know that," Lee said. "It seems as if that attraction and trust is magnified on this world."

One of the Egroms squatted by Brian. He grabbed a handful of moss and plopped it in Brian's lap. Then he grabbed a male hosk and settled it on the moss. Brian was thrilled to watch the hosk eat while it allowed him to pat its fur.

Brian looked up at the Egrom. "Thanks. They're so soft." After they rested they resumed their trip.

CHAPTER TWO

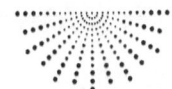

The Egroms, Lee, Brian, Jamie and Stanley stepped from the dark forest into the clearing. The Egrom village was spread out before them. Lee and Stanley stopped outside of the forest canopy and stared in awe at the tremendous mushrooms which were the size of a three-story house. The large village appeared to be deserted; then, as if a magical moment passed, they spotted Egroms out and about.

"Stanley, did you notice the slight change? One minute no one was here, then all of a sudden there's Egroms all over," Lee said.

"This area is protected," Ghury said. "Only those who are *invited* can detect the village. What you experienced was your *invitation* being accepted."

"Huh," Stanley grunted. He took in the massive mushroom houses. "How interesting. They're just like the agaricus bisporus, which are the young white mushrooms sold in the grocery store, only ten thousand times larger."

Chacoodi, an Egrom boy-child, noticed the group. "Humans! I'll bet that's D'laine's family!" He ran to the group, excited when he saw Brian and Jamie. "I'm Chacoodi! We can be friends!"

Brian and Jamie were thrilled to meet Chacoodi. The young Egrom was the same size as Brian, but they couldn't understand anything the Egrom boy said.

"Chacoodi, there will be plenty of time to get to know Brian and Jamie," Ghury said. "They can't understand you yet. Do not be a pest. Return to your duties."

Disappointed and embarrassed at being chastised by the elder Egrom in front of potential friends, Chacoodi disappeared inside a mushroom house.

After a few grumbles, Ghury led the group to his mushroom house and gestured them inside. He walked to the ledge and retrieved four translator devices. He showed them to the group.

"That looks like the clip on a pen," Lee said.

Beginning with Lee, he pressed the tiny device onto the flesh behind Lee's right ear.

The little clip settled into the flesh with a wiggle.

Lee's hand went up to the spot. "Oh! That felt so strange, almost like it was alive."

Ghury installed the translators in the others. "You require translators so you can communicate with the people of Thol."

"Oh! These are remarkable little devices." Stanley touched behind his ear. He turned to Brian and held his ear back so he could see the translation device embedded into his flesh. "Interesting."

Lee checked out Jamie's device. "I have no idea how this works."

"We'll figure it out between the two of us," Stanley said.

Ghury spoke to Brian. "When D'laine healed you, she acclimated you to Thol." He turned to Lee. "She probably didn't realize this happened, but it is good. His body is still processing. This healing will continue when he is sleeping or resting."

"Who was that little kid?" Brian asked excitedly.

"That was Chacoodi. He is anxious to get to know you so he has human companions," Ghury said.

Kestrum entered Ghury's house. "Hello, Earthlings! I am so happy to meet D'laine's family." She looked Stanley over. "And friend."

"This is Kestrum. She will take care of all your needs and make sure you settle into the village properly," Ghury said.

The Earthlings looked over the new Egrom. They noticed the female was smaller than Ghury and she had a marsupial type pouch across her belly.

"Before Ghury explains everything about Thol, why don't I show you where you will be staying and where you can wash up?" Kestrum said.

She ushered the group out the door. They walked two mushroom houses away. The larger of the two was for Lee and the boys. There were three nests, and the table was large enough to accommodate four chairs.

Kestrum walked over to one of the nests. "These are your beds. The material is gauze, woven from the silk that the hosks spin."

Jamie gawked. "Those little spider things made these?"

"Yes, they are very industrious creatures, as you will learn," Kestrum said. "Their silk is utilized in every form of material."

She showed them a lantern, the wicks and a lighting stone and demonstrated how to use them. Kestrum also warned about the dangers associated with the lighting stones.

Stanley picked up the lantern, which was like an old fashioned hurricane lamp. The round holder was carved out of a smooth polished stone that contained a trench that held the tube. The thin and translucent tube wasn't plastic or glass. Stanley didn't know what it was made from.

"Be gentle with the stones. Lighting stones do not need to be dry to light. Never bang two together because that will cause an explosion."

Next, she ushered them out the door to the next mushroom. "This is your house, Stanley. It is identical to the other houses."

They soon left Stanley's new temporary residence. Kestrum led them to an area along the edge of the village with mounds of dirt and a long stretch of a ditch. "This is where the males relieve themselves."

At first, Jamie and Brian didn't understand the concept. They watched as their father and Stanley nodded to Kestrum.

"We have to go to the bathroom outside?" Brian burst out.

"Like camping," Lee said. "What's the difference?"

"And like camping, you always cover up your business," Stanley said. "Nothing like inviting the wild animals to find you."

"Yes, as you can see here, nothing is exposed," Kestrum said.

Lee took in the dirt place then swung around and studied the tremendous size of the village with the mushroom houses. "I'm amazed this doesn't smell."

"We use a process of crushing rocks into a fine powder and mixing it with the soil," Kestrum explained. "All impurities are neutralized so there is no odor."

"Like charcoal," Stanley said. He and Lee nodded.

They left the dirt place. Kestrum led them down a path in the forest among the huge tree trunks. The Earthlings stumbled around hanging vines, exposed roots and ground cover and arrived at a large, steaming pond.

"This is the bathing pond."

A quokin bobbed to the surface.

"Wow! Look at that!" Jamie squealed. "It's like a small dragon!"

"An animal lives in hot water?" Brian asked. "Huh."

"That's a quokin. They love to play in the hot water. When you bathe, they will come up to you—as I explained to D'laine, quokins love to touch, but they will never harm you."

They returned to the village. Kestrum led them to a large mushroom where Ghury awaited them. "Ghury will provide you with information for your stay here." Kestrum ushered them inside the mushroom house then left them in Ghury's capable hands.

"Please sit. We have much to cover." Ghury held out one hand toward the chairs around the much larger table. He informed them about the Egrom species, exactly as he had when D'laine had come through the portal to Thol.

"Because there are four of you, we have changed the way we typically do things," Ghury explained. "Brian and Jamie will be taught by Bensol. Adrum will teach Stanley, and I will teach you, Lee. This is nothing like how you were taught on Earth. There are no school books, no classrooms, just our houses. No memorizing information that will surely fade with time. After breakfast tomorrow, your education and training will begin."

Kestrum entered the mushroom house carrying an armful of material. "These are the garments the Ciertrons wear." She handed out the jumpsuit-type uniforms along with the deflated boots. She showed them the buttons for inflating and deflating the clothing. "Do not touch the other buttons. They will be explained when you move to the palace in Ebscalon."

Brian and Jamie exchanged excited glances. "We're going to live in a palace?" Jamie asked. He had a vision of the Disney palace in his head.

"Yes, you are D'laine's family," Kestrum said. "And friend."

"Wow!" Brian said. "I can't wait to see what it looks like."

"It does not look like that picture in your head." Ghury provided them all with the picture of the beautiful sandstone palace in Ebscalon.

"You will learn more in the morning." Kestrum shooed them out the door to their mushroom houses. "I will come for you again after you have changed your clothing. You will meet the village elders when we eat our evening meal."

They returned to their new homes. Lee spread the clothes out on the table. They undressed. Lee stepped into the jumpsuit and pulled it up until he could slip his arms into the sleeves. He pressed the button Kestrum showed them to inflate the suit. It molded to his body.

"Do you think we're going to roast in these suits?" Brian asked as he stepped into his suit.

Lee stopped pulling on the boots and thought about the question. "Huh. So far I don't feel hot."

Jamie dropped his clothes on the table and wiggled into his jumpsuit. He inflated his suit. "This is so cool."

They all sat and put on the boots and inflated them. Then they tested them out.

Stanley appeared in the doorway. "It's like wearing work boots without the bulk. I like these clothes."

LEE, BRIAN AND JAMIE SAID "ME TOO" AT THE SAME TIME WHICH brought on the giggles.

Unlike D'laine's arrival where many things seemed to be secreted away, flying creatures were abundant.

"Look at that!" Jamie pointed to a gagu. The bat-bird screeched as it flew over the village.

"Jamie! There's a flying cocker spaniel!" Brian shouted.

The floff flapped its wings leisurely.

Kestrum led the Earthlings to the eating place where the village elders sat on the moss and silently studied them.

A male server scooped stew from the large black kettle. He filled bowls, placed a spoon in each, and passed them to a helper. The smaller male Egrom handed the first bowl to Lee, then Stanley, and finally the boys.

Lee picked up the spoon and studied it. "Stanley, does this look like one of those spoons at a Chinese restaurant?"

The scientist picked up the spoon and turned it this way and that. "Sure does. Same color and shape. Just doesn't have the Chinese lettering. Huh."

Brian and Jamie saw the bland-looking food and grimaced.

"Yuck, this looks gross," Jamie said.

"What is this?" Brian asked.

Lee drilled his eyes into his sons. "You will eat your supper and not embarrass yourself or me. This is the food offered by our hosts and you're going to eat it."

They each dipped their spoons into the stew and sampled. Eyebrows raised in surprise.

"This is awesome!" Jamie licked his spoon.

"Very tasty," Lee said.

"I think there are rutabagas in this stew," Stanley said.

Brian was too busy shoveling the stew into his mouth to comment.

The elders studied D'laine's family and friend.

Do you detect any special abilities? Bensol asked the Egroms silently.

The young boy has an affinity with animals, Absadul said.

It's too soon to tell, Drusta said. *We will observe them.*

THE NEXT MORNING, LEE AND THE BOYS STOOD AT STANLEY'S doorway.

"You awake?" Lee hollered. The problem with the mushroom houses was there was no way to knock to let anyone know they had company.

"Just getting up." Stanley sounded tired, but there was a slight echo to his voice. "I've never slept so late in my entire life." He shuffled over to the door and greeted Lee and the boys with a little wave of his hand.

Lee took in Stanley's appearance. There was definitely something wrong with the shape of his head. It looked larger, and his forehead protruded slightly.

"I can't put my glasses on." Stanley held up his glasses. "I'm not sure what's going on, but I can't see without my glasses."

"Brian, go get Ghury. Tell him something's wrong with Stanley." Lee tried to keep his concern to a minimum so as not to worry the scientist, but his voice ratcheted up a week.

About the time he got the words out of his mouth, the Egrom leader stood beside Lee. Ghury visually examined Stanley.

Kestrum joined them a few moments later.

"We will restore your eyesight and determine what is going on to cause your head to expand." Ghury ushered them into Stanley's house.

"My head expanded? Is that even possible?" Stanley asked.

Ghury set the eyeglasses on the table. He performed an Egrom scan on Stanley's cranium. He held his four hands about an inch away from Stanley's skull—front, back and both sides then was joined by Kestrum.

Lee, Brian and Jamie watched as Ghury and Kestrum enclosed Stanley in a circle between their long arms, fingers not touching. They heard a slight hum of energy, then all was quiet. When they finished, Stanley began to slump. The Egroms caught him and helped him onto a chair.

Stanley grasped his glasses. Kestrum took them away from him. "You won't need these vision enhancements," she said. "Rest is called for. Then your vision will level out and you will see perfectly, the way you are supposed to."

For a long moment, Stanley's mouth hung open. He snapped it shut. "Okay."

Lee was thoughtful. "Come to think of it, D'laine wasn't wearing her glasses."

"We restored her," Kestrum said.

Ghury pulled a chair out and sat opposite Stanley. "Your brain required growth, which pushed out your forehead some-what. This is due to the knowledge you possess and your thought processes. As time goes on, your head may again make changes. You are unique in your intelligence. Do not be alarmed when you see your reflection. It is you, just a new you."

Stanley felt his head. "I hope I don't look like a Neanderthal or Frankenstein's monster."

"It's noticeable, but not horrific," Lee said.

"Let's eat our morning meal then you will return here to rest," Ghury said. "Your training will have to wait until tomorrow."

"I feel like I could use another ten hours of sleep," Stanley said. "I've never been so exhausted."

"The healing you received requires rest to complete the process," Kestrum said. "That, along with your brain growth, will demand your body shut down soon. Food is important. Let's get you fed right now."

Stanley and Ghury got up and headed toward the door. Stanley almost crashed into the wall. Ghury grabbed his shoulders and steered him slightly to the left to avoid disaster.

Lee stepped up and took one of Stanley's arms and guided him outside. They followed Kestrum and Ghury to the eating place. Lee helped settle Stanley on the moss. The elders stared at Stanley, silently communicating among themselves.

This one is far superior.

We will have to guide him until he understands his abilities.

He will not require much training. He will absorb it from Thol.

The male Egrom cook stood at the giant cauldron stirring a thick stew. He served Stanley first, then the rest of the guests, the elders and members of the tribe. He refilled Stanley's bowl twice.

After shoveling in his last spoonful of stew, Stanley's eyes drooped, and he swayed where he sat.

"I think we need to get you back to your bed," Lee said.

"So tired..." Stanley said.

Lee stood and grasped one of Stanley's arms. Kestrum joined

him and took Stanley's other arm. They hauled the scientist to his feet.

"I will relieve you of your friend," Kestrum said. "You won't want to miss your lessons." She wound one arm around Stanley's waist and guided him to his house. They disappeared inside.

Kestrum returned moments later. "Your friend is sound asleep. His healing and new brain development have sapped him of his strength. He will sleep through the day."

Lee glanced in the direction of Stanley's house, a worried expression on his face. He hoped the scientist was going to be okay.

The elders stood. Bensol escorted Brian and Jamie to his house, and Lee and Ghury walked to Ghury's place.

WHEN THE JACKSONS EMERGED FROM THEIR TRAINING SESSIONS, Stanley was still sound asleep.

Ghury stood at Stanley's door and scanned him. "He will require much more sleep. By tomorrow morning he should be refreshed and hungry."

"Is this normal?" Lee was concerned for the scientist.

"Your friend is not normal so his situation is not normal. I can feel a tremendous amount of energy being emitted from him," Ghury explained. "Tomorrow we will be able to determine if he is ready for training."

STANLEY EMERGED FROM HIS MUSHROOM HOUSE TO THE SOUNDS of hundreds of conversations trolling through his head. He looked about. He saw the Egroms at various cook pots for their morning meal, spied Lee and his sons at the eating place and walked over and joined them. He was ravenous.

Lee watched Stanley as he marched over to the group. "Hey, Stanley. How are you feeling?"

"Good, but there's this racket in my head. I'm guessing I can hear everyone's thoughts."

Lee turned to Adrum. "Is that normal?"

Adrum stared at Stanley. "His brain is much different from other humans we have encountered."

As Stanley got closer, Lee noted that his head had expanded even more and his forehead jutted out.

Ghury and the elders studied him.

Stanley took his place on the moss between Lee and Ghury. The cook handed him a bowl and a spoon and he dug in.

"I'm starving! I can't remember ever being so hungry. It's as if I haven't eaten in a week. Did I miss anything?" Stanley asked.

"We finished the first part of our training," Brian said.

"Yeah, it's like watching a movie in your head," Jamie said. "It's really cool."

"What'd you learn?" Stanley asked between spoonsful of breakfast stew.

"It's quite a fascinating process," Lee said. "By the time the training is over, you'll know just about everything regarding the citizens of Thol, animals, plant life—too many things to outline."

The elders evaluated Stanley's appearance and chatted around the circle.

Bensol said *There have been more physical changes.*

Swezek said *His brain activity is hyperactive.*

Trabet asked *Did you feel that spike?*

Drusta said *Yes, I did. I don't think his brain has completed the changes.*

The cook refilled Stanley's bowl.

"Oh, thank you so much," Stanley said. "This is excellent. I can feel my body absorbing the nutrients down to the cellular level."

Lee scrunched his face as he scrutinized Stanley shoveling in the food. "Explain that."

Stanley stopped. "Huh. It's bizarre. I've never paid any attention to eating food. I get hungry, I eat, I continue with what I was doing. Now, though, I can sense my body utilizing this food. It's difficult to explain. Maybe I'll be able to address this later."

Lee studied Stanley. "When your changes have completed, maybe things will settle down and smooth out."

"I hope so," Stanley said. "Right now, there's a current running through me and I'm able to see all the connections like roads on a vast map."

Ghury and Adrum nodded. "Perhaps after another night's rest, your system will have quieted down. How is your vision?"

Stanley blinked at Ghury. "I just realized I can see you perfectly. Actually, I believe I can see better than at any time in my life. And farther. I can see through the trees! I'm not sure how I could have not noticed that."

"It sounds as if you are adapting, as it should be." Adrum looked pleased. "When you are finished with your breakfast, we will begin your lessons."

STANLEY SAT ACROSS FROM ADRUM AT THE TABLE IN ADRUM'S house. His eyes were closed, and all was peaceful.

The Egrom elder had just begun the initial training with the surface of Thol. He observed the smile on Stanley's face. The Earthling was enjoying the lesson.

The lesson went through everything people before Stanley had experienced, learning the basics of Thol. Understanding friends and foes, whether human or animal.

An hour into the session, Adrum experienced a slight tugging sensation in his head. He had never felt that before but made a mental note to discuss it with the elders.

Before he could snap to what was happening, Adrum started to feel like his brain was being pulled from his skull. He tried to break the connection with Stanley, but the Earthling's brain would not detach.

A RACKET FROM INSIDE ADRUM'S HOUSE HAD EGROMS RUNNING to the distress signals.

Lee and the boys joined the rush. Something was wrong with Stanley's session.

The modest mushroom house was filled with Egrom elders. Lee stood in the doorway watching a scene that could only be from an M. Night Shyamalan horror movie. While the student and teacher sat four feet away from each other, Stanley held Adrum's brain in captivity.

The Egrom elders' acute vision had honed in on the electrical connections and were using their powers to zap Adrum free. Stanley sat serenely with eyes closed; he had no idea about the havoc he was causing. When Ghury sent a massive electrical charge into Stanley's brain, the scientist was startled and opened his eyes. He blinked, looked at the collapsed teacher across the table from him and regarded the elders staring back at him. Only then did he get the sense something was wrong.

Two Egroms lifted Adrum from his chair and settled him in his nest.

Then the headaches began. One elder rubbed his right eye. Another held a hand to the top of his head.

Ghury focused on Stanley. He detected right away that Stanley's forehead had extended farther. It was now sticking out a full inch, with his eyebrows under this new ledge of bone.

"Stanley, go outside. If anyone feels achy in the head or eyes, move away from them," Ghury said.

Lee moved away from the doorway, too dumbfounded to speak.

Stanley stood and left Adrum's house. "What happened?" Lee asked.

"I'm not sure. I hope Adrum is okay. I must have done something wrong, but I don't know what." Stanley's voice echoed. It was distinct.

Lee rubbed the back of his neck.

"Are you getting a headache?" Stanley asked. "Ghury said I should stand back if anyone shows symptoms."

Lee doubled over in pain.

Stanley jumped toward Lee to provide assistance, then thought better of it and moved back five feet.

"Lee needs help!" Stanley called out.

Ghury came out of the mushroom house and appraised the situation. He waved a hand at Stanley, motioning him to back further away.

The scientist was crestfallen. He walked to the edge of the forest and sat on the moss. Defeated, he held his head in his hands.

CHAPTER THREE

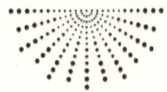

D'laine lounged on one of the sofas in her sitting room with Pup at her feet. She struggled with the Tholian scroll in her hand, trying to teach herself the written language. There was a fully stuffed library in the palace and she wanted to be able to learn about this world in greater detail.

A tap on the outer door announced a visitor. The diwal dog was on his feet, teeth clacking a warning. Trakon stuck his head into the room. "D'laine?"

Chatter scooted around Trakon and rushed into the room. He and Pup romped around as if they hadn't seen each other in forever, although it had only been a couple of hours.

"In here," she called out.

Pup bounded over to Trakon and whined a greeting. He expected his head to be scratched. Most of the time he got what he wanted.

Diwal dogs were not quite trusted one hundred percent because of the species' inherent killing trait. Their muscled bodies were similar to a Rottweiler, gray in coloring with long snouts. Their four powerful legs ended on armadillo-type feet with thick, strong claws. Instead of short-cropped hair, diwal dogs had gray oily skin. The only hair was in the form of tufts on their frightful faces. Their three layers of razor teeth were eerily similar to the monster in the movie *Alien*. Their tails ended in a pod similar to the Plotals.

Trakon entered the sitting room with the dogs on his heels and flopped next to D'laine. He snatched the scroll out of her hands. "Why are you reading this dusty thing?"

She grabbed it back. "I'm trying to teach myself your written language. One thing I miss from my world are books. I love to read, and your parents' library contains a lot of material."

"Have Twum help you," Trakon suggested. "She's always reading."

"Really?" D'laine asked, excited. "I'll ask her if we can start tomorrow."

"Want to go to the Cember Forest? Your family has been there for two weeks."

"Adrum said they should stay for one month so they could adjust properly," D'laine said. "Do you think it will be okay if we visit?"

"I don't see why not," Trakon said. "We don't have to stay long; you could just see how everyone is doing."

D'laine was on her feet and ready to go. "I wonder if everyone will be like me—do you think their gifts will be different?"

He shrugged. "This is all new to me so I don't have a clue."

They stood face to face, inches apart, deeply drawn to each other. Trakon gently grasped D'laine's shoulders and drew her in and kissed her, barely brushing his lips against hers.

Her eyes closed, lips parted as he took a step back.

"I... Was that okay?" Trakon stammered. "I didn't mean to...!"

D'laine swayed slightly. She stepped forward, wrapped her arms around his neck and kissed him back. They molded to each other. After several long, steamy moments, they parted.

"Guess that was okay," Trakon said with a goofy grin.

She swatted him playfully, but her heart was pounding.

Pup and Chatter yawned, impatient. They both bored their eyes into a pleading message: *let's go already!* They headed to the door. Pup looked over his shoulder and saw that their humans were not moving. The dog returned to D'laine and Trakon and nudged them individually.

"Okay, you don't need to be so bossy," Trakon said.

"Should we bring Scooby?" D'laine asked.

Trakon shook his head. "Nah, he won't leave my father's side. He's set on protecting his king."

THE CRESTRIDER ROSE ABOVE THE TREES AND TRAKON GUIDED IT toward a clearing at the edge of the Egrom village. Pup's front paws were braced on one of the railings as he took in the sights while Chatter snoozed on the deck. When the crestrider settled a foot above the ground, Pup jumped down to the deck and waited for the command. Chatter jumped up and stood by Trakon, who lowered the stairs.

"Come!" D'laine said.

Pup was on her heels and down the stairs. Chatter stayed by Trakon's side.

Pup ran around D'laine and Trakon in full joy mode.

"Heel!" D'laine said. Pup ran back to her and stayed by her side while they walked toward the gigantic mushroom village.

"How did you train Chatter?" D'laine asked. "He seems so calm compared to Pup."

Trakon rubbed the tuft of hair on Chatter's head. "We have a sort of understanding. Plus, I use hand signals and brain-talk which will come in handy at times when silence is necessary."

"Huh. Can you teach me?" D'laine asked. "There can't be anything worse than a diwal dog out of control."

Brian, Jamie and an Egrom child ran to meet them. D'laine noticed that her brothers were dressed in navy and silver Ciertron clothes. Their uniforms were slightly different from what she and Trakon wore.

"D'laine!" Brian and Jamie yelled out.

"Hi, boys!" D'laine said in English. "You remember Trakon, right?"

"You can talk the native language." Brian bent his right ear forward and showed D'laine his translator.

"Who's your friend?" Trakon asked.

Brian pulled his new friend forward. "This is Chacoodi!"

"I've heard that name before," D'laine turned to the Egrom boy-child. "We didn't officially meet, but I remember seeing you when I first arrived here."

"You were the first human I had ever seen!" Chacoodi said excitedly. He glanced warily at the dogs. "These diwal dogs don't attack?"

"She tamed them and one other dog in the pack who's with my father," Trakon said.

"The king of Ebscalon has a diwal dog?" Chacoodi asked with disbelief.

Jamie slumped down to the ground and patted his thighs. "Come here."

Pup and Chatter approached Jamie, teeth clacking in a threatening manner.

"Pup! Chatter!" D'laine scolded. "Jamie, diwal dogs are deadly. Remember that movie you had nightmares about with the piranha fish? Diwals are like those fish. They can strip a person down to their skeleton in moments."

Jamie stared at the dogs. The clacking stopped. Pup did a transformation as he approached Jamie, tail wagging and butt wiggling. Chatter was a little more reserved, but was curious.

"It's no big deal," Jamie said. "They'd never hurt me."

Chacoodi watched as Jamie and Pup appeared to become instant friends. "I've never seen a diwal dog so happy." He backed up and kept a respectable distance.

"My brother likes animals, and they all love him," Brian said. "I guess they can tell he's friendly."

"Where are daddy and Stanley?" D'laine asked.

"Daddy's with Ghury and Stanley is with Adrum," Brian said, bursting with excitement. "D'laine! Too bad you weren't here last week! Stanley almost drained Adrum's brain!"

"What!" D'laine and Trakon said at the same time. Brian and Chacoodi competed to tell the story.

"Yeah, he got into Adrum's head and was pulling information into his own head," Brian said.

"The elders had to drag Stanley out of Adrum's head!" Chacoodi said. "Adrum didn't fully recover for two whole turns!"

"Don't stare, but Stanley's head is bigger!" Brian said.

"And his voice echoes," Chacoodi said.

They nodded to Trakon and D'laine. "It's true!"

Kestrum walked across the village and joined them. "Are you two still telling stories?"

"Kestrum!" D'laine said. They hugged. "This is Trakon, Kestrum."

Kestrum nodded to Trakon. "Hello, prince of Ebscalon! Welcome to our village."

"Hello, Kestrum," Trakon said, contemplating something. "I've flown out here many times, but I've never seen this village."

Kestrum laughed. "That is as it should be."

"I don't understand," Trakon said.

"This village is hidden," Kestrum said. "You can only find it if you are invited to do so, or with someone who has been here." Kestrum nodded in D'laine's direction.

"D'laine!" Lee shouted across the way as he stepped out of Ghury's house. He saw her and waved.

"Hi, daddy!" D'laine waved back. "Hi, Ghury!"

Ghury and Lee walked over and joined them.

Lee drew D'laine into a hug and rocked with her. "Hi, honey." His eyes met Trakon's over D'laine's head. "Hi, Trakon."

"Hello, Lee Jackson," Trakon said respectfully.

Lee and D'laine parted. He attempted to greet Trakon with the customary hand-to-the-arm shake. "I'll get the hang of this yet. Just call me Lee."

D'laine sidled up to Ghury and hugged him. "Hi, Ghury. Are my family and Stanley keeping you busy?"

Ghury grumbled. "Your smart Earth friend is a challenge."

D'laine became serious. "That's what the boys said. What exactly is the problem?"

"He has a very active, big brain." Ghury grabbed Chacoodi and demonstrated. He used two of his hands on Chacoodi's head. "Adrum discovered that Stanley's brain is lit in areas where no human or Egrom brain has much activity. We had to abort the first lesson when Stanley attempted to pull the lesson right out of Adrum's brain into his own."

D'laine's jaw dropped open. "Is Adrum okay?"

Ghury grumbled, but nodded. "It took all the elders to dislodge the connection."

"How did they do that?" Trakon asked.

"You have seen the vines that climb and cling to the agrin trees. We had to find all the tendrils that Stanley wove into each part of Adrum's brain in the lesson then—" he paused while choosing the correct words. "We had to send shocks to each tendril before they would release."

Ghury shared a mind movie that showed electrical shocks releasing Adrum from Stanley's mental hostage situation.

Trakon and D'laine could hardly believe what they watched.

Lee shook his head. "It was several scary moments!"

"We definitely know what Stanley's gift is," Ghury said. "His brain absorbs knowledge just as the moss absorbs moisture. I suggest keeping a healthy distance."

D'laine snorted out a half laugh. "Back home someone would probably wrap his head in aluminum foil."

Lee and Trakon shared a thoughtful moment.

"We could make a helmet that would shield his powers from harming anyone," Trakon said.

Lee nodded. "Here's an idea. Let's allow for a lever that could open holes about the size of the circumference of a thumb. That will give him the opportunity to take in information, won't it?"

Trakon became excited. He tapped his communicator and brought up a holographic screen and sketched what they discussed.

Lee stepped up, and using his fingers, pulled the hologram into a 3D vision. He and Trakon were lost in diagramming a solution for Stanley while everyone watched.

"What are you doing in the meantime so he doesn't hurt anyone?" D'laine asked.

"We found a temporary solution." Ghury smiled, which, for an Egrom, meant showing all his pointy, deadly looking teeth. D'laine remembered the first time Ghury smiled at her. She thought he was going to attack.

"Oh, I can't wait to see what you came up with," she said. At that moment, Stanley emerged from Adrum's hut wearing a cooking cauldron on his head. He waved to the group and headed over to them.

Brian and Chacoodi backed away, then ran off to play.

D'laine stared at the cauldron. "I'd give anything to be able to take a picture and send it to Victor and Dr. Joplin!"

"So not funny." Stanley's voice echoed just as the boys had insisted. His forehead seemed much larger than either D'laine or Trakon recalled from just two weekes earlier.

"We may have a solution." Trakon showed Stanley the holo-

33

graphic design he and Lee had created. "I should measure your head." He looked to Ghury for guidance. "Will it be possible to take measurements safely, or will it be too dangerous if we remove the cooking pot?"

"I suggest you not use your device. You should shut it off to be safe. You will be able to use pieces of vine." Ghury clicked and chirped in Egrom. A sentry came out of the forest with a long vine trailing behind him. He and Ghury exchanged nods, and the sentry went back to his post.

"You hold it around his head and I'll cut it to the exact length." Lee pulled a knife out of his uniform. "Measure around his head, then measure from the top of his shoulder over his head to the other shoulder." Lee demonstrated.

Trakon nodded. "Good idea."

Ghury lifted the cauldron in the air. Trakon quickly wrapped the vine around Stanley's head and Lee cut it with a minimum of overlap. Trakon did the same with the over-the-head measurement. He wavered a moment and his eyes went slack. Lee quickly stepped in and snipped the vine at the second measurement.

Ghury slapped the cauldron back on Stanley's head. "Ow!" Stanley complained.

Trakon shook his head like a dog.

"Are you okay?" D'laine asked. Trakon still looked woozy.

"Huh?" After a moment, Trakon came out of the stupor. He backed away from Stanley. "Don't remove that cauldron! I'll be back with a prototype as soon as possible. Lee and I can make adjustments."

The tension eased among the group.

"I can't sleep in this thing," Stanley complained.

Lee studied Stanley. "Maybe we can make a soft version, like a bonnet, but with shielding on the outside." He rubbed the material of his suit. "Yeah, I'm sure that would work. This material is strong. We could have the inside padded so it would be comfortable to sleep in."

Ghury nodded. "Our tribe can create this bonnet. We work with the material to create many things."

"Good," Lee said. "Trakon will work on the metal helmet and we'll see how the prototype works."

"Now that that's settled, do you know what your special gifts are?" D'laine glanced from her father to her brothers.

Brian pouted. "I don't have any special ability!"

D'laine ruffled his hair. "Don't worry, it will come. Mine sort of flopped around for a bit."

She turned her gaze to Jamie. He shrugged.

"I just figured out my gift," Lee said. "When Trakon had that holographic program up, I saw the helmet drawing in my mind in a complete 3D, all layers."

Ghury nodded. "That will probably develop over time, as D'laine's gift emerged."

Stanley's face broke out in a huge grin, making him look pretty freakish with his distended forehead. "Guess there's no doubt about what I'm good at."

CHAPTER FOUR

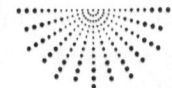

The Ciertrons kept their distance from Stanley. They eyed the Earthling wearing the strange helmet with distrust. The entire back, top and sides of his head were shrouded in a gunmetal gray material that fit snugly with a slight flare where his neck met his shoulders.

Trakon and Lee had designed the helmet so there was enough room for Stanley to shrug his shoulders comfortably. They also took into consideration stretching so there was no interference when the scientist raised his arms above his head. The front of the helmet covered part of his forehead—the distended abnormality.

Upon meeting Stanley, Scooby—renamed La'gar'ish, after a great Tholian warrior—threw himself in front of Jor-Dan. He launched into pre-attack mode to protect his king from what he considered a threat.

"At ease, La'gar'ish," Jor-Dan commanded.

La'gar'ish reluctantly quieted down, but stayed in a protective mode in front of Jor-Dan, leaning into the king's legs.

"Why doesn't he like me?" Stanley asked, crestfallen.

"It's not that he doesn't like you. He isn't familiar with your scent, and he doesn't understand how you fit into palace life," Trakon suggested.

Kitry tut-tutted. "Lee and the boys have a familial scent he recognizes from D'laine. Trakon has a connection to my family and the palace."

Stanley appraised this information. "But what about all the people he doesn't know?"

"You're putting too much thought into this," Lee said. "He's a dog. They do things their way and have their own ideas about how they should work. His self-appointed job is to protect the king."

Stanley grumbled for a few moments then let it go, eyeing La'gar'ish warily. "Okay, I guess."

Two Egroms and a handful of Ciertrons walked through the entryway and disappeared up a staircase.

Stanley's new suite of rooms on the top floor in the rear of the palace was being insulated with a protective material. During the first few turns in the palace, Stanley had been in rooms on the second floor. That was when it was discovered if the sleeping bonnet slipped completely off his head, people in rooms nearby, or downstairs, woke with terrible head-aches. The problem had been discussed with the Egroms, and Ghury sent four of his tribe to work with the Ciertron craftsmen.

"Want to test your new suite, Stanley? Lee asked.

"Might as well, while the Egroms are here," he said.

Lee, Stanley and Trakon excused themselves from the table and climbed the stairs. They walked down a long hallway to the rear of the palace to where all the activity was taking place. They approached the room.

"Can we test the suite to see if Stanley needs to keep his helmet on with company?" Lee asked the closest Ciertron.

"Sure. That's a good idea so we know if the place will require more padding," the Ciertron said.

Stanley, Lee and Trakon entered the room. "Ready?" Stanley asked.

"Take it off!" Trakon said.

Stanley removed the helmet. He eyed his friends, the Egroms and Ciertrons anticipating if he needed to replace the helmet. So far no one was bowled over in agony.

"Thank you, Thol!" Stanley whooped with joy.

They all high-fived. Even the Egroms participated in the simple celebratory antic.

Trakon, Lee and Stanley returned to the dining room to partake breakfast with the family.

"We tested Stanley's suite, and he won't have to wear the helmet or the sleeping bonnet!" Trakon announced.

"I'm so happy for you! I can't imagine having to wear that helmet all the time," Kitry said.

The palace staff was polite to Stanley, but they felt challenged around him. As he joined the family for breakfast, the majordomo set a small carafe of Stanley's favorite juice in front of him. It tasted like mango with a hint of passion fruit.

Platters of food were placed on the table. They served themselves and ate the scrumptious food.

"I'm going to take a look at those robots this morning," Trakon said. "Why don't you two join me? We'll see what secrets they hold."

Lee and Stanley were enthusiastic.

"Where do you have them? And did you get the big one? He must be the master and the others the slaves," Stanley said. He saw the raised eyebrows on the Ciertrons. "That's what we called them in electronics back on Earth. The one with all the controls is the master. The others are programmed to follow the master's commands."

"That makes sense," Jor-Dan said. "We call them leaders and followers."

"I like that terminology a lot better," Lee said.

"So, where are they?" Stanley asked.

"They're in one of the hangars," Trakon said.

Lee rubbed his hands together. "I can't wait to see how they're constructed."

"We need to be sure they're totally dead and offline," Stanley said. "When Victor, Dr. Joplin and I performed our little experiment, we inadvertently discovered that the beam generator on their chest is very powerful. That thing could drag a crestrider to the ground!"

Kitry's eyes darted back and forth between the men. "What precautions will you take?"

Lee teepeed his fingers in thought. "We'll have to make sure the circuitry is effectively dead. I'm sure Trakon has a tool to check circuits. If not, we'll have to devise something similar to what I used back home."

"A lot of our Earth tools are inferior to Tholian technology, daddy," D'laine said. "But I understand what you're suggesting. I'll bet Trakon has something like that."

"At the end of the month, we're having a formal dinner," Jor-Dan said. "We have invited the leaders of nearby kingdoms to meet all of you."

Kitry took the helm. "It will be a pleasant affair. I've arranged for each of you men to have more formal attire." She turned her attention to Brian and Jamie. "Would you two like short sleeves and short pant legs, or the full length for each?"

Brian and Jamie shared a glance with raised brows. Jamie shrugged.

"I like the long legs and sleeves," Brian said. "I've seen boys with those other clothes. I don't know if I'll like them or not."

"I'll have Remit prepare both." Kitry turned her gaze to Trakon and Lee. "Perhaps someone would be able to create a dressier helmet for Stanley?"

The men blinked, then exchanged glances among themselves. *Women! They were always mindful of fashion.*

"Okay," Trakon said. "We'll work on that." He stared at Lee with a questioning plea.

They finished the morning meal and everyone went on their way. Jor-Dan, with his dog at his side, hurried off to a meeting with his advisors.

Trakon, Lee and Stanley left the palace with Chatter romping ahead.

D'laine and Pup searched for Twum to continue her reading lessons.

Brian and Jamie hurried out of the dining salon in a controlled gait so they wouldn't get yelled at for running in the palace.

THE MEN HEADED OVER TO THE WORKSHOP WHERE TRAKON'S team was still working with the crestriders and the crystal energy problem for night flying. Chatter sniffed along the floor among the men, looking for fallen tidbits of food. "Hexlon, I've got a project for you," Trakon said as he faced an older man. His face sported a wry grin.

"Am I going to hate this project?" Hexlon studied Trakon's face.

"Your queen insists that Stanley requires a dressier helmet for formal dinners and other occasions," Trakon said.

Hexlon stared at Trakon to make sure he was wasn't joking, then swung his gaze to Stanley. He walked around the man, examining the helmet.

"Show me the original plans and I'll see what I can do," Hexlon said. "How fancy does it have to be?"

"Not quite royal, but dressier than what he's wearing," Lee said. "This one was created rather quickly so Stanley wouldn't kill anyone."

Stanley scowled. "Not my fault!"

Trakon tapped his communicator and pulled up the holographic plans. He tapped Hexlon's communicator. "Here you go. I know you'll come up with something better than what we threw together. We're going over to the hangar where the robots are."

Stanley stared at the layer of crystals on a crestrider wing. He walked the distance of both wings, holding one hand several inches over the crystals. He grabbed a stepladder off the wall and climbed it so he could look down on a wing.

"What are you thinking about?" Lee tried to assess Stanley's interest.

"See how the crystals all point in different directions?" Stanley asked. "I'm pretty sure that's the cause of the failure. These should be removed, and all of them should be reset so that every one of them points at precisely the same angle."

"That makes sense," Lee said. "All the solar panels I've ever seen face the same direction."

"Exactly," Stanley said.

The team of workers looked to Trakon for his thoughts.

He was silently studying the wings.

"Right now, all the crystals are bouncing energy off each other in a nonconstructive way. They need to be aligned so they absorb the energy from the suns, collect it and store it in the ship's battery backup system," Stanley explained.

"That makes sense." Trakon turned to his team. "This first model will be tedious. Once we have a working unit with all the kinks worked out, we should be able to get the fleet prepared for nighttime flying."

Lee pulled in a breath. He concentrated on a wing, and pulled up a holographic image of the current configuration. He studied the plan then tweaked it in 3D, showing the new configuration along with a battery bank. "Here you go. This is what's needed."

Trakon and Stanley looked over the holograph along with the team of designers.

A murmur of agreement spread through the team. Lee transferred the diagram to the team lead.

TRAKON, LEE AND STANLEY WALKED OVER TO THE HANGAR WHERE two regular robots and Zandal, the much larger robot, leaned against the wall. Lee ran his hand over the surface of a common robot. He examined it searching for seams and didn't find any.

"Huh, these things are seamless," he said. "Help me lay this thing on the floor."

Trakon grabbed one of the robot's arms and Lee grabbed the other. It was too heavy to move.

"We need a hoist," Lee said.

"Wait a moment," Stanley said. "I think I've got this. You two better go over by the door."

Stanley moved the lever on top of his helmet and opened the holes to expose part of his head. He stretched out a hand and stared at the robot. It lifted off the floor, wobbled a bit, then moved horizontally and settled on its back on the floor.

"Holy smokes!" Lee said. "You can levitate things!"

Lee and Trakon started forward. Suddenly they both got a little wobbly on their feet.

"Close the lever!" Trakon held his head while staggering. "You're pulling on my brain!"

"Oops! Sorry." Stanley flipped the lever and closed off the holes.

"I still don't understand why just the back and top of your head has to be shielded. What about your face?" Trakon asked.

"That's just the way it is," Stanley said.

"Yeah, very scientific," Lee joked. He examined the robot

closer and found a tiny hole in the side of one arm. "Look how they did this."

Trakon and Stanley examined what looked like a pin-prick. Lee discovered similar holes along the torso and legs. "Do you have anything I could pop in there?" he asked Trakon.

Trakon turned to a tool cabinet and opened one drawer after another. He picked up a thin piece of metal that looked like a needle. "This should work." He handed it to Lee.

Lee popped the needle into the hole in the arm. He pushed the needle then wiggled it. "I think I need to be able to turn it."

Trakon returned to the tool cabinet and opened the drawer. He pulled out a small ratcheting device. "Here, see if this is the correct size or if it's too big."

It fit. Lee started to work on one side, and Trakon found another set of tools and tackled the other side. In less than an hour they had the entire front of the robot's structure separated from the back. All three men poked and prodded the insides of the robot and gently touched the circuitry.

"Why don't you use that big brain of yours and pull out this guy's brain?" Trakon joked.

"That big one's the leader. He's the one who would have all the programming," Stanley said. "But the followers should have some data that might be interesting."

They all turned and stared at Zandal. Lee and Trakon walked away toward the door while Stanley levitated the big monster onto the floor.

The men tackled taking Zandal apart. Once they had his front structure removed, Stanley studied the circuitry and components.

"I think you two should stand outside for this one," Stanley said. "I'm going to remove my helmet."

Trakon and Lee quickly distanced themselves from the hangar. "Do you think this is far enough away?" Trakon gauged the distance from the closed door.

"I don't have a clue, but I'll venture to guess we'll find out pretty quick," Lee said.

An odd sound came through the hangar door. Lights glowed through the high windows.

"What's going on in there?" Lee asked, flushed with concern.

"You don't think he activated it, do you?" Trakon asked, mildly panicked. "They're formidable! We barely stopped them!"

The door opened and Stanley waved them over. "It's safe."

"What the heck were you doing in there?" Lee asked. They walked back inside the hangar.

"Let me tell you." Stanley pointed to Zandal. "This guy here was a terminator if there ever was one!"

Lee tried to explain the movie to Trakon, but gave up. Thol was eons over anything like Hollywood. He thought about the sessions with Adrum, but since there were no actors involved, he let go trying to explain the concept.

"What did you extract from it?" Trakon asked.

"Their world developed this technology and it got away from them. The machines became smarter than their human creators. They were developed to learn and change from their experiences. It got to the point where the machines took over, hunted humans and persecuted them," Stanley said. "This is like that movie *Terminator*. But this is scarier because this parallel world developed these monsters who killed almost all of their creators."

"This is not anything I am willing to share with anyone here on Thol, or back home on Earth," Stanley said. "Self-evolving technology is the ultimate destroyer."

They stared at the dismantled robot. "Is there anything left of its programming?" Lee asked.

"No. I took everything—I didn't want to take any chances." Stanley kicked the robot's foot. "I looked at the followers programming as well. There's nothing there to be concerned about. Just some binary coding so it followed orders from the leader."

"Why don't we re-create their programming to be helpful?" Trakon asked.

"That's probably how they started out," Stanley said. "Then the scientists saw more opportunity for other uses. And things progressed over the years until these machines turned on them."

"Oh, right," Trakon said. "Let's not repeat history."

D'LAINE WALKED OUTSIDE OF THE PALACE AND STRETCHED, PUP by her side. Her reading lessons with Twum were exhausting, and she didn't feel as if she was making progress. The written language was symbols and squiggles like ancient Egyptian hieroglyphics. She hoped it would make sense soon.

There's got to be a better way to learn this. If only I could absorb information like Edgar Cayce, that man who was known as the sleeping prophet. I remember he was called the father of holistic medicine, and was the most documented psychic of the 20th century.

She pressed her communicator to find her brothers. "Where are you two?"

Jamie chimed in. "We're with a group of Youngmen. Brian's practicing strategies."

D'laine found them. She watched as Brian and the Youngmen interacted. She noticed that her brother was not comfortable with the war strategies.

The difference between these Tholians and her brothers was vast. Jamie and Brian were still young children and wanted to play games whereas the Youngmen were fully mature Tholians in growing bodies. These strategies were actual combat sessions. D'laine stepped forward.

"Brian, Jamie, let's go for a ride," she said.

Her brothers said goodbye to the group and walked away

with their sister. Pup pranced around until they paid attention to him and gave him a scratch on the head and a pat on the rump.

"You have to understand that, even though those Youngmen are your size, they are fully matured men, like Trakon, and they don't play games," D'laine explained. "Maybe we can ask Ghury if Chacoodi can come to visit."

"I don't understand," Jamie said. "Don't they ever have fun?"

"This is a different society. I understand how confusing this can be. Youngmen look like kids, but they aren't. I wish you had regular boys and girls to play with, but other than Egrom children, I'm not aware of any possible playmates."

Brian scratched Pup's head as he sulked.

They walked to the pakow holding pens outside of the city gates. Lulu, D'laine's pakow, came to the fence and lowed at D'laine. She stuck her fingers through the rails and rubbed Lulu's face.

"Hey, girl. Want to go for a romp?"

She approached the man who attended to the pakows. "Would you be able to prepare Lulu and two pakows for my brothers?" she asked.

"Of course, princess. It will only take a moment," the attendant said.

"Why does everyone call you *princess*?" Jamie asked with exasperation.

"Because one of these turns Trakon and I will marry," D'laine said.

"But you're not married yet," Brian said exasperated, "so there's no reason to call you that."

"It's just their ways." D'laine was getting irritated at the whole *princess* thing.

The attendant led the three pakows over to them. "Thank you. We won't be long."

She turned to her brothers. "Do you remember how to

mount?" D'laine whispered to Lulu. Her pakow lowered itself so D'laine could climb up the animal's front leg onto its back and get into the saddle.

Brian tickled his pakow on the chin and asked it to kneel. The pakow knelt and Brian climbed up the leg and settled into the saddle.

Jamie threw his arms around his pakow's neck and giggled. The creature lowered itself and Jamie climbed aboard. They set off at a gentle pace with Pup running ahead.

Once they were comfortable with the pakows gait they sped up and raced across the amber-colored moss, completely care-free, then settled into a comfortable pace. After they had been riding for a while, they heard the loud bellowing, growling and grunting of animals fighting.

"Stop! Brian, Jamie, pull on the reins or tell your pakow to stop, right now!" D'laine saw Pup bound off. "Pup! Return to me! Now!"

Pup stopped, turned his head toward D'laine, then back at the battle up ahead. His teeth clacked in the deathly hypnotic advanced state of killing mode.

"Down, Pup!" D'laine yelled.

Reluctantly, Pup submitted and dropped to the ground, barely containing his frenzy to join the fight.

Up ahead they saw a bull pakow fighting off an animal. As they got closer, D'laine recognized the fearsome og. The bull grabbed the og by the scruff of its neck and shook it like a rag doll. They watched as the mighty bull flung the og toward a cluster of trees.

The og screeched in pain as it hit the trees and fell to the ground. It attempted to stand, but collapsed.

The bull pakow ran at full speed in the opposite direction. He bellowed his success so all the cows would be aware of how big and brave he was.

The group moved slowly forward. Pup was on his feet. He

squealed as he circled the huge moving lump on the ground, his teeth clacking a warning of attack.

"Pup, away!" D'laine motioned for her brothers to stay back. She urged Lulu forward, but the cow would not move another inch toward its dreaded enemy.

"D'laine, that animal's hurt!" Jamie urged his pakow to kneel. He jumped out of the saddle and almost ran down his mount's front leg.

"Jamie! Get back here!" D'laine screeched. "That og is hurt, and they are extremely dangerous!"

Jamie ran to the animal and fell to his knees. He pushed Pup out of the way. "Pup, go away!"

The og growled and snapped at Jamie. Pup lurched at the og.

Jamie smacked Pup. "Go sit down! You're scaring him."

Jamie turned back to the og. He *shushed* at it, reached out and stroked the lumpy bluish fur on its side.

D'laine screeched in terror while running toward him.

The og made a mewling noise as Jamie stroked it and looked it over. He noticed the og's right rear leg was bent oddly.

D'laine stopped short of her brother and watched him, hardly believing what she witnessed.

"I think he has a broken leg," Jamie said. "Do they have vets here?"

"I'm not sure. We can ask the pakow handler," D'laine said. "You should move away from it. They're normally dangerous animals, but being in pain with a broken leg, he could kill you!"

Jamie turned to his sister. "Honestly, D'laine, does it look like he's going to kill me? Brian, go back and see if that pakow guy can fix a broken leg."

Brian took off on his pakow back to the pens.

Jamie turned to D'laine. "Don't worry about this animal. He's just happy that someone's going to help him."

"Jamie, ogs are not like puppies or ponies. If this guy weren't hurt, he could take down Lulu!"

"No one understands them, that's all!" Jamie gave his sister a belligerent glare and continued to rub his hands on the og. He lifted the og's large knobby head onto his lap and stroked its face. It licked his hand and continued to mewl in pain.

After ten moments, Brian and the pakow attendant arrived.

When the man saw the og, he reached for his laser pistol. "Get away from that og!" the man yelled.

"It's okay," Jamie said. "Can you fix his leg?"

"I'm not going to touch that thing. He'll kill us," the man said.

Jamie let out a frustrated breath. "Does it look like he's killing me? Come on, help him. I'll keep him calm, I promise."

The man hesitated. He returned to his mount and grabbed a bag hanging from the saddle horn. He approached Jamie and the og.

The og growled ferociously at the man.

Jamie tapped its snout. "Stop it. He's going to help you." The og mewled in agony as it gazed into Jamie's eyes.

The attendant knelt and evaluated what he saw. "Looks like a bad break. I can set the bones and wrap his leg, but he won't be able to fend for himself."

"If you can fix him, can we get a cart and take him back to the palace? I can take care of him until he's okay."

The man shook his head, bewildered. "You want to take care of a wild og?"

"Animals sometimes need our help," Jamie said.

"Let's see how this goes first, okay?" The man set his bag on the moss.

Jamie started to sing softly to the og. The animal seemed mesmerized by the sound. Jamie waved his hand at the attendant to alert him he should get to work on the broken leg.

The man straightened out the leg. The og never even flinched. Next, the handler removed a woven cloth from the bag and wrapped it around the leg, pulling it tight. He stretched the leg until he felt the bones align. He fastened the material by taking a laser tool and sealing the end of the cloth to the wrapped area.

The og never paid any attention to what was happening to his leg. The creature was transfixed on Jamie's singing.

"Huh, you sure have a way with animals. I've never seen anything like it." The attendant stood, brushed off his knees and returned to his pakow. "I'll be back with something to haul him. Won't be able to keep him near the pens, or the pakows will stampede."

"Okay, we'll figure something out," Jamie said.

D'LAINE STEPPED OUT OF HER CLOTHES AND WALKED DOWN THE stairs to the bathing pool. She relaxed in the soothing water for a moment, then got busy cleaning up and washing her hair. She loved the bathing pool for its dual functions of bathing and swimming. And, no quokins! Although she did miss the creatures' inquisitiveness back at the hot pool in the Cember Forest. She finished her laps, wrapped herself in a thick gauze towel and grabbed another to dry her hair.

She wandered into the other room and looked in her restorative chamber. For the evening meal she chose a sari-type gown like Kitry wore, plus a pair of sandals with ties that wrapped around her calves.

She entered the dining salon just as everyone was seating themselves.

"You look lovely," Kitry said.

"Thank you for this beautiful gown," D'laine said. "It's so comfortable."

Trakon couldn't take his eyes off her.

Lee cleared his throat rather loudly and Trakon's eyes snapped over to Lee's. Trakon felt his face growing hot.

Suddenly there was a loud, distressed lowing and the sound

of falling debris. Everyone jumped to their feet and ran out of the room. They discovered D'laine's pakow, Lulu, attempting a break-in.

"Lulu! What are you doing here?" D'laine asked the animal.

"She's probably jealous of the dogs," Trakon said through a wicked smile.

D'laine approached Lulu and tried to get her to back out of the archway. Lulu would have none of it.

Jamie pushed D'laine aside. "Move. I'll get her back to the pens."

Everyone watched as he talked in whispers to the pakow and patted her chest. She backed out of the archway, grabbed a chunk of the fallen building material and crunched away.

"Come on," Jamie urged her. "Leave that. It's not your coral rocks."

Lulu obeyed Jamie. He asked her to kneel, and he climbed up her leg to settle on her bare back and grabbed hold of her long hair. They trotted toward the gate and out to the pens.

"We definitely know his gift," Lee said.

"I've never seen anything like it," Jor-Dan said.

"You should have seen him with the og!" Brian said. "He was singing to it while that guy fixed its broken leg."

"An og?" Trakon said in a raised voice.

D'laine cringed. "It's okay. He has it in a corral on the other side of the gate so the pakows won't smell it."

"The og allowed the attendant to fix the leg?" Jor-Dan was shocked. He shared a disbelieving glance with Kitry. She shrugged.

Jamie came skipping back to the palace.

"Go wash," Lee said. "Everyone's waiting on you."

"Well, young man, what are you going to do with that og?" Jor-Dan asked after Jamie rejoined them in the dining salon. "What are you feeding it?"

"Did you know they're vegetarians?" Jamie asked. "They don't eat meat."

"What do you mean?" Jor-Dan challenged him. "They attack animals all the time."

Jamie made a face. "That's because they're territorial. They only eat grass and leaves and stuff."

"Are you sure, Jamie?" Kitry asked.

"Of course. He told me so himself," Jamie said.

All eyes were on Jamie. Eyebrows were raised on six faces, not including the majordomo. His mouth was open wide enough to catch flies.

"What do you mean, *he told you so himself?*" Lee asked.

Jamie shrugged. "Animals talk in my head. We talk to each other."

Brian scowled. "How come I can't do special things? It's not fair."

CHAPTER FIVE

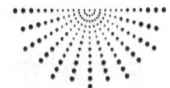

*J*amie spent the next few turns occupied with the og. Jugdaak, the pakow attendant, looked in on the enclosed pen.

"He's not healing properly," Jugdaak said. "We should put him out of his misery so he doesn't suffer." His fingers itched to pull his laser pistol out of his holster and end the dreadful creature's life.

Jamie balked. "I'm going to go find my sister. I'll bet D'laine can help him!" He jumped to his feet, climbed the fence and ran off toward the palace. D'laine wasn't in her room. Jamie had a moment of near panic as he backtracked toward the busier areas. He raced into a room filled with citizens, Jor-Dan and his advisors.

Two ornate thrones were on a raised dais in front of a wall of beautiful scenic tapestries. Globes floated inside the room, providing an almost natural light. Jor-Dan and his advisors sat at a long, intricately carved table near the base of the thrones. La'gar'ish snoozed at his feet.

Marrak, the documentarian who wrote the decisions of the

petitions and applied the king's official seal, sat to Jor-Dan's left. He already had a stack of documents in a box on the table.

Ignoring citizens lined up to meet with the king, Jamie raced around the people and interrupted a farmer seeking advice about his flock of bobboes.

"Jor-Dan! I can't find D'laine! Jugdaak wants to kill my og because his bones aren't healing the right way and I know D'laine can fix him!" Tears streamed down Jamie's cheeks.

La'gar'ish jumped to his feet and nuzzled Jamie.

Jor-Dan turned to the farmer. "Excuse me a moment." He turned to Jamie. "What's this about the og?"

Jamie was in full upset mode and couldn't stop crying. "He's in a lot of pain and the bones aren't going back together the way they're supposed to. Please don't let Jugdaak kill him! Let D'laine try to heal him first!"

Jor-Dan rested his hand on Jamie's shoulder. "Calm down. Go to the workshop area. D'laine and your father are over there with Trakon."

Jamie threw his arms around Jor-Dan's neck. "Thanks, grandpa." He took off running and disappeared out the door.

The dog settled on the floor and resumed his nap.

Jor-Dan turned his attention back to the farmer. "He has a big heart for all animals." His face lit up in thought. "I'm willing to bet Jamie can help you with your bobboes. When this crisis with the og is over with, I'll have Dannin bring him to your farm."

"I don't understand how a boy can help my flock," the farmer said.

"Animals talk to him," one of the advisors explained.

The farmer just stared for a moment, turned and walked away.

Jor-Dan motioned for Dannin. "You'd better go and make sure your man doesn't get itchy fingers while Jamie is gathering D'laine."

"Jamie's gift could be very useful," Dannin said. "I'll alert my team to seek out any problems with animals."

JAMIE FOUND D'LAINE. THEY RETURNED TO THE PEN AND FOUND Dannin talking to Jugdaak, the pakow attendant. Jamie and D'laine entered the pen, followed by Dannin. Jugdaak was atop the corral fence and watched as D'laine pulled crystals out of her pouch and ran her hands over the og. She focused on the broken leg.

"I need to remove the bandages," she told Jamie. "You keep him occupied, okay?"

"Don't worry about him. He knows you're going to heal him." Jamie lifted the og's head onto his lap and stroked its lumpy blue face.

"Let me assist you." Dannin cut the bonded end of the cloth and gently unwound the material and cast it through the rails. "Should I do anything else?"

D'laine assessed the animal. "I don't think so." She closed her eyes and moved the crystals and her other hand above the broken leg. Jamie, Dannin and Jugdaak watched as the leg moved by itself. With D'laine's deep concentration, the leg straightened out with the proper alignment for the knee and foot. One damaged claw appeared to reposition itself, bringing a whimper from the og.

"Sshh, Oggy," Jamie said. "She's all finished and now you're going to be okay. You can go back to your family soon."

D'laine breathed deeply, returned her crystals to the pouch, then stood. "He'll be okay. Can you tell him to rest here until tomorrow morning? Then he can attempt to stand and try out the leg and foot. He should be able to go home in a couple of turns."

"Thanks for fixing him, D'laine!" Jamie threw his arms

around her in a fierce hug. He turned to Jugdaak. "See, my sister can heal people and animals. There's no need to kill them."

"That's a real talent!" Jugdaak said with respect. "You both have been blessed by Thol."

A Ciertron guard rushed to the palace. He entered the crowded room and saluted the king with his fist to his heart.

"Your Majesty, Plotals are approaching!" the guard reported, somewhat anxious.

Jor-Dan and the advisors jumped to their feet, alert. "How many?"

La'gar'ish threw himself in front of the king at the abrupt movement. He sensed the kings stress. His teeth chattered a warning.

A murmur of concern spread throughout the room of petitioners.

"From what we could discern, there are five of them. They are not in battle dress," the guard said.

Jor-Dan and his advisors exchanged questioning glances.

"Send the head of the guard to meet them and find out what they want," Jor-Dan said. "Alert Trakon."

The guard saluted and hurried from the room.

"What could this be about?" Hal-sa-Bin, the head of security, asked. He gestured for a soldier. "Have two squadrons throughout the city—inconspicuous; no battle gear. We'll find out what they want without appearing to be confrontational."

"Do we meet with them here, or in front of the palace?" Jor-Dan asked.

"Let them come to us, here," Hal-sa-Bin said. "We don't want them to think we are preparing to slaughter them. If we stood in front of the palace, blocking entry, that would send the wrong message."

Marrak stood and addressed the room. "All petitions will continue tomorrow. Please vacate the palace and go to your homes and businesses."

There was a grumble throughout the room as the petitioners left.

TRAKON, IN FULL BATTLE GEAR, DODGED EXITING PETITIONERS AS he and Chatter ran into the throne room. Jor-Dan and Kitry sat on their thrones with the advisors in their positions. D'laine, Lee and Stanley sat in less elaborate chairs to the left of Trakon's chair.

D'laine rushed to Trakon. She pressed a button on his suit. "They aren't in battle gear so there's no need to look hostile." His suit clacked back to normal.

"We can't let them just waltz in here and catch us unprepared!" Trakon bellowed.

"Son, listen to D'laine," Kitry said. "Take your place. There are only five of them."

Trakon grumbled to himself, but followed D'laine to the platform. Instead of sitting in his chair beside his father, he stood behind D'laine's chair with Chatter at his side. Pup's tail beat the floor by D'laine.

TWO TWO-MAN CIERTRON CRESTRIDERS FLANKED THE PLOTALS AS they rode their pakows toward the entrance to the city. Jakla Bosakin appeared regal in an elaborate long black and gold vest over a red tunic. He sat atop his beast with its decorated saddle. He wore thigh-high shiny boots with tribal markings down the side; his legs hugged the sides of his mount.

The crestriders escorted the Plotals through the gates to a

courtyard. Two attendants rushed forward to tend to the pakows. Jakla and his envoy dismounted. A palace guard came forward. He and Jakla spoke for a moment.

"Follow me," the guard said. He led the party into the palace.

Jakla studied the palace interior with great interest as they entered the throne room.

"Jakla Bosakin with Pra-yor, Bist, Wegore and Ystap Olu in attendance, Your Majesty," the guard announced with his fist to his heart.

La'gar'ish was on his feet ready to attack.

Jor-Dan motioned for the dog to settle down as he stood and stepped down from the dais. La'gar'ish walked with the king and stayed at his side. "Greetings, Jakla Bosakin." He nodded to the four Plotal advisors. "Welcome to Ebscalon."

Jakla pounded his heart with his fist. "Jor-Dan." He turned to face Kitry. "Queen Kitry." He nodded to Trakon. His eyes took in the diwal dogs.

Kitry stood and joined Jor-Dan. "Welcome to our fair city."

The majordomo entered with a helper carrying a tray of tankards and glasses of kahl. After the king and queen were served, the tray was presented to Jakla.

"Thank you for considering our large hands," Jakla said as he grabbed a tankard. His advisors were served next then the rest of the room in attendance.

"Why don't we get comfortable and discuss what brought you here?" Kitry gestured to a seating area with sofas and tables.

"We are going to rebuild Ta'Byu'Vohon," Jakla said. There were exclamations of surprise from the Ciertrons.

D'laine, Lee and Stanley were slow to catch the significance of the announcement.

"Oh!" D'laine said. "You haven't had a permanent city since the big war."

Jakla nodded in her direction. "We have come to the conclusion that we have been fools for not rebuilding. My people have also looked hard at the lifestyles we chose after the Great War of Taylon, and more recently with the battle against our mutual enemy, the robots. We have discussed these things in detail. We desire a more civilized way of life than what we currently have with our traveling tent cities—one in which we can raise our families."

Jakla drank from his tankard. "We have chosen land that is forty miles from Ebscalon. It would put us in an alignment with Patrosym, Mer, Lansobar and Caradon. The kingdoms would form a six-pointed star."

"This is indeed a major change," Jor-Dan said. "A very good decision for future generations."

"How can we help you?" Kitry asked.

Jakla nodded to Bist. "Bist and Ystap Olu are our city planners. Even with our tent cities there is the need for structure and planning."

Bist stood and hit his chest with his fist and nodded to the people in the room. "Would it be possible to meet with your city planners and construction engineers? We would also like to tour your buildings. Ebscalon is known to be the best designed city since the war."

Jor-Dan caught the attention of one of the palace guards. "Send for Dreboo and his team." He turned to Bist. "Dreboo is Ebscalon's architect. He and his team will work alongside you."

"We thought that in the center of this star, which is wide open land," Ystap Olu said, "our communities could build tributes to our ancestors."

D'laine noticed that Ystap Olu was smaller than the other Plotals and had much more delicate features. She determined Ystap was a female, similar to how Kestrum was smaller and more refined than the male Egroms.

"That's an excellent idea," Kitry said.

Jakla's eyes wandered over to Stanley. Hexlon had indeed

created a fancy helmet of a shiny metal in black and grey for the big-brained earthling.

"Why does this human wear his helmet in the palace?" Jakla asked.

The Ciertrons, D'laine and Lee all exchanged glances. Lee cleared his throat. "If I may?" he asked of Jor-Dan and Kitry.

Jor-Dan chuckled. "Be my guest."

"On Earth, Stanley was highly intelligent—a renowned genius. The scientific community read every paper he wrote and many discoveries of outer space and inner space were due to his studies," Lee said. "When we came to Thol, we never realized how this world would affect his brain. He almost killed one of the Egrom elders by practically draining his brain. The only thing that keeps Stanley from complete isolation from all life on Thol is the helmet that shields his brain."

"And don't forget his shielded quarters," Trakon said. "We had to have help from the Egroms to shield his living area completely with the same type of material."

Jakla studied Lee and Trakon. "So, if he were to remove the helmet, what would happen?"

"You would feel your brain being drained," D'laine explained. "It's like feeling someone pull strings out of your head!"

"Not only that, but you would have an excruciating headache as if your head was hammered," Trakon said. "I know this from experience."

"If you want to understand what we're talking about with a demonstration, which I don't advise," Lee said, "there's a lever on the top of the helmet that shields holes. Stanley can flip the lever to *sense* something. But he'll have to flip it closed immediately, otherwise we would all be on our knees."

Jakla walked over to Stanley and looked down on the top of his helmet. "I would like to test this on Plotals. Perhaps this is just a human problem."

"Good idea," Stanley said. "I would advise the rest of you to leave the room—Earthlings and Ciertrons. All the Plotals should stay so we can find out if they are immune."

Jakla and his three advisors stood in front of Stanley. When everyone except the Plotals left the room, Stanley opened the vents partially. He watched the five in front of him but didn't detect any problems.

"It appears Plotal brains are significantly different," Stanley said. He reached up and opened the vent all the way. Immediately, Jakla covered one of his eyes, and his advisors doubled over.

Stanley flipped the vent closed. "Guess not! Are you okay?" He watched as the Plotals recovered from his brainy presence.

Jakla kept his hand over one eye. "That was a very painful experiment," he said. He looked his advisors over. The four Plotals held their heads while the agony drained away.

"You can come back into the room," Stanley hollered out to everyone else. "It's safe."

The group entered the room cautiously, followed by the dogs.

"I noticed there seems to be something like a static electrical charge in the air when the helmet is vented," Lee said.

Kitry and Jor-Dan rushed over to the Plotals. "Sit," Kitry said. "Would you like kahl, or water?"

"Behind my eye is very painful," Jakla said.

The other Plotals still clutched at their heads.

Trakon took D'laine's elbow and steered her over to a chair. "Do you think you can do something to help them?"

"I can try," she said. D'laine pulled her pouch open and removed her crystals. "Remember how I healed you on the battle field?"

"Please try," Jakla said. He bent forward on the chair.

D'laine closed her eyes and circled Jakla's head with her hand clutching the crystals. She took deep breaths in and blew out. Within a few moments Jakla relaxed. D'laine moved on to the closest advisor. She repeated the process on the other three until the Plotals returned to normal.

"Looks like that little experiment proved this problem is not species-dependent," Lee said.

Stanley shrugged.

Jor-Dan clasped Stanley's shoulder. "I do like the fancy helmet. You'll steal all the ladies' hearts."

"I can't see how I'll ever get a girl if I have to live in this helmet," Stanley wailed.

"Your living quarters don't require you to wear the helmet," Kitry said with a suggestive wink.

"Do you really think some girl is going to come to my place to get to know me?" Stanley asked. "I don't think so. I should just go out in the wilderness and live in a hut."

"You have only been here for one month," Jakla said. "Perhaps this problem will go away, or maybe it will settle down a bit."

"I don't think these special gifts work like that," Trakon said.

"Now that everyone is back together again, why don't I give you a tour of the palace?" Kitry hooked her arm around Jakla's large scaly arm and led him out of the room, his advisors and the rest of the group following.

JAMIE CLOSED THE PEN WHERE THE OG RESTED AND HEADED BACK to the palace. Halfway there, Dannin hailed him.

"Do you think you can talk to a farmer? He seems to be having a problem with a flock of bobboes," Dannin said.

"Sure. I can give it a try," Jamie said. "Not sure what a bobboe is, though."

"It's a domestic farm bird that lays eggs that we eat," Dannin explained.

"Oh, like a chicken from my world," Jamie exclaimed.

"Probably. We'll take a crestrider," Dannin said.

"Awesome! I love crestriders!" Jamie said.

They walked over to a hangar and climbed aboard a one-man crestrider, which was big enough to carry the two of them. Dannin eased the craft out of the hangar. It rose in the air, then took off at a moderate pace. They flew to the east until a modest farm with several barns and fenced areas appeared. Dannin guided the crestrider to the largest building and landed the ship. He and Jamie hopped to the ground.

Jamie walked over to the fence and stared at the birds in the enclosure. They appeared to be related to chickens, but they were more like turkeys because they were bigger than Earth chickens by more than twenty pounds. These birds had large chests, and blue and purple furry feathers. Dannin went in search of the farmer.

"You guys sure are odd looking," Jamie said to the birds. "What? No, I'm not!" He and the birds were having a conversation when Dannin and Farmer Jovee appeared.

Jamie gave the farmer a big smile. "Have your birds stopped laying eggs?"

"Yeah, how d'you know that? You just got here," Farmer Jovee said.

Jamie giggled. "They're on strike! They don't want to lay any more eggs because they saw you club one of their friends with an axe."

"They're just dumb birds!" Farmer Jovee said. "Whatcha mean?"

Jamie pointed to the tree stump with the axe buried in the wood. "They want you to move that. It scares them."

Farmer Jovee looked at Dannin for confirmation that this wasn't a joke.

"Do as the boy says," Dannin said. "Your bobboes explained what the problem is. If you want them to start laying eggs again, move the stump and the hatchet. Don't kill any birds near them."

The farmer looked around, scratching his head. "Not sure where I can move it where they can't see it."

"Just put it behind a building," Jamie said.

Dannin grabbed the axe out of the stump and handed it to the farmer. Then he hefted the tree stump and hauled it up in his arms. They walked around the corner of the barn and placed the stump so none of the bobboes would be able to glimpse it again, or the axe they dreaded. The men walked back to the main corral.

"Ask them if they're happy now and if they'll start layin' again," Farmer Jovee said.

Jamie squatted by the fence. Two bobboes faced him and a silent conversation commenced.

"They're glad the death thing is gone—that's what they call the axe," Jamie said. "They want to know if you can give them more of those little nuggets. They really like them."

"They like 'em, huh?" Farmer Jovee asked. "I make 'em myself. They're dried bugs mixed up with chopped agrin leaves. I stir 'em in a pot with a little honey and let 'em cool down."

"You could probably sell that at the market," Dannin suggested. "If your bobboes like it so much, other farmers may want some."

Farmer Jovee's face lit up. "I make this stuff by the barrel. I 'spose I can sell it in a clay pot to other people who only have a few bobboes. Farmers'll want to buy it in larger quantities if they've got a lot of bobboes."

"Looks like you've got a new business thanks to your birds," Dannin said.

Jamie stood. "Your bobboes like living here."

Farmer Jovee clapped Jamie on the back. "Who woulda thought my bobboes knew how to talk?"

Dannin and Jamie said goodbye and flew back to the palace.

"Please?" Brian begged, his eyes pleading with his father, D'laine and Trakon.

"It's not up to me," Lee said. "You should ask the king and queen if they would mind if Chacoodi came to visit for a week. And the majordomo would need to have the kitchen staff prepare his special food."

"Let's go ask right now!" Brian jumped out of his chair and raced to the door.

"Not so fast," Lee hollered. "The king and queen aren't just sitting around doing nothing. They keep this vast city and the palace, running smoothly. And people seek their guidance. You will have to stand in line with the other petitioners and present your request."

Brian thought it all through and nodded. "I can do that! Can I go to the big room now?"

Lee silently communicated with D'laine and Trakon. They nodded consent. "Okay, but no running in the palace, and you make sure you stand in line, no matter how long that line is. No complaining or whining, understand?"

Brian was itching to get out the door. "Okay, I promise."

"Off with you then," Lee said.

CHAPTER SIX

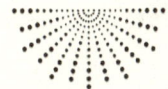

*B*rian stood in line with the petitioners in the throne room. There were at least twenty people in front of him and probably fifteen after his place in line. He tapped his communicator and pulled up the crestrider program. It was the closest thing to a game he could come up with. He shuffled forward as the line moved while playing with the crestrider controls. Slowly but surely, he was learning how to fly a ship. He hoped someday soon he'd be allowed to fly to the Cember Forest by himself in a single-man flyer so he and Chacoodi could spend more time together.

As he moved forward again, Brian looked up to see only five men in front of him. He figured he'd better pay attention to how he was supposed to act and present his case in this formal setting. He wondered if Marrak, the documentarian, would record his petition on paper like that of the others before him. The idea of showing his father and Trakon his official document brought a smile to his face.

He was next up and his excitement was evident. The man in front of him finished and moved aside. Brian now stood before the king and his advisors. Jor-Dan lifted an eyebrow. Brian hit his chest with his fist, then presented his case.

"King Jor-Dan, I would like to petition to be able to bring my Egrom friend, Chacoodi, to the palace for a week... I mean a notch. He's my best friend and I don't have anyone to play with." Brian was almost whining. "I'll even help the kitchen people with his food!"

Brian was on the brink of tears as the king studied him without a word.

Jor-Dan controlled his face to keep his expression neutral. "Why can't you play with Jamie? He's your brother and your closest companion, after your sister."

"Jamie?" Brian balked. "He's just a little kid!"

"I see." Jor-Dan kept his features serious. "What would you and this Chacoodi be doing—if you were allowed this visitation?"

Brian's head filled with so many things that words tumbled out of his mouth. "We'd go exploring through the city—I'd like to show him the market. And, you know what? I bet Egroms never, ever ride pakows because when they're full grown they're too big to ride. Chacoodi's just a kid, like me, and he'll most likely never get this chance again!"

Jor-Dan turned to Marrak. "What a noble gesture, don't you think, Marrak? To offer this once-in-a-lifetime opportunity to this Egrom child!"

"Sire, I feel it is your duty to award this petitioner." Marrak tried to stifle a smile.

Jor-Dan turned to face Brian. "Your petition is granted, Brian Jackson. Marrak will provide a clause to have Trakon escort you to the Cember Forest to gather Chacoodi."

Brian's face practically melted with happiness. Marrak finished writing the document and applied the king's seal. He folded the document and handed it to Brian.

"Here is your petition with the king's seal. I hope you have fun with your friend."

"Thank you so much!" Brian grasped the paper. "Thanks, grandpa! I promise we won't get into any trouble."

Jor-Dan winked at Brian. "Be sure to talk to the majordomo and let him know when to expect your guest."

Brian stepped out of line and ran from the room, his petition in hand. He remembered he wasn't supposed to run in the palace so he settled into a fast walk. He found Kitry and D'laine in a sitting room and showed them his document.

"You petitioned the king?" Kitry asked, somewhat amused. She read the document and turned to D'laine, then back to Brian.

"Well, you have the king's seal so you have permission. I see Trakon has been chosen as your escort," Kitry said as she read Marrak's scrawl. "And you are to speak with the majordomo about your guest. When do you propose to take this journey?"

Brian eye-pleaded with Kitry. "Would Trakon be able to take me tomorrow?"

"Let's check his schedule, shall we?" Kitry tapped her communicator and pulled up her holographic address book. She tapped Trakon's name. "Trakon, what is your schedule for tomorrow?"

"Why, what do you need me to do?" Trakon asked.

"Brian has permission from your father to fetch his friend, and your father chose you as his escort," Kitry said.

Trakon chuckled. "Sure, tomorrow will be fine. Tell Brian to see who else wants to come along so I can get the right size crestrider." Trakon ended the communication.

Kitry turned to D'laine. "Will you be going on this short journey?"

"Yes, I always enjoy returning to my first home on Thol," D'laine said.

"Why don't you check with your brother, father and Stanley and see if they want to go along?" Kitry said.

"Okay." Brian took off out of the room. "No running inside!" D'laine called out.

"That poor boy was probably a nervous wreck while waiting in line," Kitry said.

"Trakon and I thought it would be a good idea to teach him how petitions and approval worked," D'laine said. "And I didn't want Brian to assume that just because he was my brother he would get special treatment. But I realize that Jor-Dan most likely thought Brian's being in line was a little odd. I mean Brian could have asked him at the dinner table."

"I agree. It's not too soon for him to observe some of the details involved in being a king and running a kingdom," Kitry said.

EARLY THE NEXT MORNING TRAKON MANEUVERED THE TEN-MAN crestrider in the courtyard. Jor-Dan and Kitry surprised their extended family by joining them for the journey to the Egrom village in the Cember Forest. The dogs were left behind, locked in D'laine's suite. She hoped La'gar'ish wouldn't destroy anything. He wanted to protect his king and didn't like to be separated from him.

As they neared the Cember Forest, Trakon told his parents what Kestrum had said about the village: unless you were invited it was undetectable. Jor-Dan and Kitry didn't see the large mushroom village clearing until Trakon was landing the crestrider.

"Interesting," Jor-Dan said. "When you flew here with D'laine, you saw the clearing from the sky. Why didn't I see the clearing?"

"I'm not sure," Trakon said. "You'll have to ask Ghury."

The Egrom elders approached their guests. Chacoodi raced around them to the ship. He and Brian jumped up and down with excitement while Jamie looked on, feeling left out.

Ghury stepped forward. "Welcome, rulers of Ebscalon. You honor us with your visit."

Ghury introduced the elders, and they all walked to the area where the elders met and ate. D'laine noticed benches were in place around the circle. Typically, everyone sat on the moss in this area so the Egroms were making an effort to make their guests comfortable.

Kestrum and another female Egrom brought carafes of water and drinking vessels.

D'laine introduced Kestrum to Jor-Dan and Kitry. "Kestrum took care of me when I lived here. Needless to say, I was a challenge when I first arrived on Thol."

"You Earthlings are so shocked without your familiar trappings," Kestrum said. "Look how you have adapted! Isn't this a much better world? Earth is so noisy and dirty."

D'laine wanted to challenge Kestrum about her view of Earth, but she knew this was not the time. She would discuss Kestrum's views with her father and Stanley later.

Brian and Chacoodi ran wild in the distance. Lee kept an eye on them while Ghury, the elders, Kitry and Jor-Dan talked about their different lifestyles. Ghury showed the royal couple his mushroom house, and Adrum gave them an example of the lessons D'laine and her family learned. He could now joke about his near-death experience with Stanley.

Adrum walked to his house and returned with the cauldron. "Stanley's first helmet."

"A cooking pot?" Kitry laughed until she almost cried. "We are having a formal dinner at the end of the month,"

Jor-Dan said. "We would be honored if you would attend."

The Egroms communicated in their own language. "We

accept your invitation, but suggest that you include a represen-tative of the Kudaja so they are not offended."

"Yes, of course. I will extend an invitation to them immedi-ately," Jor-Dan said. "How do we contact them?"

"If you are agreeable, I will speak to them," Ditol said. "They will most likely want to come transformed so they can commu-nicate and be seen as equals."

"We understand the Plotals are rebuilding their city," Bensol said. "You are comfortable with their being so close to you?"

"That's a fair question," Jor-Dan said. "As you know, long ago we were at peace and traded with each other. As a Youngman, I had a Plotal friend who was my steady companion."

Trakon stared at his father as if seeing him for the first time. "You had a Plotal friend? How come you never told me?"

"Those times have been long gone, son," Jor-Dan said. "It would be nice to have that peace once again. I've always wondered what happened to my friend Orongo."

"Perhaps it's time to find out," Kitry said.

"We should get going," Trakon said. "We don't want to get stranded!"

"I'll make sure Chacoodi and Brian stay out of trouble," Lee said.

"A big challenge," Ghury joked. He scared Kitry with his loud grizzly bear laugh which made the entire circle chuckle.

They all stood. Lee looked around for the boys. Jamie sat quietly nearby, but Brian and Chacoodi were nowhere to be found. Ghury called out to Chacoodi telepathically.

"They are on their way," Ghury informed his guests. He grumbled. "You will have your hands full with those two."

Brian and Chacoodi ran around the mushroom houses to the circle.

"You will behave like a good Egrom boy," Kestrum scolded.

Chacoodi looked duly chastised. "I will do nothing to dishonor the tribe!"

"See that you don't!" Kestrum said with a firm nod.

BRIAN AND CHACOODI HURRIED INTO THE DINING SALON. THE family was already seated.

Lee grilled the boys with a harsh expression. "Go clean up. We'll discuss your tardiness when you return."

Brian led Chacoodi down the hallway to the bathroom. While Brian used soap and water, Chacoodi groomed himself like a cat. He licked his hands and rubbed them over his face and ears repeatedly.

"That's so neat," Brian said as he watched his friend. "Back on my world we have animals called cats. There are big wild cats that live outside in forests and jungles, and domestic cats that people keep for pets. Most of those live inside houses with their humans, but some go in and out of the house. Some become feral cats. Anyway, cats wash up just like you."

"We have an aversion to water." Chacoodi glanced at the running water in the sink as Brian washed. "If we have to cross a river or stream, it makes us very nervous."

"Later, before we go to bed, I have to take a bath. You can come with me and see what Ciertrons and Earthlings do to clean their whole bodies," Brian said. "We'd better go. Everyone's going to glare at us because we're late for dinner."

They rushed out of the bathroom and returned to the dining salon. The family had forgone waiting. At a table setting beside where Brian normally sat was a pot of thick vegetable stew and a large spoon. The boys took their place at the table. Brian glanced at the majordomo.

"Thank you for preparing my friend's special meal," Brian said.

The majordomo nodded.

Chacoodi dipped his spoon into the stew and sampled it. He nodded. "It's very good! Thank you!" Chacoodi said.

"Now, explain why you were late." Lee grilled Brian and his friend with a harsh parent stink-eye.

Both boys sat up straight and glanced at each other before turning back to Lee. They competed with their top reasons as words tumbled out of their mouths.

"We explored the marketplace...," Brian said.

"I showed Brian all the different vegetables...," Chacoodi said.

"There were hosks spinning the moss..." Brian said. "We visited Jamie's og..." Chacoodi said.

Brian swung his wide eyes to his brother. "Oggy was standing."

"He still has a limp." Chacoodi looked around Brian to stare at Jamie.

Lee held up his hand. "That's enough! Make sure you are cleaned up and at this table no later than five moments before mealtime, morning, noon and night."

"If you aren't going to be here for lunch, you need to let someone know so food isn't prepared for you," D'laine said. She scolded them with her intense expression.

"The next time you're late, you two will find yourselves in the kitchen washing dishes after the meal," Kitry said. "Do you understand?"

Both boys nodded like rear window bobbing head dogs, eyes wide as they thought about the consequences. They finished their meals and sat quietly, waiting to be dismissed.

"How many people do you expect for the formal dinner?" D'laine asked.

"We will prepare for one hundred fifty guests, not including Ciertron officials and family," Kitry said.

"Patrosym, Mer, Lansobar and Caradon will most likely be

represented by ten or twenty of their people. Sometimes more than high officials attend. I'm sure the Plotals will send at least that many. And we expect all the Egrom elders. We're not sure how many of the Kudaja will come," Jor-Dan said.

At the mention of the Kudaja, Trakon snorted his displeasure.

Kitry glared at him. "You will be cordial to the Kudaja. They joined the fight against the robots and lost many of their people and borjos."

"It's not like he has anything against the Kudaja," D'laine said. She grumbled at Trakon. "It's Herish."

D'laine and Trakon openly glared at each other at the mention of Trakon's tiny rival.

"That little miscreant!" Trakon growled.

"Herish and I were just friends until all of this *intended* and *princess* talk began," D'laine snarled. "I lost my first friend because of that!"

Trakon stood, pushing his chair back forcefully. He grabbed it before it toppled over. "It's not my fault. I'm not the one who started those rumors!" He turned his scowl on his parents.

Jor-Dan stood. "Sit down!"

Trakon stared down his father for a long moment, then sat.

"Can we be excused?" Brian squeaked out. Jamie nodded beside him. "Me, too?" Chacoodi waited, breath held. "Play with your brother," Lee directed at Brian.

Brian harrumphed. "Come on, Jamie." The three boys quickly left the stormy dining salon.

Lee looked around the table. "Does someone want to explain this situation to me?"

Everyone started talking at once. Lee held up a hand. "One at a time, please." He finally got the full story from the four perspectives.

Stanley was fascinated by the fact that the Kudaja males

could morph into full-sized adults from their tiny persons. "There must be something in their genetic code that allows for this transformation. By any chance does anyone know if the females morph?"

"I haven't heard of any females *morphing*, as you call it," Jor-Dan said, "but that doesn't mean they don't. The Kudaja keep to themselves in their forests."

"Morphing aside," Lee said, pointedly to D'laine, "if this Herish was a regular man, like Trakon, would you be interested in marrying him?"

Trakon's temper exploded. He bashed the table with both fists. "D'laine will NEVER marry that... that insect!"

Lee halted Jor-Dan and Kitry from lashing out verbally at their son. "Trakon, let's be civil. It's an honest question."

Everyone watched D'laine. Before she could respond, Trakon jumped back into the discussion, even-tempered.

"I'm the one D'laine dreamt about, not Herish! She and I shared the same dreams, which is why we recognized each other when we first met at the oasis."

D'laine nodded. "That's right, daddy. Trakon and I are connected through this prophecy. I like Herish a lot." She glared at Trakon. "But, I like him as a good friend, not a boyfriend, or a potential life partner. I'm pretty sure he felt threatened by Trakon. He most likely thought we would not be able to continue to be friends if Trakon and I married so he figured he'd better get in line."

Trakon calmed down as he digested what D'laine said. "That makes sense," he said, reluctantly. "I'm sorry I got all *warrior* over him."

Kitry appeared appeased by Trakon's response. "You will have the opportunity to make amends at the formal dinner. I suggest you approach the Kudaja delegation and request a meeting with Herish. There is no reason the three of you can't be friends."

"Now, about this marriage talk," Lee said. "I don't know your customs. The Egrom education stops short of many things. Your race was glossed over; all I learned were very basic details about the humans of Thol."

"Why don't we adjourn to my sitting room where we would be more comfortable?" Kitry said.

"I'm going to excuse myself," Stanley left the group and took the stairs to his quarters on the fourth floor.

D'laine and Trakon recognized that his mother was pleased with the discussion and wondered what she had brewing. They all left the dining salon and walked to the royals suite.

Once everyone was seated, Lee explained the engagement and marriage process of Earth. "It all depends on the two parties' stations in life. On our world, when a couple decides to get married, the man proposes and gives the woman an engagement ring. The ring stone is typically a diamond, which I don't think you have on this world. A diamond looks like a crystal, but is significantly more valuable and quite beautiful in the right setting."

Kitry, Jor-Dan and Trakon listened in rapt attention. "Then there's an engagement announcement, parties, planning for the wedding, then the wedding," Lee explained. "As I said, depending on the social standings of the couple, the engagement parties and the wedding can be modest or extravagant. Sometimes, if the status of the couple is significantly uneven, there may be a prenuptial agreement."

"Your society does not have a dowry system?" Kitry asked.

"In different parts of the world dowry systems still exist, but in the United States where we lived, most marriages are based on love, not property. Where there's a significant imbalance, as I mentioned before, there may be a prenuptial agreement. The prenup specifies what each party brings to the marriage, and what each party should leave with if they get divorced."

"Divorce?" Kitry squawked out. "Whatever does that mean? Isn't marriage for life on your world?"

The discussion continued for quite some time when Kitry steered it in the direction she wanted it to go.

"Now, about our children," she said. "Jor-Dan and I feel D'laine is a perfect match for Trakon. Do you agree?"

Trakon and D'laine squirmed as they were both in the proverbial hot seat of the discussion.

"They seem well-suited for each other," Lee agreed.

"Jor-Dan and I started our marriage late in life. As a result, we only have one child," Kitry said. "For the past two years, we have fretted over making a match for Trakon, but he always found fault with the young women."

Trakon waved his hand in dismissal. "They've all been shallow, and not very intelligent. Would you want me to suffer my life with a wife I couldn't have a conversation with? People should marry for love."

D'laine nodded in agreement. "I'd never allow my father to arrange for me to marry someone I never met, or didn't know. That sounds like a lifetime of torture!"

"For heaven's sake!" Lee said. "As if I've ever interfered with your boyfriends."

D'laine wagged a finger at him. "You didn't like Billy!"

"Billy treated you like a servant. You were always fetching things for him and making all the arrangements for every conceivable whim he suggested," Lee snapped.

She shrugged. "Okay, you're right. But, he was the only bad boyfriend I ever had."

"That's because you lost several years from the accident, recovery and your mother's death," Lee said. "Connor was the first boy you brought home that fit into my ideals of decency and an even match."

"Our kingdom would suffer if Trakon did not provide an

heir," Jor-Dan said. "While we have relatives to choose from, if it came to that, we would prefer a direct heir."

"Does it make any difference what gender the children are?" Lee asked.

"None whatsoever. The Ciertron people have been ruled by queens in the past," Jor-Dan said.

"Speaking of children, how do we know if I can even have children here?" D'laine asked. "We have live births, you pass an egg. I may not even be able to provide an heir."

Trakon harrumphed. "We talked about this when you first came to Ebscalon. I'm sure you have evolved, and not just your new abilities and powers. It may sound crazy, but I honestly think we're together for more than one reason and that includes our future children. I've loved you for years through the dreams and not only are we together, but your family is here as well."

D'laine thought quietly. "You're right. There's so many missing pieces. I love you too, Trakon."

Kitry stared at Trakon and D'laine with longing. "Their children will be beautiful! Shall we set a date?"

"It's up to them," Lee said. "While I like the idea that my daughter would be provided for, D'laine is not helpless. She certainly would not stand by while Trakon made all the decisions. He'd eventually end up with a black eye."

Everyone snickered at the picture in their heads. Then the three parents focused on their children.

"Will you marry me?" Trakon asked D'laine. Worry wafted off him.

The room was quiet as all eyes were centered on D'laine. "Yes… yes, I will," D'laine said, breathless.

Four huge breaths were released. Trakon wrapped her in his arms.

"This calls for a celebration!" Jor-Dan mentally called for Kitry's manservant. "Bring out the abrajaii!"

The servant entered the room with a tray of glasses and a lovely carafe containing a golden colored beverage, the equivalent of champagne. He placed the tray on the table and discreetly left the room. Jor-Dan grabbed the carafe and filled the glasses. They raised their glasses in a toast.

"To the future of Thol," he said.

CHAPTER SEVEN

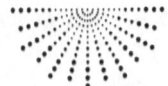

*J*amie tagged along after Brian and Chacoodi. He wished he had his own friend, but there were no children for him to play with that he was aware of. As they traipsed through the city, he found a discarded lighting orb on the ground.

"Hey, Brian, why don't we teach Chacoodi how to play baseball?" Jamie showed them the lighting orb.

Brian's face lit up. "Oh, Chacoodi, you'll love baseball! We need to find something to use as a bat, and we need to make a ball that won't break."

"Show me in your head," Chacoodi suggested.

Brian thought about one of his games and specifically showed the ball being thrown, the batter hitting the ball, then running around the bases.

"Oh, I like this game!" Chacoodi said. "The ball will need to be strong so it doesn't break from the force of the bat. Let's go over by the market and see what discards we can find. Maybe everything we require is in one place!"

The boys dashed over to the marketplace, now empty of the crowd from earlier. They pawed through boxes and bins of throwaways behind each shop or booth. Jamie dug out a branch that was discarded in a firewood bin from a vendor selling black kettles.

"How about this, Brian? Doesn't this look like the right size?" Jamie held out the branch.

Brian grabbed it and studied it. "Yeah, Jamie. Let's get some tools and carve it into the shape of a bat."

Chacoodi grabbed the branch away from Brian. "Show me that bat in your head."

Brian thought hard to bring forth a bat in full detail. Chacoodi stared straight ahead; his features went slack. Then his four hands ran over the surface of the rough branch. Within moments, the branch was transformed into what looked like a standard baseball bat.

"Wow!" Jamie and Brian said at the same time.

"How did you do that?" Jamie asked. "It's practically perfect!"

"Adrum showed us how the Egroms could make that furniture and stuff in his movies," Brian said. "That is so cool!"

"What do you think we could use for a baseball?" Jamie asked.

"We could take some material the hosks make and form it into a ball and wrap it with something," Brian said. "Why don't we ask daddy or Stanley to help? Baseballs have to be just right."

The three boys giggled—Chacoodi's sounding more like a high-pitched *hihihi* than an outright boy-giggle. They took off running, bat in Brian's hand, back to the palace.

"Where do you think they are?" Jamie asked.

"They were having one of those *family* discussions," Chacoodi said. "Those get pretty serious."

They first looked in the throne room. Empty. Then they decided to retrace their steps and go to the family wing. They heard light laughter through the large double doors of the king and queen's suite.

"They're in here," Jamie said.

Brian knocked on the door. An attendant opened the door.

"Is my father here?" Brian asked.

"Yes, they're all here except Stanley. Go through there," the attendant pointed.

The boys followed the voices coming from an inner room. Everyone seemed happy. Brian noticed Trakon and D'laine holding hands. He raised an eyebrow.

"Is that a baseball bat?" Lee asked, incredulous. He got to his feet and approached the boys. "Where did you find this?"

"Chacoodi made it!" Jamie said. "We need a baseball!"

"Daddy, can you or Stanley figure out how to make a baseball? We want to teach Chacoodi how to play!" Brian said.

"You know what? I'll bet you can get those Youngmen to play!" Lee said.

D'laine came over to inspect the bat. She rubbed her hands over the smooth wood. "Wow, Chacoodi, this is beautiful, and full of detail!"

Chacoodi puffed out his chest in pride. "Brian showed me what a bat looked like and I recreated it from the piece of wood Jamie found. It was a team effort."

"We'll need bases and gloves, too." Lee turned to the others. "You're going to love baseball. It's one of the favorite sports on our world. Brian was on a Little League team before he became sick. His coaches thought he was good enough to have a career as a professional baseball player. Here, I'll show you one of Brian's games."

Lee concentrated on the second-to-the-last game Brian had played.

Jor-Dan and Trakon enthusiastically watched the play-by-play in Lee's head.

"I don't understand. There are a bunch of boys running in a square, and those others throwing the ball at one another." Kitry looked questioningly at D'laine, the boys, then Lee.

"It's not a difficult game to learn, and you might enjoy the sport once you understand the rules. Plus, the skill to play it well," Lee said. "Here's a baseball." He projected the picture of a baseball for the group to see. "We need to figure out how to make one."

AFTER SCROUNGING AROUND THE MARKET SEARCHING FOR material for the ball, gloves and bases, Lee, Stanley and the three boys headed to one of the workshops.

Trakon joined them while Lee spread the supplies on a bench.

"The first thing we'll need is the ball. Once we get that made, and it doesn't fall apart, we'll need gloves." Lee showed Trakon and Chacoodi what the gloves looked like in a 3D view so they could understand the padding and molding of the gloves.

"I don't understand why we need these gloves," Trakon said.

Lee showed him a baseball game in his head so Trakon would understand the impact of the ball speeding from the bat to a glove. "In a professional ballgame with adult males, the ball can travel one hundred ten miles... droks per hour... uh, per hour."

"One hundred ten droks per hour?" Trakon asked. "That's incredibly fast for this ball."

"That's why you need a glove to catch it," Stanley said. "We're talking over four thousand pounds of force. No one can catch that ball with his bare hand without breaking bones."

Chacoodi studied the pictures of the ball and glove again. He looked over the materials on the bench. He nodded to Brian and Jamie. "We need to get a lot of moss. I can create these things."

Trakon handed Brian a large pouch. Brian, Chacoodi and Jamie took off and headed toward the fields outside the city gates.

D'LAINE AND TWUM SAT AT A TABLE IN THE LIBRARY, A LARGE book between them. Twum ran her finger across a line of symbols and squiggles and stopped at one.

"This symbol means *around*," Twum explained.

"Out of all these books and scrolls, why isn't there something that teaches the written language? If I were back home and didn't know how to read or write, I would get a set of elementary books. They would teach me how to form the letters and shapes. I would start with short words and graduate to larger, more complex words and sentences."

Twum gazed at D'laine sadly. "That sounds so difficult. We are born with this knowledge. I don't think I could figure it out if I had to learn reading from scratch."

D'laine had a tablet of paper that contained symbols and their meanings. She picked up the writing instrument and drew the shape of the latest Tholian word she was trying to learn. "This could take the rest of my life."

Twum stood. "Let's go for a walk. When we come back, you'll be able to tackle this with a clear head."

D'laine pushed her chair back and stood. "Good idea. This is so overwhelming."

They left the palace and walked around, ending up at the marketplace. They wandered through the stalls and came to one with beautifully crafted jewelry. D'laine picked through pieces and found a necklace with two suns and two planets. Eerily, it made her think of Thol and Earth.

"Look at this, Twum."

"I'm sure you will find many such things now that the people know where you have come from," Twum explained. "Everything they learn about you will be depicted in their craftsmanship. Just wait until you get married."

D'laine held the piece out to the vendor. "How much is this necklace?"

The tall man hit his fist to his chest. "Please, a gift, my princess. I would be honored if you wore my creation."

"You made this?" D'laine ran her finger across the beautiful design. The suns looked like gold and the planets were each represented realistically. She wondered how the man could create such an accurate portrayal of her home world. "Thank you so much. I will wear this in honor of your craftsmanship." She slipped the necklace over her head. The design settled near her breastbone.

They left the marketplace and returned to the palace and the dusty books. "How do I write necklace and jewelry?"

Twum scrawled them across a piece of paper. "This is how you write necklace and this is jewelry."

D'laine studied the words. "They're very similar, aren't they?"

Twum's face lit up with an idea. "I know what might help." She faced D'laine. "Why don't we go to the throne room and you can watch as Marrak writes the petitions?"

"Do you think that would be okay?" D'laine asked.

"Of course. You can hear the petitioners, what the king decides, and see how Marrak documents and seals the petitions."

They stood and walked over to the throne room. About thirty people stood in line. Twum led D'laine around the line of people to the back of the table and stopped at Marrak's chair.

"Marrak, the princess D'laine is studying our written language. I thought it would be a good idea if she sat by you, heard the proceedings and watched how you wrote out the documents," Twum said.

Jor-Dan turned to Marrak then nodded to Twum and D'laine. "That is an excellent idea." He motioned for one of the guards. "Bring a chair for the princess."

The other advisors sitting beside Marrak moved their chairs down to fit in a chair for D'laine.

The guard brought the chair.

D'laine sat between the king and the documentarian. "Twum and I have spent hours going through books and scrolls. I've made lists of words, but I now understand how difficult it is for someone who isn't a native Tholian," she said.

D'laine sat and watched the proceedings of a dozen petitioners. She listened carefully to the citizen, what Jor-Dan said, and what Marrak wrote on the official letterhead. The document ended up stamped with the seal of the king.

A middle-aged woman approached the king. She saluted the king, appraised D'laine, then presented her case. "My husband returned from gathering agrin leaves and became very sick overnight. The healer can't heal him. My husband's skin is all cracked and dried. I don't know what he encountered. I would like to petition for the princess," she nodded to D'laine, "to heal him."

"Of course, I will try to heal him," D'laine blurted. Then she realized her faux pas. "Oh, I'm sorry for stepping in when you hadn't responded to this woman." D'laine felt her face heat up as she stared at the king.

Jor-Dan patted her hand. "It is quite all right." He turned to the woman petitioner. "We will adjourn for a short break to determine what ails your husband."

Marrak stood. "Petitioners, we will resume in one hour. Remember your place in line."

The next petitioner sat on the floor. He dug into his pouch and pulled out some dried food and munched.

The woman led the king, D'laine, Marrak and the advisors out of the palace. They walked through the city, down lanes between houses and businesses to the small, clean house where she lived with her family.

When they stepped into the bedroom everyone stared in

shock as their eyes locked on the tortured form on the bed. The man's face was frozen in a silent scream. His skin was cracked like a dried-up lake bed from the top of his head to his toes. It was unlike anything anyone had ever witnessed.

Jor-Dan pulled his eyes from the vision on the bed. "Has the Visionary seen this man?"

The woman shook her head. "No, just our healer."

Jor-Dan turned to Marrak. "Someone fetch the Visionary." He turned to D'laine. "We should wait until the Visionary is here before you attempt to heal this man. I have never seen anything like this and I don't want to take any chances if this is infectious."

D'laine nodded. "I understand, but I can't catch any diseases from the people I heal." She observed the man while they waited. He was still, locked in his position. She did not notice his chest rise and fall with each breath.

The Visionary entered the room and stopped at the edge of the bed.

"Have you ever seen anything such as this?" Jor-Dan asked.

The Visionary walked around the bed, observing all aspects of the patient. "Never." He addressed the wife. "Tell me everything that happened. Where did your husband go, and what did he say or do when he returned?"

"Yesterday morning, my husband and our son went to the forest to gather agrin leaves from the ground. They filled five barrels of leaves and returned," she recalled. "Shortly after they returned, my husband started scratching. He said he was itchy all over. I made him bathe, but it did little to relieve the itching. His skin began to crack as if he hadn't had liquid nourishment in turns. At that point, I panicked and checked our son from head to toe, but he appeared to be okay. I sent for our healer, but he could not do anything."

"Let's examine those barrels. Perhaps there's something

there that will give us a hint as to what happened," the Visionary said.

They followed the woman and her son out of the house to the backyard where several large vats filled with water and leaves stood.

The Visionary circled the vats with an arm outstretched. "I don't detect anything out of the ordinary. Let's go back inside and determine what we can do for your husband."

The Visionary and D'laine stood at the bedside. The old Visionary swirled his hands over the bed. There appeared to be no progress. He nodded to D'laine for her to proceed.

She removed her crystals from her pouch and moved them over the length of his body. She stopped and pressed a hand to his heart.

As her hand touched the man's skin, tens of thousands of tiny, parasitic creatures scampered up her arm and invaded her. She let out an agonizing sound as a weblike structure formed over her entire body. Everyone in the room screamed her name.

Jor-Dan reached out to D'laine, but Marrak slapped his hand away, and the Visionary held him at bay.

"No one touch her!" the Visionary hollered. "I don't know what these creatures are, or where they came from." He scanned her form. She appeared as frozen in her pose as the man on the bed.

A guard slipped out of the room.

Several moments later Trakon and D'laine's family, along with Stanley and Chacoodi, raced into the room. Jor-Dan held his arm out, barring them from getting close. He looked at Jamie.

"Jamie, can you try to talk to these things? Find out if they talk back to you." Jor-Dan said. "If you can communicate with them, ask them what they want, what they are, and if they will release your sister and this man."

Jamie looked at his sister then the man on the bed. He thought words at both of them, but did not receive any response. "They're not talking to me. I don't think they have words or can communicate, but they could be ignoring me. I'm not sure."

The Visionary turned to Chacoodi. "Ask Ghury if he can help with this."

Chacoodi nodded. He locked his vision onto D'laine and the man, sending his request for help. Before he could report to the Visionary, Ghury and a delegation of ten Egroms stood outside the small house.

"It will be best to move D'laine and this man outside, far away from the city," Ghury said.

"Are these things biological or bacterial?" Lee asked.

"I should try to get a reading on them," Stanley said.

Ghury held up two hands. "No, Stanley. You would only draw them into your brain and that might be the end of you."

Stanley took a step back. "You're right. I'll stay out of this one, but I can levitate them to the field."

"There's a clearing about three miles from here," Trakon said. "That might be a good place. Since we don't know what these things are, do we have to worry about contaminating the moss or the ground? Or endangering the hosks?"

"We will protect the clearing," one of the Egroms said. "I am sure these creatures came through a portal. I don't believe they are native to Thol, and we won't know if they can survive here in our moss or soil."

Stanley motioned for people to leave the house. "Stay back and make sure everyone is at least ten to fifteen feet away. I may have to remove my helmet."

The guards jumped into action. They cleared the gathered people far back from the street where the house stood and along the route to the city gates. When the house and area were empty, Stanley opened his helmet vents, held out his arm and tested the response. It was not strong enough to move both

D'laine and the man at the same time. Puffing, he removed his helmet. Both subjects rose in the air effortlessly.

Stanley backed out of the bedroom, through the house and out the door. He guided the two frozen people ahead of him while he held his helmet in his other hand.

People who had moved closer to get a better look at the oddity found themselves clutching their heads in pain. They immediately moved back, away from the Earthling with the big head.

Stanley projected himself and his two charges to the clearing. One giant step, and they were there. He settled D'laine and the man on the ground, flipped his helmet on his head and called out to the Egroms.

"My helmet is in place; you can approach safely," he said.

Within moments Ghury and the ten Egroms formed a circle around the infected people. Several moments later, crestriders arrived with the family, the woman and her son, guards and others.

"They don't even look like they're breathing," Lee said. "Are you sure they're still alive?" A shiver of panic shook him.

Brian, Jamie and Chacoodi stood close by. "It's going to be okay," Jamie said.

The Visionary placed his hand on Lee's shoulder. "Their life force is strong, just captured, if you will. I don't know what else to call it."

Kitry had joined the group. She fretted in Jor-Dan's arms with Trakon by their side.

"Don't worry, everything will be all right," Jor-Dan said.

Trakon's expression was grim. His hands were clenched into fists by his side. He watched as the Egroms closed the circle, getting nearer to the two people. Each Egrom had all four hands extended, focused on just those two.

A large boom sounded and a deep, wide pit appeared in the ground. Soil flew in all directions, raining down on the group standing nearby. Ghury and two Egroms grasped the mass of alien parasites from the man and flung the twisting, writhing things into the pit. Another Egrom left the group and spontaneously created fire. The mass of parasites burst into flames amid the sounds of its death throes.

The Egroms returned to the two people. The man's skin appeared to be normal. He was unresponsive, but alive. His wife and son rushed to him. Two guards carried him away from the circle and settled him on the moss.

D'laine had not been released from the parasitic hold. She was still covered with the weblike structure with her crystals clutched in her fist. The Egroms formed a tight circle around her and each raised his four arms.

"Stop!" Jamie shouted. "Stop, stop. They're talking to me. They don't want to die. They want to go home. They don't know how they got here."

"Tell them to release the human and we will take them to a portal," Ghury said.

Jamie stared at his sister and relayed the silent message. Within moments, tens of thousands of the tiny creatures dropped to the ground and swarmed into a large replica of themselves.

An Egrom caught D'laine before she collapsed. Her two crystals dropped to the moss.

Trakon rushed forward and gathered her in his arms and brought her back to the family.

The Egrom retrieved her crystals and brought them to Lee.

"Oh, thank you. I know she would have been distressed if those crystals were lost."

"D'laine, can you hear me?" Trakon said.

"Honey, if you can hear us, can you move a finger or blink?" Lee asked.

Neither D'laine nor the man responded to being released from the parasites.

The giant bug-creature spoke in an echo of a thousand voices. "We mean you no harm. We only required nourishment. We want to go back home."

The creature had six arms and legs and several antennas on its head. The oval face featured a strong beak. When it turned its head from side to side, there were no visible eyes that could be detected.

"What about the two beings you fed from?" Ghury asked. "Their normal life force has not returned."

"Should they be allowed to absorb water, their life force will prevail," the creature said.

"Let's get them to the palace where we can float them in the bathing pool," Kitry said. "Guards, bring the man and his family."

Ghury turned to the boys. "Jamie, you should come with us." He stared at Brian in his Egrom way. "Brian, you will come with us as well."

"I'm coming along," Stanley said. "I want to communicate with them."

Ghury nodded. "There's a portal not far from here." He turned to the creature. "Shall we transport you?"

The creature echoed *Yes*.

The Egroms levitated the creature, and they strode across the field with the humans following. The portal was less than a mile away.

Ghury waited until everyone was present.

"This human would like to communicate with you. His brain is all-powerful so we will have to stand back," Ghury told the creatures.

Stanley approached the aliens. He waited until all the Egroms and the boys were far away, then he opened the lever on his helmet partially. A loud chattering began as the creatures responded to Stanley. They didn't seem to be in any pain, and

Stanley did not appear to be affected by them. After several moments, Stanley flipped the lever closed.

"All safe," he called out.

One of the Egroms waved a hand at the portal. Life forms appeared, but not from the home of the creature.

Brian scrunched his forehead.

"There!" he pointed. "Move to your right a tiny fraction. That's where their home is. I see their friends!"

Ghury nodded. "That is your gift. It will grow into something much bigger. We shall discuss this later."

The Egrom moved as Brian instructed, and waved his hand. Sure enough, the portal showed the creatures' world. The creature collapsed into individuals and swarmed through the doorway and returned home. The Egrom sealed the world doorway.

"They will not be returning to Thol," he announced.

"What did you learn from them?" Ghury asked Stanley.

"They're called Triculated Cribustals. Somehow, they live on a diet of humidity and what they call damp air, but they consider them as two different things. They do have a life structure and a government, and they live purposeful lives. There are billions and billions of them. I feel bad that we destroyed half of their group," Stanley said.

"It is unfortunate, but they were late in communicating with us," Ghury said.

CHAPTER EIGHT

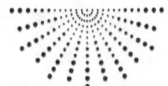

itry organized the group in the bathing pool in a guest suite.

Trakon and Lee floated D'laine in the pool, and the woman and her son floated her husband. Their heads were kept above water, but their bodies were kept submerged horizontally.

Twum arrived with drinking vessels that had a V-shaped spout for pouring. She stepped into the pool and gave one to Lee and the other to the woman. Lee tilted D'laine's head slightly and put the spout to her mouth. He poured the water slowly, but it ran out into the pool.

"I need someone to open her mouth." Lee nodded to the woman. "She's going to need help."

Twum stepped forward and helped Lee while a guard got into the bathing pool and helped the woman. Twum gently pried D'laine's lips apart and worked to get her teeth apart. That accomplished, she trickled water into D'laine's mouth while Lee and Trakon hoisted her head higher. She seemed to be swallowing the water.

The same healing was taking place with the man.

GHURY, STANLEY AND THE BOYS JOINED THE GROUP AT THE bathing pool. The air was heavy with worry and frustration because of the lack of change in either victim. The Egrom assessed the situation.

"You must let go of the bodies," Ghury said.

Everyone balked at the suggestion.

"They'll drown!" the woman said.

"They will not drown," Ghury said. "They must be totally submerged to allow the water to be completely absorbed into their bodies. Pouring water into their mouths isn't going to work."

Lee and Trakon stared at each other, fear etched on their faces.

"I trust him," Trakon said. "We need to do what he says. Otherwise D'laine and this man will die."

Lee shuddered at the grim thought. He nodded, his face washed with the pain of his decision. "Okay." He checked in with Trakon. "Ready?"

Trakon nodded, biting his lip.

They removed their hands from under D'laine. She drifted to the bottom of the pool and remained motionless. No air bubbles were visible.

The woman and her son followed suit; her husband's body laid on the bottom of the pool. Her face twisted in anguish as she stared at him through the water. Her son placed his arm around her shoulders and whispered to her.

Kitry clutched Jor-Dan.

Brian and Jamie were speechless at the edge of the bathing pool.

Time seemed to stand still. The hours passed with agonizing slowness with no progress.

"Have I lost her after all she's been through?" Lee asked.

"She's still here," Stanley said. "She's just in a form of stasis."

"At least when she was in the coma, we could see she was breathing. The machines that monitored her heart showed it was still beating," Lee said. "This looks so—final!"

"They will recover," Ghury said.

Trakon kept focused on D'laine, his nerves wrung so tight he had to force himself to breathe. He rubbed his eyes. One tiny air bubble emerged from D'laine's nose and floated to the surface.

"An air bubble!" Trakon yelled.

Lee returned his attention to his daughter. Another bubble surfaced, then another. Suddenly D'laine's arms flailed about and she shot up to the surface. She breached the top of the water and coughed, eyes wild, trying to empty her lungs of water.

Trakon held her by the waist as she spewed water though her mouth and nose.

One of the guards jumped into the pool to aid the woman and her son as her husband revived.

Trakon rested his forehead against the back of D'laine's head and whispered. "D'laine. D'laine, I thought I lost you."

"Honey, are you okay?" Lee asked.

D'laine's wild eyes focused on her father, befuddled, not recognizing him for a lengthy moment. When she took another long look, she nodded through the coughing.

Trakon lifted her in his arms, walked up the stairs from the pool, and set her on a bench.

Kitry wrapped her in a towel as Lee trudged up the stairs, his uniform dripping water across the tiles. He knelt in front of her, took one of her hands in his and patted it.

"We'll talk later when you're all rested up." Lee nodded to Trakon, patted him on the shoulder, and left his daughter in his capable hands.

TRAKON SAT BESIDE THE BED WHILE D'LAINE SLEPT. A TAP ON THE door announced Twum. She carried a tray of food and placed it on the side table. She pointed to a covered bowl of soup then nodded to D'laine. She motioned to the remaining food—a feast for Trakon. He nodded, grabbed a plate and a fork and shoveled the food in his mouth. He hadn't eaten anything throughout the whole ordeal.

D'laine stirred in the bed. She opened her eyes and saw Trakon. "Hi."

Trakon shoved the plate back on the tray, climbed onto the bed and took her gently in his arms. "I thought I'd lost you."

"Still here," she said with a raw voice. Her stomach growled loudly. She glanced at the tray of food. "Hungry. Did you leave me any?"

Trakon slipped off the bed and propped up the pillows.

She scooted back to sit against the pillows. He spread out one of the cloth napkins on the side table, set the bowl of soup in it and stuck a spoon into the bowl.

"Twum just brought the food so it's still hot." He gingerly placed the wrapped bowl in her hands.

D'laine balanced the bowl, grabbed the spoon and slurped down a spoonful of broth. Pushing the spoon aside, she tipped the bowl and drank most of the broth.

"I'm famished," D'laine said, her voice a little husky.

"I guess being invaded by an alien species from another world will do that," Trakon said.

A tap on the door announced visitors. Both families swarmed the bed. Stanley, Marrak, Ghury, the Visionary and Chacoodi joined them.

"You are well?" Ghury raised his four hands and did an Egrom scan. "I find all of your systems fully functional, but your brain is sluggish. Deep rest is called for."

D'laine nodded to Ghury. "I'm tired, hungry and a little achy."

"What do you remember?" Stanley asked.

Her eyes darted around in thought. "I remember the sick man. I've never seen anyone with cracked skin like that. I think I touched him, but I don't remember anything after that."

"They swarmed all over you and had you in this web," Lee said.

"Yeah, it looked like that Spider Man web," Jamie said. "You remember that, Brian?"

"Yeah, it did look like that!" Brian said. "It was scary, D'laine."

Her eyelids drooped.

Kitry patted her arm. "We'll let you sleep." She shooed everyone except Trakon from the room.

Trakon climbed on the bed and tucked D'laine into the curve of his body. "Rest, my love."

A SMALL GROUP WALKED OVER TO CHECK ON THE MAN AND HIS family. Kitry, Lee, and Stanley carried trays of food.

"Knock on the door, Brian," Kitry said.

The young boy came to the door. He was surprised to see the delegation and the food.

"How is your father?" Kitry asked. "May we come in?"

"He's resting, Your Majesty." The boy opened the door wide, stood aside and called out. "Mother, we have company."

Kitry, Lee and Stanley placed the trays on a table.

The woman entered the crowded room and was taken by surprise at the delegation. She pressed her fist to her heart. "Oh! Your Majesty! How nice of you to come check on my husband. How is D'laine doing?"

"She's exhausted. Bed rest is called for," Kitry said. "And your husband? He is well?"

"He doesn't remember anything other than gathering leaves and coming home," she said.

"They must have invaded him differently, or with a different motive." Stanley met Ghury's glance. They conferred silently.

Ghury nodded to Stanley.

The Visionary asked the woman, "May we see your husband?"

"Of course." She led them back to the bedroom.

Her husband was on his side covered with a gauze blanket. His eyes opened. He started when his eyes landed on the Egrom in his room.

"Jawget, these people brought you back to life," she said.

"The Egroms helped me?" Jawget asked weakly.

"The princess actually took the bugs out of you," his wife said.

"Actually, the Triculated Cribustals—what your wife called bugs—had used up all of your resources. When the princess attempted to heal you, most of them transferred from your body to hers," the Visionary explained.

"Resources?" Jawget asked, confused.

"All your body fluids," Stanley explained. "There were tens of thousands of bugs. It wasn't a pretty sight."

Ghury studied Jawget then turned to the son. "You don't remember seeing bugs all over your father?"

"No, but a bunch of leaves fell from the trees all over Da," the son said.

The three visitors thought about the scenario. Ghury asked the man, "You don't remember swallowing anything that made you cough?"

Jawget shook his head. "Didn't swallow anything, but I had this leaf dust all over me."

Ghury nodded to Jawget then the others. "We will leave you to rest now."

The delegation left the house and returned to the palace. Ghury, Lee, the Visionary and Stanley settled in a salon. A servant brought beverages.

"I didn't detect any entry points or pinpricks on Jawget," Ghury said.

"I'm willing to bet that the leaf dust was their original form in a dehydrated state," Lee said.

"That makes sense," Stanley said. "There hasn't been any rain for the past week so they were probably starving."

"Precisely so," the Visionary said. "That is why we saw so many of them when they swarmed D'laine. They had fed off Jawget until his reservoirs were dry. With so many of them eating they probably didn't get enough individually to web him."

"I hope we got them all," Lee said. "We don't know how they reproduce. If one's left behind, and if it's asexual—if it can reproduce without a mate—we could have a problem. On Earth, there are insects and lizards that are asexual, and other animals that I can't recall."

Stanley pondered what Lee said. "Unfortunately, one bug could turn into tens of thousands, or millions because of the number of eggs they might lay."

"Egroms can purify D'laine and Jawget without destroying tissue," Ghury said. "We will wait until they are completely recovered."

"In the meantime, we should monitor the citizens of Ebscalon carefully for any unusual itching," the Visionary said. "I will send word to the king and queen. They will see to it that Jawget and D'laine are watched as well as the entire community. We don't want an epidemic on our hands."

Lee pondered a moment. "Changing the subject, Jawget's son is a regular boy, am I correct? He's not a Youngman?"

"You are correct," The Visionary said. "There is an equal number of regular children here, both male and female, and Youngmen."

"Where are they?" Lee asked. "All we've seen are Youngmen. Jamie needs a friend."

"They're all about," the Visionary said.

"We haven't seen any except for Jawget's son," Lee said.

"They're most likely working with their parents," the Visionary said.

"Do they play... entertain themselves with games?" Lee asked.

"I'm sure they do," the Visionary said.

"I'll talk to the queen and king about it," Lee said.

BRIAN, CHACOODI AND JAMIE DUMPED SACKS OF MOSS ONTO THE workshop floor. Earlier, they had found discarded pieces of leather at the market. Now, Brian had a square of the skin on the ground and had heaped moss into the center of it.

"How are we going to make this into a ball?" Brian whined. Moss kept spilling out the openings as he tried to close the material around it.

"Just put it down and let me try to create this ball," Chacoodi said. "Show me that ball again."

Brian visualized the picture of a baseball.

Chacoodi studied it. He focused on the moss-piled square on the ground. Within a finger snap, the mess transformed into a ball.

"Whoa! Will you look at that!" Brian yelled.

"That looks like a real baseball," Jamie yelled. "Look at the stitches!"

A TREMENDOUS AMOUNT OF WORK WAS SPENT ON THE BASEBALL project, and Lee didn't even know if the Ciertrons or Egroms would ever *get* the sport. Lee, Stanley, Brian, Jamie and Chacoodi cleared a field for the baseball diamond outside the city walls. Trakon lent a hand when he could get away from his other responsibilities.

Finally, bases were set in place, benches for spectators were finished, several gloves, as well as baseballs, were tested, created and re-tested. The first ball Chacoodi created didn't hold up after being whacked more than a dozen times. Lee and Stanley took control with the design and materials, and resolved the problem.

Next up was recruiting. Lee was positive Tholians would catch on and want to compete and have fun. They discussed making up each team of ten to twelve players. Lee created a list:

- Starting pitcher
- Relief pitcher
- Starting position players
- One extra catcher
- Bench players who could pinch-hit, pinch-run, and become defensive substitutes in the later innings.

Between Trakon and Chacoodi, they devised a way to show one of the games from Lee's head in a holograph. Then they showed each position to make it easier for recruits to think about what position they might like to try out for. They decided the big courtyard by the palace would be the perfect place to show the holograph along with an electronic signup sheet.

Lee was adamant that two games be displayed: major league and Little League. He wanted people to observe not only the game, but the sports fans.

Stanley agreed that the Ciertrons would understand the sport once they saw the game in action, and they'd really like the way the fans supported the teams.

Only five people watched the first hour the holograph was displayed. Those people studied the holographic game. They even went so far as to stop the holograph and back up to replay whatever drew their attention. Evidently, those five people recruited their own friends, and before long there were dozens of interested people.

"If we can get two teams together and practice every turn, maybe by the formal dinner we can play a game. Once the other kingdoms attend a game I'll bet they will want to create their own team and compete," Lee said.

Jor-Dan agreed enthusiastically. "We've never done this before, but it looks like tremendous fun."

Two turns later they had their teams. Lee was the undisputed coach. Everyone met at the new baseball diamond and Lee explained the rules, and then some.

"We want an honest game," Lee said. "That means, if you have any special abilities, you can't use them." He watched as players murmured among themselves. "You will have a huge amount of fun if you just be yourself. No projecting to get to the base or home plate. No fiddling with the ball to align with the bat for a hit. And no making the ball fly where you want it to go so no one can catch it. This game is for honest players only. Leave all those other skills at home."

The teams appeared enthusiastic, accepting the rules. They practiced daily then played a game. The spectator benches filled and the excess people either stood or sat on the moss to observe the odd Earth sport. Once the game got underway, both players and fans became exuberant.

Teammates jumped, hooted and called out to batters or runners. Family and friends got into the team spirit and cheered for their people. All in all, the first game was a huge success.

Afterwards, Jor-Dan and his advisors, along with many others, slapped Lee on the shoulder. A lot of women liked the game. Others such as Kitry, hadn't connected the dots yet. She had rallied as Trakon hit the ball, ran and made a home run, but she didn't *get it* yet. Jor-Dan grumbled as he realized that Kitry was not interested in the game.

"Don't worry, she may come around," Lee told him.

Everything was in place for the formal dinner. Everyone shone in their formal attire. Stanley wore his fancy helmet. Invitees arrived at the palace and the throne room, which had been transformed into an elaborate dining salon, filled quickly.

Delegates from Caradon, Mer, the Cember Forest Egroms, Patrosym, and Lansobar fell into conversations. The Egroms were swarmed by people welcoming them back from obscurity.

The Kudaja arrived and swept into the room, their black silk cloaks flapping as they walked, Herish among them, in his formal uniform. He scanned the room searching for D'laine.

He found her across the room on Trakon's arm. His jaw clenched. He felt stupid for jeopardizing their friendship and didn't know how to make peace. He cursed silently, stood tall and strode across the room.

Trakon glared at Herish as the Kudaja approached. D'laine elbowed him in the ribs.

Herish bowed to D'laine, saluted to Trakon and held out his hand. He waited as warring thoughts raced through Trakon's head.

Trakon relented and clasped Herish's arm.

"Hi." Herish forced his face to relax so he could present a smile.

"Hello, Herish," D'laine said. "I'm glad you could attend the formal dinner."

A man approached and bowed to Herish. "Your father requests your presence, prince Herish."

"I'll be right there." Herish turned to D'laine and Trakon.

"Prince Herish?" Trakon asked. His face showed warring emotions.

Herish stood taller. "Yes, Trakon, we're of equal standing."

"Why didn't you introduce yourself as such?" Trakon accused.

Herish and Trakon inched closer to each other posturing aggression.

"I don't have to justify myself to you or anyone," Herish growled. "Perhaps D'laine will reconsider my offer for her hand." He shifted his eyes to D'laine with longing.

Trakon's eyes blazed. He grabbed the front of Herish's uniform. The Kudaja prince was ready to fight. They scuffled.

D'laine shoved herself between the two men and pushed her hands against muscled chests. They didn't back down. To avoid a scene, she sent a jolt of electrical shock to each of them. "You two just settle down, will you? You're acting like imbiciles."

"Ayi!" Trakon shouted as he jumped back. He glared at D'laine.

"What was that?" Herish asked, wide-eyed as he stared at her.

"You two are lucky I didn't turn up the heat! What are you thinking? This is a formal dinner!" D'laine whispered forcefully.

People glanced their way wondering what was going on.

Herish tugged at the front of his uniform and straightened himself out. "I'd better go find out what my father wants." He turned and strode off.

"Well, isn't that interesting? Herish is a prince!" D'laine said.

Trakon glared. "You still like him, don't you? Regardless of his actions! And lying about his station in life."

"For heaven's sake, will you quit acting like a child?" D'laine said. "He's just a friend. Or he was until you went berserk. And what difference does it make if he's a prince? I chose you."

Trakon clenched his mouth shut. He knew better than to continue that conversation.

Kitry flitted from group to group, making sure everyone was having a good time. She was happy to discover that the widowed queen of Jekorba was in attendance. She made a mental note to approach Lee to find out if he would be interested in an introduction.

There was a roar of conversation, laughter and exchanges of salutes and arm shaking.

Jor-Dan drifted among the people greeting friends from neighboring cities.

The room fell quiet as the Plotal delegation, led by Jakla Bosakin, showed up.

Jor-Dan hurried over to Jakla and grasped his arm. He took that time to speak to the quieted room. "This is an exciting time for everyone. Not only are the Egroms back among us, but the Plotals are our new neighbors!"

Jor-Dan continued and formally introduced Jakla, which was unnecessary since Jakla and his army had attacked everyone in the room at one time or another except for the Cember Forest people.

Jor-Dan's announcement about the Plotal city, lifestyle changes and community was well-received by all. The Plotal delegation found themselves surrounded by various groups of people, and discussions about changes were keen.

Kitry took charge. "Neighbors, let's be seated, shall we? We have much to relay to you, and I'm sure you came with your own news to share. I hope everyone is hungry."

Everyone settled down.

Kitry stood at the head table where her family sat and addressed the room. "You may have noticed people of a different color among us." She held out her arm to the Earthlings. "And one of them with a helmet on his head. These people come from Earth, another world that is parallel to our own."

She introduced everyone then walked to Trakon and D'laine and stood between them. Kitry grabbed one of D'laine's hands, then Trakon's, and held them up in the air.

"The prince of Ebscalon has chosen a wife," she announced.

Trakon smirked in Herish's direction.

Herish tightened his lips and glared back at Trakon. Everyone clapped their congratulations to the royal family and the engaged couple.

"Some of you have seen the princess, most likely in the battle of the invaders. She will be a welcome addition to our family. Expect a wedding invitation soon."

Kitry left Trakon and D'laine, and approached Lee. "This is D'laine's father, Lee Jackson." She whispered in his ear, "I'd like to introduce you to Queen Kansing."

Lee eyed Kitry.

Kitry moved to Brian and Jamie and placed a hand on each of their shoulders. "These are D'laine's brothers, Brian and Jamie."

Next, Kitry approached Stanley. "Stanley was a scientist on Earth, and his powerful brain must be shielded from the rest of us. Otherwise we will all be on the floor in excruciating pain." She turned to Jakla, "Even Jakla found out that Plotals are not immune to Stanley's brain pull. If that helmet is ever removed, everyone within a quarter of a mile will be completely incapacitated."

A delegate from Caradon stood. "How is this possible? The other Earthlings do not seem to require a helmet."

Trakon jumped into the conversation. "Earthlings bring their own special powers when they cross over to Thol." He explained Lee's ability to visualize complex designs in 3D. Then he discussed D'laine's powers, Jamie's ability to communicate with animals, and Brian's newfound skills.

The king of Mer stood. "Can we see a demonstration of this helmet?"

Ghury stood. "There is a lever that opens the holes in the top of the helmet. We can have Stanley demonstrate, but understand that everyone in this room will be affected by his brainpower."

The delegate from Caradon snorted. "That's all well and

good for you to explain this, but we need to understand this a little better."

People glanced at each other. The consensus was that a demonstration was called for.

Stanley stood. He moved the lever just a pinch. People grabbed their heads or pressed their hands into their eyes. He quickly closed the holes.

"Don't ever try to be funny and remove this helmet from my head," Stanley said. "Your brain will quickly drain into mine, and you may not survive the experience."

An army of servers brought plates of food. The Egroms were served their special dietary food with large bowls and spoons. The Plotals food was the same as the majority of diners but their plates and utensils were extra large.

The majordomo oversaw plates delivered to each group of attendees.

Across the room, Trakon and Herish had a non-verbal war. D'laine noticed and jabbed Trakon in the ribs. She sent a slitted eye look Herish's way. He just glared at Trakon even more.

After much fanfare, many speeches from the various king-doms and a lengthy meal with several courses, Jor-Dan intro-duced the subject of baseball.

"Friends and neighbors, our new family from Earth has introduced a delightful game. I'm sure once you see it being played, it will change the way we spend our leisure time," Jor-Dan said.

Many of the delegates were unsure what was expected of them.

Trakon and Jor-Dan urged everyone to the field where the two teams were itching to show off their skills.

More seating had been built to accommodate the attendees of the formal dinner. Jor-Dan introduced Lee to explain the sport and to show the holographic game so people would understand that this was a time for fun. After some grumbling about *inappropriate Tholian affairs,* Lee persuaded everyone to stay and watch.

Trakon's team wore gold and brown. The other team wore blue and silver. Lee slipped on a newly created black-and-white striped T-shirt over his uniform. Trakon stood on the pitcher's mound. He wound up and let the ball fly toward the batter. The player swung the bat and connected with the ball. He stood surprised as it sailed in the air.

"Run!" Lee yelled from the sideline.

The batter jerked into action. He threw the bat to the ground and started running toward third base.

Lee waved his arms in the air. "The other direction!"

The runner's team players yelled and waved their arms at the runner to get him to turn around. He made a wide arc and ran toward first base.

An outfielder tracked the ball as it flew toward him. He danced around in anticipation of catching the ball in his glove. The ball connected with his glove then flopped to the ground. He looked stunned for a moment, then looked around.

"Throw the ball toward second base," Lee hollered.

The outfielder saw the batter running toward second base. He threw the ball with all his might toward the second baseman.

The second baseman caught the ball, but it slipped out of his glove. He snatched it up and ran after the runner who ran around all over the field trying to avoid being tagged with the ball. He slipped by the second baseman and made it safely to the base.

Trakon's team members all started yelling at the second baseman for letting the runner slip by. Lee broke up a nose-to-nose argument.

"Play ball!" Lee said.

By the end of the game, some of the stuffy delegates who thought their time was being wasted were jumping at the chance to have their own team. Even the Egroms, Plotals and Kudaja were on board.

Lee told Herish that for them to have a team to compete with everyone else they would have to play as full-sized beings.

Herish met Trakon's gaze across the field and glared. "We would love to compete."

"As I've told our players, you can't use any special abilities, so think about that before you create your teams," Lee said.

He enlisted Trakon to provide everyone with the holographic game, the image of him explaining rules, and a few added images.

- Plotals could not use their tails to hit the ball, or the players.
- Egroms could not use energy for anything.
- The Kudaja could not transform and use their borjos.

Once everyone understood the rules, there was a high buzz of excitement running through the crowd about the opportunity to compete.

"When I know how many teams there will be, I will create a schedule," Lee said.

He explained about refreshment stands, team colors, and souvenirs. Vendors would have to sign up for each game. Each city would use its own vendors for food and souvenirs. Each team would choose its team colors and let Lee know, so that no two team colors overlapped.

CHAPTER NINE

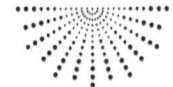

*J*amie wandered through the corridors of the palace and knocked on his father's door.

"Come in," Lee called out.

Jamie poked his head in the room, swung the door open and entered. "Hi, daddy. What're you doing?"

"Working on some baseball details." Lee pushed his chair back from the desk, stood and stretched. "If we can get some children together for Little League, would you want to try out?"

Jamie scrunched his face. "I like watching baseball, but I don't know if I want to play."

Lee observed Jamie. "You're remembering what happened to Brian when he got hit by the ball, right?"

Jamie nodded. "I don't like sports. People get hurt."

Lee hugged Jamie to him. "You don't have to play. Not everyone likes sports. Look at Kitry. She can't tolerate the game."

"I want to go see if Oggy's close by," Jamie said.

"Okay, but don't get lost, and be back in time to get cleaned up for dinner," Lee said. "You remember how to project your thoughts if you get into trouble, right?"

"Yes, daddy. If I need help, I'll holler at you," Jamie said. They hugged and Jamie skipped out of the room. He ran out of the palace, through the courtyard, past the market and through the gates.

Jamie stopped by the pen where the og had recuperated from its confrontation with the bull pakow. He kept to the outer walls of the palace for a while, then tromped through fields, calling out to the og. He never heard a response and was disappointed. He walked alongside a patch of woods, discovered an animal path and explored.

A rustling of underbrush sounded nearby. Jamie turned in that direction but didn't find an animal. He squinted, smiled and stood still.

"I see you," Jamie said into the animal's head.

An elusive kumbora bear changed its colors and showed itself. It approached Jamie and sniffed. He scratched the bear's ears and under its chin. The brown and green animal had the ability to blend with its environment, making it nearly invisible unless you stared long enough to discern its outline.

The kumbora bear had a thick, long monkey tail and flexible fingers and toes. It could scoot up a tree and swing from tree to tree overhead, escaping predators.

"Are you foraging for food?" Jamie broke a small leafy branch from the underbrush and held it out to the bear. He patted its head. "See you later."

Jamie continued walking through the patch of woods and came to a clearing. The two suns shone brilliantly and the small pond sparkled. He walked to the water, got down on his hands and knees and scooped up a handful of water. He sipped greedily, thirsty from his long walk.

A shadow fell over him.

He swung around and stared. A strange being stood before him holding a staff. He hadn't seen anything like this creature in Adrum's movies. It was as tall as the Plotals, with the same type of body. This creature didn't have the tail or the same type of snout as they did. His Mohawk was a fiery orange and his face seemed wider than the Plotals'.

The top of the staff held a brilliant crystal knob. The wooden rod was longer than Jamie was tall. A large ruby was located several inches down the wood from the crystal leaving enough space for the large hand to grasp the shaft.

"Do not fear me," the creature said.

"Who are you?" Jamie asked.

"I am Maldi Amadal, and I have been on a long journey," he said.

Jamie stood. "Where are you going?"

"I am here now, resting," Maldi said.

"Do you want to come back to Ebscalon with me?" Jamie asked. "You can rest there."

"I don't know that place," Maldi said.

"Well, a long time ago it used to be the city of Ciert. Then there was this big war with the Plotals and everything was ruined and a lot of people and Plotals were killed. So, they built a new city and called it Ebscalon," Jamie said.

Maldi was lost in memories. "Yes, I do remember Ciert. The Plotals started the war?"

"Yeah. I know they're sorry now, but it had something to do with a Ciertron rescuing a banished Plotal—you know, stupid stuff," Jamie said.

"Is there a wise man in Ebscalon?" Maldi asked.

"The Visionary?" Jamie asked. "Sure. He's really cool."

Maldi handed the crystal ruby staff to Jamie. "You will take this to him. He must protect the staff."

"Why don't you come with me? You can explain everything to the Visionary yourself," Jamie said. "He's real nice, like the king and queen."

Maldi shook his head. "No, I can't enter the city." He held his hand in the air and twirled his fingers.

An enormous shadow appeared on the ground, moving gracefully. Jamie looked up and gasped. A full-sized borjo flew overhead and spiraled down to the ground, landing and folding in its wings. It puffed smoke through its nose.

"Wow!" Jamie shouted. "Is that a borjo or a dragon? Borjos don't breathe smoke."

"Ekka will take you home. He likes you," Maldi said.

Ekka nudged Jamie.

Jamie's excitement was hard to hide. "You're beautiful! I can't wait to ride you!"

"Be gone with you now." Maldi waved his hand toward Jamie.

Ekka bowed down and Jamie climbed onto the borjos back, grasping the staff. When he looked back, Maldi was gone. Jamie looked all around, but the creature had vanished.

"Huh. Where'd he go?" Jamie asked. "Let's go to Ebscalon, Ekka. Do you know where it is?" Jamie listened to the words in his head. "I'll guide you. It's not far."

THE WALL GUARDS TRACKED THE GIANT BEAST FLYING TOWARD the city. The royals and D'laine's family were alerted. As the borjo flew over the gates, Jamie guided it to the courtyard in front of the palace. Trakon ran through the city, anger plastered on his face. As Ekka alighted in the courtyard, Jamie dismounted.

Trakon ran up to him, staring at the borjo, then back to Jamie. "Where did you find this borjo? Is Herish with you?" Trakon didn't see the Kudaja; he was confused as he panted to get his breath under control.

"I haven't seen any Kudaja," Jamie said.

D'laine, Lee, Jor-Dan, Kitry and the Visionary approached Jamie and Trakon.

The Visionary took one look at the crystal ruby staff, then at Jamie. "Where did you find this staff?"

"What is it?" Jor-Dan asked.

"It is a relic we were told had been destroyed hundreds of years ago," the Visionary said.

"Son, where did you get this staff, and the borjo?" Lee asked.

Jamie shrugged. "I was walking in the woods and came to this clearing where this little pond was. This creature showed up as I was drinking from the pond. He gave me the staff and said to give it to the wise man." Jamie handed the staff to the Visionary.

"Creature?" Lee asked. "What do you mean? What did it look like?"

Jamie projected a picture for everyone.

"That's a Plakado! They were thought to be extinct. They are distant relatives to the Plotals," the Visionary said.

"His name is Maldi Amadal, and he gave me this borjo. His name is Ekka. He likes me." To prove the point, Ekka rubbed his head against Jamie's back.

"How do we make it transform?" Trakon asked.

Brian and Chacoodi came running up through the crowd. "Wow! A dragon!" Brian said.

"It's a borjo," Jamie said. "He's mine."

"You should contact Herish and have him come get it," D'laine said.

Trakon's nose flared and his face turned shades of red as he stared at her.

D'laine swatted him. "For crying out loud, there's no reason for you to be jealous, Trakon! Contact Herish!"

"No!" Jamie said. "You're not giving away my borjo!"

"Look, son, this is not the same thing as your og," Lee said. "Where do you expect to keep him? What's he going to eat?"

Jamie eyed Ekka. "He said he won't eat the people or the pakows. He'll fly far away to eat."

Lee shared a glance with Kitry and Jor-Dan.

Ekka flew up to the roof of the palace and settled down. He let out a puff of smoke.

"He said he'll protect the city." Jamie shielded his eyes and watched his borjo.

Chacoodi looked the animal over. "This isn't a borjo. They don't make smoke."

"Are you sure?" Kitry asked. "It looks like one."

"I'll summon the Kudaja and Ghury," Chacoodi said.

GHURY AND ADRUM STEPPED INTO THE COURTYARD FROM THE Cember Forest.

"Chacoodi said something significant happened," Ghury said.

Adrum noticed the Visionary holding the ruby staff. "Where did you get the staff?"

Everyone talked at once. The Egroms finally got the whole story and understood that Jamie met with the Plakado.

"Jamie, show me in your thoughts where you met this Maldi Amadal," Ghury said.

Jamie showed the Egroms the clearing.

Adrum stepped away and was joined by several Egroms to search for the Plakado. After several moments, Adrum returned to Ebscalon.

"It appears that this Plakado has vanished," Adrum said. "Evidently this Maldi Amadal doesn't want to be found."

Ghury turned to the Visionary. "You have been charged with protecting the sacred staff."

Ghury looked from D'laine to Trakon, then the rest of the group. "The ruby staff is related to the prophecy. It is imperative that we find this Plakado so we understand what he knows about the prophecy."

Trakon and D'laine stared at the Egroms. This concerned them personally. It was frustrating that no one seemed to be able to explain the prophecy to them in detail. They figured it had all played out with the battle of the robots, but now there was another element. Would it never end?

Trakon stewed. "Can someone explain how this prophecy will affect us?" He pointed to himself, then to D'laine. "What about our future? How are we supposed to get married and plan for our own family when we don't know what this means for us?"

D'laine held onto Trakon's arm. Her face was etched with concern.

"Does this prophecy pertain to only D'laine and Trakon, or are we involved?" Lee looked from Jor-Dan to Kitry then to the Visionary and finally the Egroms for an answer.

"The prophecy does not concern you or your sons," Ghury said.

A SQUADRON OF KUDAJA, HEADED UP BY HERISH, FLEW TO THE courtyard. They dismounted and saluted the royals.

"Hi. What's wrong?" Herish looked warily from Trakon to D'laine. He heard a loud huff and his eyes traveled up to the roof. His temper spiked as he looked all around.

"Where is he? Who is it? Who dared—?" Herish demanded.

Trakon cackled loudly.

D'laine swatted Trakon. "Will you stop?" She turned to Herish. "Hello, Herish. How are you this turn?"

The Kudaja fumed. "D'laine, who dared show up and disrespected you after everyone at the formal dinner heard the announcement of your impending wedding?"

"Relax, Herish. No Kudaja warrior transformed and rode the borjo. Jamie rode him home," she explained.

Herish turned to Jamie, surprised. "Where'd you get him?"

Jamie explained. Herish and his squadron stared at the beast on the roof.

"Is he a dragon?" Brian asked.

"No, he's never been neutered," Herish said. "Our borjos would be spewing fire and smoke if they hadn't been neutered after they hatched. They're extremely dangerous and unpredictable. Get two males together and they could burn the forest down."

D'laine snorted. "Two males? Reminds me of someone."

Herish and Trakon scowled at the reference to them.

"Can you transform him?" Trakon asked.

"No. They have to go through the transformation while they are young, otherwise they're like this huge beast," Herish said.

"Can we build him a home?" Jamie made eye contact with Jor-Dan, pleading to keep Ekka.

Jor-Dan walked out into the plaza. He looked over his shoulder as he walked, keeping the palace roof in sight. When he was far back from the palace entrance, he pointed.

"The old tower would be an ideal home for him. It has openings on all sides, giving a view of all directions. He would be protected from the weather," Jor-Dan said.

Jamie ran over to the king and looked, but he was too short to find the tower.

Jor-Dan swooped Jamie up to his shoulders, holding onto the boy's hands. He positioned his body in the correct direction.

"Do you see the tower now?" Jor-Dan asked.

"That's perfect!" Jamie said.

Trakon and the others joined them. "We should go check it out. That tower hasn't been used since before I was hatched."

Jor-Dan settled Jamie on the ground. "You go explore. I have petitioners waiting."

Lee nudged Jor-Dan as he shook his head. "How many

animals are enough? Jamie has you wrapped around his fingers. Who knows what he'll bring home next?"

Jor-Dan gave a meek nod. "I just can't say no. He's so happy with his animals."

THE GROUP TRUDGED UP THE STAIRS AND WOUND THROUGH corridors until they reached the location of the old tower. Trakon opened a door, and they climbed up another set of stairs.

The old tower was enormous. It was similar to the tower on the Visionary's building, but larger. Trakon, Herish and Lee studied the height and width of the space. Lee used his Tholian gift, and the men determined it was more than adequate for the borjo.

"Can we make him a bed?" Jamie asked.

"We can pile up gauze like the Egroms do in their houses," D'laine said. "Remember how comfortable that was?"

"Yeah, that'll do!" Jamie said.

"That's a full-turn's worth of work for about five hosks," Chacoodi said. "Let's go get it!"

They left the tower and went over to a large building across the city. Hundreds of male hosks spun moss into silky gauze.

D'laine drifted over to a large hand loom where a woman was crafting a rug. She observed for a few moments, fascinated by the whole process.

"That's so beautiful. You must be so proud of your work," D'laine said.

"It's nice peaceful work. I enjoy creating these rugs and other things," the weaver said.

D'laine wandered over to find out how the raw silk was washed, dried and twisted into threads.

She returned to where Trakon and Herish were stuffing gauze into large sacks. Trakon handed her a full sack.

"It's not heavy, just bulky," he told her. "Can you find your way back to the tower?"

D'laine grabbed the sack and spied Lee leaving the building. "I'll follow my father." She trotted off with the bag over her shoulder. It bounced off her heels as she made her way through the door. "Daddy! Wait up."

Lee stopped. He shifted his two sacks. "Your brother!" He shook his head. "The next thing he'll want is boots for his pakow!"

"You'd better take that back. If he hears you, he'll suggest it to anyone who will listen." She giggled.

They climbed to the tower just as Brian, Jamie and Chacoodi emptied their sacks. A corner of the area was piled with gauze. Lee and D'laine shook their sacks upside down and added their gauze to the pile.

"Maybe two more trips each to make a sufficient bed," Lee said.

Stomping up the stairs announced Herish and Trakon, each hauling three sacks. D'laine watched as they emptied their sacks. They seemed to be getting along, even enjoying themselves.

"Two more trips?" Lee asked them.

"One should do it," Trakon said. With that, he and Herish thudded down the stairs while everyone followed at an easier pace.

When the last sack had been added to the pile, they stood back and assessed the large area. The gauze pile was enormous. Jamie called to Ekka. The borjo flew over to the tower, flying around inspecting it then sailed through a large rounded opening. He pulled his wings in to his sides. He shuffled over to the gauze pile, climbed on top, scratched it to make a pit then settled down.

Jamie turned to the group. "He's never had a bed before. He's so grateful. He said he'll protect Ebscalon."

Trakon stared at the creature. He figured it was at least three pakows tall and who knew how many pakows long. The animal was a tremendous deterrent for any invading force. He imagined what this fire-breathing creature looked like in a defensive mode and shuddered at the thought.

"Let's hope he never has to defend us," Trakon said.

Herish elbowed Trakon. "You should go for a ride. Once you ride a borjo, you'll never want to fly a crestrider."

Trakon evaluated what Herish said. "That good, huh?"

Herish grinned. "There's nothing like riding a borjo. It must be the power of their wings, or just the freedom of not having a mechanical device that can break down."

"What do you think, Jamie? Would your borjo let me fly him?" Trakon asked.

"I'd probably have to go with you to communicate with him," Jamie said. "Should I ask him?"

Jamie looked to Lee for permission.

"Do you think your father would approve, Trakon?" Lee asked.

After sputtering for a moment, Trakon got his wits together. "I'm pretty sure my father wouldn't stop me."

"Since Jamie rode him here, I know it's safe so I won't stand in your way," Lee said. "But if you get into trouble, you're on your own."

Jamie rubbed the borjos snout. "Come on, Ekka. Let's take Trakon for a ride."

Ekka allowed Trakon to climb up and sit behind Jamie.

"Okay, we're ready," Jamie said.

Ekka waddled to the opening, and leapt out of the tower. His mighty wings opened and flapped as they flew up and away from the city. They flew over the land where the Plotal city was being built. From the back of Ekka, the fierce Plotals looked to

Jamie no bigger than twigs. Jamie steered Ekka in a wide berth around the other cities, then headed back to Ebscalon.

Trakon's hair was windblown and his face erupted in a gigantic smile as they sailed through the tower opening. He and Jamie hopped down.

"You can take a nap now." Jamie patted the borjo on the snout and watched as a trickle of smoke escaped its nose.

"Well, what'd you think?" Herish asked.

"I wonder if my father will let us have some borjos." Trakon said. "You were right. There's nothing like riding on the back of a borjo."

Trakon and Herish smiled like two boys on an adventure.

They nudged each other playfully. "Told you," Herish said.

D'laine was happy that Trakon and Herish were becoming friends.

CHAPTER TEN

*D*annin entered the palace and went to the throne room where Jor-Dan was sitting at the table with his advisors. Marrak documented the meeting. Dannin approached, thumped his chest and waited to be acknowledged.

"Dannin, what seems to be bothering you?" Jor-Dan studied the man's face.

"Sire, the hosk gatherers returned from the meadow with empty crates. They reported that there were no hosks—none whatsoever." Dannin was clearly mystified as to where thousands of hosks could have gone.

Everyone stared at Dannin as if he had lost his mind. Hosks reproduced like Earth rabbits. It was impossible to walk ten paces in the meadow without stumbling upon a hosk colony.

"Did they expand their search?" Jor-Dan asked.

"They spread out and covered a five-mile area," Dannin said. "I'm not sure what's going on, or how to proceed."

Jor-Dan fretted in exasperation. "No hosks for five miles? That's impossible."

"Is there something wrong with the moss? Perhaps an enemy drove them away," Marrak said.

Jor-Dan thought for a moment. "That might be a possibility. Marrak, summon the agriculturist. Have him study the meadow moss to see if there's some type of infestation. Ask him to report back as soon as possible."

Marrak worked his communicator and contacted Forador, the agriculturist. Thirty moments later, a middle-aged man entered the room.

"Sire." Forador pressed his fist to his chest. "I've completed an examination on the meadow moss and I find nothing out of the ordinary. I brought back samples of the moss and soil to do further studies, but the moss appears to be healthy."

The group discussed the problem for several moments, not making any progress.

"Jor-Dan, perhaps your young grandson can help with this," one of the advisors said. "Perhaps he could take a hosk from the weaving building and bring it out to the meadow and find out what the problem is."

"That's an excellent idea!" Jor-Dan turned to Marrak. Marrak held up a hand. "I'm on it. I've summoned Jamie."

THE MIDSIZED CRESTRIDER HOVERED ABOVE THE MEADOW. Dannin, Forador, Jamie, Jor-Dan, Marrak and several of Jor-Dan's advisors descended the stairs. Jamie jumped off the last step, clutching a male hosk from the weaving building.

Everyone gathered in a circle as Jamie set the hosk on the ground. The little creature squealed in fright and climbed up Jamie's leg to his hands. Its tiny body trembled.

"What's the matter?" Jamie listened to the silent dialog, his face screwing up in disbelief.

"He says a big crawling enemy is near. All the colonies have fled to a safer place," Jamie said.

"Can he show you what this enemy looks like?" Jor-Dan

asked. "If we can capture it and take it somewhere, the colonies will return."

"Show me what it looks like," Jamie said to the hosk. He waited a moment. Then he shared a picture in his mind with the group. "This looks like an earthworm from back home. Those are only about this big, though." Jamie spread his fingers showing the size of the earthworms back home, even slipping in a night crawler to be on the safe side. "How would something like this scare them? They're bigger than this worm."

"Maybe it has teeth and bites them!" Dannin suggested. "You know, if that's the case, it might ambush them from under the moss and bite their tiny legs."

"I guess that's possible," Forador said. "I'm not sure how we're going to find these worms though. We'd have to dig up the entire meadow!"

"For now, the gatherers will have to travel to the far side of the meadow until we get this sorted out," Jor-Dan said.

They all rode the escalator up to the crestrider and headed back to the city.

STANLEY AND LEE SAT IN LEE'S SUITE IN DEEP DISCUSSION.

"If we could find Greg Claymore, we might discover something significant about his comings and goings prior to leaving Earth permanently," Lee said.

"I can't imagine someone abandoning his family like that," Stanley said. "I wonder if there are others like him scattered around Thol. There's a possibility the Egroms aren't telling us everything."

Lee pursed his lips. "He'd be pretty old by now, if he's even still alive. The first time he disappeared was 1952. He was in his thirties. It's been over sixty years."

"Yeah, but then I read through the report and saw those

snapshots. When he returned in 1975, he still looked thirty," Stanley said.

"We need to talk with Ghury," Lee said.

TRAKON AND D'LAINE SLIPPED OUT OF THE PALACE AND WALKED hand in hand through the marketplace and hastily out through the gates of the city. They passed Oggy's old pen, each looking over their shoulders every once in a while, as they entered the copse of trees. As soon as they were out of sight of prying eyes, Trakon wrapped his arms around D'laine and they kissed passionately.

They parted momentarily, eyes glazed with longing. "This seems to be the only place where we can be alone," Trakon said, filled with desire.

"Everyone's always watching us—not just our families, but the entire city!" D'laine said. "If I trip over a pebble, it's reported back to the palace and your mother wants to have the Visionary examine me!"

Trakon held D'laine's face and rubbed his thumbs gently over her cheeks. He leaned in and kissed her again. They were melded to each other, fingers running through each other's hair. Moans of longing escaped their lips. Trakon slipped his hands down to her butt and lifted her to him. She wrapped her legs around his waist. He knelt with D'laine enfolded around him.

Someone cleared his throat nearby.

Trakon and D'laine untangled themselves, sprang apart and jumped to their feet, panting slightly, eyes wild with having been caught in their fervent display of passion.

A lone guard stepped forward around a tree, somewhat embarrassed.

"What are you doing here, Biggan?" Trakon croaked.

D'laine placed her hand on his arm, calming him. "Trakon."

"I'm sorry, my prince, princess, but I'm just doing my job." Biggan's reddish bronze skin appeared a little redder from bearing witness to the couple's kissing session.

"Your job? What do you mean?" Trakon asked, more rational.

The guard stood tall. "My duty is to make sure the princess is safe at all times." He stared Trakon down. "Even if that means making sure her honor is upheld until your wedding turn."

D'laine gasped. "Ohmygod! This is so embarrassing! And here we were convinced we were fooling everyone."

Biggan looked from one to the other. "Your parents have your best interests in mind." He held out his hand. "Shall we?"

Trakon grabbed D'laine's hand, and they marched out of the trees, followed by their guard. As they entered the city, they parted, Trakon heading toward his work area and D'laine running into her suite in the palace.

As she opened her door, Pup blinked his eyes and raised his head. He sensed her mood and jumped to his feet. He sniffed all around her making sure she was not harmed. He sat at her feet as she threw herself on a sofa.

"I've never been so embarrassed in my entire life!" she ranted.

THE EVENING MEAL WAS UNCOMFORTABLE. BOTH TRAKON AND D'laine's cheeks were stained with color as all three parents stared knowingly at the couple. There seemed to be an undisputed agreement of unity among the parents as their eyes darted from the amorous couple to the younger children at the table.

Stanley watched the family groups, trying to figure out what was going on.

After very little small talk, Brian and Jamie asked to be

excused. They rushed from the room, not wanting to be hit by emotional shrapnel. One of Jamie's hands tried to hide a couple of morsels for Chatter and Pup. Everyone was aware of the offering and no one said a peep.

Once the boys were out of sight, the truce was lifted. "Your guardian reported a rather interesting scene," Kitry said.

D'laine cringed. She knew the queen was exasperated, and her father was incensed, but Jor-Dan tried hard to hide a smirk.

"You had us followed!" Trakon all but bellowed.

"And it's a good thing!" Lee roared.

Kitry raised her hands, beckoning the men to keep the peace. "D'laine, you don't have a mother to guide you. I took it upon myself, with your father's permission, to make sure you were protected from your emotions in regard to my son." She nodded in Lee's direction to emphasize their solidarity on the matter. "And from Trakon's enamored feelings."

"Uh, I better go to my room now." Stanley slunk out of the room and dashed up the stairs.

Once tempers cooled, Kitry continued. Her eyes bored into Trakon. "Biggan will be your shadow—whether you like it or not. Do not take your anger out on him. He is just doing as instructed, and he takes his job seriously."

"And no more locking up your dogs to try to sneak out." Jor-Dan tried to keep a serious disposition to support his wife and Lee, but he couldn't help letting a chuckle escape.

Kitry whirled her attention to her husband. Her eyes turned to slits of anger and she was about ready to lash out at him.

Jor-Dan raised his hand in surrender. "Wife, your memory seems to have lapsed. I recall your father practically running me out of the city when we were discovered in a rather compromising situation."

Kitry's face flamed.

Trakon sputtered.

D'laine's jaw dropped.

"You were much older than we are!" Trakon stuttered. "By more than twenty years!"

"Jor-Dan!" Kitry exclaimed. "Don't you think it's our responsibility to keep our children chaste until they marry?"

"It sounds to me as if you two were not innocent before you were married," Trakon said. "Perhaps I should ask one of your friends about this."

"Oh, for Thol's sake! See what you started?" Kitry yelled at Jor-Dan.

Lee scrutinized D'laine and Trakon. "You two need to consider all the ramifications of your actions. Do you want to take a chance and get pregnant before your wedding? It's not as if there's birth control here, D'laine."

D'laine's jaw dropped. Trakon's chair moved back a couple of inches. They exchanged a shocked look. It was obvious to all that those thoughts had never occurred to them.

BREAKFAST WAS AN EASIER MEAL WITH TEMPERS UNDER CONTROL. Brian and Jamie gauged the situation by studying the faces of the adults, their sister and Trakon.

Jamie nudged Brian.

Brian shrugged back. He didn't know what was going on. He decided there were times when it was best to be ignorant in the dealings with adults. Brian figured this was one of those times. He turned to Stanley.

Stanley gave Brian the thumbs up as if to say that everyone was okay and whatever had happened was under control.

As the meal was ending, family members and Stanley left the table to begin their turn. A loud squealing of hundreds of male hosks erupted from the weaving building.

All three dogs jumped to their feet, teeth clacking in attack mode, ready to spring out of the room.

"Down!" D'laine commanded, using The Voice.

The dogs all went down on their bellies, heads submissive.

"To me!" she commanded.

All three dogs obeyed. They crawled to her side. D'laine held her hand out, palm down—a signal telling them to stay.

"What's going on?" D'laine asked as everyone ran out of the palace. She waved her hand, and the dogs were on their feet, but they stayed at her side, teeth clacking.

"That was a smart thing you did," Jor-Dan said. "The dogs are all riled up and could easily attack anyone."

Lee and Stanley stood back, away from the pack, eyeing them warily. Trakon and a small squadron of guards ran through the city to the weaving building.

"Surely an animal didn't get into the weaving building!" Kitry was alarmed.

"Trakon will find out what's going on," Jor-Dan put his arm across Kitry's shoulders. "Those buildings are completely secure. Someone may have been careless and left a door open."

"That's a very unnerving sound," Lee said. "I had no idea hosks squealed."

Trakon's voice sounded through the communicators amid the deafening squeals from the hosks. "There's nothing in here. I don't know what's wrong with them. We've searched everywhere."

The Visionary joined the family. "Danger approaches!" The ground shook and a loud rumbling sounded.

The right side of the city gate and the wall shattered as a monstrous head and partial body erupted from the ground. The creature looked like a gigantic worm until a split tongue darted in and out of its mouth. Large, pointed teeth filled the monstrous cavern. The segmented, tube-like body was a brownish color and appeared more wormlike than snakelike.

People screamed in panic and fled in all directions. Market stalls flew into the air and crashed around them. Guards and soldiers activated their suits into war mode. Jor-Dan was wearing his meeting robes, which would not protect him. Palace guards grabbed Jor-Dan, Kitry and the Visionary and pulled them back into the palace to keep them safe.

"Release the dogs," Jor-Dan yelled over his shoulder.

D'laine snapped her finger. The dogs sprang toward the giant worm-snake creature.

"Activate your suits!" D'laine yelled to her father, brothers and Stanley. She showed them which button to press on their wrists.

They watched their suits as they clacked into war mode. Trakon came running through the city, laser weapon in hand. A battalion of soldiers attacked the creature. Trakon joined in the fight.

D'laine watched as the dogs jumped at the monster. She saw that they were not able to grip the sides of the worm-snake. The creature rolled from side to side, crushing anyone who got too close.

D'laine screamed as she watched.

Come to me! She commanded. The dogs did not want to leave the fight. "*COME TO ME!*" she bellowed. The Voice thundered louder than ever before. The dogs momentarily dropped to the ground then reluctantly returned to her side, teeth chattering. "*INSIDE!*" she commanded as she pointed to the palace.

Jamie ran toward the worm-snake. "Jamie!" Lee screamed. "Get back here!"

"Oh, God! He thinks he can talk to it!" D'laine said.

Jamie stopped out of reach of the worm-snake. He focused on the creature. *Stop! You're hurting people! What do you want?*

The worm-snake suddenly turned its head in his direction and moved forward in a rolling thrust.

Stanley, D'laine, Brian and Lee screamed in horror for Jamie to run, but it was as if he was rooted to the spot. They ran toward Jamie. Trakon ran from the opposite direction, swinging his laser at the beast.

A large shadow appeared on the ground. Ekka swooped in, talons extended and grabbed the worm-snake and jerked it fully out of the ground. The worm-snake twisted and turned, but couldn't wrap itself around the borjo, or bite it. Ekka shook the creature furiously, then flew off away from the city.

"Are you crazy!" Brian yelled at his brother.

"That thing could have crushed you!" Lee yelled.

"I should have tried to remove my helmet," Stanley said. "That might have stopped it in its tracks."

Lee breathed heavily as he crushed Jamie to him.

More rumbling sounded. A hundred Plotals rode their beasts hard toward the city, lasers ready. Jakla Bosakin and a squadron of Plotals jumped from their pakows and ran through the ruined city gates as others waited for instructions.

"Did the creature escape?" Jakla yelled. He approached Trakon and the family.

"The borjo captured it and took it away to eat," Trakon said.

"We were attacked at our site. There were two of them. One got away and we followed it here," Jakla said.

Jor-Dan and Kitry emerged from the palace surrounded by the guards. Jor-Dan had changed into his war suit. He approached Jakla with his hand extended. They exchanged the customary greeting.

"There were two?" Jor-Dan asked.

"We killed the other one," Jakla said. "What are they? I have never seen anything like it."

The Visionary came forward. "It's called a fhahadda. There have not been any sightings of these creatures in over five hundred years."

Jamie scowled. "It didn't want to talk to me."

"Don't you ever do that again," Lee said. "You have to understand that not all creatures are happy-go-lucky and want to talk with you, Jamie. Always approach cautiously."

D'laine nudged her father. "Didn't that look almost like the giant worm in the movie *Dune?*"

Lee reflected for a moment. "Yes, very similar, except for the snake-like tongue and those teeth."

Lee noticed that everyone was looking at him, waiting for an explanation. He considered how to explain a movie. "The easiest way to explain this is that on the fictional desert planet Dune, also known as Arrakis, there are these gigantic worms. They are much, much larger than this snake creature."

"Is this Dune Arrakis another dimension shared with our planet?" Jor-Dan asked.

"They didn't come through a portal, if that's what you're worried about," D'laine fibbed. "Dune is far away in deep space, not anywhere near our galaxy."

"Wherever they came from, we may have a big problem," Stanley said.

All eyes swung to Stanley, waiting for the bad news. "Snakes reproduce once or twice a year. These fhahadda may either have live births, or lay eggs—anywhere from one to a hundred."

"Oh, no!" Trakon said.

"They lay eggs. You must find the nest and exterminate them," the Visionary said.

Jakla held up a gloved hand. "It would be wise for us to find where they came from. If we trace their route from the first attack, we might be able to find the nest and destroy them."

Jor-Dan nodded. "A good plan. Let's take a platoon and go to Ta'Byu'Vohon. I think it would be wise to take crestriders—we may be able to see their trail better from the air."

"Yes, that sounds practical," Jakla said. "We should also send crestriders to the other cities and find out if there have been any sightings."

Trakon turned to one of the guards. "Send two-man

crestriders to Patrosym, Mer, Lansobar and Caradon. If they haven't seen these creatures, they should be warned, just in case there are others."

A large shadow announced Ekka's return. He flew in a circle over the group, then returned to his tower nest.

Jakla and his platoon of Plotals watched.

"You have a full-sized borjo living in your tower?" Jakla asked.

"Jamie seems to attract animals," Jor-Dan said. "Most creatures like to interact with the boy. Ekka is his latest pet. Oggy, his og, was the first stray he brought home."

Jakla looked down at Jamie. "You had an og for a pet?"

"He's gone back to his family," Jamie said. "Ekka is here to stay. That worm-snake wouldn't even talk to me."

"Let's hope the cities won't have to contend with adult worm-snakes," Lee said. "The younger ones may be easier to deal with. Not everyone is going to have a full-sized borjo on hand to take care of the problem."

"Jakla, would you and your small platoon want to come with us in the ship?" Trakon asked.

"That might be beneficial," Jakla said. "I would like to get a broader view of where the creature emerged before it attacked." He turned to his warriors. You two come with me. He motioned to another one of his warriors. "Ride with our army back to the city—be on the lookout for any more worm-snakes. We will join up with you shortly."

The big Plotal warrior ran back through the city to the ruined gate and mounted his pakow. He led the army back the way they had come.

A PLATOON-SIZED SHIP SKIRTED ACROSS THE MOSS HIGH ENOUGH in the air for the passengers to determine whether there was any ground movement. They passed up the Plotal army making its way back to Ta'Byu'Vohon on their pakows.

As they hovered over the city, they saw massive holes in the ground near a collapsed building.

"There," Jakla said pointing. "The creatures came out of two separate tunnels. As you can see, they smashed their way through the construction as if it were a box of leaves."

Trakon leaned over the side of the ship and pointed. "Steer the ship that way."

Ta'Byu'Vohon was several miles away from the Ikley forest, and it appeared the tunnels came from that direction. The midsized ship slowed as it approached the forest. Everyone aboard, except for the pilot, stared over the sides of the ship.

Lee and Jor-Dan conferred, side by side as they hung over the edge of the ship gripping the hand railing. "It doesn't appear as if they came from the forest," Lee said.

"The tunneling shows they skirted the edge of the forest," Jor-Dan said.

D'laine squealed. "Look! The ground is moving over there!"

Everyone rushed to the side of the ship where she stood. A large area of meadow moss, about the size of the baseball field, undulated.

"Raise the ship!" Trakon shouted to the pilot. "We don't know what's going to emerge from that action. Might be adults, or a lot of hatchlings."

Within moments, the ground opened and dozens of worm-snakes, tangled together in a large writhing ball, surfaced. Unhatched eggs could be seen from the air along with eggs cracking open.

The fhahadda appeared to be four to six inches in girth. Their length was impossible to determine as they were inter-twined in the gigantic ball.

"Start shooting!" Jakla shouted to his warriors.

"Wait!" D'laine said. "I can handle this." She looked over her shoulder. "Everyone stand back. Go to the other side of the ship to be safe."

D'laine spread her arms wide and turned her face toward the suns for a moment, eyes closed. Then she snapped her eyes open and pointed a finger at the nest. A beam shot from her finger to the nest. A loud boom sounded. As the dirt and moss settled, all that was left where the ball of fhahadda had once roiled, was a crater and decimated worm-snake bits.

A cheer rose up from the ship's passengers.

"It would be wise for a crew to sift through that rubble and make sure no eggs survived," Lee said. "Do you have any material to use as a sifter?"

"What is this device you're talking about?" Jakla asked.

Lee conjured up a picture of a wire mesh sifter and shared the vision with the group.

Trakon studied the image. "We can easily fabricate that. I'll send this image to Hexlon."

As Trakon assembled the image and explained what they needed, his communicator squawked an incoming alert message.

"Prince Trakon! One of those creatures is rampaging through Lansobar!"

"We're on our way!" Trakon said. The pilot headed southeast.

Lee shook his head in confusion. "I don't understand what's going on. Earthworms don't bother people. Worms are creatures that live in and consume soil. They help to oxygenate the dirt. Gardeners love them."

He noticed confused faces. "Soil, you know, dirt—the ground you walk on, what's under the moss."

When he noticed that everyone was on board with that explanation, he continued. "Snakes, on the other hand, eat small rodents and, depending on the type of snake, some attack humans and animals. Back on Earth, if we had hosks, the snakes would eat them. This is most likely what caused the hosks to panic."

"Yeah, but these fhahadda look like our earthworms and snakes rolled into one," D'laine said. "That doesn't make any sense. I wonder where they came from. The Visionary said that no one has seen them in five hundred years."

No sooner had the conversation finished than the ship arrived at the outskirts of Lansobar. Large furrows in the ground showed the path of the fhahadda. The worm-snake travelled through the meadow and into the city, where it seemed to have stopped to rest.

They saw massive damage to buildings and inner-city roads and walking paths. A mammoth hump near the center of the city was visible from the air. As the passengers of the crestrider watched, it appeared the hump of ground seemed to undulate.

"Looks like it's getting ready to rise," Lee said. "We should warn everyone to stand back."

Trakon hit his communicator and opened a channel with the people on the ground. "Fall back from the creature. It is getting ready to break through the ground."

The land erupted as the head and several feet of the body broke through the dirt and pavement.

"This is a younger worm-snake," D'laine said. "It probably escaped from the nest we destroyed."

Jakla studied the creature. "This one is much larger than the worms in the ball, which makes me think there must be another nest."

"Not only that, but we didn't see any ground disruptions between Ta'Byu'Vohon and Lansobar," Jor-Dan said. "That's quite a distance."

The worm-snake was now fully out of the ground, but not writhing.

"Huh," Trakon said. "It's not doing anything."

"Daddy, we should send for Jamie and see if he could talk to this one." D'laine said.

Lee watched the worm-snake. He let out a sigh. "He does have this gift. As long as we can keep him safe, we should let him try to talk to it."

Trakon turned to Dannin. "Have someone bring Jamie here."

Dannin tapped his communicator and passed along the request.

"Let's land the ship so we can find Youndon," Jor-Dan said. "Trakon, open a communication channel to Youndon, if you can."

The pilot veered the ship to a landing area outside the damaged zone.

"Keep the ship in hover mode," Trakon said. "If it looks like there's a threat, get way up in the air."

The pilot acknowledged the orders. The passengers descended the stairs. Youndon of Lansobar and a small delegation approached them.

"You have come about the creature?" Youndon asked.

"Jakla's city was hit first. The Plotals managed to kill one of the adults, and the other hit Ebscalon. My grandson's borjo killed the other adult," Jor-Dan explained after he and Youndon greeted each other.

"You have a full-sized borjo?" Youndon asked.

"It's a long story," Lee said.

Ekka's shadow covered the ground. They all looked up and saw the giant borjo floating through the air with Jamie and one of Dannin's men on his back.

Lee pointed to where the crestrider hovered. "Land there."

Jamie had Ekka land. He and the guard climbed down to the ground.

"You stay here, okay, Ekka?" Jamie asked. "I'll go see if this worm will talk to me. If not, I guess he'll be your dessert!"

Ekka looked like he smiled. A stream of smoke blew out of his nose.

Jamie and the guard approached the group.

The guard had a huge smile on his face from the wonders of flying on the back of the borjo.

Trakon grinned, knowingly.

"That worm isn't as big as the other one," Jamie said.

The worm continued just to lie on the ground.

"Do you think you can try to talk to it?" Lee asked.

"Sure," Jamie said. "I hope he wants to talk to me."

They walked over to the area where the creature seemed to be resting on top of the ground. Jamie walked to the head of the creature, the others following him.

"Make sure you stay way back, in case it gets irritated," Lee said.

D'laine placed her hand on Jamie's shoulder. "Do not try to be friends with this thing. Look how much damage it can do, just because of its size."

"Okay, I get it. I made a mistake with the other one," Jamie said. "Stay here."

Jamie walked toward the worm-snake. He stopped to where he was not directly in front of the creature. He stood silently, trying to communicate with his mind. After a few moments, he jumped back, startled.

"His name is Jum," Jamie yelled out.

The group talked among themselves, excited at the connection.

"He's twelve years old, and he's just starting out on his own, away from the nest," Jamie said.

"Ask him why he's here, destroying our city," Youndon called out.

Jamie stood silently, communicating with the creature. "He says he didn't mean to do any damage. He's looking for a place to build his nest. His kind doesn't know about the ways of humans or cities," Jamie said.

"Okay, we need to send him someplace away from cities, where he won't disturb the hosks," D'laine said.

"What about near the Jaffre Forest?" Jakla suggested.

"Isn't Aveldon near there?" Youndon asked.

Trakon pulled up a map from his communicator. They conferred for a moment as they studied the map of cities and forests. He tapped a holographic spot.

"What about here? This is about 50 miles on the other side of the Cember Forest. The Egroms should be able to keep them under a watchful eye," Trakon said.

They all studied the area.

"That should be a good place." Jor-Dan turned to D'laine. "Should we ask the Egroms about this?"

D'laine stood unfocused for a moment in a silent communication. She blinked then focused on Jor-Dan. "Ghury said that would be a good place for the fhahadda. The worm-snake shouldn't bother the Kudaja. She turned toward her brother. "Jamie, would Ekka be able to take the worm-snake there without hurting him?"

"Sure, but I need to talk to Jum first." He approached the worm and placed his small hand on the side of its face. He pointed to Ekka then patted Jum.

"Yeah, he's okay with Ekka taking him there, but he wants to make sure he won't be hurt. Can we make some kind of sling?"

Youndon hailed one of his guards. "We need a large, strong piece of material so the borjo can transport the worm out of the city."

"That's one big piece of material," Trakon said.

Jakla took a step toward Jamie, then thought better of it. "Jamie, the worm needs to understand it has to sense the surface before coming above the ground. If it detects people or structures, it needs to move away. Would it be able to recognize things like that?"

"Huh. I don't know. Let's see." A few moments later Jamie passed on the information. "He said they do use a type of sonar to navigate, but he didn't understand what he was sensing. Now that he knows about these cities, he'll make sure his young ones understand. He said they eat dirt."

Youndon's people returned, hauling a large heavy canvas roll of material and a sack of grommets. Two guards had thick rope over their shoulders.

"How are we going to do this?" Jor-Dan asked.

"Clear away all the debris from this side of the worm, then lay the canvas out on the ground. Once we have the grommets in place, Jamie can tell the fhahadda to roll onto the canvas. We can get it secured with the rope through the grommets, and Ekka can lift it off the ground and get it out of here." Trakon smiled like a kid with candy. "I'll ride with Jamie."

"I'm coming for the ride!" D'laine said.

EKKA HOVERED OVER THE WORM-SNAKE THAT WAS WAITING ON the canvas. Two men held out the rope so the borjo could grasp it and lift the sling into the air. After two tries, Ekka grasped the rope and the worm-snake lifted off the ground in the sling.

Jamie patted Ekka's back. "Good job. Let's go now."

D'laine sat behind Jamie, and Trakon sat behind D'laine. Ekka didn't waste any time. His mighty wings beat.

They soared through the air, across the meadows, over the Ikley Forest and beyond the vast meadows of moss. They approached the Cember Forest. D'laine heard hundreds of greetings from the Egroms as Ekka passed over the village.

The area Ghury suggested for the fhahadda's new home was fast approaching. It was a vast, uninhabited meadow. Ekka lowered himself until the canvas sling touched the ground. He landed several feet away from his live cargo and allowed Jamie, Trakon and D'laine to climb down to the ground.

Jamie patted Ekka's snout. "We won't be long. Go fly, if you want, or you can wait here."

Trakon and D'laine stood on either side of the huge sling. They each grabbed a rope and pulled the material flat to allow the worm-snake to crawl off the canvas.

Hosk squeals sounded throughout the meadow. Jamie stood near the fhahadda. He called out to the hosks.

"Hosks! The fhahadda isn't a meat eater. He's not a predator. He eats soil, what's underneath the moss. You can live in harmony!"

A female hosk popped out from under the moss. She approached the fhahadda. Shaking with fear, she sniffed it. They seemed to commune for a moment, then the hosk popped back under the moss. The male hosks stopped squealing.

Jamie stood by the fhahadda. "This is your new home. Live in harmony with the hosks, okay?"

He patted the side of the fhahadda. "Everybody stand back. Jum's going to tunnel now."

They watched as the gigantic creature stretched its body up, pointed its head to the ground and plunged into the earth.

All three were splattered with moss and dirt. "Gross!" D'laine sputtered as she wiped her face.

"Thanks for the warning, Jamie!" Trakon said, spitting dirt out of his mouth.

Jamie shook himself to dislodge the debris.

"Let's go to the warm pool in the Cember Forest where we used to bathe," D'laine said.

They gathered up the canvas and ropes, approached Ekka and climbed aboard. Jamie directed the borjo to the pool. "You can go hunt now," Jamie said. "I'll call you when we want to go home."

D'laine stood at the edge of the pool. The quokin bobbed to the surface.

"Jamie, did you get to play with the quokin when you were here?" D'laine asked.

"Yeah, he missed you," Jamie said.

A dragonfly-sized borjo zoomed over and around them.

Laughter sounded.

"Herish, is that you?" D'laine called out as the borjo sped away.

Herish and a girl appeared, full-sized. He laughed at the sight of the three in front of him.

"What happened?" Herish asked.

Trakon's eyes darted from Herish to the Kudaja girl.

"A fhahadda dove into the ground and we got splattered," Jamie said.

"Fhahadda? What's that?" Herish asked.

"Our people have those documented," the girl said.

Trakon and D'laine waited to be introduced. Suddenly it dawned on Herish.

"Oh, sorry. This is Meeri, my betrothed," Herish said. "Meeri, meet D'laine, Trakon and Jamie."

"So, this is D'laine," Meeri said, nodding. She didn't appear to be jealous, just curious. "And the two of you are also betrothed, aren't you?"

Herish grinned widely.

Trakon suddenly became possessive as he wrapped his arm across D'laine's back. "Yes, D'laine and I are to be married soon."

D'laine elbowed him in the side. "Knock it off, will you?"

Bored, Jamie waded into the pond and silently talked to the quokin.

"I didn't know girls morphed to full size," Trakon said.

"Not all Kudaja females morph. I was lucky enough to get those genes, so our children should be full-sized Kudaja," Meeri said. "Most people in my village are normal."

"How will that work?" D'laine asked. "Can you stay fullsized, Herish? I thought you only morphed on occasion."

Herish and Trakon stared at each other a moment, and it bordered on hostility as Trakon suspected the truth. Finally, Herish gave in.

"Okay, perhaps I wasn't one hundred percent truthful before, but now we both have our betrothed so we can be friends," Herish said.

Trakon grumbled slightly. He turned toward the water and dove in. He surfaced and flung his dripping hair back out of his face, then bobbed down under the water again.

D'laine and Meeri shook their heads.

"What idiots." Meeri walked back to the borjo.

"That's our men," D'laine said.

CHAPTER ELEVEN

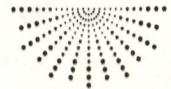

D'laine, Lee, Brian and Stanley focused on Trakon as he prepared to instruct them on the ins and outs of flying a crestrider.

Jamie stood to the side, arms tightly folded across his chest. "Why can't I learn to fly?" He pouted.

Exasperated, Lee turned to his younger son. "For one, you're too young. Two, you can't even see above the controls. When you're Brian's age, you'll learn to fly."

"Fine!" Jamie shouted as he stormed off. "I'll just fly Ekka! He's way more fun, anyway!"

"He's such a weenie," Brian said.

"Young man, perhaps you have a touch of amnesia? When your sister got her driver's license you had a fit and wanted to know why you couldn't drive a car." Lee stared daggers at Brian. "Be thankful you've grown taller, otherwise you'd be whining alongside your brother."

D'laine turned to Trakon. "Aren't you glad you don't have siblings?"

"I can understand the benefits of having a brother or sister, but I don't think I could take the competition," Trakon said.

"Well, that's pretty obvious," D'laine said.

Trakon gave her a funny look. "What do you mean?"

"Just think. If Herish were your brother, you'd both be dead by now," she said.

Trakon's jaw set in a scowl.

"Let's focus on the training, shall we?" Stanley said.

Trakon grounded his thoughts and commenced with the training. He tapped his forehead. "First off, everything is in here, from your brain integration with the Egroms. So, if you are out there flying and something goes wrong, or you can't remember how to do something, get into your head and pull up the information."

He pointed to the control panel. "This engages the power. These levers control raising the ship in the air and lowering it. If you want to hover, this should be in the horizontal position. The stick is similar to your gaming devices, from what D'laine showed me, so shouldn't require any explanations."

Trakon glanced to his audience. Everyone seemed to be onboard.

"How do you stop it?" Brian asked.

"This switch. The ship will simply hover in place," Trakon said.

"Now, to lower the stairs, press this button. There's another button at the bottom of the stairs to make them rise up," he explained. "Remember, your communicator will bring the stairs down again."

D'laine looked everything over. "What about if you've raised the stairs back up, you're on the ground, and your communicator doesn't respond? How do you get back on the ship?"

Trakon stared at her as if she'd lost her mind. "That's never going to happen."

D'laine crossed her arms across her chest tightly. "Remember when you crashed the ship? Your communicator and everything quit."

"That's different," he argued. "Your powers were interferring with the electronics and controls."

D'laine scowled. "Let's pretend that something strange happened, and this situation is real. How would the stranded pilot get back on the ship?"

They had a standoff.

"How do I know?" Trakon yelled.

Lee walked up to them and placed a hand on one of each of their shoulders. "Look, you're trying too hard." He turned to Trakon. "Take that up with your design team, okay?" Then he turned to his daughter. "While we appreciate this new possible situation, can we return to the lesson so we can all learn to fly without killing ourselves and everyone around us?"

Trakon rolled his shoulders to de-stress. "To be on the safe side, hover your crestrider *low enough* so you can get back on it —if your communicator should fail."

D'laine gave him a dirty look, but kept her mouth shut.

"Shall we get started?" Trakon asked. "We'll go by age. Lee, you're first."

Lee stood at the controls and studied the panel. He started the power and lifted the ship off the ground. He tilted the stick forward, and the ship sailed through the air. He turned to the right, then left, tried the hovering feature and felt comfortable with his new skills.

"This is so much easier than driving a car."

Stanley was up next. He passed his flight test with flying colors, same as D'laine.

Brian stood before the controls. He closed his eyes and held a hand out in front of him. Without his touching anything, the ship started, rose and flew. He hovered the ship and settled it gently on the ground.

Lee stared at his son. "How'd you do that?"

Everyone stared at Brian in awe.

Brian shrugged. "Just seemed the easy thing to do." He hopped down to the ground and walked away.

The small group stared at each other.

"Oookay…" D'laine said. "I guess he has two gifts. I wonder what other tricks he has up his sleeves he hasn't bothered to mention."

"Remember, he was the last one to discover his gifts from Thol so maybe they're still cooking inside," Stanley said.

"Sounds like a good conversation to have with Ghury and the elders," Lee said. "When we see them, we'll bring that up." He turned to Trakon. "Which reminds me, Stanley and I want to take a trip to the village. Where do we go to get a ship?

"If you press your communicator and bring up the menu, you'll find where to sign out a ship," Trakon said. "Just mention where you want it delivered and one of the guards will bring it."

Lee rubbed his hands together, happy that it was a simple procedure.

"Let's go finish up our planning session," Stanley said to Lee. The two men walked back toward the palace.

D'laine and Trakon stood silently. She fidgeted with a spot on her sleeve while he stared at the ground.

"Look, I'm sorry I acted like a jerk." Trakon looked up, stepped in close, took her in his arms and kissed her.

D'laine wrapped her arms around his neck and deepened the kiss. She grabbed the hair on the back of his head and ran her hand through his thick mane.

They jumped apart as they heard Biggan clearing his throat. Both turned to glare at the unwanted guardian.

"Shall we go inside, princess?" Biggan asked. "I'm sure Prince Trakon has work to do."

D'laine stomped off toward the palace with Biggan following a short distance behind.

Trakon grumbled as he hopped aboard the ship and flew off toward the storage building.

LEE AND STANLEY SAT IN LEE'S SUITE IN DEEP DISCUSSION ABOUT their upcoming trip to the Egrom village.

"I've integrated all the information that I had access to about Greg Claymore," Stanley said.

Lee stared at the scientist, his brows furrowed with many questions. "How, exactly, did you do that? If I understand you correctly, you have access to everything you read?"

Stanley shrugged. "I have a photographic memory. Everything I've ever looked at is in here, and I figured out how to do an upload to this new Tholian technology." Stanley tapped the side of his head. "All here. You probably could upload everything you ever worked on from NASA."

Lee stared into space a moment, thinking of the wealth of information he'd accumulated over the decades of his distinguished career. "Oh, wow. I'm going to have to try that."

"This new technology is exhilarating. I wish Victor and Ben could experience this," Stanley said.

"Let's go over the report on Claymore. We might be able to determine where he is, or if there's anything documented about why he left Earth for good." Lee shook his head. "I just can't get over his abandoning his family like that. There's definitely something missing. I wish we had records on his family. There's most likely some explanation."

"He was gone a long time. His wife most likely had him declared legally dead so she could move on with her life. There's also the possibility she had another husband when he finally returned to Earth in 1975. He would have been gone for twenty-three years," Stanley said.

Lee pondered the whole situation as he had done when he discovered the information in the secured file in Houston. "Even if he's no longer living, if we can find out where he stayed all these years on Thol, we might discover something useful. He might have kept a journal."

Stanley slapped his thighs. "Okay, it looks like we're ready to go talk to the Egroms. Sign out a crestrider. This is better than renting a car!"

Lee pulled up the menu in his communicator. He and Stanley looked over the options and he requested the next size up from the single-man crestrider.

"Let's go get lunch. We can tell everyone our plans," Stanley said.

They headed out the door to the dining salon.

THE FAMILY WAS GATHERED IN THE DINING SALON, BUT JAMIE'S chair was empty when Lee and Stanley made their appearance.

"Where's your brother?" Lee asked his children.

"I haven't seen him since he stomped off," D'laine said. Brian shrugged.

Lee let out a sigh. "I guess he'll show up when he's hungry." He explained the situation with the crestriders to Kitry and Jor-Dan.

"At least Ekka will keep him safe," Kitry said.

"Stanley and I are going to visit Ghury and the elders after lunch," Lee said. He turned his focus to D'laine. "You and Brian are going to have to pay closer attention to your brother while I'm away. It could be a full turn, or a week. We're not sure."

Stanley went on to explain the mystery surrounding Greg Claymore.

"And he never returned?" Jor-Dan asked. "That is odd. I hope you can solve this mystery."

"He would be ninety-six years so we don't know if he's still alive," Lee said.

THE PLOTALS LOOKED SKYWARD AS EKKA FLEW OVER THE CITY with Jamie on his back. The borjo landed in a clearing and Jamie slid off its back.

"I won't be long."

Several Plotals approached Jamie.

"What business do you have here in Ta'Byu'Vohon?" One of the Plotals asked as he warily watched the borjo.

"I'm here to see Jakla," Jamie said.

"Our commander is very busy," the warrior said.

"He won't be too busy to see me," Jamie insisted.

The Plotal harrumphed. He hit his communicator and contacted his commander. "There's a small human boy here and his borjo..." The warrior stood taller. "Yes commander!" He looked down at Jamie, mystified. "Come."

Jamie followed the Plotals over to some new construction. He saw Jakla with a small group of Plotals and Ciertrons.

"Hello, Jamie. I am honored that you came to visit my city," Jakla said.

"Hi, Jakla. This is going to be a great place when it's finished!" Jamie looked around, eyes wide at the massive buildings. "Do you think it would be okay if I showed you and your people a better way to get your pakows to follow orders? They don't want to be whacked."

Jakla stared down at Jamie. "Show me." Jakla led the group and Jamie over to a holding pen.

Jamie stood by the gate. "Who wants to be a volunteer?"

A pakow lumbered over to Jamie. He tickled it under its chin, then he opened the gate and led the animal out.

"When you get ready to mount your pakow, all you have to do is tell it to kneel. They understand your language," Jamie said. He turned to the pakow. "Kneel."

The animal went down to its front knees.

Jakla and his men murmured among themselves.

"Let me try this technique," Jakla said. He approached the beast that had returned to its feet to stand. "Kneel!"

Jakla and his men talked to each other. Jamie saw heads nod.

"Yes, we like this method much better," Jakla said. "It's much kinder, and we are trying to change our ways. Thank you, Jamie."

BY THE END OF THE MEAL, JAMIE HAD NOT SHOWN UP. "CONTACT me if Jamie's gotten himself into trouble and I'll come home," Lee said.

Stanley and Lee left the palace and walked to the courtyard where the crestrider had been delivered. They climbed on board and Lee took the helm. The ship started and rose silently and they headed for the Cember Forest and the Egrom village.

As they flew across the meadow moss, Stanley spotted Ekka in the distance. "Want me to flag them down?"

"Yeah, tell him to get his butt home and check in," Lee said.

Stanley pressed his communicator and opened a connection to Jamie. He passed on Lee's message and told Jamie they would see him when they returned to Ebscalon.

"Am I in trouble?" Jamie asked.

"Check in with grandma or grandpa," Lee said. He and Stanley watched as Ekka turned toward his tower.

Lee turned to face Stanley. "I get a little odd feeling when I say the word 'home' as it relates to Thol and the palace."

Stanley nodded, lost in thought. After a long moment, he said, "I know what you mean. I never really felt that I fit in anywhere on Earth. Sure, I was respected by my colleagues for my discoveries and all that, but I was a laughingstock among my peers due to my complete social awkwardness. The only true friend I had was Victor... then Ben Joplin."

"How do you feel here?" Lee asked.

"At first, horrible, especially after I nearly killed Adrum, then figuring out how to protect others from my big brain magnet," Stanley said. "But more recently, I feel a peace I've never experienced. I've spent some time with the Visionary, and I'm finding my place here in this dimension."

JAMIE RAN FROM EKKA'S TOWER TO THE PALACE. HE FOUND HIS brother and sister outside with Pup.

"Where were you?" Brian asked. "You missed daddy, and lunch."

"Jamie, no one asks anything of you except for you to let us know where you are and what you're doing," D'laine said. "We have incredible freedom here on Thol. You're not in school for several hours a turn. You get to ride Ekka, discover new things all the time—we have so much more freedom here and you can't seem to follow simple rules."

Jamie scowled at his sister's yammering. "We spotted Oggy when we were flying back from Ta'Byu'Vohon."

"You flew to Jakla's city?" Brian asked. "Cool. What'd you do there?"

Jamie thought for a second. "It bothered me that Jakla and his warriors whacked their pakows every time they wanted to ride them. I figured I could show them a better way."

"Oh! That's wonderful," D'laine said. "You should do the same thing here—give lessons so people understand how loving and friendly pakows are. You'd better go inside and find Kitry."

Jamie slunk off into the palace, knowing he was in trouble with his grandmother queen. He headed directly to the dining room, which was empty. He then went down the long hallway and passed several meeting spaces and the throne room. He hurried around the corner to the giant doors that contained the king and queen's private quarters.

He knocked on the door and waited. The door swung open, and a woman greeted him. "What can I help you with, young Master Jamie?"

"Is my grandmother, the queen, here?" Jamie asked.

The woman held the door open wider. "Yes, she is. Come in and I will take you to her."

Jamie entered the beautiful suite. The woman led him though the sleeping chamber and other rooms until they came to the queen's private sitting room.

Kitry sat at a desk writing.

"My lady, young master Jamie is here to see you." The woman turned and left the room.

Jamie approached the desk looking humble. He glanced at the paper on the desk. As he did, the strange writing symbols morphed into recognizable words. He squirmed as he offered an apology.

"I'm sorry I didn't show up for lunch."

Kitry held a stern face. "Do you remember the rules? I recall you were there when I told Brian and Chacoodi what happens when little boys don't take responsibility to contact the majordomo."

A thought flashed across Jamie's face. His eyes opened wide as the memory slid into place.

"I will have Leena escort you to the kitchen," Kitry said. With that, the woman returned. Kitry held her hand out and made a little push gesture.

Leena led Jamie out of the queen's chamber, down the long hallways and into the kitchen. Jamie almost fainted as he glimpsed dirty dishes piled on the counter and in the large sink.

The majordomo approached. "Master Jamie, I assume you are here to help clean up the dirty dishes."

Jamie gulped then nodded.

One of the kitchen staff plunked a footstool down in front of the sink. Another brought an apron which she wrapped around Jamie's chest a couple of times and tied the long strings at the waist in front.

With a sad face, Jamie stepped onto the stool.

AS THE CRESTRIDER FLEW ABOVE THE CEMBER FOREST, A PATROL of Kudaja riding their borjos appeared by their side. Stanley recognized one of the warriors who was always with Herish.

"You're not lost, are you?" the warrior yelled.

"No, we're going to meet with the Egroms," Stanley said.

"You just passed the village." The warrior pointed to his left.

"How could we have missed it?" Lee asked, mystified.

"You're just a little too far to the right to find the clearing," the warrior said.

"Thanks! No telling where we would have ended up." Lee turned the ship and backtracked until the clearing became visible.

The borjos sped off in a different direction as Lee steered the ship to the clearing in the village where Trakon had landed ships in the past. He settled the ship on the ground and he and Stanley hopped down.

Chacoodi ran up to them, eyes wide, looking for Brian. "Sorry, it's just us this time," Lee said.

"Aw, I was hoping Brian came to play." Chacoodi sauntered off, disappointed.

Ghury and Adrum met their visitors at the halfway point. They greeted each other with their customary nods; Lee and Stanley nodding in return.

"You have questions about another Earthling?" Adrum asked.

Lee didn't understand how they did it, but he didn't question their mind-reading abilities. He could not read minds, but he wasn't sure about Stanley. The scientist had changed so much, no one was sure what he was capable of anymore.

Ghury led them to his mushroom house. They entered and sat at the table.

"Sixty-six years ago—your completed paths—a man named Greg Claymore disappeared from Earth. This was in 1952, Earth time. He returned twenty-three years later, in 1975," Stanley said. "Lee and I have seen pictures in files back on Earth that show this man in Tholian clothing. So, we know he's here. We want to find him and talk to him. We don't understand why he abandoned his family."

"The thing is, Greg didn't have an Egrom helping him. He seemed to be able to come and go through the portals by himself," Lee said.

Ghury and Adrum nodded.

"He did journey here and back again," Ghury said.

"Is he still alive?" Lee asked.

"The pictures of him from 1975 have caused a lot of questions. When he disappeared in 1952, he was thirty years, but when he came back—twenty-three years later—he hadn't aged," Stanley said. "Are we going to age? Or does Thol have a rejuvenating effect on Earthlings?"

"He is very much alive," Adrum said. "We don't see him often, but he does show up here in the village sometimes."

"Where does he live?" Lee asked. "Can we find him?"

"He lives with the Oolarooloo people on the other side of Thol. Many, many miles from here," Adrum said.

Ditol entered Ghury's house.

"Ditol knows more about the Oolarooloo people than we do," Adrum said. "He spent a month there several completed years ago." Adrum turned to Ditol. "Lee and Stanley are asking about the Earthling that lives with the Oolarooloo."

Ditol nodded. "The Oolarooloo took him in long ago. They

are remarkable healers and Greg has learned many of their mysteries."

"Can we go there and meet him?" Lee asked.

"He does not talk about his home world," Ditol said. "I don't know if he would welcome you or not."

Stanley snorted in exasperation. "We just want to talk to him. We have so many questions."

Stanley turned to Lee. "Just think if we could go back and forth, at will. I could fill my head with information, such as solar cell technology, and bring it back."

"I think you'd be a little conspicuous," Lee said.

Stanley thought for a moment. "I'd just tell everyone I'm in costume for a movie."

"I will guide you when you want to make this journey to meet Greg," Ditol said.

"How long would it take to get there on a crestrider?" Lee asked.

Ditol thought for a bit. "Four turns, or a week by crestrider. If you rode pakows, it would take a month."

"I suggest you take Brian on this trip," Ghury said.

Lee frowned in thought. "Why's that?"

"Remember, one of Brian's gifts is detecting portals," Ghury said.

"Oh, so Brian may be able to understand how Greg does that?" Stanley asked.

Ditol and Ghury nodded.

"Okay, then we'll return to Ebscalon and get Brian," Lee said. He looked at Stanley. "We should be back tomorrow, right?"

Stanley looked at the Egroms. "Is there anything we should bring with us when we leave tomorrow?"

"Brian," said Ghury and Ditol.

STANLEY FLEW THE CRESTRIDER BACK TO EBSCALON WHILE LEE enjoyed the ride.

"Sometimes there seems to be something lost in the translation with the Egroms," Stanley said. "They didn't seem to get that I was asking if we should bring *something* with us, *besides* Brian."

"Yeah, I've noticed that a few times. I think the problem is that they're too literal," Lee said. "They didn't answer your question about aging either."

As the ship approached Ebscalon, Stanley pressed his communicator and pulled up the menu. "Let's find out where we're supposed to return this ship."

He and Lee looked at the menu and finally figured out where the ships were stored. Stanley steered the ship over to the building and landed the craft gently on the ground. One of the workers came over and relieved them of the ship.

"How was your first flight?" the worker asked.

"Great," Lee said. "A very smooth ride."

They walked around the buildings and headed over to the palace. Lee determined that dinner would be an excellent time to discuss the trip and inform Brian of his participation.

BRIAN AND JAMIE SPENT A RARE, COMPANIONABLE TIME ROMPING through the meadow. They were intent on seeing if the hosks had returned to their homes after they had freaked out over the fhahadda and fled for their lives. To the boy's delight, the colonies were abundant.

As they sat and played with rambunctious baby hosks, Brian looked up and saw an animal lumbering their way.

"What's that?" he asked Jamie.

Jamie studied the creature. "I don't know. Sort of looks like an anteater, doesn't it?"

Brian studied the creature as it approached closer. "I don't think there're any ants here—at least I haven't come across any fire ant mounds, have you?"

"Nope, I haven't seen any mounds, or even those little normal ant places," Jamie said.

The animal came right up to Jamie. Brian jumped to his feet and kept his distance behind the animal.

"Hi," Jamie said. "What's your name? I've never seen your kind before."

The creature's long, skinny tongue darted out and licked Jamie's face.

Jamie giggled. "Ragapunga? That's what you are?"

The ragapunga nudged Jamie with its head. Jamie scratched it behind its little ears.

In the distance, Pup and Chatter announced their approach with their diwal racket. The ragapunga's head lifted.

"Pup! Chatter! No!" Jamie shouted. The dogs slowed their approach.

The ragapunga lifted its tail and sprayed. Brian was the direct recipient of the acidic, odorless spray.

Brian screamed as the acid permeated his face and hands. His clothing protected the rest of his body.

"Brian!" Jamie screamed.

He hit his communicator in a panic and screamed into it. "A ragapunga sprayed Brian. He needs help!"

His communicator popped alive with responses. "Where are you?" Trakon bellowed.

Pup and Chatter attacked the animal. They were in a dangerous killing mode. Within moments, nothing remained of the ragapunga.

"In the meadow. The dogs killed the ragapunga!" Jamie said.

D'laine ran like the wind across the meadow. "DOWN," she commanded the dogs as she ran.

The Voice boomed and echoed, the energy alive and fierce.

The dogs dropped to the ground, but their teeth were extended and clacking—a dangerous sign that their instincts wanted to take over.

Brian screamed in pain as he pawed his eyes with his sleeves. His face and hands sizzled with burning acid eating his flesh.

A crestrider landed on the ground hard. Trakon and Dannin jumped to the ground.

D'laine approached her brothers. She grabbed her water flask.

"No!" Trakon yelled, slapping her hand away from the flask. "Water intensifies the acid. Get him on the ground. We need to get dirt on everything that was exposed to the acid."

"Oh! I could have caused so much more damage!" she said.

Brian wailed in agony as Dannin and Trakon stretched him out on top of the moss. Both men tore up moss and tossed it aside. They scooped soil and covered his face, leaving his nostrils exposed.

"Don't open your eyes or mouth," Dannin said. "Breathe through your nose and try to stay as still as possible. I know it hurts."

A crestrider landed. Jor-Dan, Kitry and the Visionary rushed to Brian's side. Lee sprinted to Brian. Stanley hung back watching the activity.

Lee was sinking into a full panic attack as he heard the sizzling of the burning acid.

Jamie stood alone looking on. Kitry rushed over to him and embraced him. "It's not your fault," she said.

Jamie cried.

Lee roared at his younger son. "You are never to approach an unknown animal ever again! Do you understand? How many times do you have to be told that not every animal is friendly?"

Jor-Dan placed a hand on Lee's shoulder to calm him.

Jamie cried relentlessly. "He was friendly! It all happened so fast when the dogs were running over here and started making a racket! How was I supposed to know Brian would get sprayed?"

"Daddy, calm down!" D'laine said. "We should be thankful that Jamie and Brian didn't get killed. Once the dogs attacked and killed the ragapunga, they could have turned on the boys, but they didn't. They must have recognized them or remembered that they are off limits."

Lee did not apologize to Jamie. He was in anguish over Brian's condition.

The Visionary knelt by Trakon and Dannin. "Let me see what I can do."

The Visionary's hands flicked over Brian's face then his hands. The sizzling slowed, but did not stop.

"We have to stop the burning," the Visionary said. "D'laine, see what you can do."

D'laine already had her crystals ready. She knelt over her brother and closed her eyes. She centered herself emotionally, sidestepping her panic. She fisted two crystals, one in each hand. She placed a fist over each side of his face for several moments then repeated the process for his hands. The sizzling stopped.

"You have neutralized the acid. It is no longer burning into his flesh," the Visionary said. "We can now transport him back to the palace and check the damage."

Lee was ready to swoop in and lift Brian. Jor-Dan grabbed Lee by the upper arm and pulled him to his feet.

"Let Trakon and Dannin carry him. You're too emotional and could cause unintentional harm," Jor-Dan said.

"We need a gurney." D'laine shared the vision with the men.

"Yes, that would keep him stabilized," the Visionary said.

"Wait!" Stanley said as Trakon and Dannin were about to sprint to the forest to find sturdy branches. "I can levitate him and keep him suspended without any motion."

"That's right!" Lee said. "Do it, Stanley."

"Where should I take him?" Stanley asked.

"Take him to the temple," the Visionary said. "Rettu and Ekal will show you where he should rest."

Stanley touched the lever on his head. "Everyone, stand back."

People scurried to get far behind the scientist.

Stanley opened the levers on his helmet. He held out one arm toward Brian. The dirt-covered body rose off the ground. Some of the soil rolled off Brian's body. Stanley took one step forward, and they were gone.

People scrambled to the crestriders. "Pup! Chatter! Come," D'laine said.

The dogs ran up the stairs. D'laine angled her hand, and the dogs dropped to the floor of the ship.

CHAPTER TWELVE

*L*ee tried to keep his emotions under control as he gazed down at Brian, who appeared to be unconscious, floating above a surface.

Kitry kept her fist to her mouth as she stood nearby, eyes welling with tears. She kept her other hand on Jamie's shoulder.

Trakon embraced a silently sobbing D'laine while Jor-Dan and Dannin stood nearby, helpless to comfort anyone.

The dirt had been removed from Brian's face and hands. What was left was akin to a nightmare. From the middle of his forehead to his neck, the skin was like melted wax. His hands had received most of the acid spray as he tried to protect his face. The skin had melted from his fingers leaving exposed bone behind.

Brian appeared to be in a state of suspended animation. Ekal stood at Brian's head and Rettu near his feet, both with hands outspread. The Visionary stood beside Brian with his hands outspread. It reminded Lee of how the Egroms healed with their four hands.

"Is he still alive?" Lee asked, his voice just above a whisper. "His chest isn't rising."

"Yes, he is in a stasis period while his body recovers from shock," the Visionary said.

Ghury and the elders stepped into the room. They approached Brian and relieved the disciples and the Visionary. Several more Egroms appeared. Soon, Brian was surrounded by Egroms, each with four hands held out.

The room buzzed with energy, causing the hairs on the back of Lee's neck to stand straight out.

"It would be best if all of you returned to the palace," the Visionary said kindly. "If there is any change, I will send for you."

Jor-Dan approached Lee, placed an arm across his shoulders and led him out of the temple.

JAMIE DIDN'T KNOW WHAT TO DO. EVERY ONCE IN A WHILE, A little sob escaped from D'laine. She was wrapped around Trakon burying her grief in his chest. The room where everyone waited for news of Brian was quiet.

Lee stared at the floor from the sofa. Everyone else sat, fidgeted, stood and paced in intervals.

The majordomo entered the room and announced dinner. Like zombies, everyone followed the man to the dining salon. Everyone took smaller than usual portions. Forks and knives scraping plates were the only sounds heard.

Lee pushed his chair back and left the room. He headed for the palace entrance and stood outside. He looked up at the sky as the last sun crossed the horizon and the lights throughout the city blinked on. It was a beautiful sight, but he couldn't appreciate it just now.

Jamie came outside and stood by Lee. "I'm sorry, daddy." Lee dropped to his knees and grabbed Jamie into a hug.

He sobbed. "You're just a little boy, son. This wasn't your fault. I'm sorry I yelled at you."

Jamie sobbed into Lee's shoulder. "I didn't know the ragapunga would hurt Brian. He was nowhere near it and I didn't know they sprayed like a skunk."

Lee wiped his eyes. He held Jamie back and looked at his younger son. "Jamie, there's no way you would have known what was going to happen. It's just one of those things. You're not to take the blame, understand?"

Jamie sniveled and wiped his eyes and nodded.

"Ghury and the Egroms will do everything they can to help Brian."

D'laine and Trakon came out of the palace. She smothered her father and brother in a hug. They all stood quietly wrapped in each other's arms. After a while, they returned to the palace to wait for news.

THE ROOM WAS AGLOW WITH WARM LIGHT. JAMIE WAS SPLAYED out on a sofa, asleep. D'laine was on another sofa wrapped in Trakon's arms. Lee's legs stretched out in front of him as he slouched down in a chair. Kitry and Jor-Dan held hands on another sofa. Dannin and Stanley had left earlier.

The Visionary entered the room. Lee jumped to his feet.

Everyone else stirred alert, hopeful.

"The elders have left to recharge their energy and have been replaced by a dozen younger Egroms," the Visionary said. "Brian is stable. You should get to bed and rest."

"Can I see him?" Lee asked.

"There hasn't been any change. It would be best for you to stay away as your body is producing waves of stress that would inhibit the healing." The Visionary grasped Lee's shoulder gently. "What you can do is visualize Brian whole and healthy; focus on his healing."

D'laine stood and went to her father. "I know what to do."

She took her father's hand and pulled him down to the floor. She sat with her legs crossed. She placed a hand on each knee with her thumb and index fingers touching each other.

"Watch me and follow along as you visualize a picture of Brian healthy like he was before this happened." She took in a deep breath and let it out. "Shroud Brian with the pure white light of healing. Help him to release his pain. Heal him. Restore the skin on his face and hands. Restore his facial features. Restore any and all damaged cells. Thank you. Amen."

Lee stumbled through the meditation. Afterwards, he sat still for several minutes, then unfolded his body and stood.

Kitry and Jor-Dan stood followed by Trakon.

"I think it would be best for all of us to retire for the night," Kitry said.

Lee nodded. They all left the room and sought the privacy of their suites.

AFTER AN EARLY, GLOOMY BREAKFAST, EVERYONE RETREATED TO the sitting room to await word on Brian's progress.

"I thought I could heal him," D'laine said. She stared at the floor in disbelief, stunned that her powers had failed her.

Trakon tightened his arm around her shoulders. "You stopped the acid from doing any more damage."

Lee sat at the edge of his chair. "D'laine, don't flog yourself mentally. If you hadn't been there, your brother wouldn't have any face or hands left at all."

Pup rolled over on his back and wiggled on the rug, his legs dancing in the air. Chatter belly-crawled up to him and wagged his tail. La'gar'ish acted like their behavior was beneath him.

After a little while, the dogs got up and left the room. They headed to the kitchen where they knew the food came from.

One of the kitchen staff shrieked. The chef saw the dogs. "Bring the dogs their steaks," the chef said.

One of the helpers brought a plate with three raw steaks. He placed it on the floor and scurried back. The dogs attacked the food, and within moments, the plate was empty.

They looked at the people wanting more.

"Go hunt," the chef said. He made a shooing motion with his hands.

Pup led his pack out of the kitchen through the kitchen door and they took off running toward the gates.

JAMIE STOOD AT A WINDOW AND WATCHED AS THE DOGS RACED through the gates and across the meadow. He sighed, turned and let his eyes wander over the group in the room. "Why don't we go get that guy you've talked about?" Jamie said.

Lee's and Stanley's heads swung up. They looked at each other then back to Jamie.

"Ghury said it would take several turns to get there," Stanley said. "We should probably wait, maybe bring Brian with us."

Lee puffed out a breath. "You're right. That would be the best bet. We need to find out what shape he's in before we can plan that trip."

"Maybe I can transport us there—instantly, you know?" Stanley said. "It works around here."

"Yeah, but you know where you are here," Trakon said. "The Oolarooloo are on the other side of the planet, and we don't have any reference for you to get there safely."

Stanley fretted.

Come to me, the Visionary whispered into the room.

The hairs stood up straight on the back of Lee's neck.

"Who is that?" He looked around, nerves on edge.

"That's the Visionary!" D'laine said.

The family headed to the temple. The closer they got to the building, the more energy was present. D'laine's hair flew out about her. The air crackled, alive.

Ghury exited the temple. He held out two hands and turned them in a circle. The energy was absorbed into his hands. The air became simply air once again.

"Brian is much improved," Ghury said.

"Can we see him now?" Lee asked, stepping forward.

Ghury nodded and ushered them inside.

BRIAN WAS HORIZONTALLY SUSPENDED IN THE MIDDLE OF TEN Egroms. The first thing D'laine noticed was his face. It was partially restored—there was a nose where previously only a bone and melted skin had been. His hands no longer looked like a skeleton's hands, but there was deep scarring.

She fretted as Trakon held her tight.

Lee covered his face with his hands for a moment. "It's much better than what I expected. I'm so grateful for what you have done for my son."

Ditol placed a hand on Lee's shoulder. "It will get better. And your plan to seek out Greg Claymore is a wise one." He looked at Stanley. "You will be able to step there with a small group. I will accompany you."

STANLEY, LEE, BRIAN, D'LAINE, TRAKON AND DITOL STEPPED OUT into a lush garden. The group, except for Brian, who was unconscious, and Ditol, who had been there before, stared at the vision before them in wonder. Long hammocks hung among the trees—lots of them. They were more than twice the size of any hammock D'laine ever remembered from back home, even in Mexico where she had vacationed with Connor's family once.

This forested area was not like the dense, dark Cember Forest. Plants and trees engorged with fruits and vegetables were abundant.

A group of strange-looking people sat around a fire while others meandered among the trees. D'laine's eyes widened as she took in the tall, thin people. They were the darkest of all the people she had met on Thol, with skin the color of deep, dark brown with a bronze tinge. Their heads were oblong with long human ears.

Necks that must measure at least a foot long were ringed with metal discs. They wore hip-length sleeveless tank-type shirts, and what D'laine would consider shorts. Their feet were shod in vine-wrapped flat soles.

The group around the fire stood when they noticed the visitors.

"Welcome to our village," one man said.

Ditol stepped forward and nodded. "Oogo, we have great need of your healing powers."

Oogo and his group stared at the Earthlings. "These are Greg Claymore's kin?"

"No, not kin," Ditol said. "But yes, they are from his Earth. The boy was sprayed by a ragapunga. We have healed him to the best of our ability, but we require your advanced skills for restoration."

They came forward and studied Brian. Then they studied D'laine.

"You are a healer," Oogo said as he studied D'laine.

Tears sprang from her eyes. "I couldn't heal him."

"She stopped the acid from burning," Trakon said.

"If you hadn't stopped the acid, the Egroms would not have

been able to restore him to his current state," the man said. "You judge yourself poorly. You must let that go."

They wandered around Stanley, fascinated by his helmet. Oogo reached for the levers on top of Stanley's helmet. Ditol grabbed Oogo's hand.

"Stop! When this helmet is removed, the human's mind will pull on your brain and will drain it, leaving you an empty shell," Ditol said.

"This cannot hurt the Oolarooloo," Oogo said.

Oogo flipped the lever wide open and peered through the holes. Within seconds, Oogo and his group were on the ground rolling in agony, clutching their heads or rubbing their eyes.

Stanley flipped the lever closed. "Never, ever do that again, and never think about removing my helmet. I'm deadly."

After several painful moments, the Oolarooloo were back on their feet and keeping their distance from Stanley and his helmet.

Oogo turned to Ditol. "We will repair the boy. He will be as good as new. I will require a vision of his former self."

At that moment, a man stepped out of the trees. Lee and Stanley recognized Greg Claymore from NASA pictures. He still didn't look a turn over thirty. He stopped abruptly when he saw the people from his home world. His facial features showed an internal warring.

"Please, help my son," Lee pleaded. Greg Claymore backed up one step.

"We were told that you have great healing powers," Lee said. "Please don't turn your back on us because we're from Earth."

Greg paused, settled his eyes on the ground and had a private internal dialog with himself. He let out a sigh and strode forward toward his fellow Earthlings. His eyes swiftly took in Brian's condition.

"Bring him over here and settle him on this table," Greg said.

Stanley walked over to the table with Brian hovering in the

air, still not conscious. He eased him down onto the surface, then stepped back.

Greg stared at Stanley's helmet. He opened his mouth to speak, but Stanley waved his hand.

"It's a long story," Stanley said. "Best told at another time."

Greg turned his attention to Brian. He glanced over to D'laine. "You should have been able to do what I'm going to do. What happened?"

D'laine sucked in a deep breath. "I don't know what happened. I stopped the acid from burning, but I couldn't heal him." She dug in her pouch and pulled out her two crystals and showed them to Greg. "I used my crystals like I always do…"

"Show me a picture of your brother in good health," he said.

D'laine pulled up a picture of Brian from breakfast before the animal encounter.

"Watch," Greg said.

He kicked off his sandals and stood before Brian, closed his eyes, spread his feet apart and his arms wide. Next, he curved both hands and held them mere inches above Brian's face. A glow appeared under his hands. After several moments Greg moved his hands. Brian's face was restored. Not even a freckle was left—only smooth skin.

D'laine, Lee and Stanley gasped. Trakon was wide-eyed surprised.

Greg moved his hands to where Brian's hands rested on either side of him.

"Would you place his hands on his stomach, palms down?" Greg asked D'laine.

She gently lifted one scarred hand, then the other and placed them on her brother's stomach.

Greg repeated the healing process for each hand. They miraculously transformed to healthy, scar-free hands. Brian's fingers and thumbs were back to normal. Greg let out a long breath, rubbed his hands together and stood back.

"That... that's amazing!" D'laine stated. "Why couldn't I do that?"

Lee was at Brian's side. He ran his fingers through Brian's hair. "Why doesn't he wake up?"

"It will take his body a while to catch up," Ditol said.

"He should be back to normal by tomorrow," Greg said.

"He's had quite a shock and may require some sessions to calm his memory from the burning pain."

"Sessions?" Lee asked.

"With the Visionary." Greg turned to D'laine. "Your crystals bring you great power, but for this type of healing, you need to gather power from the elements of Thol to work with your gifts."

D'laine tilted her head in thought. "Do you mean I should forgo my crystals and use Thol energy instead?"

"Each situation is different. You may find that you need to ground yourself to the soil—take off your boots and sink your feet into the moss," Greg said. "There will be times when your crystals will be all you require. But for something as serious as the acid from a ragapunga, you would have been able to perform a perfect healing with bare feet, pulling energy from the planet."

"Okay." D'laine nodded. "Thank you so much for this information."

Greg turned away from D'laine, Lee and Trakon. He approached Stanley and Ditol. "What's the story about this helmet?"

Ditol explained what had happened.

Greg walked around Stanley and examined his helmet and his facial features. "I believe I might be able to help you so that you won't require this helmet."

"I don't want to lose my powers, or the vast intelligence that enhanced my genius," Stanley said.

"Nothing will change in that regard." Greg reached for the helmet. "May I?"

Ditol swiftly reached out and stayed Greg's hands. "To remove the helmet without forewarning would be cruel to your people and the visitors."

The Egrom elder turned to the people nearby. "Stand back to protect yourself."

"We shouldn't move Brian. Can you move way over there?" Trakon pointed across the campfire to the other side of the village.

"Greg Claymore, do not toy with the helmet!" Oogo warned.

"It will be okay," Greg said.

The Oolarooloo people fled to the forest. Stanley coaxed Greg over to where Trakon pointed. He knew the radius of his brainpowers and judged the distance to be safe.

Ditol joined Lee, Trakon, D'laine and Brian, who was still in repose. They watched as Greg pulled the helmet off Stanley's head.

Greg didn't appear to be affected by Stanley's brain. He studied Stanley's jutted forehead and his enlarged skull. He spread his fingers wide and held his hands on either side of Stanley's head. He walked slowly around the scientist, his hands keeping contact with Stanley's skull and face. Greg moved his hands to the crown of Stanley's head.

A soft pop sounded.

Stanley staggered back a half step. "What happened? What was that noise?"

"Everything is contained inside, where it's supposed to be," Greg said. He waved Lee over.

Lee approached warily. He stopped fifteen feet away, testing the distance. No headache. He crept closer and closer still without any excruciating side effects. He stood in front of his pal and looked him over.

"Wow," Lee said. "No more Neanderthal! You look pretty

good, Stan. Your head seems a little rounder, but not in a bad way."

Stanley rubbed his hands all over his face. "This is wonderful. I thought I'd never be rid of that helmet. Are you sure this is permanent?"

"I'm ninety-nine percent sure you'll never have to wear that helmet again unless you want to dress up for a party," Greg said with a smirk.

Ditol picked up the helmet. "You should keep this just in case."

Lee and Stanley cornered Greg.

"Why didn't you stay with your family when you returned in 1975?" Lee asked.

Greg kicked the ground, uncomfortable with the conversation. "Look at me. I haven't aged," he said. "My wife had me declared legally dead. She remarried. My kids were all grown, finished with college, starting their careers—what was left for me?"

They shared a moment of silence while thinking about the changes Greg had seen with his family.

"Plus, everything on Earth had changed. It was unfamiliar to me, noisy, fast-paced, different family values—I had changed. I no longer was comfortable," Greg said.

Stanley nodded. "You should see it now. If you thought it was fast-paced in 1975, your head would spin if you returned this turn."

"Practically everyone has a mobile phone, which are called cellphones. Electronics come in all forms for personal convenience, such as eBooks, iPads, laptop computers—the family structure has broken down. Kids killing other kids, gangs, terrorism from across the ocean—I'm glad D'laine returned for us," Lee said.

Greg's forehead wrinkled, trying to get his head around what they said. Lee and Stanley opened up and showed Greg what Houston had looked like when they left. Stanley also pulled up memories of front pages from several newspapers.

Greg staggered back, the influx of information and the changes too staggering for him.

"I have to ask you something." Stanley stared at Greg. "Why haven't you aged?"

"Yeah, people here are of all ages—I'm speaking of the Ciertrons and other humans," Lee said. "Even the Egroms and Plotals are different ages."

"I don't know if it's just me," Greg said. "Now that you and your family are here, we'll have to see if you age. I'm ninety-six! I feel like thirty."

Lee appeared troubled. "While I'd love to stop aging because of all the problems that come with advanced years, I wouldn't wish that on my kids. D'laine and Trakon will be marrying soon. It would be a challenge if he aged, and she didn't. Same with the boys—how could they possibly stay in a child's body for the rest of their lives?"

Stanley placed his hand on Lee's shoulder. "Don't over-think it, Lee. We have to see what next year brings. I suggest you start measuring and marking a wall for each of the boys to track their growth. Aging comes with progression unless you have a specific development problem. D'laine should be okay. She's seventeen so probably full-grown by now."

"I think it's just me," Greg said. "But I don't know why. It could have something to do with my ability to heal."

Lee's communicator crackled. He pressed the button and a holographic picture of Kitry appeared.

"Lee, Jamie took off on Ekka. He felt left out so I'm pretty sure they are heading your way," Kitry said. She was upset.

Lee gasped. "I guess we should have brought him with us. Don't worry, Kitry. Earth children are a handful. It's not your fault that he left."

"How is Brian?" she asked.

"He's healed." Lee walked across the moss to Brian. "He's not conscious yet—his body is still repairing itself."

Kitry gasped. "He looks just like he did before the accident!"

Lee turned to Greg. "We have our fellow Earthling to thank for this."

A large shadow covered the ground. Everyone looked up to spy Ekka flying overhead with Jamie sitting on his shoulders.

The Oolarooloo people pointed to the sky, nervous about the giant borjo. Ekka glided to a large space away from the immediate village and landed gracefully. He folded in his wings and Jamie climbed down.

"You can go hunt or go home, Ekka." Jamie rubbed Ekka's nose.

His family, Stanley, Greg and Oogo approached him. "How did you get here so fast?" Trakon asked. "It's a four-turn trip by crestrider."

"Chacoodi did this thing and Ekka just flew through this tunnel," Jamie said.

Ditol grumbled. "He folded space between dimensions. We will have to watch that one. Folding space can be dangerous. You could get stuck somewhere you don't want to be."

Jamie shrugged. "We're here so I guess it doesn't matter anymore."

Lee eyed Jamie. "Son, Thol is a dangerous place. You can't run wild."

Jamie ran over to where his brother lay on the table. He stood beside Brian, quietly looking him over.

D'laine joined him. She rested her hand on his shoulder. "He's going to be okay. We just have to wait for him to wake up."

Jamie sniffled. "I didn't know…"

D'laine placed her finger under Jamie's chin, raising it so they were eye to eye. "Jamie, from now on, before you approach a strange animal, go into your head where your mind-movies are and look up the information. It's all there." She tapped his forehead.

Trakon walked up to them. "Or, you can tap your communicator and check that way. You have to stay safe. There are a lot of dangerous animals—and even people—on Thol."

Jamie hung his head and fidgeted.

THEY STAYED WITH THE OOLAROOLOO WHILE BRIAN WAS HEALING. On the morning of the third turn, he stirred. Lee was on his feet, hovered over him when Brian opened his eyes and blinked.

"Where are we?" Brian looked around the strange village. He saw the hammocks, then the tall Oolarooloo walking about.

"Welcome back, son." Lee's eyes brimmed with tears. "We're on the other side of Thol. These people are called Oolarooloo. Greg Claymore healed you."

"That sounds like a name from back home," Brian said.

"It is," Lee said. "Greg came to Thol in 1952. He's a great healer here. You don't have any scars at all. He even healed Stanley—he no longer needs to wear the helmet."

Brian swung his legs over the side of the table and sat. "Wow! Is he more powerful than the Egroms?"

"No, they each have different abilities," Lee said.

Everyone rushed over to the table when they saw Brian sitting up.

"Brian!" D'laine and Jamie yelled at the same time. They smothered him in hugs.

Brian's eyebrows lifted as Stanley approached without his ever-present helmet. "Wow, Stanley, your head's almost back to normal!"

Stanley blushed and ran his hands over his face and head. "It's so nice not to have that helmet on my head!"

CHAPTER THIRTEEN

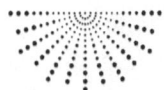

$\mathcal{A}$fter thanking the Oolarooloo for their hospitality and Greg Claymore for healing Brian, the group stepped back to Ebscalon. Once Ditol deemed the group would make it back safely, he parted from them, returning to his Cember Forest home in the Egrom village.

Chatter and Pup danced on hind legs yapping and whining as their people returned to the palace. D'laine got on the floor with the dogs. They were all over her, taking in the strange scents.

"You two better have been on your best behavior," she said.

Jor-Dan and his dog came into the room followed by Kitry. "They were a handful!" Jor-Dan boomed. "They searched every inch of the palace and the city looking for you."

"Then they decided they should protect their king," Kitry said. "La'gar'ish had his time being the alpha dog, but that didn't last long."

Jor-Dan snorted. "Pup will not step down as the leader." He patted La'gar'ish on the head. Jor-Dan clapped his hands together and looked Brian over. "So, you are all back together again, as you should be."

Brian and Jamie stood side by side in solidarity.

"We're never going to go near a strange animal again," Jamie said.

"And I'm never going to stand in back of one... just in case," Brian said.

Jor-Dan stepped forward and embraced the boys in a tight hug. He let out a loud breath. "Please don't approach any animal you don't already know!"

Kitry elbowed into the hug and extracted the boys from her husband. She kissed their cheeks. "Are you hungry?" She led them to the kitchen, all holding hands.

TWO TURNS LATER, EKKA CIRCLED HIS TOWER AND LANDED. JAMIE ran through the city and climbed the stairs to the borjos lair.

"Ekka!" he threw his arms around the borjos lowered neck. "How'd you get back here so fast? Everyone said it would take a week."

Maldi Amadal stepped out of the air. "I opened a tunnel for him."

"Maldi!" A worried expression crossed Jamie's face. "Have you come back for Ekka?"

"No, Ekka would never leave you. He has bonded with you," Maldi said.

Jamie let out a sigh of relief. "What are you doing here?"

"I must speak with the king and the Visionary," Maldi said.

"Come on, I'll take you to the palace." Jamie hugged his borjo and led the Plakado down the stairs. With his mind, he called out to Jor-Dan.

Grandpa, Maldi Amadal, the Plakado who gave me Ekka and that staff thing, wants to talk to you and the Visionary.

Jamie's communicator dinged. "Where are you?" Jor-Dan asked.

Trakon and Dannin approached the tower at a brisk run. They ran up the stairs and almost crashed into Jamie and Maldi.

The Plakado raised his hands. "I come in peace."

TRAKON AND DANNIN FLANKED MALDI AS THE THREE MADE THEIR way from Ekka's tower to the palace. Jor-Dan and the Visionary awaited them in one of the salons.

"Welcome, Maldi Amadal," Jor-Dan said.

Kitry entered the salon followed by the majordomo carrying a tray. "Please sit."

They moved to the sofas and chairs. The majordomo served kahl in deep blue drinking vessels.

The Visionary declined. "What brings you our way?"

Maldi removed his hat. His bright orange Mohawk stood straight up from the top of his forehead to the collar of his tunic.

Jor-Dan noticed the difference between the Plakado and his cousins, the Plotals. Maldi's face was round, and his snout was flat with two slits for nostrils.

"The Raagor Ice Men are on the move with their chuns," Maldi said.

Trakon sat straight, alarmed. He placed his drink on a small table. "Where did you see them? Could you determine where they were going?"

Maldi's large hand lifted his glass for a sip of kahl. "The Raagor are descending their mountain at the base of Kitchikiwon."

Trakon hit his communicator and a holographic map of Thol appeared. His fingers manipulated the map until he came upon the mountain. "That's near the Oolarooloo village."

Dannin stared at the map then turned to Trakon. "What could they be going there for?"

"What do we know about the Raagor?" Jor-Dan asked.

"They are called the ghost people because of their white skin and blue veins," Maldi said.

D'laine and Lee entered the salon.

"They're not a warring race," D'laine said. She sat beside Trakon.

"I remember Ghury saying they don't socialize with the other races of Thol," Lee said. "I wonder why they're leaving their home?"

Maldi thought for a moment. "There were about twenty that I saw. With the fog and clouds, there could have been more."

"Should we warn the Oolarooloo?" Lee asked.

"I did not see any weapons," Maldi said.

"They don't need weapons," D'laine said. "They could freeze you to death with a touch."

MALDI STEPPED D'LAINE, TRAKON, THE VISIONARY AND LEE through to the Oolarooloo's village. Greg Claymore saw them approach and met them.

"Is there a problem with Brian?" Greg asked. His eyes stayed on Maldi.

"Greg, this is Maldi Amadal, a Plakado," Lee said.

Surprise lit Greg's face. "Plakado? I thought they were extinct."

"Not quite," Maldi said. "The Raagor will be arriving soon."

Oogo and the elders joined the conversation.

"They are leaving their mountain?" Oogo called to his people in a twittering sound. Oolarooloos emerged from the dense forest opposite the visitors. They spread out and entered the forest on the mountain's side.

Stanley and Ghury *stepped* into the village.

"I hope you don't mind, but I contacted Ghury," Stanley said.

Ghury stood as tall as Maldi. They towered over everyone else.

"This is unprecedented," Ghury said. "In all my years, I've never known the Raagor to leave their mountain. I'm not sure they can survive in the heat of the lowlands."

Roars of the chuns approached through the forest.

The Oolarooloo were the first to emerge from the forest. The Raagor appeared, riding their chuns. Riders and beasts were nervous in this hot, unknown environment. Maldi had been correct in their numbers.

The beasts were the size of Earth's horses. Lee, Stanley and D'laine were convinced they were related to saber-toothed tigers.

The chuns had long hair and a mane like lions, large padded feet and thick tails. They were unlike any animal on either world. Their tusks gleamed deadly.

The skin of the Raagor was smooth, crystal white with blue veins. Their lips were also blue. The riders were completely hairless and wore no clothing. They held onto a braided part of the chun's mane and gripped the beast's sides with their knees and feet.

The Visionary waved one hand. A faint boundary was visible between the Raagor and everyone else. "Everyone back away from the Raagor, slowly."

No one was going to argue. Most of the villagers faded into the forest on the opposite side of the village clearing.

Oogo stepped forward. He twittered a greeting to the Raagor.

One chun moved out in front of the delegation. The icy male Raagor made a hissing noise.

D'laine studied the man. She cocked her head as the hissing continued. She picked up a cadence of sounds. "Does anyone understand their language?"

Even Ghury shook his head. "Perhaps Jamie would be helpful."

"He talks to animals," Lee said.

"I'll bet he can understand this language," Stanley said.

The Earthlings, Trakon and the Visionary turned to Ghury. He nodded and stepped back to Ebscalon. Within moments, he returned with Jamie.

Jamie took in the sight before him.

"I know you'll want to speak to the chuns—those white beasts," Ghury said. "But we want you to try to communicate with these people. We don't know why they left the mountain to come here."

"Okay. I'll try."

"You must not touch the Raagor people," the Visionary warned.

"Yeah, I know," Jamie said.

The Visionary waved his hand, and the barrier vanished.

Jamie stepped toward the lead chun. The large cat took one step toward Jamie.

Stanley grabbed Lee's arm, stopping him from making a protective move. *He'll be okay.*

Lee sucked in a calming breath. He tilted his head slightly to Stanley.

A magical moment ensued. The chun rubbed its head against Jamie and licked his face.

Jamie giggled. "You sure are beautiful." He rubbed the chun's head.

The Raagor hissed.

Jamie listened, face scrunched in thought.

"They need help. Their king—he's called a hadra—his son is very sick. The queen is here with their son."

Another chun pushed its way from the middle of the group. A limp young boy was held by the Raagor queen.

Jamie listened to more hissing. "He ate a raptor's egg two turns ago, then became sick. They can't heal him."

"Sounds like salmonella poisoning," Lee said. "As far as I know, only antibiotics can cure it."

"Natural medicine is what's needed," Greg said. "Jamie, can you ask them to bring the boy over there to the table?"

Jamie thought the words to the lead Raagor. He pointed to the table where Greg moved to.

The chun, with the queen and the boy walked to the table. The queen slid off the chun's back and laid the boy on the covered table.

Greg gathered leaves, seeds and other ingredients. He placed everything in the middle of a small square of gauze and tied it with a thin vine. He placed the bundle in a small bowl and poured hot water over it. He dunked the bundle with a spoon to keep it submerged in the water.

He called to one of the Oolarooloo women. "Warm some cloths by the fire. I will need three or four."

"Jamie," Greg called. "Ask the queen to lift the boy's head so I can get him to drink this tea."

Jamie thought to the queen's mind.

The Raagor queen elevated the boy, and Greg held the bowl to his lips.

"This isn't going to work—the boy is unconscious and I need his lips parted."

"Wait a moment, I'll explain." Jamie thought the instructions while opening his mouth to demonstrate.

The queen held the boy in one arm and used her fingers to open his lips.

Greg pressed the bowl to the boy's lips and poured the liquid slowly, a little bit at a time.

The boy's eyes opened, and he drank from the bowl. Greg set the empty bowl aside. "Bring two cloths."

The Oolarooloo woman brought two pieces of warmed gauze.

"Place one under his lower back—be careful not to touch his skin!"

Greg motioned for the Raagor to lay the boy on the cloth. Then he took the other warmed cloth and placed it over the boy's stomach. "Bring another warm cloth."

They repeated the process for the better part of an hour.

"Jamie, ask them if they use fire and can boil water."

Greg made up two bundles of the herbs.

"They can use fire and boil water," Jamie said.

"She saw what I did so the queen should understand what is required." Greg held up one bundle in front of the woman. "Tell her to have him drink one small bowl tomorrow and one the next turn."

The Raagor queen lifted the boy. The chun lowered itself to the ground, and the woman climbed on.

Greg wiped out the bowl and dropped the two bundles inside. He handed it to the woman, along with two cloths.

She urged the chun back to her people and handed the bowl to another rider. She turned her chun to face Greg. She nodded to him, then hissed to her leader.

"She told him what they need to do," Jamie said. The leader hissed to Jamie.

"He says they are very grateful, but they need to return to the mountain because it's too hot here."

"Tell them to come back if they need more medicine," Greg said.

All the riders hissed. It sounded like air leaking from dozens of tires. The chuns roared. Then they turned and vanished into the forest.

Jamie stared after them. "I'm pretty sure that guy in front was the hadra."

Lee patted Jamie on the back. "Well done, son."

Trakon grabbed D'laine's hand. "Let's go home."

They all said their goodbyes to Greg and Oogo. Ghury and Maldi facilitated the return home.

CHAPTER FOURTEEN

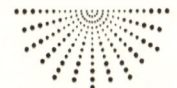

*G*hury, the Visionary and Maldi approached the temple. The Visionary and Ghury entered the temple. They noticed the Plakado did not follow them inside.

They returned to the outer doorway and discovered Maldi waiting on the other side of the threshold.

"Do you not like the temple?" Ghury asked.

"I must be invited inside," the Plakado said.

Ghury and the Visionary stared at the creature, their faces scrunched in question.

"Please explain," Ghury said.

"Plakados must be invited over thresholds, through gates and into cities other than their own," Maldi explained. "We are not like our distant cousins, the Plotals. We evolved earlier and our evolutionary journeys split from theirs.

"While our cousins developed their physical muscles and built strength to conquer, we developed mental and spiritual growth. In this evolving, we discovered a protection not only for ourselves, but for those we interacted with.

"We must be brought in as I was earlier with your prince and guard. If we determine the place to be unholy, dangerous or otherwise bad for us, we cannot or will not cross the barrier protecting all. If it would be bad for those who live there for us to cross over, we cannot proceed."

The Visionary stepped forward. He waved his arms across the doorway. "Your entry into the temple is sanctioned. Please come in and be comfortable."

Maldi let his senses open and felt the energy. He stepped forward and crossed the threshold.

THE THREE DIFFERENT BEINGS SETTLED ON THE FLOOR comfortably.

"We have much to discuss," Ghury said. He eyeballed the Plakado suspiciously.

"Yes," the Visionary said. "Are you the last of your kind?"

"Where did you come from?" Ghury asked. "Where have you existed these hundreds of years?"

Maldi teepeed his thick fingers. "The Plakado's thrive in another realm. Our leader, the great Sorgus Blaski, discovered Asbram by accident as he was stepping from our home here on Thol to another location. Asbram is our own paradise filled with peace and love."

He projected a picture of the planet realm, a thin line away from Thol. The blue sky and one large sun were very Earthlike, but the similarities ended there. The planet consisted of lush vegetation, pure air, water and soil. Predators mingled among the meek, all in harmony.

Both Ghury and the Visionary recognized the Eden-like setting.

"Please explain why you left your home," the Visionary said.

"Where did you get the ruby staff?" Ghury asked.

Maldi nodded. "I received a calling from Mount Aguberro."

Ghury held up all four of his hands. "Wait! Mount Aguberro

is on Thol. You received a calling across realms?" He paused as he thought of D'laine and her dreams, then her final journey to Thol. He nodded.

Maldi noticed the Egrom's enlightenment. "As you know, Mount Aguberro is the least explored mountain on Thol. Its massive peaks have not been reached by any Tholian I have ever heard of. A while back I began having dreams of a cave near the crest of Ingosaquille."

"I tried to dismiss these dreams as frivolity but they not only lingered, they made me feel deep guilt for ignoring the call."

Maldi shook his head. "Three years ago I left Asbram and returned to Thol. I tried stepping to the cave that was calling me. That didn't work. I had to climb the mountain."

"You climbed to the crest of Ingosaquille?" the Visionary asked. He teetered between surprise and shock. The crest was around one mile from the summit of Mount Aguberro. The mountain was six and three-quarter miles from its rocky base to the summit. Mount Everest on Earth was only five and a half miles from base to summit.

"It took me almost two complete years to reach the cave," Maldi said. "When I did reach it, I was beyond surprised. It is an enormous cavern and contains many ancient artifacts and scrolls."

Maldi shared a thought picture of what he saw as he explored the cave.

"How could these things have been transported to the cave without anyone's knowledge?" Ghury didn't expect an answer from his outspoken thought.

The Visionary shook his head in denial. "Some of those items were too large to be transported manually. If Maldi couldn't step to the cave, how were these things delivered?"

"Everything is in pristine condition. I looked at some scrolls and they are intact. The ruby shaft literally jumped into my hands," Maldi explained. "I wanted to bring one scroll with me that seemed to be about the prophecy, but I couldn't leave the cave with it in my possession."

Maldi shared what he had seen on the scroll. It contained a picture of a young couple with a great likeness to D'laine and Trakon. Their hands were on the staff and the picture showed a vibration coming off the staff. The scroll said something about their bringing change and saving something.

Maldi shook his head. "I should have unrolled the scroll more to get the most meaning."

"What do you mean you could not leave with the scroll?" Ghury asked.

"It was like an invisible wall at the entrance to the cave. I thought I was doomed to die there," Maldi said. "Once I returned the scroll to the place where I found it, the barrier lifted.

"It took less time to reach the ground than the journey up. Then I began my journey to deliver the staff," Maldi said. "You know the rest."

"Where did you get the borjo?" the Visionary asked.

"Mount Aguberro is teeming with borjos. Some live in the caves while others have nests on ledges all up and down the mountain. I met Ekka around the halfway point of my descent. He saved me another full year to get to the ground."

D'LAINE STOOD ON THE LIBRARY LADDER IN THE HUGE ROOM, HER head turned sideways reading the spines of books. After pulling books off the shelf and thumbing through them, she replaced them and continued on her search.

Jamie wandered into the room. "What are you doing up there?"

D'laine looked over her shoulder. "Hi, Jamie. I'm trying to

find a book that teaches the Tholian alphabet so I can learn to read some of these books and scrolls."

"You can't read Tholian?" Jamie asked, surprised.

D'laine stared at her brother. "No. Can you?"

He nodded.

D'laine made her way down the ladder. "How'd you learn to read Tholian?"

Jamie shrugged. "I don't know, it's just there. I figured I got that in a download from the Egrom lessons."

"I wonder why I didn't get that." D'laine grumbled.

"Are you sure? Look at some writing and just let your eyes soften," Jamie said.

D'laine grabbed a book off the shelf and opened it. She followed Jamie's instructions. Nothing happened. He grabbed the book from her. She watched as his eyes almost closed, then opened again.

"There're a lot of big words here, but I'll try to read a little to you." He slid his finger under the words. "The arch-i-tec-tural de-vel-op-ment..."

"That's okay, Jamie. That's about the architectural develop-ment of either Ebscalon or Ciert." D'laine tried again.

"I wonder what's wrong with me." she asked. "If you can read this I should be able to!"

Trakon entered the library. He nuzzled into D'laine. "What are you two doing?"

"D'laine's upset because I can read Tholian and she can't." There was just a smidgen of gloat in Jamie's attitude.

Trakon walked over to a section of books and pulled one off the shelf. "Here, Jamie. This whole section is for your age group." He handed Jamie a book that depicted a young boy in the marketplace. Jamie opened the book.

"Akelb works in the market alongside his parents. They make jewelry and sell or trade with shoppers. Akelb is learning how to make fine chains."

Jamie went over to the shelves Trakon pointed out. "Wow! There're so many books to read!"

D'laine's mouth turned down. "I don't understand why I can't read. Nothing makes sense. All I see are these squiggly lines and symbols."

"Maybe you're missing something. Have you asked Ghury about this?" Trakon asked.

Jamie brought D'laine a book. "Here. This is kind of like the Tholian alphabet explained."

D'laine took the book and opened it. She slammed it shut. She gave a little grunt of exasperation. "I wish I could put this book under my pillow and wake up and know how to read!"

Trakon grabbed her shoulders and slammed her into his chest. "Calm down. I'll bet it's up there. You just can't seem to access it." He knuckled the top of her head, which did not sit well with D'laine.

She stomped out of the library and stormed to her room. "Well, that didn't go so good," Trakon said.

"My sister likes to figure things out. She doesn't like failure," Jamie said.

"No kidding." Trakon left the library.

Trakon knocked on D'laine's door, then opened it a couple of inches. "Is it safe to come in?"

He entered the room and shut the door. Pup and Chatter wiggled up to him for scratches. That finished, Trakon joined D'laine on the chaise. He dragged her slumped body into his arms.

"Come on. Get over it," he said. "It's probably something simple that Ghury can solve. Did you call out to him?"

D'laine blustered. She elbowed herself out of Trakon's arms. "No! I'm trying to find it in my head!"

"You don't have to be so grumpy!" Trakon said. "You're taking it out on everybody."

He grabbed her and planted a kiss on her mouth. She wrapped her arms around his neck and let go of all her worries. Soon, they were sprawled on the chaise, D'laine under Trakon. The kiss was smoldering. One of Trakon's hands held her head while the other explored her body.

D'laine wrapped one of her legs under Trakon's butt.

A loud knock sounded at the door.

Trakon and D'laine sprang apart.

The door opened and Biggan stepped into the room. Pup and Chatter's tails rapped against the floor.

Biggan's eyes roved over the young couple. D'laine's hair was ratted in a mess and Trakon squirmed trying to hide his arousal. "I don't recall attending the wedding," Biggan said.

Trakon scowled. "One of these turns you'll get yours, Biggan!"

"Just wait until you have a daughter," Biggan said. "Then you'll most likely challenge her interested partners to a fight to the death."

Biggan held the door wide. "After you, my prince."

Chatter followed Trakon out the door.

CHAPTER FIFTEEN

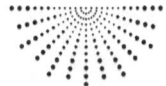

*V*ictor Bennett, one of the scientists who had investigated D'laine Jackson's disappearance in Katy, Texas, sat in his home office, his face buried in his hands.

A week ago, everything had changed, crashed down around his feet.

Kara, his wife of ten years, had received the worst news. Brain cancer, Grade IV. Brain cancer wasn't in stages like other cancers. It was graded I to IV.

No one knew it had started eating away at her brain. During the past six months, though, there had been tiny hints, things that should have added up to questions and doctor's visits. But today's busy families were always running around—children's events, sports and club gatherings—a virtual whirlwind of social activities to the point of everyone dropping into bed beat.

Only Kara's exhaustion seemed to magnify in the past two months. She had to take naps every afternoon. She added additional vitamins and home remedies in her health program. When the headaches began, she made an appointment with their family doctor.

She was convinced it was allergies. Summer brought on her

green allergies, as Kara liked to call them. If it was green, she was allergic to it. The doctor wrote a prescription and noted that she had lost five pounds. He reminded her to use the nasal pump to block the influx of pollen and other allergy cooties and patted her on the shoulder.

Just last week, Darren, Victor's eight-year-old son spent the night at his friend Bobby's. Victor ran out to the office supply place to find lead for his favorite mechanical pencil. Kara began preparing potato salad early so it would cool down for supper. When Victor returned home, the house was quiet.

"Kara? I'm home."

He went into the bedroom, but she wasn't there. He stopped at his office and deposited the bag of supplies on his desk, then went to the kitchen. He turned the stove off—the water was almost all boiled out and could have started a fire.

"Kara!" Now Victor was worried. He looked out the window to see if she was on the patio in the backyard talking on her cell, but he didn't see her. Then he noticed one of the kitchen chairs missing. He rounded the island and saw Kara on the floor.

"Oh my God, Kara! Kara!"

Victor fell down to his knees in a heartbeat. He felt for a pulse, lifted an eyelid. He called 9-1-1. Then he called Bobby's mother and asked her if Darren could stay longer until he knew what had happened to Kara.

As Victor sat at his desk, he felt cheated. Something had been going on for months. Her doctor should have been more concerned. Paid more attention. Made Kara take tests.

He should have dug deeper. Now she was at the point of no return. The only thing past Grade IV was death's door. Her tumor was inoperable.

Buffy, the family dog with a face of white hair, lumbered

over to Victor and planted her head on his thigh. He scratched her head, lost in melancholy.

"What are we going to do, Buffy?"

Victor didn't know how he would survive without Kara. He didn't know how he could bury her in the ground. How would he take care of Darren?

In one week, Kara had gone from a vibrant woman to a shell of her former self. She couldn't stand without help. Couldn't follow a conversation. Barely recognized familiar faces, including Darren's.

Darren cried himself to sleep the night she asked who he was. Victor explained over and over to him that her brain was being eaten away, that she didn't even know who he was anymore, other than a caregiver.

The pain on his heart was horrendous. Not only did he have to watch his wife die a slow, painful death, but his young son was already motherless. Darren would lose out on a lifetime of her love and advice. Victor didn't know how he could fill her shoes.

Victor used his home office two or three days a week to avoid the Los Angeles traffic, but he didn't have a clue about Darren's schedules. Kara kept a date book on the kitchen desk. He didn't know how to contact any of the people whose names were jotted in the calendar squares with times noted.

When Victor finally retrieved Kara's cellphone, he felt like he was snooping. But he had to do it. He looked through her appointments and started calling the people whose names were on her calendar. Each time he got in touch with someone, he put an X in the square.

His medical insurance was excellent, along with the additional policy that paid for two nurses. One nurse attended to Kara during the day and the other at night. The spare bedroom contained medical equipment he heard beeping in his home office.

THE FRONT DOOR OPENED AND CLOSED. VICTOR LOOKED UP AS Darren sauntered into his office. Darren pushed Buffy out of the way and slid onto Victor's lap.

Victor held him and rubbed his back. "It's going to be okay, son."

"No, it's not. Mom's dying. She's not going to see me grow up, graduate from school, or get married," Darren said.

"You're getting married?" Victor quipped.

"Come on, Dad. It's not funny," Darren said.

"Listen, son. We've all been dealt a bad hand, but you and I are still going to be here. We have to stay strong for however long your mom will be with us," Victor said.

"But she doesn't know us anymore." Tears spilled down Darren's cheeks. "I don't want her to go." He blubbered, trying to be quiet, but failing.

"She may not recognize us, but we know her. That's what matters. We know her and we love her. All we can do is make her as comfortable as possible for whatever time she has left."

Darren's eyes grazed across his father's desk. He stared at the special picture that always sat on the desk. D'laine Jackson and her family, along with his father's friend, Stanley Daigle.

"Dad! You should contact D'laine! She'll heal Mom like she healed Brian!"

Darren's voice escalated to pitch level. His excitement ran wild. He slipped off his father's lap and grabbed the picture frame and thrust it at Victor.

"Whoa! Darren, I can't call up D'laine or Stanley. They aren't even on Earth anymore," Victor said.

"Yeah, but you said that guy Greg Claymore…"

"Darren, there's no way to contact them! Believe me, if I could, I would," Victor said.

"You have to try, Dad!"

CHAPTER SIXTEEN

D'laine was still grumbling about her lack of reading skills. Everyone in her family was able to read the Tholian script. Even Stanley devoured scrolls and books from the library. As she sat across from Ghury in his mushroom house, she nudged the book Jamie had found. It seemed to be an elementary reading tool.

"Can I absorb it some way?" She was almost manic in her quest to read every book in the palace library.

"Stand," Ghury commanded. "I will scan your brain. This knowledge should be up there."

They stood in the middle of his hut. Ghury spread his four hands, fingers splayed apart, around her head. An almost imperceptible low hum sounded as he performed an Egrom scan.

After he finished, he tapped her head in four places: the forehead, the crown, and each side of her head, in back of her ears.

He reached for the book and handed it to her.

As she stared at the cover, the Tholian hieroglyphics seemed to squiggle and form words.

"Oh my God! I can read! Oh my God! Thank you so much, Ghury!"

She grabbed him in a hug and ran out the door, yelling "thank you" all the way to the crestrider.

D'LAINE LANDED THE CRESTRIDER AT THE BUILDING WHERE SHE had retrieved it earlier. It bumped to a stop. She jumped down and ran like the breeze toward the palace.

An attendant rushed forward, his face creased in worry. He looked over the crestrider then watched as the princess disappeared among the buildings. He shrugged.

D'laine raced into the palace and headed straight for the library. Stanley and Jamie were there, reading quietly.

Stanley had a stack of books and a pile of dusty scrolls on the table. He flipped through pages faster than any speed-reader on Earth.

"Hey, D'laine. Where've you been?" Jamie asked.

"I went to see Ghury! I can read!"

"What did he do? Was something missing?" Stanley's eyes never left the page of the book he was flipping through.

"He did one of those Egrom scans on my head then he tapped my head in four different places and now I can read!" D'laine was hyper excited. She stood before the monstrous shelves. "Where do I begin?"

"If you start reading now, you should finish everything in this room in thirty or forty years," Stanley said. "If I could manage to get a book and scroll count, I'd be able to narrow down the time it would take. But it depends on how fast you read a book."

"Oh, Stanley," D'laine said. "I like to take my time and digest what I've read."

"It may be different here," Stanley said.

"What do you mean?" she asked.

"I've noticed that I absorb the information at an alarming speed," he said.

Stanley turned to Jamie. "What about you, Jamie? Is your reading faster here than on Earth?"

Jamie looked up from the book he was reading. "Now that I think about it, yes. I read a lot faster than when I was back home. I've already read five books!"

D'laine rubbed her hands together. "Oh boy! I don't know where to start! I think I'll just close my eyes and pull a book off the shelf."

"Sounds like a plan." Stanley said as he flipped pages.

D'laine closed her eyes, walked to the shelves and felt the spines. She grabbed a book off the shelf. She opened her eyes and stared at the title. It was an anatomy and physiology book.

"Huh, isn't this interesting?"

Stanley stood. "What'd you pick?" He sauntered over to her and glanced over the cover. "Let me read that when you're finished."

"Okay." D'laine left the library and walked to her suite. The dogs were off hunting and the room was nice and quiet. She curled up in the corner of the sofa and tucked her feet under a pillow.

D'laine opened the book. She looked over the table of contents but decided to go from front to back so she wouldn't miss anything. She could skip around, but she thought it would be better to plow right through the book.

The pages flew through her fingers. She stopped herself, shocked. "Am I reading this material?" D'laine sat still for a moment. She closed her eyes and thought about what she had seen on those fast-flipped pages. "Uh huh, uh huh." She got it. Like Stanley and Jamie, her reading and absorption rate was phenomenal.

When she turned another fifty pages, she came to a part about Tholian mating, conception and the eggs.

D'laine gulped. She slowed to an almost normal reading speed for Earth. Tholian artists left no doubt to the imagination. It was all laid out on the page.

D'laine was totally engrossed when Trakon plopped down on the sofa beside her. She jumped.

"Oh my God! When did you get here? I didn't even hear you knock," she sputtered.

Trakon held her place while he flipped to the cover. "I sneaked in here. Biggan wasn't outside. Why in the world are you looking at this book?"

"I'm reading it! Ghury fixed me so now I can read!"

"That's good, but why are you reading this?" Trakon asked.

"Remember when I first came to Ebscalon, and you told me about the differences between our kind?" D'laine grilled him. "Well, now that I can read, I thought it would be a good idea for me to see what I need to know. Hint, since we're going to be married soon."

"Oh! I mean… you know how men and women *do it*, right?" Trakon asked. He blushed.

D'laine felt her face heat. "I know how Earthlings *do it*. I wanted to make sure Tholians *did it* the same way!"

She flipped the book open again and quickly read the text and studied the pictures. She turned the page.

Trakon grabbed the book. He turned it at an angle as he studied a picture that showed different positions. He turned the page. He and D'laine conked heads as they lowered them to see the picture better.

He tossed the book on the table, grabbed her and flung her down on the sofa. "Do you want to practice what we learned?"

D'laine screeched out a laugh. Trakon rather quickly attached his lips to hers. He moaned as the kiss deepened.

Their nemesis cleared his throat from the doorway. Trakon and D'laine split apart.

"For Thol's sake! Can't a man have any privacy?" Trakon yelled.

"Wait until you're married! Then after a few months you'll be begging for someone to interrupt you from your humdrum life." Biggan snorted.

"Never! D'laine and I are different!" Trakon boomed.

D'laine placed a hand on his arm. His fists were clenched at his sides.

"Trakon, cool down. Biggan's only doing his job." D'laine squeezed his arm.

"Yeah, cool down. You've got sex on your mind and can't think straight," Biggan said.

Trakon stormed out of her suite.

D'laine trotted over to the window and stuck her head outside. "Trakon!"

He stopped and turned, his face a mask of anger. "What?"

"Don't be mad!"

Two borjos zoomed around Trakon. He swatted at them without thinking.

"Hey! Watch it!" Herish yelled.

Trakon glared at Herish. "Sorry."

"Lovers' quarrel?" Herish looked Trakon over, then glanced up at D'laine and waved. "Frustrated?"

Herish dismounted and morphed. His tiny borjo landed on his shoulder.

"What's going on?" Herish asked.

"D'laine and I can never catch a moment alone," Trakon railed.

"Yeah, Meeri and I know how that works," Herish said.

"You, too?" Trakon asked.

Herish nodded.

The second borjo zoomed up to D'laine's window. "Hi, D'laine. Can I come in?" Meeri asked.

"Oh, hi, Meeri! Yes, come in. I hope Herish can get Trakon in a better mood."

Meeri flew into the room and dismounted. She morphed into her regular full-sized person. "Sounds like you're having our problem."

"Do you have someone watching you all the time?" D'laine asked.

Meeri stuck her head out of the window and pointed. Not one, but a squadron of borjos landed in the square.

"I guess we just have to wait until we're married," D'laine grumbled. "Come sit down."

Meeri glanced at the book on the table. She raised her eyebrows at D'laine.

"Like I told Trakon, I need to understand the difference between Tholian women and Earthlings. We have live births, whereas you pass your eggs."

Meeri's face scrunched up in a look of pain. "Live births? How big are those babies?"

D'laine did her best to give a visual of a newborn.

Meeri scrunched her face again as she looked toward D'laine's crotch. "That comes out of there? Oh. My. Thol! That must be horrifically painful!"

"I've never had a baby so I'm not sure about all the ins and outs of a live birth," D'laine said. "Trakon and I were looking at the pictures. *That* part doesn't seem different from what I've heard about back on Earth."

They perused the section of the book that showed different pictures, almost like the Kama Sutra book back on Earth. Both D'laine and Meeri blushed deeply as they explored the pictures.

"I may have to borrow this book when we get married," Meeri said.

The door opened and the men came into the room. Trakon was calm. D'laine scooted over so Trakon could sit by her, and Herish sat with Meeri.

Herish grabbed the book and glanced at the page. Then his mouth fell open as he realized what he was looking at. He looked across at the three faces watching him.

"Whoa! Where'd you get this book?" He flipped to the cover. "Can we borrow it?"

"I already asked." Meeri blushed deeply.

Trakon grabbed the book and set it on the table. "This is not doing us any good! It just leads to frustration!"

"And trouble," D'laine said.

They talked for a long while. D'laine and Trakon brought Herish up to date on everything. Since Meeri had never met D'laine's family, she didn't understand some of the things they talked about.

"Do you want to stay for lunch? You can meet my family and Trakon's mother and father," D'laine said.

"That sounds nice." Meeri turned to Herish. "We don't have to go right back to the Cember Forest, do we?"

"No, let's stay for a while. We'll tell the guards to get something at the marketplace," Herish said.

D'laine sent a telepathic message to the majordomo so enough food would be prepared. She was sure Herish was like Trakon and ate enough for three people.

Meeri and D'laine moved over to the chaise and talked about Tholian weddings and traditions. The men stayed on the sofa and poured through the book, jostling each other amid whispers and belly laughs.

EVERYONE STARED ACROSS THE TABLE AT HERISH AND MEERI, then at D'laine and Trakon. Kitry broke the silence.

"It is so nice to meet you, Meeri. When will you and Herish marry?"

"In four months," Meeri said. "Our families are going crazy.

Every female relative of mine and Herish's seems to have an opinion as to how our celebration will flow."

"Well, it is an important event for Prince Herish," Kitry said.

"All my parents talk about is *producing an heir*," Herish complained. "How about letting us get married first? Then we'll *work on it.*"

Herish and Trakon snickered.

"So, now that you are both paired up, you're friends?" Lee's eyes bored into the men.

"That was all a big misunderstanding," Trakon said.

D'laine and Kitry stared at him openmouthed.

"I seem to recall things differently, son," Kitry said. "You two were brawling right outside in the courtyard!"

"Yeah, well that was…"

D'laine elbowed Trakon in the ribs—hard. "Do you have memory problems?"

D'laine shared an exasperated look with Kitry. She turned to Meeri. "Herish was my first friend on Thol. Then Trakon and I met and they both sort of went berserk, and I lost my best friend."

"What did you expect?" Meeri said. "They revert back to our early ancestors with underdeveloped brains when they have these moments!"

Brian, Jamie, Stanley and Jor-Dan stayed out of the conversation.

"Do you have a guardian?" Jamie asked Meeri. "D'laine and Trakon can't be alone together anymore or they'll get in trouble."

"Actually, I have four when I visit Herish," Meeri said.

Lee squinted at them. "I'll bet it's because you could get into so much more trouble due to your morphing. You would be able to hide from just one guardian."

Kitry nodded, knowingly.

Meeri immediately regretted opening her mouth.

CHAPTER SEVENTEEN

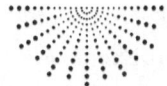

*V*ictor picked up his cellphone, scrolled through his contacts and clicked on a name. The phone rang three times.

"Ben? It's Victor."

He listened to Dr. Ben Joplin's cheery greeting. It had been at least a year since they had last talked.

"I need your advice." Victor explained Kara's dire situation. "I know this may sound crazy, but my son asked me why I didn't contact D'laine. What do you think, Ben? Would it be remotely possible to get in touch with her?"

VICTOR DROVE AROUND THE AIRPORT LOOP SEVERAL TIMES waiting for a text. When it came, he pulled up to passenger pickup at baggage claim at LAX airport in Los Angeles. He spotted Ben Joplin at the curb. He eased over to the curb and collected the scientist and his bags and they got on their way.

They arrived at Victor's house forty-five minutes later and stretched when they left the car. Victor helped Ben with his bags and they entered the house. Since Kara was in the guest bedroom with all her hospital equipment, Victor showed Ben to the fourth bedroom. He settled into the former nursery. Then they retreated to Victor's office.

Ben took in the fully functional home office with the diplomas and pictures on every wall that didn't contain a bookcase. His eyes landed on the picture of the long-gone group on the corner of Victor's desk. He picked up the frame and stared.

"If Stanley only knew the reams of paperwork his disappearance had generated!" Ben said. He settled the picture frame back on the desk. There was a hint of sadness in his eyes.

The front door slammed shut. Darren ran into Victor's office. At seeing a visitor he stopped abruptly.

"Whoa, son. What's the rush?"

"Oh, sorry! I didn't know we had company," Darren said. "This is Dr. Joplin, my friend from Houston," Victor said.

Darren stared at Ben. "You're that guy my dad worked with when D'laine Jackson disappeared!" Darren's eyes widened. "Are you going to help us call D'laine so she can cure Mom?"

Ben chuckled. "I guess your father told you the whole story."

Darren nodded. "Yes, he did. He even showed me the pictures of the creatures, that robot and Trakon!"

He turned to Victor. "You kept one of the pictures?"

Victor grabbed the picture frame, eased the backing off and unfolded the piece of paper. He handed the drawing to Ben.

Ben gripped the paper's edges. He stared in disbelief. "God! I can't believe you kept one of the pictures!"

Victor shrugged.

He took the drawing and made a copy on his color laser printer. Victor handed the drawing to Darren. "Go put this on Dr. Joplin's bag in the little room."

Darren raced out of the room, drawing in hand.

"I will cherish this drawing," Ben said. "That's quite a boy you have there. Smart as a whip."

"Yeah, he wouldn't let go of the fact that D'laine healed her brother," Victor said.

They sat and got comfortable.

"The best thing to do is to go to San Diego where Claymore seemed to have a portal," Ben said. "I only brought a couple of pieces of equipment with me. I figured you had the rest at the lab."

VICTOR CLEARED THE TABLE OF SUPPER DISHES, THEN SLID OPEN the patio door and made sure the propane tank for the barbecue was turned off.

"Thanks for the great meal. I love a grilled ribeye, and that steak was perfect," Ben said.

Darren rushed into the room. "Dad, would it be okay if I stayed over at Bobby's tonight?"

"Did his mother invite you, or did Bobby?" Victor asked.

"Mrs. Daniels invited me," Darren said.

"In that case, sure. Take your toothbrush, pajamas and a change of clothes," Victor said.

Darren lit out of the room. A few minutes later the front door closed.

Victor slid into a chair at the kitchen table. He let his face go slack. With Darren gone, he didn't have to keep up appearances.

"I don't know what I'm going to do, Ben. If we can't get through to D'laine, how am I going to raise Darren by myself?"

"It's a tough situation, but we're going to put everything into this experiment, Victor. If Greg Claymore managed a couple of round trips, then by God, we're going to do everything we can to get a message to D'laine!"

CHAPTER EIGHTEEN

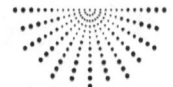

*K*itry had seemed very busy for several turns, but no one knew with what. At the dinner table that night, she dropped her bombshell.

"I have invited Queen Kansing of Jekorba for a visit," Kitry said. "I thought it would be good for her to get away. She is interested in how our hosk weaving facility operates as well as how we do other things."

Jor-Dan lifted an eyebrow, questioning his wife. He suspected she was up to something. "She was just away from Jekorba—she was here at the formal dinner."

Kitry nodded. "Yes, but that was in an official capacity. This visit is more to unwind and de-stress than anything else."

"Since when is she your friend?" Trakon asked.

A tiny blush crept up Kitry's neck and covered her cheeks. "Trakon, sometimes women come together for a purpose. Don't you worry your head off. You have your little princess and everything is as bright as the two suns."

THE NEXT TURN A ROYAL FLEET OF CRESTRIDERS ARRIVED carrying the gold, turquoise and silver flag of Jekorba. The queen's vehicle landed in the courtyard by the palace and deposited Queen Kansing and her retinue on the ground.

Kitry, Jor-Dan (with La'gar'ish at his knees), Trakon, D'laine and her entire family stood outside the palace entrance in their formal wear. Brian and Jamie squirmed.

"How come Stanley isn't here?" Jamie whispered to his brother.

"Because he isn't a part of the family. He's just a friend," Brian whispered back.

The young stately queen, who had just reached her thirty-sixth year approached the Ciertron royalty. When she spotted the diwal dog, the queen's wide smile vanished. Her guard detail stopped abruptly. A decorated guard flung his arm out in front of the queen and pushed her behind him. The rest of her detail surrounded her and aimed their laser pistols at La'gar'ish.

Jor-Dan held up his hand. "There's no need for that. La'gar'ish is my first line of protection. He won't attack unless I specifically tell him to, or he senses ultimate danger."

The guards relaxed slightly. The queen touched her head guard's arm lightly and moved in front of him. She tapped her fist to her heart in the official greeting and inclined her head slightly to the Ciertron royals.

"Welcome, Queen Kansing," Kitry said.

"Welcome to Ebscalon," Jor-Dan said.

"I am honored," Queen Kansing said.

They all entered the palace and walked to the main salon. The majordomo brought kahl and delicate pastries.

Jor-Dan's dog lay at his feet. The king reached his hand down and scratched La'gar'ish's head. His teeth clacked and his tail wagged.

Queen Kansing's guard detail stayed within a few feet of her chair, their eyes focused on the threat of the tamed guard dog.

When Lee saw his sons grabbing more than one pastry, he gave them the stink-eye. Brian and Jamie got the message.

The real purpose of the visit soon became evident.

"This is D'laine Jackson, Trakon's intended. They will be marrying in the near future," Kitry said. "And this is D'laine's father, Lee Jackson. His wife died in a horrible accident several years ago."

"Queen Kansing is a widow," Kitry told Lee. "Her husband died in a hunting accident two years ago."

Lee studied the beautiful, stately woman across from him. She had smooth skin the color of bright copper, the Tholian black hair, and dark, alert eyes. He had noticed the flow of her sari-like clothing as it fluttered across her trim hips.

The visiting queen extended her hand to Lee. He didn't know the appropriate behavior and didn't have time to access information in his head. Lee stood, bent over her hand and brushed his lips across her knuckles. He retreated back to his chair.

Daddy! What were you thinking? You've practically told her you want to marry her with that public display of affection! D'laine sent.

Lee startled slightly, then resumed his businesslike posture.

I didn't know. It all happened so quickly and I didn't know how to act so I chose a meeting with the Queen of England, Lee thought back.

That's not done anymore!

Well, what's done is done. Lee surreptitiously glanced at Jor-Dan. He didn't notice any alarm on the king's face so he thought he'd be able to undo any wrong later.

"I'm so sorry to hear of your loss," Queen Kansing said in a melodious voice. "My husband was impaled through the heart by a wild bull pakow. If it had been anywhere else, he might have been saved."

"You eat pakows?" Jamie's eyes widened in horror.

"No, no, no, my dear child. My husband, the king, was

hunting this pakow for breeding stock," the queen explained. "He repeatedly broke into the pens so the king decided to capture him."

"Oh!" Jamie was mollified.

Pup and Chatter dashed into the room looking for hand-outs from the goodies being served.

Queen Kansing screeched and jumped up on her chair.

Her guards sprang into action, surrounding her. *"TO ME!"* D'laine hollered using The Voice.

Pup and Chatter ran to D'laine, not sure what they had done wrong. They dropped to the floor, submissive.

"It's okay. You just scared Queen Kansing," she told them. She patted Pup then Chatter, whose teeth clacked in his nervous cadence.

Lee helped the queen down from her perch on the chair. "They're tame, so you don't need to be frightened."

Queen Kansing rested her hand over her heart. "I've never seen such a thing! Tame diwal dogs? Aren't you worried they will turn on you?"

Jamie got on the floor with the dogs and played with them. "They love people. They're just misunderstood."

"You might want to consider having one as part of your royal guard," Jor-Dan said. "D'laine could tame a dog for you and train it."

The decorated guard bent and whispered in the queen's ear.

"We would like that. Perhaps more than one dog?" Kansing asked. "A queen without a king is vulnerable."

"I'll take you on a tour of the hosk facility," Kitry said to Queen Kansing.

THE WOMEN ENTERED THE HOSK FACILITY WHERE THE SPINNING and weaving took place. Then they toured where the spinning was performed by the male hosks. The tiny creatures were always busy. Kitry showed the visiting queen where raw gauze was washed, dried and separated into batches. Raw gauze along with dyed, was sold in the marketplace.

Brian and Jamie were bored to tears, but they followed the entourage through the tour so they wouldn't get in trouble with their father or their grandmother queen.

One of the buildings was the place where artists drew patterns on the material and applied colors. There were hundreds of designs and color schemes.

"This is an impressive setup," Queen Kansing said. "I'm sure you sell a lot of material."

Kitry led them out of the buildings to the marketplace so the queen could see the various booths with a variety of material. She also saw craftspeople creating clothing, uniforms, and other items—everything from sheets to napkins.

"Your craftspeople are quite talented. I would like to borrow some ideas to take home with me," Queen Kansing said.

"Our craftspeople are highly prized for their creations," Kitry said.

Queen Kansing's eyes wandered the marketplace. The sheer number of people bargaining at the booths was impressive. And she noticed they were not just Ciertrons. All manner of Tholians were jammed into the large outdoor space.

D'laine spied Bok-Tor, a Safri (one of the lesser creatures of Thol), engaged in a bargaining duel with a shopkeeper. She excused herself and joined her friend.

"Hi, Bok-Tor. What are you trying to buy?" D'laine looked over the table of leather goods. There were travel pouches, water skins, weapons holders—all things leather.

Bok-Tor bowed then hit his chest when he straightened himself. "My princess! I'm trying to purchase this travel pouch. My old pouch finally retired. It was worn thin after all the years of serving me well."

D'laine fingered the leather of the pouch Bok-Tor was interested in. She looked up at the shopkeeper. "Did you make this?"

The shopkeeper bowed and hit his chest, following Bok-Tor's lead. "Yes, princess. Everything you see here in my booth was created with my own hands."

He turned to Bok-Tor. "Because you are a friend of the princess, I will offer you a bargain. I will sell this pouch to you for only ten sepiks."

"Sold!" Bok-Tor opened his money pouch and counted out the payment. Then he took the new pouch and draped the long leather strap over his head to sit across his chest. He grinned. That was amusing all by itself, since it showed his big, flat teeth.

"Where have you been?" D'laine asked.

"I found a troupe of my Safri brothers and we have been wandering," Bok-Tor said. "I decided to return to Ebscalon to rest."

D'laine patted him on the back. "I'd better get back to the queens. It was good to see you again."

QUEEN KANSING BID EVERYONE GOODBYE AND SHE AND HER guard returned home to Jekorba. Jor-Dan promised to deliver two diwal dogs within two or three months, depending on how long it took to tame and train the dogs.

As they watched the crestriders fade into the distance, everyone returned to the palace, to the salon.

"Queen Kansing's bonding will soon be completely dissolved in less than a complete year," Kitry said.

"What does that mean?" D'laine asked.

"A marriage is for the life of both parties. When one dies, their bonding must be dissolved over time if they are to take another marriage partner," Kitry said. "The longer the couple were together, the longer the bond takes to dissolve."

"How does that work?" Lee couldn't wrap his head around what Kitry said.

"The spiritual bonding between marriage partners is an intricately woven connection. The period following the death of one of the partners goes beyond mourning," Kitry said.

"As I mentioned, Kansing's bond is almost dissolved. She and her husband were only together eight years. I thought it would be good to introduce you to her. If you are interested in her as a potential partner, you would have to begin showing up to get her attention. I'm sure she was intrigued when you displayed your interest."

"About that," Lee started. He was mortified by the faux pas. "I did not have time to research how to respond to her hand so I used an old Earth custom when meeting with the Queen of England."

D'laine snorted a laugh. "I told my father that was not the right type of response for royalty here on Thol. He didn't understand."

Kitry swung her eyes over to Lee. "Oh! So you are not interested in Queen Kansing?"

"I don't know her," Lee said. "Quite frankly, I wasn't even thinking of another wife."

"Where is Jekorba?" D'laine asked.

"It's quite a ways away," Trakon piped in. "On the other side of Caradon."

Jamie and Brian's heads ping-ponged back and forth following the conversation.

"Would we have to move there?" Jamie asked.

"If your father married the queen, that's where you would live," Kitry said.

Without warning, Jamie's face screwed up, and he sobbed long and hard. "I don't want to move! I'll never see D'laine and Trakon, or you and grandpa! Ekka would have to move and he likes his tower." He bawled his eyes out.

Kitry went to Jamie and pulled him into a hug. "Oh, Jamie. I hadn't thought about how this would affect you and your brother. We will just forget about this romance business, shall we?"

Still blubbering up a storm, Jamie nodded. He dried his eyes.

D'LAINE WENT IN SEARCH OF JOR-DAN IN HIS MEETING SALON. She found him talking to Marrak. She was about to leave when he spotted her.

"D'laine, don't go. What do you need?" Jor-Dan asked.

"I've been thinking about the wild diwal dogs. I'm not sure it's a good idea for us to become the diwal dog capture and training program for the other kingdoms," she said.

"Why? Once they're tame, they're perfectly happy creatures," Jor-Dan said.

"While that's true, without The Voice, those dogs could slaughter the town. No one could stop them except me, or one of the Egroms," D'laine said.

Jor-Dan and Marrak looked frightened.

"You saw how Pup and Chatter acted this turn when Queen Kansing jumped on her chair. They were excited—which isn't good sometimes. Instinct takes over."

"Oh, dear. There are now two situations we have to back out of," Marrak said. "Jor-Dan mentioned your father's misunderstanding with the queen."

"My father is drafting a formal apology for his blunder. I'm pretty sure he will also explain that the distance from Ebscalon is too great for the family," D'laine said.

Jor-Dan sighed. "Let's hope Queen Kansing doesn't declare war!"

CHAPTER NINETEEN

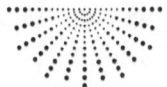

*V*ictor's wastebasket was filled with crumbled pieces of paper. The printer churned and spit out another sheet and Ben grabbed it.

"I think this will do," Ben said.

D'laine,

My wife, Kara, is dying. Grade IV brain cancer—very sudden. Please help. Come to Coronado Beach near San Diego to Greg Claymore's portal.

Latitude: 32° 41' 9.20" N. Longitude: -117° 10' 59.12" W.

Dr. Joplin and I will stay on the beach for twenty-four hours. Please try to contact me by your telepathy.

Yours truly, Victor Bennett

Ben studied the embedded map that showed the entire beach and the town of Coronado. Those locations were in relationship to the spot marked on the map with a large X where Greg had come and gone. Ben passed the page over to Victor.

The scientists had spent the better part of a week on the beach with several pieces of equipment Victor had *borrowed* from Whitting. They expended hours searching for the portal. Victor created a grid overlay on his laptop. They searched the beach systematically so as not to miss as much as a square foot of the sand.

When they found a slight waver for the portal, they set up a clever sign instead of a flag that pinpointed the portal. The sign announced the site of the Bennett-Joplin-Jackson family gathering. Ben thought it would be safe. No one would move it, hopefully, since that would be a challenge for the scientists.

It helped that Victor was on leave from his job from the prestigious Whitting Institute. He had no intention of bringing his boss into the search and details. Dr. Joseph Paxton was too much of a schmoozer and Victor and Ben worried that D'laine and Thol would be compromised. While this was a major scientific experiment that, if successful, would catapult Victor and Ben's careers, they refused to turn it into a media circus.

In addition to the unwanted attention, there was the government aspect. They were aware that if this got out, the government would put everything it had into breeching the portal and getting into Thol. Every other world that became known through the doorway alignment would be in danger of invasion.

"We should do this at night when people are sleeping so no one sees something they shouldn't," Victor said. "We can bring sleeping bags and camp out on the beach."

Victor checked with Bobby's mother to see if Darren could spend the night. He told her he had to go to San Diego overnight, but was vague about the reason. Everything was all set up. Victor and Ben gathered what they needed and loaded up the car.

Just then, Victor's cell phone rang. It was Bobby's mother, in tears. "I'm sorry, Victor, my brother passed away unexpectedly and we're going to have to drive up to San Francisco."

"I'm so sorry to hear about your brother, Beverly. Don't worry about it. Darren can come with me," Victor said.

He returned to the house and gathered up another sleeping

bag and supplies for his son. Darren ran home, his backpack dragging along the sidewalk.

"Dad?" Darren called out as he entered the house.

"In here." Victor stood at the side of Kara's hospital bed.

The day nurse busied herself looking over the chart.

"Kara, I'll be back either late tonight or early in the morning. If all goes well, D'laine will be with me. I know you don't want to hear about her, but the fact of the matter is that you have no more choices. It's either give D'laine a chance, or wither away, and I'm not willing to let you go."

Darren came into the room and listened quietly. He approached his parents.

"It's going to be okay, Mom."

Victor spoke to the day nurse. "We have to go to San Diego, but I hope to be back tonight some time. Please tell the night nurse. You both have my mobile phone number in case you need me, but keep in mind it's a three-hour drive on a good day."

When they were outside, Darren pulled on Victor's shirt. "Dad, we should take Buffy. She'd be able to let you know if D'laine was nearby."

Victor thought for a moment. "That's not a bad idea."

"I agree," Ben said.

Victor returned to the house and came outside with Buffy on her leash.

"Come on, girl. Let's see if we can find D'laine." Victor loaded the dog into the third row of seats.

At the mention of D'laine, Buffy whined.

Victor, Darren, Buffy, and Ben piled into the SUV. They headed to San Diego by way of CA-90 east, then took I-405 south.

"Are you going to try to find D'laine?" Darren asked excitedly from the back seat.

Ben turned. "We're going to try. If all goes according to plan, we hope to return to the house with her and get your mother fixed up."

"Wow! I can't wait to meet her!" Darren said.

The SUV continued on CA-73 south then merged onto I-5 south. They crossed over the Coronado Bridge and followed signs to the beach. They got out of the car and stretched their legs and looked around.

"Let's grab a bite to eat before we start setting up," Victor said.

Victor walked Buffy, then brought her back to the car. He poured water in her travel bowl, set up the travel fan, opened the sunroof and lowered the windows five inches all around.

Ben looked at his watch. "We have at least four or five hours. I figure people will not be on the beach at eleven tonight. At least I hope it will be free of tourists and locals."

They found an Italian restaurant and walked across the road and went inside.

THERE WERE A FEW STRAGGLERS ON THE BEACH AT TEN-THIRTY. Victor was getting antsy, wanting to move forward with the experiment. He checked his phone repeatedly for the time, and for any emergency messages from home.

Finally, they had the beach to themselves. Ben set up their cameras on time-delay to capture any events.

Buffy and Darren wandered the beach close by. After awhile, they all settled for the long-awaited moment.

"Should I just push the paper along the sand?" Victor asked Ben.

"Maybe roll it up?" Ben suggested.

"Yeah, I think that would work better." Victor rolled up the piece of paper. He put it on the ground and used a golf club to push it toward the portal. Ben knelt at one of the cameras.

"Four inches to your left," Ben said. Victor made the adjustment.

"Keep moving steadily forward," Ben said.

A frustrating half-hour passed to no avail. They took a much-needed break. Buffy and Darren were sprawled on a blanket.

"Don't worry, Dad. Everything's going to work out. I just know it!" Darren said.

"Shall we try again?" Ben encouraged Victor.

Victor grabbed his golf club and stood at the ready. "Should I make any adjustments?"

Ben moved between two different scientific cameras. "Move the paper an inch to the right. I know that seems insignificant, but that should put you right in the center of the portal."

Victor did as instructed, then slowly pushed the rolled-up paper.

A bright flash lit up the area. The paper was gone.

Before anyone could stop her, Buffy ran and leapt through the portal.

"Buffy!" Darren ran after her.

Victor grabbed his son before Darren disappeared through the portal.

"Darren! You have to let her go! Buffy's instincts will keep her alive. Evidently, she knew that's where D'laine and her family went. We can only hope for the best."

CHAPTER TWENTY

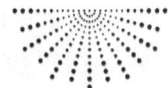

D'laine woke from a sound sleep. She sat in bed, cleared her head and held out her hand. Victor's rolled paper flew into her grasp. Before she even had a chance to read it, she had a revelation. In seconds she was on her feet and out the door with Pup on her heels.

She rushed across the hall and knocked on Trakon's door. She slipped inside. He was sprawled across the bed, one leg wrapped around a pillow. D'laine shook his shoulder.

"Trakon!" she whispered. "Wake up."

"D'laine... love you..."

She shook him again. "Wake up!"

Trakon jolted awake. "Wha... you came to my bed?"

"Something's going on. The portal to Earth has opened and I think my dog came through. Get dressed. I'm going to wake my father. You go get Stanley."

D'laine rushed out of Trakon's bedroom and up the stairs to her father's suite.

"Daddy! Wake up!"

Lee stirred, then woke when he realized he wasn't dreaming. "D'laine? What's wrong?"

She explained about Buffy and the portal. "I haven't had time to read this. I'll be back as soon as I can. I don't want Buffy killed after all she's been through."

D'laine thrust Victor's note in her father's hand and took off out the door.

Trakon, Stanley and the dogs were waiting for her. "You're sure you weren't dreaming?" Stanley asked.

"Victor sent a note. My father has it. We'll see what's going on when we get back, but we have to find Buffy."

They left the palace and went through the door by the closed main gates.

D'laine squatted and called the dogs to her. She projected a picture of Buffy into their heads. "Mine!" she told them.

Pup and Chatter took off across the moss.

D'laine, Trakon and Stanley stopped at the pakow pens. D'laine mounted Lulu bareback. Trakon and Stanley found mounts and did the same. They took off at a fast pace, searching for the dogs. They heard Buffy barking way off in the distance and headed in that direction.

"Please don't let the dogs kill her!" D'laine urged Lulu faster.

They arrived at a standoff. Pup and Chatter stood between Buffy and three wild diwal dogs in attack and kill mode. All the diwal dogs' teeth were extended and clacked loudly.

"Stay where you are," she told Trakon and Stanley. She slid to the ground.

"D'laine, you have to be careful. It's three against two, and those wild dogs are killers," Trakon said.

"I've got it," D'laine said.

D'laine held her hand out toward the three wild dogs. "*AWAY!*" She projected The Voice. The three wild diwals hit the ground, then jumped up and ran in the opposite direction.

Buffy leapt into her arms. D'laine let her breath out. "Oh, Buffy! What are you doing here, girl?"

Buffy whined and crawled all over D'laine. When she

was thoroughly satisfied that her human was within scratching and petting distance, Buffy took notice of Pup and Chatter.

The three dogs sniffed and greeted each other. The diwal dogs were not so unlike Earth dogs. Pup lowered his front paws in a playful posture. Buffy jumped to the side. They ran in a circle, playful. Even Chatter loosened up a bit and joined in the fun.

"Come on, let's go home." D'laine climbed up Lulu's leg and they started out back to the pens.

"How could this have happened?" Stanley asked.

"Something must be wrong back home. I'm pretty sure Victor wouldn't just let Buffy jump through the portal to this wild land," D'laine said.

"We need to see what his message says," Trakon said.

They rode back to the pakow pens in silence, secured their rides inside the fence, then returned to the palace.

They found Lee downstairs on the main floor in a small salon, pacing.

"Daddy! What's going on back home?" D'laine rushed to Lee, but Buffy beat her to him.

"Buffy! How in the world...?" Lee stood back and studied the dog. "D'laine, have you looked at Buffy?"

Lee, D'laine and Stanley stared at the dog. She looked old.

"How long have we been gone?" D'laine asked.

"Two-hundred and thirteen Earth days," Stanley said. "But Buffy looks about ten years older than when we last saw her."

"What did Victor's note say?" D'laine asked.

Lee retrieved the note and passed it to her. "Victor's wife needs your help. She has brain cancer."

"Wife?" Stanley appeared shocked. "Victor's married? He wasn't even dating anyone!"

D'laine passed the note to Stanley.

"We need to go as soon as possible." Stanley turned his attention to Lee. "If I could bring something back for you, what would that be?"

Lee thought about it. "My laptop. It has so much information about the projects I worked on at NASA. We'll have to figure out a way to power it here, so if you can get to my home office, grab the laptop bag. All the cords and the charger are in there."

"What if we have problems returning?" D'laine asked.

"I think Brian can help with that," Stanley said.

"Wait! You're going to leave?" Trakon was absorbing the conversation and its ramifications. "You are not going without me! If you get stranded, I need to be with you!"

D'laine thought it over. "Trakon, I don't know how you would take to Earth. It's nothing like anything you have ever experienced before. It's very crowded, noisy, polluted, and so far behind with technology you will be freaked out."

"I don't care. I'm going and that's that!"

"Where are you going?" Jor-Dan asked. He and Kitry wandered in the room, their bathrobes tied around them. "What's wrong?"

Kitry spied Buffy and squeaked out a surprise. "What is that creature?"

D'laine fell to her knees and Buffy climbed onto her lap. "This is my old dog from Earth. Her name is Buffy."

"How did your dog get here?" Jor-Dan asked. "I'm surprised the diwal dogs didn't attack her."

La'gar'ish came into the room and rushed to Jor-Dan, teeth clacking as he stared at Buffy.

"Stand down, La'gar'ish!" Jor-Dan boomed.

The diwal dog's teeth retracted back into his mouth. He stretched his neck and sniffed in Buffy's direction.

Pup and Chatter joined Buffy at D'laine's knees.

"My scientific partner sent a message to D'laine, and the dog jumped into the portal," Stanley said.

They all talked at once, explaining the situation. "Trakon,

you can't possibly go!" Kitry said. "You're the heir. What if something were to happen, and you were trapped there, or killed?"

"I can't let D'laine go without me. We belong together!" Trakon said.

"It will be okay," Stanley said. "Victor found the portal that Greg Claymore used—he returned to Earth more than once, so the portal is viable. And Brian will be here. Remember, his gift is finding and recognizing the correct portal. If all else fails, Ghury can bring us back."

"You're going as well?" Kitry asked.

"Yes. There are some things I need to do, and I'd like to see my world again," Stanley said.

"I really need to contact Victor!" D'laine said. "When can we leave?"

"Give me just a moment." Stanley teleported out of the room.

"Let me go wake the boys. They'll be happy to see Buffy," Lee said.

THE GROUP STOOD OUT IN THE MEADOW. BRIAN WANDERED around like a blind person, his hands stretched out in front of him. He stopped and turned ever so slightly.

"It's here." His fingers spread thin air in front of him and the beach appeared. "Hurry!"

"Don't worry! We'll be back," D'laine said. "Take care of the dogs."

D'laine grabbed Trakon's and Stanley's hands and they stepped forward. A bright light flashed. Then they were gone.

CHAPTER TWENTY-ONE

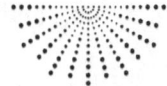

D'laine, Trakon and Stanley stepped onto Coronado Beach followed by a loud crack.

"Oh my God! They're here!" Victor, Darren and Ben rushed over to them.

Darren's mouth hung open. "You're Trakon, aren't you? Wow! I'm Darren. I'm a little kid on Earth."

Trakon chuckled. He reached out and grabbed Darren's arm in greeting.

"Yes, I'm Trakon."

Darren's eyes widened as he heard the Tholian language.

"Oh! You have to adjust your translator—no one can understand you," D'laine said.

Trakon went into his communicator settings and made the adjustment so he could communicate in English.

"Here's how we do it on Earth," Darren said. He grabbed Trakon's hand and shook it once.

"Huh." Trakon studied the hand-grasp. "I like that."

There were hugs and tears all around.

Stanley studied Victor and Ben for a moment. "There's a vast time difference between our worlds. When we saw Buffy, I determined there must be a ten to one ratio of time."

Stanley explained how long they had been on Thol.

Victor and Ben studied Stanley. "You haven't aged at all," Ben said.

"This is your son?" Stanley asked Victor.

"Yes. I met Kara, his mother—my wife—shortly after you left. Darren's eight years old. Kara and I were together for two years before we married."

"You don't need glasses any longer?" Ben asked.

Stanley shook his head. "Egrom healing. You'd love Thol."

Ben walked around Stanley. "Your head is different—it's rounder than what I remember. You had a longish face the last time I saw you."

"We have a lot to tell you," D'laine said.

Victor and Ben brought their attention to Trakon. "Trakon! I'm Victor and this is Ben. Wow. It's so good to meet you."

THEY PILED INTO THE SUV.

Trakon leaned into D'laine. "This is one of those ground-riders?"

"Yes. Try not to freak out when we get on the highway."

"Why would I freak out?" Trakon looked around. It was peaceful and quiet along the beach.

After several minutes, Victor steered the SUV onto the highway.

Trakon gripped the door on one side and the seat with his other hand.

"We're going to be killed! This vehicle can't lift up and fly?"

"Nope. Welcome to old technology," D'laine said.

After forty-five minutes, Trakon relaxed his death grip. "No wonder your people are so stressed. I could not live here with all this noise and the antiquated modes of travel."

"D'laine, will I be able to teleport here?" Stanley asked. "Your dad wants me to bring back his laptop from his home office."

"You can teleport?" Victor gawked in the rearview mirror.

"Victor, you can't imagine everything I can do on Thol! You and Ben would be amazed at the technology. Plus, you'd have gifts—special abilities brought over from Earth," Stanley explained.

"When we get to Victor's house you can practice stepping from one room to the next, or from the house to the backyard." D'laine thought a moment. "You'll need the location reference to get to my father's house."

Ben turned around from the front seat. "You've been there before, Stan, when we were investigating D'laine's disappearance."

Stanley sifted through his memories. "Yes, I see now. I do have a clear reference and should be able to get there without any problems. If I have that capability here."

D'laine and Stanley brought Ben and Victor current with everything that had happened since they left Earth. Darren listened, spellbound.

"Those diwal dogs sound scary," Darren said.

"Did you ever see the original movie, *Alien?*" D'laine asked.

Darren nodded. "That was so scary I slept with the lights on for a week!"

"Well, diwal dogs have the same type of retractable teeth that came out of the mother alien creature."

Darren's eyes widened. Victor glanced at D'laine through the rearview mirror, and Ben gaped.

"They're extremely deadly," Trakon said. "D'laine tamed three dogs and they live in the palace with us. One guards my father, the king."

"You tamed them?" Darren's mouth was opened in a *WOW* expression.

"We all have special capabilities on Thol," D'laine said, humbly.

Trakon snorted. "Don't let her fool you. She's not only brilliant, but she's a powerful warrior—she can kill you by pointing her finger at you. D'laine can do so many other things that no one else has the capability of, like using The Voice."

They arrived at Victor's house. Trakon was relieved to be out of the metal groundrider. He had repeatedly cursed the *death trap*, what he called the SUV, while riding the highways between Coronado and Marina Del Rey.

Victor escorted them into the house to the living room. "Please wait here while I walk the night nurse out. I'm not sure how to explain who you are and what you're going to do, so it's best if she just leaves."

"You can tell her we're a group of alternative healers," D'laine said.

"That sounds good. Still, she doesn't need to be here. I think we should keep this private." Victor walked down the hallway.

Several moments later, the front door closed quietly. Victor returned to the living room. "All set."

They followed him to the home hospital room. Kara was a sad sight. Her cheeks had taken on a sunken look and her previously radiant blond hair was limp.

D'laine approached the side of the bed. She held her hands around six inches above Kara's body and did an initial body scan. Then she dug into her pouch and pulled out her crystals.

"Victor, where exactly is the cancer?" she asked.

Victor rifled in a folder on a small chest of drawers. He brought out a picture of an X-ray he held up to a light. It showed the tumor and what seemed like feeder lines or cells close by.

D'laine studied the picture, then closed her eyes. She took a deep breath and released it. She ran the crystal barely an inch over Kara's head. She opened her eyes.

"Kara, I'm going to put my crystal on your forehead," D'laine said.

She placed the rock on Kara's forehead.

"Do you have a large pot or something I can put next to the bed? Even a mid-sized trash can will do. That might be better—just not plastic."

Victor left the room and returned with a small metal trash can.

"That will work. Kara, I'm going to start now. It may seem weird, but try to relax as much as you can."

D'laine rested her hands on Kara's head and closed her eyes. She took and released several deep breaths.

Kara whimpered.

"It will be okay," D'laine bent and whispered to Kara. D'laine's eyes opened wide and stared straight ahead. "Move the crystal."

They all looked at each other. Trakon approached and snatched the crystal off Kara's forehead.

"Stand back. Way back. Leave the room."

They all hurried out of the room. They crowded in the doorway, watchful.

D'laine took several deeper breaths. Her face scrunched up as if lifting a heavy weight.

D'laine's hands slipped inside Kara's head and pulled out the tumor. She threw it into the metal trash can where it sizzled. Her hands dripped with goo.

"Wet washcloth!"

Victor bolted into the bathroom. He wet a washcloth and squeezed it out, then handed it to D'laine. She wiped her hands and folded the cloth so the muck was on the inside.

"Throw that out. Maybe put it in a plastic bag first."

Victor sprang from the room. Ben followed. "Where's a bag?" Ben asked.

Victor nodded. "Pantry."

Ben pulled out a self-sealing plastic gallon bag and held it open for Victor. The washcloth was dropped inside the bag. Victor sprinted out through the garage door and tossed the bag into the trashcan. He washed his hands at the kitchen sink then he and Ben returned to Kara's hospital room doorway.

Kara stirred. She opened her eyes.

"Sshhh." D'laine held her hands just over the surface of Kara's skull.

"Crystal." She held one hand out.

Trakon came forward and placed the crystal in her hand. "Leave."

Trakon returned to the doorway.

D'laine placed the crystal between her hands and blew into it. She placed the crystal on Kara's forehead. With fingers spread wide, she wrapped her hands around Kara's head.

She looked down at Kara, meeting her eyes. "This may feel weird, but it will be okay."

D'laine thrust one hand inside Kara's head. She pulled out some tendrils of the cancer she had pinched between her thumb and index finger, and threw them into the trash can.

Victor supplied another washcloth. D'laine wiped her hands.

"You should be able to wash this one."

"Nah. It's going into the trash," Victor said.

D'laine picked up her crystal and ran it over Kara's body.

She laid her hand on Kara's shoulder. "How do you feel, Kara?"

Kara blinked for a moment or two. She met D'laine's eyes. "I feel good. Really good."

"Do you want to sit up?" D'laine asked.

Victor moved to the other side of the bed. "Let me help you."

He supported her back and sat her up. "Oh, Kara! I thought I'd lost you!"

Kara swung her legs to the other side of the bed where D'laine stood.

"You're D'laine, aren't you?"

D'laine nodded. "I've removed the tumor from your brain." She motioned to the trashcan.

Kara startled as she saw the vile oozing mess in the trashcan. "My God! That was inside my head?"

"Yeah. You don't have to worry about it anymore." D'laine and the others retreated to the living room leaving Victor to have a private moment with Kara.

Victor held Kara tenderly. "Kara. Oh, Kara. I thought all was lost. I was so scared for Darren."

Kara cried. "I'm so sorry I never believed you."

"Let's face it, that story was hard to digest. Don't beat yourself up about it. I'm thankful D'laine received my message and could travel back here to save you," Victor said.

He kissed her tenderly. Then his eyes wandered to the equipment.

"Hon, I should disconnect you from all these devices and remove the catheter," Victor said.

"Oh! Good idea." Kara scooted over and lay back down. Victor went about removing all the electrodes. He followed instructions for the catheter and removed it. "Where's Darren?" Kara asked.

"He's probably asleep," Victor said. "He was so thrilled seeing D'laine and Trakon he about passed out from exhaustion."

He helped Kara up, and they went to the living room.

Darren was on the floor pillows, sound asleep.

Victor settled Kara into a corner on the sofa. "Why don't I order pizza?"

"Oh! That sounds so good." D'laine turned to Trakon. "Wait

until you taste pizza! I'll have to figure out how to make it back home."

"Who wants something to drink?" Victor asked.

"I'll help," Stanley said. "What do you have so I know what to offer?"

TRAKON LOVED PIZZA. BUT ONLY A FEW SIPS OF WINE HAD HIM talking quite a bit louder and laughing. D'laine cut him off from wine and switched him to water. He scowled.

"Stan, why don't you practice your teleporting?" Ben asked.

"Good idea." Stanley focused and teleported out of the living room then popped back into the house. "I stepped out to the driveway and back again. I'm pretty sure I can get to Lee's home office. Should I bring anything else beside his laptop and the bag with the charger and cables?"

D'laine looked pensive. "I just had a thought. If it's been ten years, will the laptop still be there? Maybe the house is no longer my father's."

Stanley, Ben and Victor looked shocked.

"That's right. The house could belong to someone else," Ben said.

"I should go with you," D'laine said.

"You're not leaving without me!" Trakon said. "We shouldn't separate."

D'laine stood. "Okay. We should hold hands so we stay together." She faced the others. "We should be back shortly."

D'laine, Trakon and Stanley firmly gripped hands. Within a blink they were no longer in Victor's living room.

THEY POPPED INTO LEE'S OLD OFFICE. D'LAINE FOUND THE LIGHT switch on the wall and the room lit up. The desk surface was bare, the chair pushed up to the desk. D'laine looked around the room in dumbstruck silence.

"Looks like my fathers office hasn't been touched," D'laine said.

Suddenly, the ratcheting of a shotgun sounded behind them.

"Don't move, you thieving robbers!" Eric said.

"Eric?" D'laine asked. She turned around.

Rosa was half-hidden behind her husband. D'laine blinked away her shock at seeing how old her father's housekeeper and husband were. They appeared to be in their fifties.

"D'laine!" Rosa screeched. She flew around her husband and grabbed the girl in a hug. She wailed and shook as she clung to D'laine. Finally, she moved an arms length away and stared.

"You're still a young girl. How could that be?" Eric propped the shotgun against the wall.

"I'm so glad to see you, Rosa. We didn't know if the house would still be here, or if someone else owned it," D'laine said.

Rosa patted her chest to calm herself. "Your father willed the house and property to us. He was declared dead last year. It's been so sad for us."

"He also left a ton of money to be used for taxes, repairs and insurance," Eric said. "We left his office alone—Rosa packed up his things, but this is sort of like a sacred space."

"Rosa, Eric, this is Trakon, my intended—my fiancé," D'laine said. "Use the handshake, not the arm grip," she whispered to Trakon.

Trakon nodded. He shook hands with each of them.

"Rosa, do you remember Stanley Daigle? He was one of the scientists who investigated my disappearance."

"Oh, Mr. Stanley. You haven't grown older either!" Rosa said.

"We've just figured that out today," Stanley said. "Lee wants his laptop and the computer case. Do you still have it?"

Rosa crossed the room to the closet. She pushed some things out of the way and grabbed the computer case. "Yes, it's all here. I put all the little things that go to it in the case."

Stanley took the case, set it on the desk and unzipped it. He poked around. "Looks like all the cables are here. We're going to try to find a way to charge the laptop."

D'laine had a moment. "Rosa, do you know where the cord to my Kindle is?"

"It's in the wall socket by your bed," she said.

D'laine turned to Trakon. "Want to see my bedroom?"

They ran up the stairs. D'laine opened the door to her room. Nothing had changed. Trakon walked to D'laine's shrine.

"These are some of your deities?" He asked.

"These are old-world gods and goddesses, but not many people pray to them anymore," she said sadly.

She pulled the cord out of the wall. At least her device would be charged, but she didn't know if the charge would last on Thol. D'laine grabbed several of her crystals from various surfaces and stuffed them into her pouch.

"We'd better get going," she said. They went back downstairs and joined the others in her father's office.

Rosa and Eric took in the Thol uniforms.

"Where have you been? Is everyone okay?" Eric asked. D'laine thought about her response. She remembered Eric was an avid *Star Trek* fan, so she figured he'd understand. "Thol is a lateral plane of existence—another dimension, Eric. It's like a slice away from Earth, if you can wrap your head around that. I love it there. My father and brothers wouldn't give up Thol for anything."

"Trakon, show them how to change your suit to your battle suit," Stanley said. "We should show Victor and Ben when we go back to the house."

Trakon pressed the button at his wrist. Eric and Rosa's eyes widened as they watched the suit transform amid the clacking of what looked like metal, helmet included.

Eric stepped up to Trakon. "May I?"

Trakon nodded.

Eric touched the material. "Feels like steel! Isn't it heavy?"

"No, it's very light, but it's hard to penetrate," Trakon said.

Rosa gawked.

Trakon pressed another button and the battle uniform transformed into the typical jumpsuit he usually wore.

"We have to go, but I'm hoping my father can come back to see you soon," D'laine said. She fiercely hugged Rosa then Eric. "Thank you for everything you have ever done for me."

Rosa sobbed and nodded.

Trakon held one of D'laine's hands while Stanley gripped the other. He latched onto the laptop case. In a blink, they were gone.

THEY POPPED BACK INTO VICTOR'S LIVING ROOM. "HOW LONG were we gone?" Stanley asked.

"Around half an hour or forty-five minutes," Ben said.

Kara's coloring had returned. She looked healthy. She stood and took D'laine's hands in hers.

"I don't know how to thank you for saving my life." She sighed deeply. "I didn't accept the story Victor told me years ago about your returning to Earth and all that happened. He told our son, but I'm so ashamed at how I treated him. There was a point where I assumed he was borderline crazy."

Kara started sobbing. "I can't get over the fact that you cured me. Ripped the cancer right out of my brain!"

Darren piped up. "I tried to tell you she cured Brian, Mom."

Kara wrapped an arm around Darren. "I know, Darren. I just would not—actually could not accept that was anything other than a fairytale. But it looks like we have our own personal fairy godmother!"

"Now we have confirmation it's possible to travel back and forth," Stanley said.

"Not only that, but I can send telepathic messages from Thol. We didn't have any proof before," D'laine said.

Darren's face lit up. "Can I visit Thol?"

D'laine raised her eyebrows in question to Trakon.

Trakon shrugged. "I don't see why not."

Darren raised his fist in victory.

"Victor, don't forget the ten-to-one ratio of time. If you're going to visit, you'd better do it soon," Stanley said.

Darren grabbed the remote and turned on the TV.

When he saw the explosions and heard the gunfire from some action movie, Trakon jumped and reached for his laser pistol.

"Are you under attack?" Trakon pressed the button at his sleeve and his suit transformed.

"No! This is a movie, like I tried to explain to you one time. Everything you see on the screen is for entertainment purposes. The people are actors and they get paid to run, jump, shoot—all the action is made up. It's not really happening," D'laine explained.

Trakon hurried to the front door and jerked it open. It was quiet in the neighborhood. "Huh. I'll have to search our archives and see if we had entertainment such as this."

Victor, Darren and Ben touched Trakon's battle uniform.

"Wow. Just with the push of a button this transforms?" Victor asked.

"You would not believe the ease of life on Thol," Stanley said. "Oh! Before I forget. I brought you something." He dug into one of his pockets and pulled out two seed pods. He handed one to Ben and one to Victor.

"These are from the agrin tree on Thol. One seed will create a complete forest within one year. These are immense trees that dwarf the redwoods so plan carefully where you want to plant one seed. It should be placed in the middle of the area. The seed will grow into the mother tree and will communicate to her children trees.

"The sap from these trees is used in manufacturing ships, clothing—practically everything. It's almost indestructible and has its own healing abilities. For instance, if I tore my suit, it would repair itself instantly."

Stanley pulled a small knife out of one of his pockets. He slashed the sleeve of his uniform. Within moments, the fibers wove themselves together.

Ben and Victor watched in amazement.

"Wow, Dad, think of the money you'd save on my school clothes!" Darren said.

"Yeah, you should only plant one seed where a forest has been devastated by fire, or clear cut, but definitely not near any development," D'laine said.

Stanley pulled something else out of his pocket. He tapped it on Victor's palm. "This, my friend, is a holographic pen. I don't know if it's going to work here. On Thol, if you sketch something on paper or any surface, you can raise it up in the air into a holographic version of what you drew."

Stanley looked around, snatched up a magazine and sketched a crestrider with the pen. Then he pinched the drawing with his fingers and raised it up to eye level. Sure enough, it worked on Earth. The ship floated before them.

"This is a crestrider. They're awesome! Trakon's working on a solar design so they have lights and power at nighttime. They had a big war long ago that destroyed all their technology. While some things have been developed and improved upon, others, like night flying, are behind the times."

"We really should go," D'laine said.

Victor, Ben and Darren moaned.

"You just got here! There's so much I want to discuss," Ben said.

Victor grabbed D'laine into a heartfelt hug. "I can't thank you enough for saving my wife. Giving her back to us."

"Thank Thol for that. Thol gifted me these powers," D'laine said. "I'm so happy I could do that for you, after everything you did for my family."

"Don't forget, I'm coming to visit you!" Darren said.

D'laine's face lit. "I'll send you an invitation to my wedding!"

"Would it be okay to take a picture of the three of you?" Victor asked.

"Sure," D'laine and Stanley said.

They grabbed Trakon and the three stood together while Ben and Victor snapped pictures with their phones. They showed Trakon the pictures.

"Huh. That's a good picture," Trakon said. "I wonder if it could be transferred to my communicator?"

"How would you do that?" Stanley asked.

"Hold your device and I'll try to capture the picture," Trakon said. He opened his communicator and clicked on a menu. Then he aimed his communicator at the phones and clicked. After fiddling around with the controls, he displayed the pictures from the two cellphones.

"Oh, wow! It worked!" D'laine said.

She had Trakon take pictures of Victor, Kara, Darren, and Ben.

"We need to go," Stanley urged.

CHAPTER TWENTY-TWO

*T*he SUV pulled up and parked in the same place at the beach they had vacated earlier. Everyone, including Kara, got out of the car and walked to the sign for the family gathering. It was approaching dawn. Soon the beach town would be waking. The visitors from Thol had to make their exit without being recorded. The last thing they wanted was a YouTube video showing them leaving Earth.

They said their goodbyes with more than a few tears.

D'laine grabbed one of Trakon's hands, and Stanley's.

They stepped forward—only to step onto sand again.

"Oh, no!" D'laine looked around. "Let's try moving slightly to the right."

They adjusted their position and stepped forward again.

"We're not staying here!" Trakon roared.

"Calm down. You're not helping." D'laine glared at him.

"Try to get through to Brian," Stanley said.

"What seems to be the matter?" Ben asked.

"The portal doorway shifted." Stanley shrugged. "It happens. They're forever floating."

They moved away from the sign where they had entered Earth. D'laine stared ahead focused on her brother.

Nothing. No connection whatsoever.

"Don't panic. Remember, there's always Ghury!" Stanley said.

"Someone better get us off this noisy, polluted planet!" Trakon was livid.

D'laine held her hand out for quiet. She pulled up The Voice. *"BRIAN! We can't get home!"*

Several feet away, they heard Brian. "Move over here!"

"Thank Thol!" Trakon hauled Stanley and D'laine to the place where they heard Brian.

They repeated their goodbyes, stepped forward together and disappeared.

Trakon dropped to the moss and kissed the ground.

D'laine nudged him with her boot. "What a weenie!"

"Weenie? Do I even want to know what that insult means?" Trakon grumbled.

Stanley nudged Trakon. "Are you saying you didn't have faith in D'laine to get you home?"

"I can't win!" Trakon sulked.

Brian, Jamie and Lee stood in the field, arms crossed.

"What was so bad? You were only gone an hour... uh, chack," Lee said.

Trakon appeared confused. "Only a chack? Are you sure? Chacks went by on Earth."

"Check your communicator," Lee said.

"Remember, Trakon, it's a ten-to-one ratio," Stanley said. They all started walking to the palace.

"Great! We can take a nap before breakfast!" Trakon smiled at the irony.

A FULL-SIZED BORJO LANDED IN THE COURTYARD. HERISH AND Meeri jumped down and strode to the palace. A guard greeted them with the traditional fist to the chest.

"Prince Herish, Princess Meeri. Shall I summon Prince Trakon and Princess D'laine?"

"Enough with the prince and princess thing!" Herish crossed his arms. "Just contact them and tell them we're here."

Meeri poked Herish with her elbow. "Don't be a jerk."

Pup, Chatter and Buffy flew out of the palace followed by D'laine. Trakon trotted to catch up.

Meeri sank to the ground. "Oh, look at this cute animal!"

"That's Buffy. She was our family dog on Earth and managed to jump through the portal," D'laine said.

Buffy started when she saw the giant borjo. She barked nonstop.

"Buffy! Quiet!" D'laine said. "She has a lot to learn. My main concern is to make sure she doesn't run after the dogs when they go hunting. It could be disastrous once their instincts take hold."

"They look like friends," Meeri said.

"They are. Pup loves her, but diwals lose all control once they go into a feeding frenzy," D'laine said.

"Come inside. Have you eaten?" Trakon asked. They all went into the palace to the small salon. The majordomo appeared with refreshments.

"So, what have you two been up to lately?" Herish shoved what looked like pate´ on a cracker in his mouth.

"You would not believe it!" Trakon jumped into the trip to Earth story.

"Oh, my Thol! What if you couldn't get back home?" Meeri gasped.

D'laine gave Trakon the stink eye. "There was never any real concern. My brother Brian can see the portals. Then there are always the Egroms to help."

Trakon's eyes turned to slits as his anger surfaced. "You would not believe how utterly horrible her home world is! All the noise, outdated technology—they ride in ground vehicles on roadways that are full of holes..."

Meeri harrumphed. "Looks like someone needs to go through the archives and look at Thol around fifteen hundred or two thousand years ago. We were a mess until someone—I can't recall who—got us on the track to where we were before the war."

"D'laine's father and their Earthling friend Stanley are helping with the crestrider upgrades so we can fly at night," Trakon said. "Her father is very analytical and sees things in 3D."

"He worked with the space agency on Earth," D'laine said. "And Stanley is a genius." She told them about the fiasco with Adrum.

Trakon and Herish munched away.

"Yeah, but he no longer has to wear that helmet. The Oola-rooloo fixed the problem in his brain so no one has to worry he may accidentally drain them," Trakon said.

"Actually, it wasn't the Oolarooloo. It was an Earthling who lives with them who is a great healer," D'laine said.

"Why don't you get Jamie's borjo and we can all go for a ride?" Herish said.

Trakon jumped to his feet. "Let's go!"

D'laine pressed her communicator and called Jamie. "Hey, can Trakon and I ride Ekka? Herish and Meeri are here and we want to go for a ride."

"Sure. Ekka can talk to you so you don't need me to tag along." There was a noise in the background.

"What's that noise? What are you doing?" D'laine asked. Trakon raised his eyebrows.

"Oh, nothing."

D'laine let her focus soften. She picked up a clear vision of her younger brother. "What are you doing in the hosk building?"

"Stop snooping on me!"

"He should be okay there," Trakon said.

D'laine ground her eyes into Trakon. "This is the kid who made a pet of an og, brought home a borjo, and tried to talk to that worm-snake thing…"

Trakon thumped his communicator. "Jamie, tell me right now what you're doing or I'm coming over there."

"For crying out loud! I'm just talking to them! They miss their families," Jamie spouted out.

They all looked at each other.

"You should take this up with my father," Trakon said. "Tell him what the problem is and what the hosks are saying."

"Oh, okay, I will. Now leave me alone!" Jamie closed the communication down.

"Leave it to my brother to find a problem that no one ever thought of." D'laine shook her head.

"I think it's pretty awesome that he can talk to animals," Meeri said.

"Yeah, how many people do you know who can hear what the animals say?" Herish said.

They walked outside.

"Call Ekka so we don't have to climb all those stairs to his tower," Trakon said.

"Honestly, you sure are bossy this turn!" D'laine reached out to Ekka.

They looked to the sky, and the borjo soared from the turret to the ground. Ekka towered over Herish's borjo and seemed to be posturing in an unfriendly manner.

"Ekka! Be good! This borjo—Herish, what's your borjos name?"

"Name? He doesn't have a name." Herish balked.

"You idiot!" Meeri glared at Herish. "His name is Puando."

Herish and Trakon shrugged.

"Ekka, this is Puando. Be nice to him so we can have a good time flying," D'laine said.

The four friends mounted the two borjos, and they took off, Ekka in the lead.

EKKA GLIDED OVER THE FIELDS OF BRIGHTLY COLORED MOSS WITH Puando a head's length behind him. D'laine sensed the superiority attitude of Jamie's borjo. She decided to discuss this with her brother when they returned.

Both Herish and Trakon were acting like boys—albeit excited boys—flying at breakneck speeds. The borjos performed like aerial stars and their passengers hung on while the beasts tipped, dipped, and flew circles in the sky with Meeri and D'laine screaming with glee.

After more than a hour, the women took control and made the men return to the palace. They landed in the courtyard and dismounted. Neither D'laine nor Trakon had worn a helmet and their hair was a wild, tangled mess. Meeri and Herish had a little more common sense since they rode borjos all the time.

Jamie ran up to greet Ekka. "Did you have a good time with Herish and Meeri?"

Ekka rubbed his snout against Jamie's chest.

"Jamie, you need to have a talk with Ekka. Tell him how fortunate he is because he wasn't neutered when he was a newborn," D'laine said. "He was treating Puando as if he were inferior because Puando could morph."

"Huh. I'll have a talk with him," Jamie said.

Trakon rubbed his hands through his hair. "I'd rather fly a borjo than a crestrider!"

Jor-Dan stepped out of the palace with Marrak at his side. "What's that, son?"

"Father, have you ever ridden a borjo?" Trakon quickly came up with a plan. "Jamie, why don't you take the king for a short ride on Ekka?"

Jamie's face lit up. "Grandpa! You'd love it!"

"Oh, I don't know," Jor-Dan said.

Not waiting, Jamie jumped up on Ekka's back. "Come on, Grandpa! We'll go slow."

Jor-Dan let out a sigh and climbed up in back of Jamie. "No crazy stunts, young man!"

Once Jamie was sure Jor-Dan was situated and holding on firmly, he encouraged Ekka to take to the skies. After fifteen minutes, Ekka landed in the courtyard. A radiant Jor-Dan dismounted then helped Jamie down.

"That was pleasant and invigorating!" Jor-Dan said.

Trakon's face lit up. "The Plakado said Mount Aguberro was where all the full-sized borjos were. We should plan an expedition there!"

Jor-Dan patted Trakon on the shoulder. "Son, we have a wedding to plan. I think that takes precedence over your borjo expedition, don't you?"

D'laine and Meeri shook their heads. "At least you have Ekka," Herish said.

THE LARGE SALON WAS TEEMING WITH PEOPLE FOR THE END OF the month gathering. Every month, a diverse group of Ciertrons met in the salon to discuss the kingdom's growth, accomplishments, goods produced, problems (social and otherwise), and everything in between.

Lee thoroughly enjoyed these gatherings. It gave him a chance to meet more of the Ciertron community leaders and to understand what type of problems they experienced in this utopian world.

He and Marrak chatted while drinking kahl.

"Looks like Stanley is getting quite a bit of attention due to the missing helmet," Marrak said. They shared a chuckle.

Lee's eyes drifted across the room. A beautiful woman in a shimmering dress of yellow, orange and red gauze was staring at him. He was sure of it. A heart-shaped face with full lips and sparkling black eyes captivated Lee. She turned sideways after being caught staring. Her hair was in a large knot on the back of her head with strands almost to her waist.

Lee cleared his throat. He wondered how to approach this with Marrak—it's not like he and Marrak were best friends; at best they were acquaintances. The problem resolved itself.

Marrak nudged Lee. He pretended to talk into his glass.

"Lee, you have an admirer."

"I noticed. She's beautiful. Do you know who she is?" Lee swallowed hard. His mind was a whirlwind. How exactly did one go about dating on Thol? He needed to know how to avoid blunders so he didn't repeat his Queen Kansing mistake.

"Yes, her name is Ethaderia. She's rejected all suitors. Guess she has high standards," Marrak said.

Lee noticed a twinge of something in Marrak's statement. Maybe he had been one of the rejected?

"What are the protocols? Do I approach her and introduce myself for general conversation?"

"Ethaderia is Queen Kitry's cousin so you will need a formal introduction. That should be pretty easy," Marrak said.

"Oh! I wonder why she hasn't been to the palace—why I haven't seen her before," Lee said.

"Ethaderia was visiting her sister who lives far away in Kensadora. She has only recently returned after several months," Marrak said.

Lee's eyes skirted the room again. Ethaderia wasn't there. He felt disappointed.

After breakfast, Lee and Stanley joined Trakon in the workshop to review changes to the crystals on the wing surfaces of the crestriders. It had been an arduous task for the team to reconfigure the placement of the crystals. Through experimenting they also discovered that the crystals needed to be in a somewhat uniform shape.

Lee's suggestion to approach the Egroms for help paid off. Four of the white creatures gathered buckets of the crystals which grew naturally on Thol. Fields were covered with crystals. What was a challenge for the Ciertrons was child's play for the Egroms. They used their psychic laser abilities to cut the crystals for the ship's wings.

Lee, Stanley and Trakon looked over the crystal-coated wings on two test crestriders in the workshop. They were amazed at how precisely the crystals were shaped, making the positioning on the wings an easier task. They all fit perfectly like pieces in a jigsaw puzzle.

The two vehicles were soaking up the suns, charging for a test that very night.

"We'll give it another shot tonight after dinner when both suns have set," Trakon said.

CHAPTER TWENTY-THREE

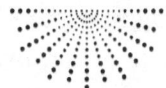

*A*t lunchtime they called it quits. Trakon, Lee and Stanley walked back to the palace, cleaned up, then entered the dining salon. Jor-Dan, D'laine and the boys were there but Kitry was missing.

Lee discovered an extra place setting on the table. He took his seat and waited for the queen to join them with her guest.

After a few moments of small talk, they heard Kitry's voice in the hallway. She entered the dining salon arm in arm with Ethaderia. Being the gentleman that he was, Lee stood as the women entered the room.

"Ethaderia, since you have been gone, Trakon has become engaged," said Kitry. "This is his betrothed, D'laine, her father Lee, her brothers Brian and Jamie, and their scientist friend Stanley Daigle," Kitry said.

Kitry smiled directly at Lee. "Ethaderia is my cousin and one of my best friends. She was away visiting her sister in Kensadora and has just recently returned."

They sat, and the majordomo supervised the serving of the meal. Ethaderia sat beside Kitry; Lee sat across the table and two seats down. His eyes kept drifting to the beautiful woman.

Boys, being what they are, Brian and Jamie jumped right in with their turn's activities.

"The Youngmen are interested in forming their own baseball team," Brian said. "We've been talking about positions, colors and stuff. We're going to find out if other kingdoms want to participate in a Youngmen's competition."

"Excellent!" Jor-Dan boomed. He was overly enthusiastic in anything regarding baseball, much to Kitry's chagrin.

"Dannin took me over to the pakow pens. One of the young bulls was causing a lot of trouble," Jamie said. "I talked to him. He was mad because a wild bull kept trying to break into the pen to steal his herd. We're going to search for the wild bull and I'll ask him to quit doing that."

Ethaderia leaned forward to see Jamie. "You talk to animals?"

The towhead nodded. "Yeah, that's my gift. All animals like me and we talk."

"You and your sister seem to have that gift. Kitry told me D'laine tamed the wild diwal dogs," Ethaderia said.

Understanding the word *dog*, Pup got to his feet and approached the queen's cousin. He rested his chin on her thigh.

Ethaderia held her hand back, unsure if it was really safe to pet the dog.

"It's okay. He won't attack," Kitry said.

Ethaderia timidly stretched her hand out and scratched the tuft of hair on Pup's head. Her eyes darted over to Lee.

"Your children have remarkable talents!"

"We are grateful for the gifts Thol has bestowed upon us," Lee said. "On Earth we were normal human beings. We did not stand out among our fellow men and women."

Ethaderia shook her head. "I seriously doubt you were common people. Greatness knows no dimensional boundaries."

Lee blushed slightly. "That's kind of you to say, but we really were regular people."

D'laine gave a little grunt. "My father is so modest. He

worked for NASA, the space agency of Earth, and has many patents—registered designs of things he has invented."

"Yeah, our dad is extremely smart," Brian said.

Jamie smiled goofily as if he had a secret. "Where do you live?"

"My home is not far. If you stand outside the palace doors and look to your right, you will see my family's banners flying. They are blue, purple and green. When my mother is in residence, you will also notice a banner with red among those colors."

"I'm glad you don't live far away," Jamie said. "I like you. You're pretty and I can tell you're smart, like the queen."

"Oh, boy." Lee waited for the laughter around the table to die down. "Why don't you go check on those pakows, Jamie?"

Jamie swiped his napkin across his mouth and scurried out of his chair. "See you later, daddy!"

"Stay out of trouble!"

After everyone finished lunch, Kitry and Ethaderia entered the small salon followed by the rest of the family.

"How is your sister settling in?" Jor-Dan asked.

"She has many obstacles in her marriage," Ethaderia said. "The palace was rather barbaric and the groom's mother is downright hostile toward her."

"Oh, no," Jor-Dan said.

"I helped her create a palace worthy of the kingdom and her husband, the new king of Kensadora," Ethaderia said. "Now it is inviting and comfortable."

Kitry patted Ethaderia on the back of her hand. "I suggested that they move the old queen to the smaller palace, where she will most likely be happier."

"Two strong-minded women shouldn't be under the same roof," Lee said. "I can foresee plenty of conflict in that arrangement. Do you think the old queen will move?"

"I hope so for my sister's sake." Ethaderia stood. "I must be going."

Kitry and Lee stood. "Lee, why don't you walk Ethaderia home?"

Lee bowed his head slightly. "I'd love to."

LEE AND ETHADERIA WALKED THE SHORT DISTANCE TO HER HOME.

"I'm helping Kitry with the wedding arrangements for Trakon and your daughter," Ethaderia said. "Everyone in the kingdom is excited. They have been waiting a long time for Trakon to take a wife."

"I like Trakon. He's a good match for D'laine," Lee said.

Ethaderia stopped walking and studied Lee's face. "And what about you? Kitry told me your wife died in a terrible accident. Please don't think I'm brazen for speaking my mind, but I'm not getting any younger and I have not found a mate that is worthy."

Lee glanced at the ground. He looked up and met her inquisitive eyes. "Back on Earth, I hadn't given any thought to remarrying. Thol has forced me to look at things differently. The entire way of life here is so much better than Earth. I would like someone to share my life with."

"Would you consider me as a prospective life partner?" Ethaderia asked.

"I am very interested in getting to know you better," Lee said. "You do realize that I have two young sons—we're a package deal."

"Your young men are adorable. They would be excellent older brothers," she said with a twinkle in her eyes.

"Ethaderia, you haven't been here to witness what they've gotten into so far. Especially Jamie, my youngest." Lee shook his head. "He can be a handful. He's wrapped Jor-Dan around his little finger. The king just can't say no to him."

They continued walking and soon came to the door of the sprawling sandstone mansion.

"Thank you for escorting me home." Ethaderia extended her hand to Lee.

Knowing full well what he was doing this time, he bent and kissed her fingertips. As he straightened, their eyes met. Before him stood a happy woman.

Lee returned to the palace. Hearing voices in the small salon, he headed that way.

Kitry's eyes jumped to him. "Well?"

"I'm smitten," Lee said.

Kitry appeared pleased. "Ethaderia and I will be planning Trakon and D'laine's wedding celebration. We could always make it a double wedding."

Lee held up a hand. "Not so fast! I need to adjust to thinking about taking another wife."

JAMIE SPIED ON HIS FATHER. AS SOON AS LEE ENTERED THE palace, Jamie ran to Ethaderia's home and knocked on the large door.

A manservant answered the door. "How may I help you?"

"I'm here to speak with Ethaderia," Jamie said.

The man opened the door and allowed Jamie entry. "Aren't you a little young to be calling on the lady?"

"Heck, no. Is she here?" Jamie asked, knowing that she was.

"Who may I say is calling?" the man asked.

"Jamie Jackson, princess D'laine's brother."

"If you'll wait here, I'll fetch the lady."

A few moments later, Ethaderia appeared with a full smile on her face. "Welcome to my home, Master Jamie. What can I do for you?"

Jamie was all seriousness. "I thought we should get to know each other better, if you're going to be my second mother."

Ethaderia brought her hands together. "Well, in that case, we should learn more about each other, shouldn't we?"

A hour later, Jamie left Ethaderia's home and skipped back to the palace, extremely pleased with himself.

THE NEXT MORNING ETHADERIA AND KITRY WERE SEQUESTERED in the sitting room of the queen's private suite. They giggled like school girls as Ethaderia related the story about Jamie's visit.

"That boy has a way not with just animals, but with people as well," Kitry said.

"He definitely seemed to be staking his claim on me as a potential mother," Ethaderia said.

Kitry made a face. "He was so upset when I introduced his father to Kansing. He doesn't want to leave Ebscalon."

Ethaderia balked. "You tried to pair Lee with Kansing? How could you!"

"For Thol's sake, you weren't here, and I had no idea when you would return," Kitry said. "I know you don't like Kansing…"

"She eats men for breakfast and doesn't even spit out their teeth!" Ethaderia spluttered the words. She was furious with her cousin. "Lee is too gentle and kind for her type."

"Will you calm down? Jamie put a stop to that before Lee could act upon it. Lee inadvertently kissed her fingertips— he didn't know what that meant and was following a custom from Earth for greeting a queen. I have already told Kansing that Lee was not a suitor and that his sons would not approve of the liaison," Kitry said.

Ethaderia dipped her head for a moment as a bit of shyness overcame her. "He kissed my fingertips."

KITRY AND ETHADERIA WALKED THROUGH THE MARKETPLACE TO an enclosed shop. Ulavia, a well-known seamstress throughout the land, welcomed them into her place. Bolts of fabric and accessories graced shelves and surfaces.

"What can I help you with, Your Majesty?" Ulavia was tall and stately with copper-colored skin that glowed. Her black hair was in a knot at the top of her head with stragglers around her oval face. Ulavia's dark eyes were lit with her smile.

"I would like to commission you to make princess D'laine's wedding dress," Kitry said. "There is no other designer I would entrust this garment to, Ulavia."

The seamstress pressed her hand to her heart. "Oh, Your Majesty, thank you for honoring me with this project. I will create the most beautiful garment for the princess!"

"Make sure there are no crystals on the fabric," Kitry warned. "The princess's energy charges them and they shock her."

Ulavia pressed her fingers to her mouth. "Oh, dear. Don't worry, we have many options."

She hurried to a section of her shop and pulled several bolts of cloth. She placed them on a large cutting table in the middle of the floor. Ulavia loosened several inches of material from each bolt so it could be rubbed between the fingers.

"Do you like any of these materials?" the seamstress asked. "This material would be for the top layer of the dress."

Ulavia returned to the shelves and retrieved more bolts of fabric.

Kitry and Ethaderia approached the table. The cloth was exquisite like the finest chiffon.

"We have similar tastes, cousin," Kitry said. They both chose a shimmering white fabric with delicate purple flowers that contained gold threads.

"These bolts are for the under layer of a dress," Ulavia said.

This cloth was similar to taffeta, but the fabric glowed with radiant colors.

Kitry and Ethaderia reached for the same bolt of material. It radiated a lilac hue that would complement the lovely upper layer of material. They giggled.

"This was easier than I expected," Kitry said.

"D'laine's beauty will be enhanced by this dress. The material is stunning," Ethaderia said.

"The final decision for fabric is up to D'laine, though," Kitry said.

"When will I be able to measure the princess?" Ulavia asked.

"I will see to it that she arrives this turn," Kitry said. "Perhaps you can show her some designs."

Ulavia bowed her head slightly. "Of course, Your Majesty."

LEE AND D'LAINE ENTERED THE DRESSMAKER'S SHOP.

Ulavia came forward. She pressed her hand to her heart.

"Welcome, princess D'laine! Welcome Lee Jackson! The queen and her cousin were here earlier and chose material for your wedding dress," Ulavia said. "These are only suggestions. I can show you many more bolts of fabric so you can make your decision."

She guided them over to the large table where the two bolts of fabric lay.

D'laine stared in wonder at the fabric. "Oh, this is so beautiful!"

Lee had been mother and father to his children since his wife Lori died, but he felt slightly uncomfortable in this particular situation. His daughter's wedding finery should have been something she chose with her mother's advice.

"Would you be more comfortable with the queen or her cousin helping you?" he asked D'laine.

D'laine glanced at her father. She sensed his discomfort—she knew he was out of his element. "Maybe Ethaderia could help me. She's younger than the queen, but she knows all the customs."

Lee nodded, relief flooding his face. "I'll contact her." He pressed his communicator as he walked out the door.

Ethaderia answered his request to talk. "Hello, Lee."

"Ethaderia, I need your help. D'laine and I are at the dress shop…"

"I can feel your stress from my home! I'll be right there," Ethaderia said.

"I can't thank you enough. I am fully aware when my decisions are useless," Lee said.

Lee returned to D'laine in the shop. "Ethaderia will be here shortly."

D'laine hugged her father. "Thanks, daddy. I know this is difficult for you. I wish Mommy were here for all of us, but I have a hunch Ethaderia is a close second."

Lee blushed. The door opened and Ethaderia entered.

She walked up to them and patted Lee on the arm.

"You look very uncomfortable in this shop. Why don't you go and find Trakon or Jor-Dan?" Ethaderia winked at D'laine.

Lee hugged D'laine. He kissed Ethaderia's fingertips. "Thank you!" He left the shop.

"Men are out of their element among bolts of fabric. Do you like the material the queen and I picked out? This is your dress for your special celebration." Ethaderia swept one arm wide. "As you can see, there are many choices."

"It's beautiful! I most likely would have chosen this same fabric," D'laine said.

"Shall we look at some dress designs?" Ethaderia asked.

Ulavia stepped up with a thick binder. She placed it on the

table and opened it to the first dress. She tapped the center of the dress, and it became a holograph that turned slowly.

"Oh! I didn't know you could do that. It makes the pictures practically come to life!" D'laine was giddy with excitement. She turned the page and tapped the next dress design.

Two dresses were in front of her.

"You have to tap the design again to make the holograph disappear," Ulavia said.

"Oh." D'laine turned back one page and tapped the center of the dress on the page. The holograph shrank back into the page.

D'laine and Ethaderia went through all the wedding dress designs. Three dresses floated in the air above the book. Ethaderia spread them out so D'laine could study each. After several moments, she decided.

"I like this one the best," D'laine said.

"Me, too," Ethaderia said. She one-arm hugged D'laine. Their faces were alight with huge smiles. "You will outshine all the princesses of Thol."

CHAPTER TWENTY-FOUR

One of the palace guards entered the dining salon. He hit his chest in greeting.

"Prince Trakon, I'm sorry to interrupt your evening meal, but a delegate from the Cember Forest is here to see you."

Trakon and Jor-Dan exchanged questioning looks. D'laine and Trakon looked at each other and shrugged.

The entire family, as well as Stanley, followed the palace guard outside. Sure enough, a lone Kudaja waited beside his full-sized borjo.

The man hit his chest. "Your Majesties. Your Highnesses—Prince Trakon. Princess D'laine." He nodded to the other family members. Reaching into his pouch, he pulled out a scroll tied with a delicate piece of green vine and handed it to Trakon. "From Prince Herish and Princess Meeri."

With that, the man jumped on his borjo and flew away.

"Open it!" D'laine nudged Trakon.

Trakon slipped the vine off the scroll and unrolled it. He read it out loud.

To: Your Royal Highnesses:

Prince Trakon and Princess D'laine
Please honor us with your presence at the Endings Celebration of
Prince Herish Cagmondoore and
Princess Meeri Glascombe
Within two weeks from this day.
Contact Prince Herish for directions to this event.

"They're getting married way before us," Trakon said.

"What's an *endings* celebration?" D'laine asked.

"It's a huge party with a lot of speeches, presents, food and dancing," Trakon explained. "Occasionally some rowdy drunken brawls, but mostly a nice gathering."

"Sounds like a combination bachelor and bachelorette party," Lee said.

"I never would have thought they would have those customs here," Stanley said.

"These aren't wild parties, are they?" Lee asked. "Some of these parties on Earth can get pretty outrageous!"

"No, these celebrations are very sedate," Kitry said.

"Why is it called an *endings* celebration?" D'laine asked.

"It's the end of their single years. They will be starting a new life together," Kitry said.

"I wonder if this party will be in the Cember Forest, or at Meeri's village." D'laine asked. "Remember, she said that most of them didn't morph. They're full-sized people and borjos."

"No, she said most of the females didn't morph, remember?" Trakon added.

D'laine thought a bit. "Oh, you're right." She turned to Kitry. "What do female guests wear to endings celebrations?"

"They're forest creatures so I'll bet Meeri's village is actually in a forest," Jor-Dan said.

"Not to worry," Kitry said. "You would wear clothing similar to what I wear. After dinner, let's look at your dresses." She turned to the group. "Shall we dine?"

THE TWO WEEKES FLEW BY. D'LAINE HANDED TRAKON A BAG WITH changes of clothes for both of them. He looked handsome in his official uniform instead of the customary jumpsuit. D'laine wore one of the flowing dresses that Kitry recommended, along with ballet slippers that laced up her calves.

These weren't the typical Earth ballet slippers. The soles were created with the silk from Hosks along with sap from the agrin tree that made things practically indestructible. With the material's ability to repair itself, clothing and shoes rarely wore out.

"I don't understand why you think we need a change of clothes," Trakon grumbled.

D'laine placed her hands on her hips. "Really? What if the crestrider doesn't work to get us home? What if we stay overnight? You don't want to get your uniform dirty. Your mother would not be happy."

Trakon colored slightly. "Oh."

"Yeah, oh! I try to think things through. Anything could come up." D'laine grabbed a heavy package and handed it to Trakon.

"What's this?" he asked.

"A present from the two of us."

"What is it?" Trakon frowned wondering what it was. He didn't remember D'laine showing him a present.

She blushed bright pink. "Something they want."

Trakon stared at her face then snickered. "The book! But—"

She ignored his guess and handed him another package. "This is an official Ebscalon present—you know, from your parents as the king and queen."

After he had stowed everything in the two-man flyer, he snickered again. "Maybe we should plan to break down so we have time by ourselves."

D'laine appeared haughty. "I'd expect Biggan to materialize out of thin air. He seems to crop up at the most unexpected and inconvenient times."

"Our parents probably think it's safe to let us go alone since we are returning tonight." Trakon nuzzled her.

D'laine jabbed him with her elbow. "Not here! You'll have our chaperone in the ship before you can blink!"

Trakon jumped back, startled. He eyed the immediate area for the guard.

When everything was stowed properly, they returned to the palace. First, they went in search of Lee. They found him in his suite absorbed in baseball. He stopped what he was doing and focused on them.

"All set for Herish and Meeri's celebration?" Lee asked.

"Yes. We're going to leave as soon as we see Trakon's parents," D'laine said.

"Did you find a nice gift at the market?" Lee asked.

"Yes! The market has everything anyone could possibly want," D'laine said.

Lee stood. He hugged D'laine, and he and Trakon shook hands. Trakon liked the Earth custom.

"Make sure you contact me when you arrive at the Cember Forest so I don't worry about you," Lee said.

"We will." D'laine kissed him on the cheek.

They went in search of Kitry and found her in her suite working at her loom. They said their goodbyes. Jor-Dan was tied up with meetings so they just waved from the doorway.

As they were leaving the palace, Jamie was coming in. "Jamie, take care of the dogs until we get back. They're in my suite," D'laine said.

"Okay. They'll be fine. Make sure you take some mind movies so Brian and I can see what the party is like," Jamie said.

"I promise." D'laine ruffled his hair.

TRAKON FOLLOWED HERISH'S DIRECTIONS TO THE KUDAJA location in the Cember Forest. As they arrived in the vicinity, there were full-sized Kudaja positioned to wave them on to the area set up for ship parking.

As the crestrider settled to the ground, another ship parked beside them to the right. An older, dignified couple disembarked. The woman stared through D'laine and Trakon and raised her nose to the air. As they walked away D'laine grumbled.

"That woman was telling her husband that we should have had a royal escort, and we were too young to understand correct protocol," she said.

"That old gagu most likely doesn't get out much. Only my parents use a royal escort," Trakon said. "I wonder who that was."

"I don't know, but when we find Herish and Meeri, we can ask them." D'laine thrust his parents' gift at him. "Here." She grabbed the package that contained the book and they followed the path to the festivities.

The woodland was lit up with tiny twinkling globes. D'laine stared at the decorations. There were no cords, just lights that appeared to have been flung up into the trees.

"We have these types of lights back home, but they have to be connected with wires and plugged into a power source," D'laine said. "How are these powered?"

"They're crystal powered. The source lasts a long time. They'll stop glowing by mid-day tomorrow, then they'll recharge all afternoon," Trakon explained.

They wandered farther into the forest along the lit pathway. They arrived at a vast area crowded with people. Tables and chairs were scattered along the sidelines.

Suddenly both their eyes were covered by hands. Trakon

didn't take too well to the surprise and almost decked Herish. They play-squabbled while D'laine and Meeri looked on.

"Don't get your clothing mussed!" Meeri cajoled Herish. The men stopped goofing off and paid attention to their women.

Herish wore his dress uniform, similar to Trakon's. Meeri's dress was something out of a fairytale as far as D'laine was concerned. The beautiful sheer white fabric was covered with tiny specs of crystals while the undergarment was a delicate shimmering material. When the suns shown on the dress, it was breathtaking.

"Endings presents." D'laine nudged Trakon.

"From Ebscalon," Trakon said with an eye roll.

D'laine made a silly face as she handed Meeri the gift from her and Trakon. "Our present."

Meeri's mouth opened in an O. "Tell me it's the book!"

D'laine giggled. "I found one in the marketplace!"

Meeri and D'laine squealed and jumped up and down. Trakon and Herish looked on, amused but confused by the girlish behavior.

Meeri thrust the package at Herish. "Quick! Take this to your suite! We can't open it in front of anyone!"

Herish searched the room. He hailed a man dressed in Kudaja livery. Herish handed him the package. "Please take this to my suite and place it on the table in the front sitting room," he said.

The man fisted his chest, turned and left the celebration.

"When are you two getting married?" Herish asked.

"No telling. My mother and her cousin are making all the plans," Trakon said.

"Tell you what," Herish said with glee. "Meeri and I will let you know what page to turn to in the book."

Meeri elbowed Herish hard in the side. "Don't show your lower side, Herish!"

"Oh, do you know who these people are?" D'laine shared a mind vision of the older couple with Meeri and Herish.

"He's a retired general. Why?" Herish asked.

D'laine relayed what the old woman had said.

"Don't worry about them. They're ancient. The worst they can do is gripe to the royals," Meeri said.

Beautiful horns sounded.

"Oh! That's our cue!" Meeri squealed. She grabbed Herish's arm. "Grab a place to sit. Have fun."

She and Herish rushed off to the dais where the ceremony would take place.

Trakon led D'laine to a table close to the dais where two seats were empty.

"May we join you?" Trakon asked an elder at the table.

"Of course, Prince of Ebscalon! We would be honored."

The old man turned to D'laine. "Is this your first Tholian Endings celebration?"

"Yes. I'm interested to see what happens. Are all Tholian Endings celebrations performed in the same manner, or will the Kudaja's be different from our's in Ebscalon?"

"They are mostly the same with slight variations by kingdom. Enjoy. Looks like they're getting started."

D'laine's eyes were focused on the dais. A Kudaja Visionary started the ceremony.

"This Endings celebration brings together two of our young royals who approach a lifelong partnership: Prince Herish Cagmondoore and Princess Meeri Glascombe. We will toast the prince and princess and enjoy a feast and dancing."

D'laine and Trakon watched and listened as dozens upon dozens of people told stories about Herish and Meeri. Some were downright embarrassing but most were funny.

D'laine and Trakon laughed at most of the escapades.

They watched as Herish and Meeri made their way through

the swarm of people wishing them well. Eventually they stood before Trakon and D'laine.

"I'm so glad you invited us. I love these traditions," D'laine said.

"When all these boring official things are finished, we'll have our fun!" Herish whispered.

D'laine raised her brows at that while Trakon and Herish shared a gleeful exchange.

A chime sounded.

"Oh, we have to go sit at the head table. They're going to serve food now," Meeri said. She hugged D'laine. "I'm so glad you're here."

Meeri and Herish rushed off to the table where their parents and important officials waited. Trakon and D'laine sat at their table and waited for the food to be served.

"We better not get into any trouble, Trakon," she threatened.

"Just wait and see."

CHAPTER TWENTY-FIVE

D'laine stared in open-mouthed shock as she watched the dancing at Herish and Meeri's Endings celebration. She tapped her communicator and connected with her father.

"Daddy, you're not going to believe this, but they're dancing the minuet!"

"What exactly are you talking about?" Lee's face was scrunched up.

D'laine turned to Trakon. "How do I show my father the dancing?"

Trakon pressed a tiny button on the communicator. "Hold it up and point it to the people."

D'laine followed his instructions. She heard her father gasp. "I told you!"

"How could that be?" Lee looked as confused as she felt.

"Obviously, someone came through the portal in the eighteen-hundreds!" Stanley said as he glanced over Lee's shoulder.

"We're all going to need dancing lessons before my celebration!" D'laine almost panicked.

"It's not that difficult," Trakon said.

Three angry faces—Stanley, Lee and D'laine—said otherwise.

"Don't worry, my mother will organize everything. She probably hasn't thought about all the little details," Trakon said. "When we get back home, you can talk with her and Ethaderia about everything you witnessed at this celebration."

Stanley shook his head. "I'm not coordinated enough to dance like that. It's graceful, and you all know I'm not graceful."

"Stanley, if you want to have female companionship, you'd better learn to dance," Trakon said.

Stanley grumbled and walked off.

AFTER THE DANCING FINISHED, THE GIFTS WERE OPENED AND displayed for the guests. D'laine didn't recognize half of what Herish or Meeri held up to the guests.

Trakon leaned in and whispered in her ear. "This is where it gets good. Everyone will look over the gifts and make a note of who gave what. Then the gossip will start." He nodded ever so slightly at two women at their table who tsk-tsked as gifts were held up. "These two are criticizing a lot of things. Bet they don't realize that people will do the same for their gift as well."

D'laine slapped Trakon's arm. "You are so bad!"

Trakon looked quite confident. "You can bet the best gift came from us!"

They snickered then couldn't hold back full belly laughs.

Herish looked in their direction. He must have figured out what they were laughing about because he whispered in Meeri's ear. She giggled and waved three fingers their way.

After the gifts were opened, the adults were in dance and party mode. Herish and Meeri ducked through the crowd. Meeri grabbed D'laine's hand and the four of them, along with a half dozen young people, hurried through the trees. They arrived where several full-sized borjos were hunkered down.

"We'll have to double up. Come on, let's go," Herish said.

They all climbed onto the borjos and Herish led the way. The short flight brought them to a small clearing where a stack of wood waited to be lit into a bonfire.

They all dismounted and walked to the center of the clearing. Herish removed lighting stones from his pocket and lit the fire. He and Meeri walked over to a table and poured glasses of kahl. Meeri handed D'laine and Trakon each a glass. Their friends joined in and the real celebration began.

After drinking two glasses of kahl, and laughing uncontrollably, people were jumping around the fire as if it were a rock concert.

"Let's slide!" Herish yelled.

Everyone squealed in delight at the suggestion and headed to the trees.

"Where's everyone going? What are we doing?" D'laine yelled to Trakon as she ran with everyone else.

"You'll see. It's fun!" Trakon hollered to her.

Next thing she saw was Herish flying through the trees on a zip line, followed by Meeri and others.

"Oh! Me first!" D'laine hollered to Trakon.

They climbed the stairs of an enormous tree and the guy who was in charge of the zip line helped D'laine into the harness. He waited as she tucked her dress under her butt and away she flew, screeching in delight.

After several flights, they returned to the bonfire where everyone went into jumping mode as if they were listening to some secret tunes.

D'laine grabbed Trakon's arm to stop him from jumping. "Why is everyone jumping? Do you hear something I don't hear?"

"Oh!" He fumbled with her communicator and suddenly her

head was filled with the closest thing to music—resonating tones that was very close to rock and roll.

D'laine's eye bugged wide. She jumped with wild abandon.

"WE SHOULD BE GOING SOON," D'LAINE SAID.

Trakon glanced up at the sky through the treetops. "We have around three hours before the suns set."

"Let's go say goodbye to Herish and Meeri," D'laine said. They stood and made their way over to their friends.

"Leaving?" Meeri asked.

Trakon scowled. "If we don't get home by sunsfall, they'll send a search party."

Herish grinned. "Pretty soon we won't have to worry about that anymore!"

"Rub it in, why don't you?" Trakon shoved Herish gently. "What's next tonight?" D'laine asked.

"Herish and I will leave when you do. Everyone else will continue to enjoy the celebration," Meeri said.

"Will you have your own place to live, or will you live in the palace?" D'laine asked Meeri. She really didn't know how the forest people did things, or for that matter, even the people of Ebscalon.

"Herish never showed you around?"

D'laine shook her head.

Meeri grumbled. "Why am I not surprised? Come on, I'll show you the suite where we'll live, then you can take off."

They flew back to where they found the borjos and dismounted. Meeri linked her arm with D'laine's. Trakon and Herish followed. Meeri led them around a giant agrin tree until they came to a winding staircase built into the tree. They climbed up and up until they came to a wide walkway.

D'laine's eyes widened with astonishment. An entire city

stretched throughout the trees, unseen from the ground. Beautiful structures. She spotted what she thought was the Kudaja palace with its breathtaking architecture. It resembled the Taj Mahal with domes and spires, rounded archways of windows and doorways but on a much smaller scale. It took her breath away.

She noticed there were large structures and very small places. She figured it was because not all Kudaja could morph between the two sizes. D'laine thought back to her first encounter with them upon her arrival in the Cember Forest when hundreds of the tiny Kudaja had attacked her. If she hadn't used The Voice she wondered where she'd be this turn.

The two couples entered the palace. They walked what seemed like forever until they came to the suite where Herish and Meeri would live after their wedding. It was larger than D'laine's own suite, but she figured it was because they would both be living there. Other than that, it was similarly furnished.

"Oh, this is gorgeous!" D'laine said.

"We will each have our own private sitting areas along with a more public area for company," Meeri explained.

D'laine and Trakon stayed for another ten moments then bid their friends goodbye. Herish summoned an escort so they could find their way back to the crestrider.

They climbed aboard and Trakon guided the ship out of the still-crowded parking area. They noted the empty space where the ship of the nasty older couple had parked.

"Guess they left to go complain about something else," Trakon snipped.

After they had been traveling for a good half hour, Trakon hovered the ship.

"What's wrong?" D'laine looked at the controls. There was nothing out of the ordinary. All settings were in the normal or best performance range. She looked over the side of the ship to the ground below—only moss as far as the eye could wander.

"Nothing." Trakon swooped her into his arms and laid a passionate kiss on her.

They parted. Trakon lowered the escalator to the ground. He grabbed her hand and led her down the stairs. He tugged her to the ground where they wrapped around each other in a smoldering kiss.

Trakon kissed her face. He stared into her eyes, burning with passion. "I can't wait to marry you, D'laine. Do we really have to wait?"

Chest heaving, D'laine ran her fingers through his black hair. "Yes. It won't be long."

He gave her another quick kiss and rolled off her. Trakon stood, reached for her hand and pulled her to her feet. He brushed himself off, then swiped his hands down her sides and back, not daring to touch anywhere else.

"We'd better get back before we get into real trouble," D'laine said.

D'laine and Trakon stood smashed together staring into each other's eyes for several long moments. Then Trakon grabbed her hand and led her back to the ship. They climbed the stairs and Trakon put the ship in motion.

Arriving back at Ebscalon, Trakon landed the ship in the courtyard. He opened a compartment and grabbed their travel bag.

One of the guards hopped into the crestrider and zoomed it over to where the ships were stored.

Trakon and D'laine went into the palace to the small salon where the family typically spent time. Pup and Chatter rushed over to them. They squealed and squirmed as if they hadn't seen their people in months, instead of hours. Buffy rolled around the floor at D'laine's feet. She earned a belly rub.

"Did you have a good time?" Kitry asked.

"It was beautiful and interesting," D'laine said. "My family and I need dance lessons!"

"Yes, your father mentioned that as well. Your brothers don't like that idea at all." Kitry laughed.

Lee got to his feet. He glanced from Trakon to D'laine. He walked up to D'laine and dug a piece of moss out of her hair. He held it in front of Trakon.

"Would you like to tell us how this managed to get into my daughter's hair?" he asked.

Trakon swallowed. He and D'laine started talking loudly at the same time, each offering wildly unbelievable explanations.

Finally, D'laine blurted. "We were trying to make snow angels in the moss, daddy!"

Kitry and Trakon looked at her wondering what snow angels were.

D'laine dropped to the floor and started moving her arms and legs. "Moss angels—you know? Like snow angels! You should try it in the field sometime!"

Trakon jumped into the tale with his own embellishments. "D'laine taught me how to make a moss angel. It's fun!" His eyes swept the room. His mother raised an eyebrow while his father smirked behind his hand.

"Perhaps we should discuss the wedding date, Kitry, and let's not think in terms of months... uh kelds. It may be prudent to consider weeks," Lee suggested.

Kitry nodded, her eyes slitted at her son and future daughter-in-law. "D'laine's gown will be ready for a fitting in a week as well as the dress uniforms for you, Stanley, and the boys. I'll arrange for dancing lessons. There will be enough time for everyone to practice so you'll be proficient at the Endings and wedding ceremonies."

"We already have dress uniforms from the formal dinner," Lee said.

"Weddings require much more elegant wear," Kitry said. "These are our children, after all, the future king and queen of Ebscalon."

Lee nodded. He knew when to shut up.

"So, when will the wedding take place?" Trakon asked. "We need to tell Herish and Meeri."

"I will let you know tomorrow after I speak with Ethaderia," Kitry said.

"Where will Trakon and I live once we're married?" D'laine asked.

Jor-Dan finally came out of his silence. "Dreboo, the city planner and architect, has a team working in the West wing of the palace preparing your new quarters. I'm sure you will approve—he has an eye for detail and creates comfortable living spaces."

"Which way is west?" D'laine asked Trakon.

He pointed. "That way."

"I'll find out if he can give you the grand tour tomorrow," Jor-Dan said.

Jamie ran into the room and flopped on the floor by the dogs.

"Where have you been?" Lee asked. "You're all sweaty."

"I saw Oggy! He's doing great. You can't even tell he had a broken leg. He introduced me to his family," Jamie said. The dogs sniffed him from head to toe.

Lee just stared at his younger son. "I'm glad he's back on his feet." Lee and Jor-Dan shared a disbelieving glance and both men shrugged.

Brian entered the salon and flopped onto a sofa. "I'm bored. There's no one to play with."

Kitry tapped her lips with a finger. "We will have to arrange for a meeting so you and your brother can make friends with the boys and girls in the city."

"Where are they? I never see anyone except those Young-men, and they don't like me," Brian said.

"It's not that they don't like you," Jor-Dan said. "They're men, growing into their bodies. They don't play. Which reminds me, I should arrange for you to have fighting lessons."

Brian's face lit up. "That would be cool!"

Jor-Dan appeared thoughtful. "It's not just about looking important. What it amounts to is that you should be able to protect yourself if we were ever invaded by a foe. Currently, you don't have those skills and I've been remiss in seeing to your training—all of yours in fact."

Jamie jumped to his feet. "Can I learn, too?"

"Of course," Jor-Dan said. "It's good you can communicate with animals—they may be able to help you in a fight. You and your brother need to know how to use our weapons."

"He's awfully little," Lee said.

Jamie glared at his father.

Jor-Dan silently agreed with Lee. "While he's little, it's my responsibility as king to make sure all of my people can protect themselves, including you, Lee. As soon as the wedding is out of the way, we will begin training. I guess dancing takes precedence."

"Brian, you will most likely meet some children at the wedding, but after things have settled, I will plan some events. When is your emerging turn?" Kitry asked.

Brian, Jamie and Lee looked clueless.

"Your birthday," D'laine said.

"Oh! I need to get up to speed with the terminology," Lee said. "Brian's is April fifth, and Jamie's is March twenty-fifth."

Kitry raised her eyebrows.

"Marsus and Aviril," D'laine said. "Mine is Janswary seventeenth." She swung her eyes to her father. "Daddy, you should see the Kudaja village. They have beautiful structures way up in the agrin trees! It's a whole city with a palace and everything!"

D'laine focused and showed her father a mind picture. Brian and Jamie piped up. "Show us!"

They watched the mind picture D'laine presented.

"Wow, that's like the Ewok village from *Star Wars*," Brian said. "Can we go there sometime?"

"Next time we go, you and your brother can come with us," Trakon said. "You may even find playmates there."

SOMEONE TAPPED ON D'LAINE'S DOOR.

"Coming!" D'laine trotted to the door. She opened it to Ethaderia and Kitry's big smiles.

"Are you ready to try on your gown?" Ethaderia asked.

D'laine's face lit up. "Oh! I can't wait to see what Ulavia created! Come in while I go put my boots on."

"We'll go for your fitting, then we can take a tour of your new living quarters," Kitry said.

"Oh! I can't wait to see the new place!" D'laine pulled on the boots and inflated them.

Ulavia was waiting for them, all smiles. "I hope you will be happy with my creation."

She placed her hands on D'laine's shoulders and guided her to the fitting area in another room. Ulavia turned to Kitry and Ethaderia. "Ladies, make yourselves comfortable while I dress the princess."

D'laine gasped at the gown hanging on a dress form. "Oh, it's so beautiful! I can't wait to try it on!"

D'laine scampered out of her uniform. Ulavia helped her into the bottom layer that was similar to taffeta. It hugged her figure, but wasn't binding. Next came the wispy top part of the dress made of layers of the gossamer material.

Ulavia produced a pair of lace-up ballet-type slippers. They were made from the same wispy material but, with the agrin tree sap that was used in clothing manufacturing, the slippers were sturdy, yet comfortable.

D'laine gasped when she saw her reflection. "I love it! I look like a storybook princess!"

"Let's show the queen and her cousin, shall we?" Ulavia asked.

The dressmaker opened the door and let D'laine exit. They found Kitry and Ethaderia sitting in a waiting area talking quietly while looking at a long list in Ethaderia's communicator. The two women looked up and gasped.

"Oh! You look beautiful!" Kitry exclaimed.

"D'laine!" Ethaderia was out of her chair and grabbed D'laine in a hug. "How I wish your mother could see you now!"

D'laine teared up. "She should have been here."

Ethaderia rubbed D'laine's back. "At least your father is here."

"And you're here," D'laine said softly.

CHAPTER TWENTY-SIX

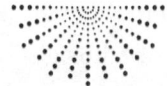

*I*t was a good thing the dance wasn't a traditional waltz. D'laine stumbled and fumbled. She hopped when she was supposed to glide. Trakon was patient until the end then fled the palace when dancing practice ended.

Lee, however, had eyes only for Ethaderia and didn't pay enough attention to the dancing instructor. His partner tried to steer his mind back into the dance, but failed each time.

Stanley surprised everyone. He took to the dance like a dandelion puff to a breeze.

Lee and D'laine grumbled as they cornered the scientist.

"How did you learn to be so proficient with this dance?"Lee demanded.

Stanley snickered. "I slept on it, literally. I watched that mind movie D'laine captured and played it in a continuous loop last night. When I woke up, it was like a part of my DNA."

"Huh." D'laine thought about that. "Makes sense. I'm going to do that tonight. Daddy, you should try that so you can dance with Ethaderia."

Stanley's partner beckoned him. His chest puffed out with pride.

"Looks like you've found a great dance companion," Lee said.

"I hope more than a dance partner," Stanley said as he left the group.

When the adults left the room, the instructor turned to Brian, Jamie and the two girls chosen to dance with them. The boys had watched the adults. It was hard to determine whether they liked the steps or not.

Brian was partnered with Yucovia, a pretty ten-year-old girl with shiny long black hair and bright black eyes. She had beautiful light bronze skin and straight teeth.

Galgason was Jamie's partner. The six-year-old wore her dark hair in a ponytail and a huge smile on her face. She was a whiz at the dance. For one so young, she tutored Jamie expertly.

Brian was happy to meet an Ebscalon child who wasn't a Youngman, even if it was a girl. He pranced around the floor as if he danced the minuet every turn.

"You boys don't need any more lessons," the instructor said. "I hope your father and sister are better tomorrow."

"They're going to be fine after tonight," Jamie said with confidence.

"I WISH VICTOR AND BEN COULD COME TO MY WEDDING," D'LAINE said as they all visited in the small salon. "I told them I'd send a wedding invitation."

Lee thought about it. "It's not an improbability. You could send an invitation. Remind them of the ten-to-one difference in our time so they could plan accordingly. I know Victor, Darren and Ben would jump at the chance to see Thol. I'm not so sure about Kara, since I never met her."

"Brian would be able to find the exact portals for both of them if they are at different locations," Trakon said.

"Better make a list of anything you want them to bring from back home," Stanley suggested.

Lee opened his communicator and started a list.

Trakon's eyes widened. "We need pizza and chocolate so the chef can replicate them!"

D'laine and Trakon belly laughed at the memory of Trakon's introduction to the Earth foods he couldn't get enough of.

They wrote an invitation that D'laine could send to Victor. Lee suggested they arrive two full turns before the wedding so they would become accustomed to the world of Thol.

D'laine included the list: pizza and chocolate, some manuals her father and Stanley wanted, and a photo album from her childhood.

"How do we print this? I need a physical piece of paper to send to Victor," D'laine said.

"Are you sure?" Stanley asked. "Maybe you can just think it into Victor's brain."

"I think it would be best to have the printed version. The mind-sharing between Earth and Thol is iffy," she said.

Trakon showed Lee how to get a physical copy. The sheet of paper just sort of dropped out of thin air.

"Huh. How did you do that?" Lee asked. "What is it printed on?"

"If you feel the material, you will recognize it has the same consistency as all other hosk-spun materials," Trakon said.

D'laine snatched it out of her father's hands and read it. It seemed complete. It included Victor and his family, and Ben. The list was noted. The time factor was there as a reminder, plus a note for them to communicate with D'laine for explicit instructions on their arrival to Thol.

Her eyes softened as she held the invitation. In a blink, the sheet of hosk silk paper was gone.

Next, they discussed the locations where their Earth friends should materialize. They needed to get that worked out before hearing back from Victor.

Lee clicked his communicator and located Brian. "Son, would you come to the small salon? We need your help with something."

Brian and Yucovia entered the salon. "Hi, daddy, what's up?"

"Some friends from Earth are going to attend the wedding. Do you think you might be able to find the best place for them to arrive? Or do you need help from an Egrom?"

Brian thought for a moment. "I'd better have an Egrom on standby, just in case."

"Okay. We don't have all the details yet, but as we get closer to the date, you can work that out. I'd have to send them coordinates so they understand exactly where to go," Lee said.

"Were you two practicing your dancing?" D'laine asked.

"No, we were just hanging out," Brian said.

Two turns later as D'laine was eating breakfast, a strange feeling came over her. For an instant, her eyes went out of focus. Lee witnessed the oddity from across the table.

"Are you okay, D'laine?"

"Incoming!" D'laine raised her hand in the air. A piece of paper flew into her hand.

"Is it from Victor?" Trakon leaned toward her to read over her shoulder, but gave up at trying to translate the English into Tholian.

"Ben will fly into LAX. Then they'll all drive down to Coronado Beach and use Greg Claymore's portal," D'laine said. "So, it will be Victor, Kara, Darren and Ben."

"Excellent!" Lee turned to the boys. "Darren is right between your ages. He likes anything scientific, but he's a kid so you can show him around. Just keep him safe."

"It will be good to spend some time with Victor and Ben," Stanley said.

Jor-Dan nudged Stanley. "I'm looking forward to meeting your Earth scientist-friends."

Kitry looked thoughtful. "Will your Earth friends gain Tholian gifts? We do not need any disasters so close to the wedding!"

Both Lee and Stanley balked at Kitry's question.

"Maybe we should have Ghury close by," Stanley said. "They're going to need translators while they're here."

"Brian, since they're coming from Coronado Beach where Trakon, Stanley and I portalled back and forth, you should have all the coordinates, right? Will you need one of the Egroms to help out with the right doorway?" D'laine asked.

"No, I'm good. Ghury told me I can see doorways better than the Egroms," Brian said. "Go figure."

Everyone raised an eyebrow.

"I'll contact Ghury and get everything coordinated," D'laine said. "Do you want me to move to the new quarters, Kitry? Victor and Kara can stay in my suite, and Darren can stay with either Brian or Jamie, whoever he fits in with more. Then we'll only need one more suite for Ben. He's older than my father."

Kitry thought. "Yes, that would work out. Lee, would you want Ben to stay in your suite?"

"Yes! That's a great idea. Not that we'll get any sleep— there's so much to discuss."

"Excellent!" Kitry said. "I'll make sure Biggan is notified of the change of rooms."

D'laine and Trakon both frowned. Lee and Kitry smiled slyly.

BRIAN'S EYES SCRUNCHED UP AS HE PEERED AT WHAT NO ONE ELSE could see, other than the Egroms. Everyone waited patiently in the field of moss for the visitors to make an appearance. A mid-sized crestrider hovered nearby.

"Are you sure we have the right turn and hour?" Brian asked for the fifth time.

"They are coming!" Ghury grumbled.

"Yes! How many times do I have to tell you..." D'laine's words were interrupted by a loud BOOM.

Victor, Kara, Darren and Ben stumbled forward onto the moss, slightly freaked out. They all had backpacks strapped on.

Stanley and Lee rushed forward to the two scientists. Brian and Jamie welcomed Darren.

D'laine hugged Kara.

The Earthlings gawked at Ghury.

"Wookies are real?" Darren asked.

Their eyes wandered the sky noting the two suns and some of the flying species of Thol. Then their eyes sank to the never-ending moss. But what really got their attention was the crestrider.

"Wow! Dad, look at the ship!" Darren hollered. Sweat beaded on his forehead. He noticed how unfazed Brian and Jamie were with the heat. "Aren't you sweltering in those clothes?"

"Nah," Jamie said. "We love this material. It keeps you cool."

"Before we do anything or go anywhere, you all need trans-lators," D'laine explained. "This is Ghury. He's the Egrom leader, and he's going to insert your translators. It's easy and doesn't hurt so don't freak out."

Ghury squatted beside Darren and pressed the translator behind his ear.

"Can you understand me?" Ghury asked. Darren's eyes sprang wide.

"Yes! Hi, I'm Darren."

"Yes, I know."

Ghury moved to Kara. She was fearful but allowed him to press the device into her flesh. Ghury asked the same question.

"Oh, my goodness! I understood you," Kara gasped. Ghury repeated the process with Ben and Victor.

"I will leave you to your visitors," Ghury said. He *stepped* back and was gone.

"Whoa!" Victor exclaimed as Ghury vanished.

The ground rumbled. A platoon of Plotals led by Jakla Bosakin riding pakows thundered across the meadow and stopped close to the site.

Kara screamed. She backed into Victor tugging Darren against her.

"I detected a disturbance and feared we were being invaded by those robots again," Jakla said.

He slid off his pakow and joined the group. He tapped his chest with his fist.

The Tholians responded similarly.

Lee diffused the situation by approaching Jakla and grasping his arm in friendly greeting. "No robots. Visitors for D'laine and Trakon's wedding."

Jakla eyed the group and nodded. "Welcome to Thol. I am Jakla Bosakin, commander of the Plotal army."

Kara was frozen with fear.

Victor stepped up to the giant alligator-like being and extended his hand. "I'm Victor. This is my wife Kara and my son Darren. And this is another Earth scientist, Ben Joplin."

Jakla gripped Victor's arm in the customary greeting. He studied Kara for a moment. "You have no need to fear me. We have settled our differences and are living in peace."

Kara swallowed. "I'm happy to hear that, Mr. Bosakin."

"Why don't we all get going?" Trakon suggested. "We can visit at the palace and you can have refreshments." He turned to Jakla. "Would you like to join us?"

"Perhaps another time. I am working closely with the architect and city planners," Jakla said. "I will return for the wedding festivities."

Jakla mounted his pakow and led his platoon back toward Ta'Byu'Vohon.

Ben slapped Lee on the back. "Oh, man! We get to ride in the ship?"

"Wait until you experience this!" Lee said. "There's so much to show you."

Trakon lowered the escalator via his communicator and everyone boarded the ship. Trakon raised the stairs, elevated the ship, and they zoomed off to the city. He landed the ship in the courtyard and he and D'laine ushered everyone into the palace.

Victor, Kara and Ben's eyes were wide as they took in the palace. They noticed there wasn't any glass in the windows. The floating globes of light and murals practically stopped them from making any progress down the hallway.

"It's so beautiful!" Kara exclaimed.

Brian and Jamie tugged at Darren. They passed up the grownups and headed down the wide hallway.

"Go to the big salon," Lee called out. He turned to Ben, Victor and Kara. "Trakon's parents are the king and queen of Ebscalon—that's the name of this kingdom."

Kara's mouth opened in an O. "Oh my God! I don't know what to do to meet royalty!"

"Don't even worry about that nonsense," Trakon said. "My parents are practical rulers. They mix and mingle with their subjects. They're not like some of the other kingdom heads who have a strict protocol."

They entered the big salon and slid their backpacks off and settled them in a pile on the floor, out of the way. The major-domo and two servants brought refreshments. After a few moments Kitry and Jor-Dan arrived with La'gar'ish at his side.

"Welcome!" Jor-Dan's voice boomed out.

La'gar'ish threw himself at Jor-Dan's legs in a protective mode, teeth clacking out a warning.

Jor-Dan scratched the tuft of hair on the dog's head. "At ease, La'gar'ish."

The visitors' eyes went wide.

The dog didn't quite want to obey. He didn't recognize these strangers or their scent.

Jor-Dan tapped La'gar'ish's head. "That's enough."

The dog blew out a sigh and shut up.

"Not so loud." Kitry nudged Jor-Dan with her elbow. "You'll scare them."

Jor-Dan approached the men and extended his hand. He liked the Earth greeting. Kitry mentioned that it was less like grappling.

Kitry approached Kara. "You must be Kara. I'm Kitry. I'm happy you will be attending the wedding."

"Thank you for allowing us to come. Your world is beautiful," Kara said.

Kitry nodded. "Yes, it is beautiful, but you must make sure you are always escorted by someone to avoid danger."

Pup, Chatter and Buffy scampered into the room. Chatter's teeth clacked a hard warning. Pup looked like he was going to attack. Buffy ran to Darren.

"*DOWN!*" D'laine boomed using The Voice. All four dogs dropped to the floor.

"Huh, even Buffy dropped," Trakon said. "That could be a good thing if there's danger around."

"Pup, Chatter, *To Me*," D'laine commanded.

The dogs crawled across the floor to her. She stared into their eyes. "Friends!" D'laine made them stand, and led them over to Ben and Victor.

"They need to catch your scent so you will be safe," she explained. "Please hold out your hand, one at a time."

Ben stared at the frightful diwal dogs. "Their teeth are like the teeth of the creature in the original *Alien* movie with Sigourney Weaver!"

Trakon wandered over. "Diwals have always been feared across Thol. They can strip a person to the bone in a matter of moments. But, D'laine tamed these three and showed us they could be trusted. They like our companionship."

"That is so, but we still need to be extremely firm with them," Jor-Dan said. "One wrong move and all that will be left of you are the buttons and other metal of your clothing."

"Show your hands," D'laine said.

Ben lowered his hand toward the dogs. He held his breath. Pup sniffed the hand and wagged his tail. Chatter sniffed and chattered. Victor followed Ben's lead. Then D'laine led the dogs over to Kara.

Pup licked Kara's hand. "Oh! He likes me!"

"This is Pup and Chatter," D'laine explained. "Pup is the alpha of the pack. Guess why I named this one Chatter."

The dog's teeth clacked away in a nonthreatening manner.

D'laine finished up with Darren.

D'LAINE BROUGHT VICTOR AND KARA TO HER OLD SUITE.

Kara wandered with her mouth open and eyes wide. "This is the most incredible suite of rooms I have ever seen! How lucky for you to live here!"

D'laine explained all the technology: restorative chamber, lighting globes, bathing pool, and window grids.

Victor was practically giddy. "This chamber is something else!"

"Everything here seems so much more progressive, Victor!" D'laine said. "I thought we were so far ahead of everyone else in the United States, but compared to this, we're playing with

Tinker Toys back in that dimension. And don't get me started on healing and medicines."

"We both know first-hand how advanced your healing abilities are," Kara said, wistful.

Lee gave Ben the grand tour of his suite. They stood before the closet.

"So, this restorative chamber cleans and repairs clothing?" Ben was stupefied.

"Yes," Lee agreed. They returned to Lee's office and sat. "One of the most advanced things is the translator. I don't understand how this device can take all these languages and translate them into English."

Ben slid his finger over the tiny clip behind his ear. "This technology is truly incredible. Earth won't catch up for who knows how long."

"Then there's the whole educational aspect. When we first arrived, we stayed at the Egrom village in the Cember Forest so they could bring us up to speed. They gave us what seemed like hours of content in mere minutes." Lee shook his head, mystified.

"And you would not believe the contrast between this beautiful city to the mushroom village of the Egroms. It is truly rustic, to say the least. No electronics. Nothing but these gigantic mushroom houses, cook pots over fires in the village, outside privy, bathing in hot-springs—for humans. They groom themselves like cats. I'll take you and Victor there. I want you to see the forest so you fully understand the scope of these trees."

"My head is spinning!" Ben said.

CHAPTER TWENTY-SEVEN

*B*rian, Jamie, Darren and Buffy ran through the gates of Ebscalon into the field. They stopped when they were five hundred feet from the gates.

"Come meet my friend," Jamie called out.

Several adult hosks peeked out from under the moss. A riot of hosk babies scampered all about.

Jamie sat on the moss. Brian and Darren followed suit. The hosk babies scampered all over Jamie. He giggled up a storm.

"Play with my brother and our friend," Jamie told the babies.

Several babies ran up Brian's legs, his chest, over his head and down the other side. He laughed as their tiny feet tickled him.

Darren stared in wide-eyed wonder as the fluffy balls of fur with tiny spider legs darted about. "What are they?"

"Hosks," Brian said. "The females have the babies and the males create silk that's made into our clothes and stuff."

Jamie grabbed a handful of moss and plopped it in Darren's lap. Then he grabbed a big male hosk and settled it on the moss.

"You can pet this one. The females won't let you pet them— they get too excited, but the males like to be petted."

Darren cautiously reached out and touched the hosk. "Oh, wow! It's so soft!"

"Brian, let's take Darren to the pakow pens!" Jamie yelled.

He grabbed the male hosk out of Darren's lap and set it on the moss.

"Come on. You remember those giant beasts the alligator men rode? Those are pakows. They're awesome!" Jamie bubbled over with glee.

The boys ran toward the pakow pens and climbed the fence.

"Lulu! Come over here," Jamie called. D'laine's big pakow cow lumbered over.

"Wow! They have six legs!" Darren squealed when Lulu licked his face. He lifted his T-shirt and wiped the slop off his cheek.

Jamie scratched Lulu's head.

"Her eyes look like a fly's eyes!" Darren exclaimed.

"Yeah, they're strange looking, but they're fun to ride,"Brian said. "Jamie, let's show Darren Ekka! Can all three of us ride him together?"

Jamie's face filled with happiness. "Oh, sure. Wait until you see my borjo!"

They scampered down the fence and took off running back to the city.

"What's a borjo?" Darren asked.

"It's sort of like a dragon!" Brian said.

Kitry and Ethaderia brought Kara to the marketplace. People stared in open wonder as they took in Kara's light skin and hair along with her Earth clothing.

Ethaderia whispered in Kara's ear. "The people are surprised to see a foreigner. But don't worry. They are respectful and friendly."

Kara took in the sights. The marketplace was teeming with merchants barking out their wares and shoppers searching for bargains. Kara stroked jewelry, clothing, housewares and all manner of things.

"Your clothing is so beautiful," Kara said. "Why is it D'laine wears what the men wear?"

"D'laine is a warrior," Kitry explained. "Most women here are of the domestic nature, but we also have women warriors."

"A warrior?" Kara was amazed. "She's just a young woman."

"Thol seems to bring out special qualities in the humans who cross over from Earth," Kitry said. "When the robots came through a portal, we were being decimated—all the different peoples of Thol were involved in that war. Plotals, Egroms, the Kudaja, other kingdoms—even together they could not stop that foe. Yet D'laine singlehandedly saved us.

"She was the one who brought peace between the Plotals and the human Tholians," Kitry went on. "That war changed things. Jakla Bosakin was severely wounded by a robot, but D'laine saved him. Jor-Dan said Jakla should have died from the laser blast to his chest."

Kara appeared thoughtful. "I feel so bad. When I met Victor, he told me about D'laine and Stanley. He told me about Thol, but I didn't believe him. It seemed way too fantastical to be true. Yet here we are, visiting in another dimension! My son will never want to return home."

"No one can afford to be naïve about this world. Thol is a very dangerous place," Ethaderia said. "There are creatures, such as the diwal dogs, out in the wild that would tear you to pieces because it is their wild nature. And as my cousin mentioned, we now have peace with the Plotals. Previously, they were blood-thirsty warmongers. They captured weaker beings and people and turned them into slaves."

They returned to the palace and discovered Ben, Victor, Lee, Stanley, D'laine and Trakon were just leaving.

Neither D'laine nor Kitry missed the silent exchange of glances between Lee and Ethaderia.

"Where are you heading off to?" Kitry asked.

"I want to show Ben and Victor the forest and the Egrom village," Lee said. "Maybe we can also visit the Kudaja."

"Don't be late for dinner," Kitry said. "Ethaderia will be joining us."

The small group left the palace and walked to the crestrider holding area. Trakon selected a midsized ship, and they all climbed aboard. Trakon flew out of the city, slowed down over the pakow pens, then zoomed off toward the Cember Forest.

The group stood at the base of the trees looking up. It was impossible to spot the tops of the agrin trees from the ground. Even if one was lying on the ground, it would be a challenge because of the the dual suns in the flashing sky.

"Good grief. I see what you mean," Victor said. "Redwoods are the biggest trees I've ever seen, but these agrin trees are immense."

"The sap is one of the strongest substances on this planet," Lee said. "It's used in almost every type of manufacturing you could imagine."

"The ships are cast with an agrin resin base and metals," Trakon said.

"Don't forget the clothing that heals itself." D'laine demonstrated by taking her knife and ripping it down one sleeve.

Ben and Victor watched in wonder as the material knitted itself back together.

"That's mind-boggling!" Ben cried out.

"One of the reasons I cautioned you about the seeds was due to the tree's rapid growth and perimeter of the trunks at one year old," Stanley said. "This is old-growth forest. The Egroms showed me a new-growth area a couple of miles from here. It started with one seed that a bird must have dropped. Wait until you see what sprang up!"

They returned to the crestrider and Stanley pointed Trakon in the direction of the new grove of trees.

"If you bring us up to the tops of these new trees, and point us in the direction of the old growth, you'll understand what I mean," Stanley said.

Trakon hovered the craft at the top of the trees. They all looked across to the other trees, which had disappeared into the clouds.

Ben looked over the edge of the crestrider to judge the distance to the ground. "I looked up statistics regarding the California redwoods," he said. "The tallest is the Hyperion Coast Redwood. It's three-hundred seventy-nine feet tall (one-hundred fifteen meters). Compare that to the Statue of Liberty, which is three-hundred five feet tall. Think about it! Also, the Hyperion is considered a young tree, somewhere between seven-hundred to eight-hundred years old. Redwoods live for a couple of thousand years."

D'laine translated the numbers for Trakon.

"Let's take a reading of the height." Trakon made sure the ship was settled on the ground. He showed Lee, Stanley and D'laine which screen to use to track the height.

He flew the ship to the top of the new trees—three hundred fifty feet, then they flew over to the old-growth trees. Trakon settled the ship on the ground, restarted the counter and raised the ship straight up to the very top of the trees. Nearly eight hundred feet tall. They truly were in the clouds.

"No wonder I could never see the tops of the trees," D'laine said.

"I'd like to collect a sample of that sap," Ben said. Trakon dug into a bin and produced a small, round container and handed it to Ben. "Will this work?"

"That's perfect!"

"I wish my cellphone worked so I could take a picture," Victor said.

"Let's go visit Herish and Meeri," D'laine suggested. "Wait until you experience their city, daddy! You're going to think you're on the Endor moon!"

Trakon settled the ship on the ground and they hopped out. He approached a tree. He placed his hand on the enormous trunk. "We need a sample of your sap."

Victor raised his eyebrow. "You talk to trees?"

Trakon swung his head to make eye contact with Victor. "They're alive."

D'laine's heart swelled. She didn't know Trakon had similar thoughts.

Trakon pulled a knife out of a pocket and scraped away a circle of the bark. Then he twisted the knife into the flesh of the tree until sap flowed.

"I need the container!" he barked.

Ben stepped forward, the container open.

Trakon held the container under the wound and let the sap flow into it. He handed it back to Ben, who capped it.

"Watch closely," Trakon said.

They all crowded around Trakon and gasped loudly as the wound closed. Within five minutes there was no trace that the tree had been molested. There was new bark in place.

"That's unbelievable," Ben said.

Trakon patted the tree. "Thanks for your sap."

They piled back into the crestrider and lifted off the ground. Five tiny borjos zoomed around the ship. Two landed on the rail as the others hovered close by.

Herish raised his hand in greeting. "Hold on!"

He flew several feet away and dismounted, as did Meeri on the second borjo. They morphed into full-sized beings.

Victor's and Ben's mouths dropped open. "Whoa!" Victor said. "How did you do that?"

"Not all Kudajas can morph," D'laine said. "Herish's people and some of Meeri's people have the gene."

They all headed toward the Kudaja city in the Cember Forest.

Victor, Ben, Lee and Stanley were all agog as they stared up at the boardwalk way above their heads.

"My son would love to live here," Victor said.

"Never mind Darren," Ben said. "I'd like to live here!"

Lee nodded knowingly. "Believe me, Ben, you'd never regret it."

Ben and Lee shared a glance.

Victor nudged Ben. "Don't get any wild ideas."

They let the discussion drop, but Lee knew he and Ben would have a quieter, more serious talk later that night in his suite.

Herish and Meeri showed them around the Kudaja elevated city. D'laine was glad to have come for the ride. She hadn't seen all the buildings they were seeing.

"We'd better get over to the Egrom village or we'll be late getting home for dinner," Trakon said. "I really don't want my mother getting upset."

They all piled into the crestrider and Trakon maneuvered it up into the sky to look for the hidden village. D'laine pointed to the clearing and Trakon steered the ship and they landed.

Chacoodi came running toward the group. "Where are Brian and Jamie?"

"Sorry, Chacoodi," Lee said. "It's just us adults this time."

Chacoodi harrumphed and walked away.

Ghury and Adrum approached.

"Welcome!" Ghury said. "Are you enjoying your visit?"

Victor and Ben's gazes were drawn up almost two feet over their heads to meet the Egrom's eyes.

"Thol is a dimension filled with wonder," Ben said. "I'm glad to be here."

"I know you've seen Earth," Victor said. "I'm amazed at your technology here and the beauty of your planet. No pollution. No wars. No overcrowding."

Ghury led them to a larger mushroom hut so they could all fit inside. "Make yourselves comfortable."

Victor's hand slid across the top of the chair then the table. "This is precision craftsmanship. How is this manufactured?"

"The Egroms create this through the powers of their minds," D'laine explained.

"No way!" Victor examined the surface of the table closely. "This is truly beautiful."

"Just think of Superman times ten," D'laine said.

Ben studied the mushroom house. "It seems odd that the other inhabitants of Thol have technology but your people live more simply."

"We have no need for it," Ghury said. "Our powers are all that are required for us to keep the planet safe. D'laine and her family brought their own special gifts when they came to Thol. Right now, you have things stirring in your own heads, but when you go home, they will fade with time."

"I wonder what your gifts would be." Stanley looked from Victor to Ben.

"Wouldn't that be interesting to discover?" Ben asked. They stayed for a half-hour more then returned to Ebscalon to prepare for dinner.

CHAPTER TWENTY-EIGHT

*L*ee and Ben stopped by D'laine's old suite to gather Victor and Kara. Lee pressed his communicator and called Brian.

"Where are you boys? Are you getting ready for dinner?" He heard a racket in his communicator. Brian's voice sounded far away.

"We're riding Ekka! We'll come home now," he said.

"You get back here right now, do you understand?" Lee asked.

There was a swooshing sound and all three boys laughed. "Okay, Ekka just landed in his tower," Brian said.

"You're all probably filthy. Hurry and get cleaned up. Loan Darren one of yours or Jamie's suits."

"Where were they?" Victor asked.

"Riding Ekka, Jamie's borjo," Lee said.

"What's a borjo?" Kara asked.

"It looks like a cross between a dragon and a dragonfly," D'laine said as she and Trakon joined the group.

"Aren't they tiny?" Victor asked.

"Ekka is a full-sized borjo—he was never neutered when he

was first born," Trakon said. "Otherwise he would be like the tiny ones the Kudaja ride, unless they morph."

"The borjos can morph as well?" Ben asked.

"It's a long story," Trakon said.

"They were riding this dragon?" Kara's voice hitched with fright.

D'laine patted her shoulder. "It's okay. Jamie communicates with animals, and Ekka would never let anything happen to the boys. He's assigned himself to protect Ebscalon."

Kara patted her chest to calm down.

They walked to the dining salon and were greeted by Kitry, Ethaderia and Jor-Dan. Stanley sauntered in after them and took his regular place at the table.

Kitry introduced her cousin to the newcomers, and they all sat waiting on the boys.

Thundering feet brought unwanted attention as Lee mentally scolded his sons. They slowed down immediately and entered the dining salon. Lee glared at his boys.

"We will have a discussion about how to behave yourselves while in the palace, later," he said. "You obviously need a reminder."

Brian and Jamie cringed.

Ethaderia placed a hand on Lee's arm. She held back a laugh. "Just be thankful they didn't get into any trouble, and they're here—relatively on time."

"I suppose you're right," Lee said.

Kara took inventory of Darren. Satisfied he was in one piece, she let the dragon-riding discussion go.

"What about their education?" Kara asked Lee.

"I've been thinking of homeschooling them so they won't be behind, if we ever have to return to Earth for whatever reason," Lee said.

Panic floated across Ethaderia's face.

Lee caught the expression and patted her hand. "I don't

foresee ever returning to Earth, but if the boys ever wanted to return to their home planet as adults, they should be prepared."

"We don't want to be homeschooled," Brian said.

"You have nothing to keep yourselves occupied," Lee said. "You have no careers. You have not finished traditional Earth schooling. What do you plan to do for the rest of your lives?"

"What about D'laine?" Jamie asked.

"What about her? She's getting married. She finished high school," Lee turned to Victor and Ben. "Do you think either of you could root around back home and find school books? Elementary through high school, and beyond. Rosa has access to funds for all these purchases."

"The boys are six and ten, right?" Kara asked.

"Yes," Lee said.

"I'll get online when we get back home and make a list of books for you," Kara said. "I know exactly where to go to get them. Victor can box them and let D'laine know when they're ready to be shipped via dimensional express."

Kara snickered at her little joke.

Brian and Jamie looked downright forlorn.

"What exactly do you propose to do every turn, turn in and turn out?" Lee asked. "I don't think there's going to be much demand for finding the dimensional doorways when you're an adult. You have to have something to focus on."

"Your father is right," Kitry said. "You may be young boys now, the older you get time goes by faster. You can never have too much education."

"I'm going to be an animal communicator," Jamie announced. "I've already helped a couple of farmers with their problems."

"Whether you like it or not, you will be homeschooled. End of discussion," Lee said.

D'laine seemed thoughtful. "I wonder if the Egroms have a

way to take all the Earth education and make one of their mind movies."

"That would be an excellent idea," Lee said. "But there's still the problem of what Brian and Jamie would do every turn. They can't just run wild."

"I think there are lots of ways to keep them occupied while they learn about their new home," Kara said. "I'll make a list and we can discuss this after the wedding."

THE TURN OF THE WEDDING FINALLY ARRIVED. KITRY AND Ethaderia attended to D'laine, helping her dress. She slipped into the first layer of the exquisite gown, a radiating lilac colored fabric that was similar to taffeta. Once that was in place, they helped drape the top layer. The delicate shimmering white fabric, similar to chiffon, held delicate embroidered purple flowers laced with gold threads.

"Oh! I love this dress," D'laine said as she gazed at her reflection in the full-length mirror.

D'laine gathered her long white-blond hair in her hands. "Should I wear my hair up?"

Kitry shook her head. "The people love your hair. I think it would be better to keep it loose and flowing down your back."

Ethaderia agreed. "Women would give anything to have your hair color!"

There was a tap on the door and Meeri entered. She squealed when she saw D'laine in her dress. She ran across the room and grabbed D'laine in a hug.

"You look beautiful!" Meeri said. "But you always do so I should amend that to 'you appear more beautiful than ever!' Your dress is lovely!"

"Meeri, this is Ethaderia, the Queen's cousin," D'laine said. "And, my father's *almost* intended."

Ethaderia blushed. "Hello, Meeri. I've heard a lot about you."

"Hello, Ethaderia. D'laine's my best friend," Meeri gave D'laine a quick hug and studied her hair.

"Why don't you take a wisp of hair from each side and braid it so it doesn't fall into your face at the wrong moment?"

"That's an excellent idea," Kitry gathered the hair and braided the strands. "Ethy, find me a tiny fastener."

Ethaderia looked through a box of trinkets and pulled one out.

"Not that one!" Kitry said. "D'laine can't have any crystals on her person! They spark."

"Oh! Good thing you reminded me." Ethaderia dug into the box once more. She pulled out a nugget of what looked like gold with a looped cord of a gold and silver color. She handed it to her cousin.

"Perfect!" Kitry fastened it to the braided hair. The long braid reached to D'laine's waist.

The three women stepped back. They smiled in approval.

LEE AND JOR-DAN WERE OFFERING TRAKON SUGGESTIONS WHEN Herish entered the room.

"Not bad. You clean up pretty good," Herish smirked.

Trakon grunted.

Jor-Dan adjusted the gold braids on the shoulder of Trakon's dark uniform. His wedding suit was dressier than his state garments. The fabric was a dense purple, almost black. It was chosen by his mother and cousin to complement D'laine's dress.

Next, Jor-Dan eyed the ribbons, medals and braids on Trakon's chest to be certain they were straight.

"You're almost as handsome as I was in my wedding suit," Herish joked. "Are you nervous?"

Trakon smirked. "I just want to get the ceremony over so I can have a glass of kahl!"

"You're sure to be disappointed then," Jor-Dan said. "We will be serving abrajaaii."

"That will do, father!"

Jor-Dan and Lee appraised Trakon. "You're all set."

"I'm going to see if D'laine is ready." Lee left the room.

Herish leaned in and whispered in Trakon's ear. "Page one-thirty-six." He winked.

LEE KNOCKED ON D'LAINE'S NEW SUITE OF ROOMS.

Ethaderia whisked the door open, a wide smile on her face. "Don't you look handsome." She admired Lee's white dress uniform.

His eyes wandered over Ethaderia's wispy dress. "You are stunning."

Ethaderia opened the door and invited him in. "Wait until you see your daughter!"

Lee stepped into the room and gasped. D'laine was a vision of beauty and elegance. Blinking back tears, he crossed the room and gently hugged her.

"I don't want to mess anything up, but honey, you look beautiful." He blinked back tears.

THE TIME HAD COME TO LEAVE THE SUITE.

"Nervous?" Meeri asked.

D'laine grabbed Meeri's hand and pulled her to the side. "How long do we have to keep the thread on our hands?" D'laine asked.

"Until you leave the celebration," Meeri said. "Then it's cut off outside your suite. It's a keepsake of your vows."

"What if you have to... you know..." D'laine blushed crimson.

"You have to go together!" Meeri said. Her face flamed. "It's embarrassing, but you'll be married so it's not like you won't see each other in various forms of disarray."

"I'd better go now!" D'laine said. She hiked up her dress and ran to the bathroom. Moments later she returned. "I can't wait to see how Trakon looks."

"He's very handsome in his uniform," Lee said. "Are you ready?"

Ethaderia and Kitry brushed down the material of D'laine's dress in the back.

"You're ready!" Kitry said. "I leave you in capable hands."

Meeri opened the door. Kitry and Ethaderia slipped out of the room. Kitry rushed to join Jor-Dan and Trakon.

Lee held his bent arm out and D'laine slipped her hand through and latched onto his sleeve. They left the room.

Ethaderia led them to the palace entryway.

D'laine sniffed. Lee patted her hand and kissed her on the cheek.

They were joined by Trakon, Jor-Dan and Kitry. All five of them walked abreast out of the palace to the courtyard. Meeri and Ethaderia waited until the royals were through the doorway, then they scooted to where Jamie, Brian, Stanley and the visitors from Earth stood.

The entire main corridor from the main gates to the palace was decorated with colorful wedding banners. People flanked the corridor a hundred deep, all vying to see the prince and princess.

The Visionary motioned the wedding party forward. Trakon and D'laine were delivered to their places and faced each other.

Their parents stepped back and joined the rest of the family and friends.

Trakon's eyes latched onto D'laine's, filled with love.

D'laine smiled back at Trakon, tears dribbling down her cheeks.

The Visionary was dressed in a long, flowing white garment. A glittering multicolored cloth across the back of his neck draped to his waist.

He tied one of Trakon's hands to D'laine's hands with thin red threads.

"Prince Trakon Bramstone of Ebscalon willingly receives D'laine Jackson of the Cember Forest Egrom tribe as his wife and life partner. From this moment forward your dreams of accomplishments are willingly shared between yourselves until one or both depart this life."

The Visionary repeated the same in reverse, with D'laine receiving Trakon. After that, he painted a gold triangle symbol in the third eye area on each forehead.

He bent and whispered to both of them. Trakon and D'laine rearranged their hair behind their right ear.

The Visionary painted the rim of their right ears with the same gold paint.

"You shall listen to each other and openly discuss the turn's and future events, problems and successes, not dwelling on the past.

"As husband and wife life partners, you shall honor each other with truthfulness and loyalty, as equals. Your children will strengthen your bond to each other. May you be blessed with as many children as you desire.

"You will protect one another, your kingdom, and Thol itself from danger. You will respect the elders of your kingdom, for one turn you, too, shall be an elder seeking the same respect you gave."

The Visionary turned and picked up a chalice that contained

dirt. He dipped his finger into the dirt and touched Trakon at one temple then the other. He repeated this on D'laine.

"This dirt symbolizes the very ground of the planet Thol that you stand upon. You are her stewards. Keep her safe for all inhabitants. May you bless her with your love and respect for all beings who share our space."

"May you have a wonderful celebration of your joining! From this moment on, D'laine Jackson shall officially be known as Princess D'laine of the house of Bramstone of Ebscalon."

With that, Trakon and D'laine held hands and turned to face the guests. They raised their bound hands together.

The crowd cheered.

Lee wiped tears from his eyes.

The adventure continues.

Creatures of Thol

Ghury
Egrom elder of the Cember Forest Tribe

Jakla Bosakin
Plotal Commander

Diwal Dog

Borjo

MAP OF THOL

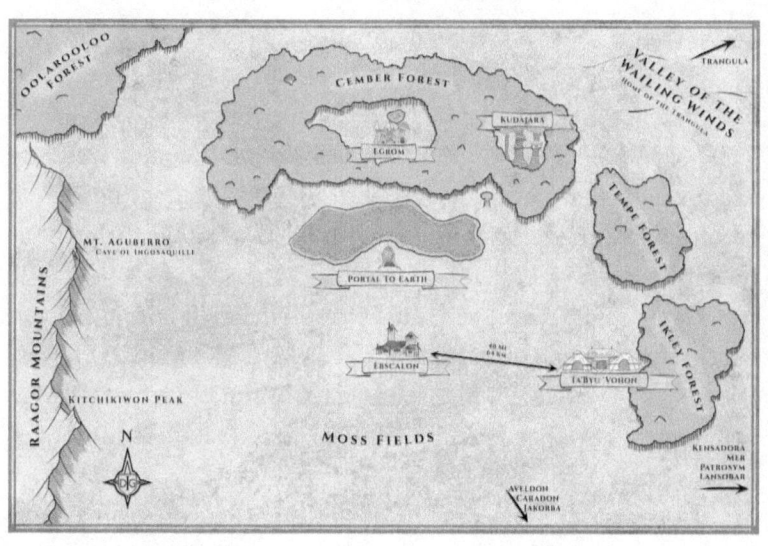

WANT MORE THOL?

Get ready for Book 3:
Love of Thol

THE MARKETPLACE contains replicas of D'laine's wedding dress, and jewelry even depicts Buffy, the Earth dog the people are now used to seeing romping with the diwal dogs throughout the city.

D'laine and Trakon are mushy in love. Brian and Jamie can barely stand to be around them. Herish and Meeri are their best friends and the two couples spend a lot of time together. D'laine is happy to have her friend back now that Trakon is no longer jealous of Herish.

Ekka gets sick. The large borjo appears to be on deaths door. Jamie is frantic. The Visionary, Ghury and D'laine determine what is wrong—poison!

Back on Earth, Ben Joplin and Victor Bennett have many discussions about Thol. Ben decides to immigrate. He can't get Thol out of his head and he really wants to live among the Kudaja. Victor and Kara discussed their immigrating as well, but Kara fears the wildness of Thol and the challenge of keeping Darren safe.

Before Ben leaves Earth for good, Al Jordan, the reporter from Houston, contacts him about all the disappearances: the entire Jackson family, almost a year after D'laine vanished. Ben feels guilty knowing he's next.

Romance and marriage are in the air. Lee and Ethaderia head to the alter. Stanley has a serious girlfriend after many failed dating attempts. His new girlfriend is a Tholian scientist and they are a perfect match.

The Plotal city of Ta'Byu'Vohon is nearly completed. Jor-Dan discovers his old friend Orongo and they reestablish their friendship as if no time has passed.

Maldi Amadal, the Plakado, flies with Jamie on Ekka and leads an expedition to the Aguberro mountains. The Visionary, Ghury, Trakon, D'laine, Stanley and Adrum plan to explore the caves to find scrolls with information about the prophecy. Trakon wants to convince some borjos to return to Ebscalon with them.

While Trakon and D'laine fly to see Herish and Meeri, a large insect-man whose human shape has huge butterfly wings, swoops down and snatches D'laine from the ship. Trakon pursues while calling for help. The Kudaja and Ciertrons take chase but lose the creature.

The adventure continues

Book 3 ~ Love of Thol
Book 4 ~ King of Thol
Book 5 ~ Earth Calling Thol

Did you miss Book 1?
Prophecy of Thol

Gifts From Thol: A Glossary

A * indicates a new character, creature, or thing introduced in Gifts From Thol.

Characters

Absadul	One of the Egrom village elders.
Adrum	One of the Egrom village elders, he is tasked specifically with teaching D'laine the history of Thol.
Akubel	An ancient Egrom leader from long ago who received a prophecy.
Al Jordan	A junior staff member at Houston Daily News looking to make his big break, and a science fiction fan at heart.
Ben Joplin	The head of Rice University's physics department. He gets enlisted by Victor Bennett for a desperate plan to save the man's wife.
Bensol	One of the Egrom village elders tasked with helping and training D'laine to realize her destiny.
Biggan*	An Ebscalon guard assigned to D'laine and Trakon as the amorous couple's chaperone.
Bist*	A city planner and one of several Plotals accompanying Jakla on his visit to Ebscalon.
Bok-Tor	A Safri prisoner D'laine saved from the Plotals.
Brenda	D'laine's childhood friend since 3rd grade.
Brian Jackson	D'laine's younger brother; at 10 years old, he plays in the Little League, but a sudden health complication might put a stop to it all. Traveling to Thol, he is the last to come into his powers: detecting the portals between the alternate earths.
Buffy	The Jackson family's tan and white pit bull.
Chacoodi*	A young Egrom from their village, he is quick to befriend both Brian and Jamie, becoming best friends with the former.
Chatter	Trakon's pet diwal dog.
Connor	Tall, dark-haired, and D'laine's ex-boyfriend.
Dannin	One of Ebscalon's council members, he is in charge of livestock, food and water, and hosk gathering.
Darren Bennet	Victor Bennet's son, this 8-year-old is both space obsessed and loves a good story.
Ditol	One of the Egrom village elders tasked with helping and training D'laine to realize her destiny.
D'laine Jackson	Smart and resourceful, D'laine was in for more than she could have ever imagined when her mysterious dream became reality. Now fully settled into Thol along with her family, D'laine's relationship with the prince of Ebscalon might progress to become something more.
Dreboo*	Ebscalon's architect.
Drusta	One of the Egrom village elders tasked with helping and training D'laine to realize her destiny.
Dupree	An inventor defensive about his achievements; he comes up with a device to pick up spectral images.

Characters, *Continued*	
Ekal	One of the Visionary's only two disciples.
Ekka*	A full-sized borjo gifted to Jaime by a mysterious traveler.
Eric Villarreal	Rosa's husband.
Ethaderia*	Cousin to Queen Kitry, she might just find shared feelings with one of the newcomers from Earth.
Forador*	The agriculturist of Ebscalon.
Ghury	A key member of the Egrom village elders, Ghury became D'laine's mentor and guide for the path that lay ahead.
Greg Claymore*	An Eartholian who abandoned his former home and family many decades ago, Greg has come to terms with his new life on Thol; however, the newcomers to the planet find themselves suddenly in desperate need of his healing abilities.
Hal-sa-Bin	A member of the Ebscalon council, he is in charge of security.
Herish Cagmondoore	A Kudaja warrior of Cember Forest. Revealed to be the prince of his race, Herish tries to make amends with D'laine; all while getting into the occasional tussle with Trakon.
Hexlon*	Usually seen working on the crestriders, Hexlon's various skills come in handy when he receives an unusual commission.
Jakla Bosakin	Once a pillaging warlord, Jakla has since turned to more peaceful ways, his goals switching from using D'laine's powers to rebuilding his people's kingdom.
Jamie Jackson	At only 6 years old, he's D'laine's youngest brother. Always having a special kinship with animals, Jamie's talent gets taken to new heights once his Tholian powers are realized; however, his innocence may mean learning the hard way that not all animals are perfectly friendly.
Ja-Toy-Anic	Despite being a citizen of Ebscalon, his loyalties may lie elsewhere.
Jawget*	A Ciertron farmer infected by a mysterious ailment.
Jor-dan	Despite his age of sixty years, the King of Ebscalon doesn't shy from being both venerable ruler and fearless warrior.
Jubulon	The ruler of Aveldon.
Jugdaak*	The pakow handler of Ebscalon, he comes to verbal blows with Jamie over an injured og.
Jum*	A young fhahadda saved and later relocated.
Kara Bennett*	Victor Bennett's wife, and the receiver of a horrible medical diagnosis; the ripple effects of which will affect both Thol and Earth.
Kestrum	A female Egrom who lets D'laine stay at her mushroom house; the two quickly become fast friends.
Kitry	The motherly Queen of Ebscalon, always looking to make those under her care as comfortable as possible.

Characters, *Continued*

La'gar'ish	One of the diwal dogs tamed by D'laine, formerly called Scooby. Upon becoming King Jor-Dan's guard dog, he is given the Ciertron name of "La'gar'ish."
Laoife	Mother to Ja-Toy-Anic, she shares both his leanings and vices.
Lansing*	The widowed Queen of Jekorba.
Lee Jackson	Father of D'laine, Brian, and Jamie, this former NASA scientist's faith was tested when his eldest mysteriously vanished. Now reunited in a new world, Lee turns to using his career skills and his gift of holographic envisionings to help the Ciertrons with their technology.
Lori Jackson	Lee Jackson's late wife, and the victim to a tragic accident.
Lulu	A female pakow that becomes D'laine's mount.
Majordomo	In charge of the dining salon.
Maldi Amadal*	A Plakado traveler and wanderer, he has found several secrets on his journeys, including a mysterious staff.
Marrak*	A member of Jor-Dan's council, his role is that of a documentarian, recording petitions made to the king, the decisions taken, and applying the royal seal to the finished documents.
Mark	Victor and Stanley's tech assistant.
Mayaar	Jor-Dan's manservant.
Meeri Glascombe*	One of the Kudaja, she becomes Herish's betrothed and later his wife, befriending D'laine along the way.
Oggy*	An injured og rescued and later adopted by Jamie.
Oogo*	The leader of the Oolarooloo village who took in Greg Claymore.
Pra-yor*	One of several Plotals accompanying Jakla on his visit to Ebscalon.
Puando*	A neutered borjo serving as Herish's mount.
Pup	D'laine's diwal dog.
Quark Zerfre	One of Jor-Dan's advisors, he heads Ebscalon's crestrider fleet.
Rachel	D'laine's childhood friend since 3rd grade.
Rettu	The second disciple of the Visionary.
Rosa Villarreal	The Jackson family's housekeeper.

Scooby	One of the diwal dogs tamed by D'laine. Upon becoming King Jor-Dan's guard dog, he is given the Ciertron name of "La'gar'ish."
Sorgus Blaski*	The leader of the Plakados and the one to discover Asbram.
Stanley Daigle	Victor Bennet's old friend and fellow physicist, this genius's enthusiasm with the alternate dimension theory is unmatched. Perhaps one of the most powerful of the Eartholians, once his powers of telekinesis and telepathy develop, Stanley must figure out a way to either control or suppress his mental abilities for the good of everyone around him.
Swezek	One of the Egrom village elders tasked with helping and training D'laine to realize her destiny.
The Visionary	Both healer and spiritual guide, the old Ciertron man is one of only three inhabiting Ebscalon's sacred temple.
Trabet	One of the Egrom village elders tasked with helping and training D'laine to realize her destiny.
Trakon	The Prince of Ebscalon. Despite his hasty temper, Trakon is willing to befriend once adversaries; and maybe take his relationship with D'laine to the next level.
Twum	D'laine's handmaiden assigned to her during her stay at Ebscalon's palace.
Ulavia*	A Ciertron seamstress, she is hired to make D'laine's wedding dress.
Victor Bennet	An accomplished physicist and best friends with Stanley Daigle, he's one of few who found out what happened to D'laine Jackson. When personal tragedy strikes, Victor is in for the shock and adventure of a lifetime once another portal to Thol is finally discovered.
Wegore*	One of several Plotals accompanying Jakla on his visit to Ebscalon.
Youndon	The ruler of Lansobar.
Ystap Olu*	One of several Plotals sent as diplomats, she is a city planner with her sights set on helping her people rebuild.
Zandal	The cruel leader of the robotics forces of Zan, he aimed to conquer all who stand in his way.

Locations & Places

Asbram	Another separate realm, and the place to which the Plakados migrated to, vanishing from the surface of Thol.
Caradon	A city-kingdom, and home to the Caradonians.
Cember Forest	Home to the Egroms and Kudaja, this giant, colorful forest is filled with massive, unknown flora and fauna.
Ebscalon	A Ciertron city of diamond-like roofs and colorful banners rebuilt in the wake of a devastating war, its name means "knowledge".
Egrom Village	Home of the Egroms of Cember Forest, visitors must be invited to it; else the village and inhabitants remain invisible to them.
Ikley Forest	A forest located nearby Ta'Byu'Vohon, the city-kingdom of the Plotals.
Ingosaquille	A crest on Mt. Aguberro, it is located one drok from the summit and hides a cave containing mysterious artifacts and scrolls from times lost.
Jekorba	A neighboring kingdom to Ebscalon.
Kensadora	A neighboring kingdom and the place where Ethaderia's sister lives.
Kitchikiwon	This mountain serves as home to the Raagor, the ice people living on the cold slopes and terrain.
Lansobar	A neighboring kingdom to Ebscalon.
Mer	Kingdom of the Mers.
Mount Aguberro	The least explored mountain on Thol, Mt. Aguberro is home to an impressive population of borjos, the untamed creatures able to reach their full-size without outside interference.
Oolarooloo Forest	Home to the Oolarooloo people's village. While this forest on the other side of Thol has no official name, it is certainly unforgettable, with lush flora and an abundance of fruits and vegetables like a garden.
Patrosym	A neighboring kingdom to Ebscalon.
Raagor Mountains	A large mountain range home to the Raagor Ice people.
Ta'Byu'Vohon	The city-kingdom of the Plotals, it was destroyed in the Great War, leaving nothing behind. However, nothing states that it must remain that way.
The Visionary's Temple	The sacred Ciertron temple is set in the middle of Ebscalon.
Thol	An alternate Earth, Thol is the third planet in orbit; but this is where similarities end, with two suns, four large moons, vibrant landscapes, and a plethora of unique creatures and races.
Valley of Wailing Winds	Located on the opposite side of Thol.
Zan	Another alternate Earth, this world has been reduced to a barren wasteland by its robotic inhabitants, humans made into slaves and prey.

Races

Caradonions	Another of the many races of Thol.
Ciertrons	Most resembling Earth's humans with their bronzed skin and dark hair, the Ciertrons are a technologically advanced society, defenders of justice who value honor despite their constant conflicts with Plotals. Their offspring are split between being born with childlike minds and those of adults.
Egroms	A wise, ancient race possessing wonderous abilities, the long-lived Egroms have since faded into myth and legend, isolating themselves in the Cember Forest while they continue to carry out their self-appointed duties. Recently, they have become more involved in the affairs of Thol's other races, interacting and aiding those they can.
Kudaja	Described as tiny peoples who inhabit the Cember Forest, the Kudaja ride borjos as their mounts and wield wyres. Despite their stature, they possess a significant ability to morph to a larger form. However, not all Kudaja are able to do this.
Mer	A very similar race to the Ciertrons, Mers only differ by their square jaws and pronounced foreheads.
Oolarooloo	Distinctive by their tall and thin appearance, dark bronzed skin, oblong heads and long ears, and lengthy necks, the Oolarooloo live on the opposite side of the Thol, renowned for being great healers and keepers of the knowledge of many mysterious of Thol.
Plakado	Long thought extinct, the Plakado are distant relatives of the Plotals, differing slightly with their lack of a snout, along with other features. Interestingly, they are physically incapable of entering places or past thresholds without first being invited in.
Plotals	Tall reptilian bipeds that appear both human and alligator with the addition of hidden barbs on the ends of their tails, their society was destroyed by the Great War, leaving the survivors to live a nomadic life of plundering and slavery across Thol. Recently, they have switched to a more peaceful way of living, trying to rebuild their old kingdom.
Raagor	Living in the mountain range of their namesake, the Raagor wear little clothing without fear of the cold. Also known as the "ghost people" because of their hairless pale skin and blue veins, the Raagor avoid socializing with other races. They can freeze a person with a single touch, but cannot withstand high temperatures, preferring to live high in the frigid mountains.
Safri	An intelligent race of Thol, the Safri have friendly relations with the Ciertrons and trade with them. Their appearance resembles a blend of human and goat, with horns, pointed ears, and cloven hooves; the small wings and three-fingered hands being an exception.
Triculated Cribustals	Tiny, parasitic organisms that feed off an individual's life force; they are foreign to Thol and come from another alternate Earth.
Zan Robots	These robots began as self-evolving technology built by the humans of the alternate Earth called Zan. Later, they took over the world and either enslaved or exterminated their creators.

Creatures

Augugal	A large spiked, hard-shelled animal, augugals are capable of blending into their environment, but these herbivores will prove to be both quick and dangerous when threatened.
Bobboes	Large, flightless birds raised by Ciertrons for their eggs, bobboes have large chests and a fluffy plumage of blue and purple.
Borjo	Resembling small dragons unable to breathe fire, the dragonfly-like borjo are used as mounts by the Kudaja. They are neutered upon hatching; otherwise, an unneutered borjo will grow to be large enough to ride by full-sized humans, capable of breathing fire with a wild temperament. These large borjos are unable to transform to a smaller size, unlike neutered ones.
Diwal dogs	Roaming the sponge plains, diwal dogs are widely considered vicious carnivores, capable of stripping their prey in seconds with their layered, razor-sharp teeth. However, some find the gray-skinned, tufted canines to be misunderstood creatures.
Fhahadda	A giant snake-like worm, the fhahadda burrows through the ground with the use of its many teeth. An odd creature, it is capable of both live births and egg-laying, with the number of offspring ranging widely in number. Despite this, no fhahadda has been sighted in over five centuries.
Floff	Despite its cute, wide-eyed appearance and fluffy limbs, this is a carnivore that hunts on the wing.
Gagu	Brightly colored feathers cover most of this flying creature, with its clawed membrane wings being the exception.
Grophie caterpillar	Living in the Cember Forest, its sting results in itchy purple spots that must be soothed with an Egrom antidote.
Hosks	This spider-creature's palm-sized, fluffy body varies in color, and contrasts its black legs and eyes. Living in colonies, it produces plenty of silken webbing from the moss-like sponges of the plains; a material widely used by both Egroms and Ciertrons alike.
Kumbora bear	While usually brown and green-furred, kumbora bears can change their colors to blend into their surroundings. Their long tails and flexible digits allow them to traverse the trees with ease.
Mruck	Appearing a mishmash of creatures with its lidless eyes, long trunk, split hooves, and short ears, mrucks are surprisingly edible and enjoy water.
Og	Large, lumbering animals with blue-tinged fur and knobbed heads that live on the sponge plains. Despite being prone to attacking other animals, ogs are in fact herbivores, their aggression stemming from being highly territorial.
Orich	A large flying creature with a heavily built body and broad wings.
Pakow	The epitome of gentle giants, pakows are bulky, wooly beasts with six legs, wide faces, and compound eyes. They are used by several races as mounts, transportation, and labor.
Par	A type of scarlet-winged bird.
Quokin	This draconic creature makes its home in water, recognizable by its green-tipped black scales and curious personality. It is said a person touched by a quokin will find their true love.
Ragapunga	Resembling an anteater, the ragapunga should never be startled, as it sprays a deadly acid when frightened to protect itself.
Saber-toothed chun	Large, saber-toothed felines the size of horses that inhabit the Raagor mountains, they serve as comfortable mounts for the Raagor people, their thick manes and paws suited for the cold environment.
Sidel	A rabbit-sized creature that lives on the sponge plains; its meat is an easy source of food.

Measurements

Chack	A Tholian hour
Complete path	A Tholian year
Drok	Tholian unit of distance; equivalent to a mile
Dunct	A moment
Full turn	A Tholian day
Keld	A Tholian month
Notch	A Tholian week
Sepiks	Copper coins used by Ciertrons as currency.

Technology

Crestriders	Flying ships invented by the Ciertrons for travel and city-wide defense against intruders. They are capable of "beaming up" objects and people inside, can both fly and hover, and are controlled with a series of levers, switches, and a joystick.
GSB	Short for "gravitational synchronizing beam," crestriders use it to enable flight and store solar energy in crystal cells.
Jumpsuit	A Ciertron type of clothing made from breathable fabric and worn by its warriors. It has multiple different "forms", including an armored one for combat.
Light healer	A Ciertron invention that uses a beam of light to heal injuries.
Restorative chamber/Smart Closet	A glassed-in multi-purpose chamber serving as wardrobe, washer, and restorer for clothing.
Sonicate box	A Ciertron invention used to assess injuries.
Translator	A small metal clip placed behind the ear which then settles into the flesh and serves as an automatic language translator.
Wyre	Bows used by the Kudaja, they form an arrow made of pure energy when the glowing string is drawn. Arrows can be set to either stun or kill.

Miscellaneous

Abrajaii	A golden Ciertron drink resembling champagne; it is drunk during celebrations.
Agrin trees	These trees produce large amounts of sap, which is tapped and blended with hosk webbing to create many durable items like footwear and banners. Entire forests can grow from one seed, reaching heights tall enough to touch the clouds.
Bonding	The spiritual bond formed between partners in a Tholian marriage; once it has been broken, only time may heal it.
Cribbage	A Plotal board game played with markers, octagonal dice, and dowels.
Kahl	A thick, sweet alcoholic drink consumed by Ciertrons.
Lantern-wick plant	The exact name of this plant is unknown. It grows in large clusters among shaded areas of the Cember Forest, and its thick, oily blue stalks are used in lanterns due to their slow-burning nature.
Lightning stones	A special type of rock that produces a purple flame when gently tapped against itself. Banging them together creates an explosion.
The Great War of Taylon	A lengthy Ciertron-Plotal war that left both sides decimated.
The Staff	A sacred relic thought to have been destroyed centuries ago.
The Voice	A mysterious ability that allows one to control others with verbal commands.
Youngmen	Not all Ciertron children are the same; Youngmen are those that emerge from their eggs in child-like bodies but with the minds of fully functioning adults.

A NOTE FROM THE AUTHOR

If you discover a missing element that should be included in the Glossary, or any Errors whatsoever, please let me know at dawn@degreenfeld.com

ABOUT THE AUTHOR

 D.E. Greenfield, aka Dawn Greenfield Ireland, is the award-winning author of 22 published novels which consists of 5 series: cozy mystery, sci fi/fantasy, billionaire shapeshifters, and dystopian. There's also a stand-alone sci-fi romantic adventure, and currently 7 nonfiction books (1 hardcover). she adapted 4 of her screenplays into book format. She also has created over 50 themed notebooks.

Two of her screenplays were optioned, and she worked on a screenwriter-for-hire project. Dawn has a certificate from the Professional Program in Screenwriting from UCLA (2002) and with ScreenwritingU.

D.E. Greenfield's business, Artistic Origins, has been around since 1995. Besides writing, she coaches writers, edits, formats and publishes clients' books.

Her former day job as an award-winning technical writer played a major role in her fiction writing. She is detailed-oriented, the organizational queen of the known universe, and never misses a deadline.

Actions Appreciated

Please leave a review on the website where you bought the book. Reviews help authors get recognized, get the word out and sell more books. I will love you forever if you leave a review!

HINT: don't regurgitate the synopsis for your review. Just tell people what you liked, didn't like – that's what people want – your opinion.

http://degreenfield.com

facebook.com/dawn.ireland.18
x.com/dawnireland
instagram.com/DawnGreenfieldIreland
linkedin.com/in/dawnireland
goodreads.com/dawnireland